BREAKING POINT

Ian Holland

BREAKING POINT

Copyright © 2020 Ian Holland

All rights reserved

The characters and events portrayed in this book are fictitious. Any similarity to real persons, living or dead, is coincidental and not intended by the author.

No part of this book may be reproduced, or stored in a retrieval system, or transmitted in any form or by any means, electronic, mechanical, photocopying, recording, or otherwise, without express written permission of the publisher.

ISBN-9798573447421

Cover design by: Art Painter

Library of Congress Control Number: 2018675309

Printed in the United States of America

Ian Holland

For Pat, with love and thanks.

BREAKING POINT

'...for to travel hopefully is a better thing than to arrive, and the true success is to labour.'
- Robert Louis Stevenson

Ian Holland

Cast of Main Characters

Concorde IV; *Harmonie, Orange Free State, South Africa*
Danny Core (40) Chief Engineer
Steyn Broed (55) Mine Captain
Piet Reiss (42) Maintenance Supervisor
Embele Ngozi (24) Boss Boy

Rinto Gold Mining; *Johannesburg, South Africa*
Thys van Heerden (60) President

Mathers Engineering; *Crossways, South Wales, UK*
Billy Jones (36) Technical Director
Terry Socket (42) Engineering Manager
John Dread (32) Senior Engineer

Heron Inc; *Houston, Texas, USA*
Rik Last (58) CEO
Luca Majori (43) Financial Controller
Fred Stremsen (55) Senior Deputy Vice-President of Engineering

Ian Holland

Prologue

Twelve thousand feet below ground, Don Colville was surrounded by gold. Over two million years old and indistinct from the contiguous rock, it was neither pure nor noble… and was crushing the life from his broken body.

He crimped his eyes shut against the pain, afraid to imagine the damage below his waist. And around him nothing but darkness; dense, underground darkness.

His hands thrashed out, trying to make sense of his surroundings, but nothing moved… nothing changed as choking dust crackled in the atmosphere, drawing moisture from his lips. His tongue was a dry, alien entity, stuck to the roof of his mouth.

'Jack, where are you?' he whispered.

The words scored the back of his throat. As he coughed, a shuddering pain seared across his chest and his bowels emptied, filling the space with a choking mix of shit and blood.

Straining to hear a reply, there was nothing except the sound of rushing water and cold steel pressed across his chest. A twisted metal rail ripped from its fastenings, held him down with a giant's grip. His arms were free, but useless within the constraints of the destruction around him and every new breath was shorter than the last.

He tried again. 'Help me, Jack.'

The raking cough, the excruciating pain.

Only silence answered.

He opened his eyes, trying to focus and sensed something to his left. Turning his head, he pushed as far forward as the metal rail allowed and saw a pale light reflecting off the rock.

I'm not alone, he thought… *hope*.

BREAKING POINT

Craning his neck, he saw his safety helmet. The lamp was still attached, sending an eerie glow onto the hanging-wall beyond a small opening.

At that moment his head cleared and he remembered the explosive force pouring down on him... and why Jack couldn't help him?

For a moment, he'd been eight years old, lying on the road with his toboggan in pieces. His pal, Jack, had been standing next to him, crying inconsolably; turning away from the horror of Don's shattered leg. Snot, tears and blood, puddled onto the floor, and Jack was calling for his mother, over and over.

Hard rock and crippling pain had wrenched Don back to the present.

His head was bursting; stars shooting across his eyes in painful constellations. He blinked hard as the realisation came. He was in his place of work, twelve thousand feet beneath the earth, when something catastrophic happened.

'Marius, Ray, Johannes. Can you hear me?' He barely recognised his voice, his eardrums bleeding from the detonation.

The coughing fit returned, and with it, the metallic taste of blood.

'Jesus, Don, is dit jy? Watter bloedige het gebeur, man?' *Jesus, Don, is that you? What bloody happened, man?*

Somewhere behind him, the familiar voice of, Marius van der Merwe, the Maintenance Team Leader. *He wasn't alone!*

'Marius, thank God... I can't move, please help me.' His coughing tapered into sobs.

'Okay, Don, stay calm, I'm coming!'

Marius' clawed at the loosened rock. He cursed the mining company, grunting for the oxygen his body craved.

'Don, can you hear me?'

Ian Holland

The sobbing was close and drove him to more considerable efforts. But the air was foul, and he struggled at every constricted movement. The ground beneath him was saturated, and he could hear the surge of high-pressure water pumping in. Somewhere very close by.

'Keep talking, Don, I need you to guide me.' Marius could barely get the words out.

'Follow the light...' Don's voice was fading.

'I'm not far away; hang on, man.'

Marius shifted one of the larger rocks and a gap opened to reveal a chamber, faintly lit from the glow of a lamp. He was able to glimpse his friend for the first time, forcing his bloodied hands to work faster.

'I'm almost with you, I just need to clear more of this... Oh, my God! Oh, my God!'

His hands had fallen into something soft and unfamiliar amongst the splintered rock, and he pulled back; his torn skin stung by the moisture. He hoped his friend couldn't hear him vomit and gasp for the diminished oxygen.

When he recovered, he cleared the debris to reveal two bodies. There was enough light to recognise his colleagues Ray and Johannes, and enough to see they were both dead.

'What's happening, Marius? Jesus, man... no more, please no more!'

Marius couldn't help himself; he was crying uncontrollably.

'I don't understand it, Don.' His body shuddering. 'We were all here... right here... talking... breathing.'

He composed himself and cleared enough rock to squeeze into the chamber where Don was laid out; barely visible in the chaos. The floor was filled with over half a metre of water... and rising.

Crawling toward him, he pulled at the metal rail constricting his friends breathing, but it was futile and risked further collapse. He lay down, immersing himself in the cold water to hold Don's hand.

BREAKING POINT

Beyond the light, he could see the whole of the roof had collapsed, closing off space in the haulage that now imprisoned them.

'Don, wake up,' he said. 'It's me, Marius. I'm going to get us out of this.'

Futile words were all he could offer.

Don was calling for his mother. Marius instinctively held him tighter until the pain was gone.

And the water continued to rise.

Ian Holland

Chapter 1

I stepped from my car and looked up at the bright, South African sky. My head was clear, and for the first time in five years, I was feeling comfortable in my new country. Memories of my old life in South Wales, six thousand miles away, had started to heal and I was *contemplating a return… no matter what sort of welcome awaited.*

It was Saturday morning, but mining didn't have weekends off. Shifts were planned with everything covered 24/7, fifty-two weeks a year. This was my weekend on, but it still felt good.

On my way to work, the car radio had been playing *London's Burning*, by The Clash, and I'd been matching Joe Strummer's vocals at the top of my voice. At forty, I was too old for punk, but the rebellious lyrics resonated with me. My body tingled, and my eyes were wet. I was still Danny Core but somehow changed since fate had intervened and led me to this controversial country.

Blessed with the world's richest seams of gold, it had everything, except peace. I wasn't comfortable being part of a minority using segregation in such an unambiguous way, but it wasn't a debate I was ready to have with myself. For now, Rinto Gold had given me a chance.

The land stretched beyond the boundaries of my home town of Harmonie; a level panorama of scrub and thorn trees. The dusty N1 Highway lay hidden in the distance, connecting the major cities of this vast country. From its southernmost point in Cape Town, it stretched north through Bloemfontein to Johannesburg and Pretoria, before ending up at Beit Bridge on the border of Zimbabwe. The road had been my introduction to South Africa and had carried me on the dusty journey south, from Jan Smuts Airport, in Johannesburg, to here, in the Orange Free State.

In the distance, the ubiquitous mine dumps, shimmering in the heat, broke up the conformity of the flatlands. These

BREAKING POINT

pyramids of waste were by-products of the gold making process and scarred the landscape of the goldfields. Relics of a bygone age, they were gradually being reprocessed to remove more minerals. Still, the resultant slimes dams were no less ugly. Mining was a greedy process and would continue to extract every last cent from the broken ground.

I tasted grit in my mouth, as a warm breeze ran across the tarmac. Above one of the dumps, a brown cloud of sand swirled against the cloudless sky, waved on by a wind I couldn't feel as I walked across the car park. Hundreds of feet above me, the grey, concrete tower of the winding house cast a welcome shadow as I entered the mining compound. A white sign clung to its side emblazoned with *Rinto Gold* in black letters, visible from a mile away. Beneath it in smaller, red script, *Concorde IV*.

I showed my identity card at the Security Gate like every one of the five thousand workers employed on the mine.

'Morning, Boss.'

The gateman waved me through with a massive smile. He had on a grey uniform, black tie and cap; the latter emblazoned with the company logo. His right hand was tucked into his jacket while his left hand clumsily did the work of two.

'Today looks like a perfect day, Sir.' He spoke in a baritone and gave another broad toothed smile.

'I hope so, Marshall, I hope so. How's the hand?'

He looked at it with disdain. 'Not a problem, Mr Core, healing nicely. I'll be back very soon.'

Marshall lost three fingers and part of his thumb when he caught his hand in a cutting tool, working on the underground *stopes*. A vacancy on Security after he was released from the hospital meant he was one of the lucky ones. Typically, injured men like him were jettisoned and replaced without breaking step.

'That's good, Marshall…' We both knew he would never work underground again. 'I'll see you later.'

Ian Holland

I continued walking up the concrete path toward the Engineering Office. The perimeter of the walkway was edged with a low, wooden fence, partially covered with green bushes and flowers that looked out of place against the industrial backdrop. A dusty, green lawn separated the path from a covered walkway, which ran a serpentine route a hundred yards away. Another nightshift of underground workers was making their way along. Having exited the *man-cages,* they were headed toward the washrooms, protected from the heat of the morning sun.

On the far side of the compound was the Central Reduction Plant and I could hear the conveyor belts rattling away inside their sheet metal enclosures. They were crisscrossing their payload from one process to the next, effortlessly covering the distances in between. The light blue colour contrasted with the concrete grey winding house in the foreground; like a painted landscape.

As I approached the main buildings, the winding gear kicked in, obliterating every other sound, as it drew the hoist cable around the headgear and raised the man-cages to the surface. Another shift of men and materials delivered from the subterranean levels of Concorde IV. Subconsciously I chalked up another *Fatality Free Shift*.

It was 8.30, and the engineering team were already busy at their desks as I walked into the office. I said good morning to everyone before settling into my chair to go through the nightshift reports. I was one of fifty staff on the dayshift, with half that number on each of the afternoon and nightshifts. The office was a single storey building furnished with draughtsmen, surveyors and a multiplicity of engineers; every technical discipline was covered. The maintenance teams were run from a separate office but remained my responsibility.

Laura, my secretary, brought in a cup of coffee and handed me the extraction figures from the previous night, along with the shift rotas for the following week.

BREAKING POINT

'Anything untoward, Laura?' She would have already transferred the numbers onto a spreadsheet.

'No, Mr Core. Figures are pretty good, what with holidays and absence.'

We were about to reach the *One Million Fatality Free Shift* milestone. Remarkable, considering we were increasing output and excavating at record depths.

She passed over the Safety Report. 'And no accidents reported,' she said with a smile.

My predecessor had taken risks. His nickname, *The Butcher*, said everything about his methods. Three years ago, the fatalities were uncomfortable, and the company demanded change. It had taken three years, but we saw results. Concorde IV was the most productive mine in the Orange Free State and the flagship of the Rinto Gold Mining Company. Not bad for a *Soutie.*

As I sipped my coffee, the hoisting cable ground to a halt with an ear-splitting screech, and the winding engine fell silent. Then the siren let loose, and the air was saturated with a piercing shrill, vibrating through the building.

Everyone in the office froze, and conversations stopped. For a millisecond, there was paralysis and then fear as the realisation of an emergency hit home. Some people ran to the windows while others just stared at one another. I was already out of the door and running toward the Mine Captains office.

I seemed to be sprinting in slow motion. Labouring in my heavy boots, I was gasping through dust made airborne by scores of others dashing toward the alarm above the headgear. They hadn't experienced the sound for over twelve months, and the surface was alive with people. Voices shouted across one another, fighting to make themselves heard.

Already lightheaded with the adrenaline, I pushed my way through a group gathered around the safety fence of the main shaft; their eyes looking skyward toward the metal framework. I stopped to look up and shivered. The red alarm light was flashing on top of the steelwork, reminding me of gallows; gaunt and soulless against the clear sky. I ran on to a remote office at the edge of the changing rooms and rushed through the door.

'What's happening, Steyn?' I coughed the words out.

Steyn Broed had been a miner for thirty-five years. From cutting the ore at the deepest levels, he'd advanced through every underground discipline to become a Mine Captain; the first-line supervisor for all underground workers. Fifty-five years old, the duration underground had taken its toll. He was my closest friend.

'I've just got off the phone, Danny.' His eyes were bloodshot, his face creased like folded leather.

'There's been a collapse on Level 120, near the proposed sub-station. We're overriding the headgear alarm so the men on Level 130 can make their way up.' I noticed a forgotten cigarette perched on the edge of his desk, branding the surface. 'I've contacted the rescue team, and they're making their way to the collapse.' His hand was stroking the back of his mahogany coloured neck, shining with perspiration.

'Are they following the emergency protocol?'

'Yes,' he said. 'But nothing prepares you for the real thing.'

'You've taught them well, they'll be okay.' I tried to put his mind at rest. 'Is it on 120 East or West?'

'East,' he replied, rubbing his eyes.

'Who's at risk?'

He adjusted his glasses to look at the shift log. 'Marius van der Merwe's team.'

'How many men? Come on I need the facts… quickly, man.' I was jumpy. *Calm down*, I told myself.

'Sorry, Danny.' His stubby fingers scrolled down the names on the sheet of paper, silently counting them. He looked back up, and I could see the edge of his mouth quivering.

BREAKING POINT

'There are thirty-two men in that area.' He wiped the sweat from his forehead.

'Do we know what they were doing down there?'

He turned more pages. 'The work log says there was a production team of twenty-six men, excavating. And a maintenance crew of six, including Marius.'

'Do we know what the maintenance crew were doing down there?'

He turned the pages back and forth. 'The production team were drilling out the new sub-station...'

'Yes, I know that Steyn, but I'm asking about the maintenance crew. What were they doing down there?'

'Erm... they were checking the seismic sensors in that area.'

I looked at him, confused. *Seismic checks were always organised through the Engineering Office.*

His eyes stayed fixed to the sheets of paper.

'Didn't we run a full check in that area, less than a month ago?' I asked.

'I don't know.' His answer didn't make sense, but time was moving on. I looked at my watch, it was 9:30.

'I need to get down there, Steyn. The rescue team are going to take at least thirty minutes to get here, and that's too long. Give me two good men and have them meet me in the changing rooms.'

He grabbed my arm as I made my way outside. 'Are you sure that's a good idea, Danny?' I pulled away, and he looked startled.

'What I mean is... you haven't been underground for a while. Maybe we should wait for the rescue team.'

I pressed my face close enough for him to feel my breath. 'Two good men, Steyn. I'll be ready to go in ten minutes.' His comment had stung me.

As I stepped from his office, a crowd closed in around me. I held up my hands to quieten them and shouted above the noise of the alarm.

'At this stage, I can only tell you there's been a collapse on 120 East. We don't know how bad, and the rescue teams are on their way. They'll be looking for volunteers, so you must stand by until they arrive.' I spoke in English. I'd learned enough Afrikaans to get by but found it easier to listen to, than speak.

As I pushed my way through the crowd, I could hear the different dialects translating my words. Zulu, Tsonga and Xhosa, among others from the black workers and Afrikaans from the whites. Even some European languages were mixed in, all their racial and tribal differences put to one side.

I pressed through and ran to the main changing rooms. Once inside, it felt like a sauna. The smell of sweat and disinfectant oozed from the tiled floors and walls, turning my stomach. I took the white boiler suit offered by the cleaner, a black man of about fifty wearing a tattered vest and shorts. His curly hair was more salt than pepper, and he had a wispy beard. As I stripped, I saw him leaning against his mop, watching me from the shower room.

'I got some cream for that, Boss,' he said.

I self-consciously pulled up the boiler suit to cover the dry patches of scaly skin around my shoulders and lower back. 'No thanks,' I said. 'It's fine.'

I was embarrassed by psoriasis that had invaded my body in recent years. I sat on the wooden bench to tie my bootlaces, but my hands were shaking so much, I couldn't make the knot and sweat was stinging my eyes.

'Let me help, Boss?' His voice was urgent, and before I could reply, he was at my feet, his hands working feverishly at the laces.

'Here's your lamp, Boss.'

He helped adjust the belt and battery, before taking a helmet from the rack and placing it gently on my head. The sound of his movements and the touch of his hands had a calming, almost hypnotic effect. My nerves steadied, and I was grateful for his attention. It had distracted me from thinking about the journey ahead.

A gentle tap on the shoulder broke my trance.

'You're ready, Boss.' He beamed up at me with a three toothed smile, and I couldn't have been more grateful.

'Thanks,' I said. 'What's your name?'

'Tumelo.' he replied.

'That means, *Having Faith*, doesn't it?' I enquired.

He nodded. 'A good omen, sir.'

'I hope so, Tumelo, and I appreciate your time.' He seemed to grow in stature with my comment.

Steyn was probably right to question my decision, but I needed to help... I was responsible for the men down there.

'Is it a bad accident, Boss?'

Before I could answer, the door flew open and Steyn rushed in followed by a black giant.

'This is Embele,' he said. 'He's the Boss Boy for 110 and 120 and knows his way around that area better than anyone. I could have had a hundred volunteers, but I told them to be patient.'

'Embele.' I nodded toward him.

'Boss,' he said, behind a fierce stare and a mouth that didn't readily smile.

He was about the size of a light-heavyweight, well over six foot and weighing about two hundred pounds. His shaved head shone like polished coal, indented with enough scar tissue to make a brave man wary, and his boiler suit strained to contain his shoulders.

Beyond his impressive physique, I noticed the large holes in both his ears, the loose skin dangling like strings of soft liquorice. *Probably, Zulu,* I thought. *Christ, I wouldn't want to cross his path at night.*

'You're okay with this?' I asked.

His face was impassive; a characteristic he carried with ease. 'My brother is down there, Boss.'

His eyes settled on me for a millisecond longer than was needed, before he put his helmet on, impatient to go.

Ian Holland

A man of few words, I thought, trying not to be swayed by my first impressions.

I thanked Tumelo again before turning to watch Steyn, grunting and groaning into his boiler suit.

'I suppose there's no point in telling you, you're too old for this?' I said with a smile. I was keen to make up for my earlier irritation.

'None at all, someone's got to look after you, eh.'

He hopped halfway across the room, trying to fit his leg in. 'Jesus, this boiler suit has shrunk a bit,' and laughed as he fastened the buttons over his ample stomach. 'I wish I could stay in shape like you youngsters.'

He gave me a wink, and I knew we were okay.

'The man-cages are being kept clear to bring up the injured,' he said. 'So I've arranged for us to go down in the service skip. It'll be full of emergency pit props and other shit. You okay with that?'

'Whatever works, Steyn. Let's go.' I crossed my fingers.

BREAKING POINT

Chapter 2

Calm down, you *stupid bastard; you can do this.* Steyn was right… he usually was. The last time I'd been underground was over twelve months ago, and I was already having doubts about my decision to return. Twelve months since being caught up in the fallout from a *pressure burst*.

The deeper gold mines excavated, following the gold-bearing reef, the more significant the profits. But mining at those depths amplified the risk of pressure bursts, as the weight bearing down on the open workings increased exponentially. In deep-level mines, like Concorde IV, the stress concentrations could reach a pitch where the rock would explode, causing catastrophic collapses. They were unpredictable, and the larger ones could produce surface tremors miles from the epicentre.

Fortunately, I'd experienced a small pressure burst. Unfortunately, I'd been right underneath it. With a broken leg and dislocated shoulder, I was told I was lucky… but it didn't feel like it then. The physical pain was excruciating, but the mental suffering of being unable to move was worse and reignited a personal tragedy from over five years ago. And a loss I hadn't come to terms with.

The experiences left me with a profound fear of confinement that my pride wouldn't allow me to admit, even to Steyn; though he obviously had his suspicions. In my hospital bed, I'd pledged to do all I could to prevent the same thing happening to any other man working below ground on Concorde IV.

The three of us climbed through the entrance gate of the service skip; a metal cage constructed like a medieval prison. It contained the three hydraulic pit props which were being sent to help the rescue teams. We squeezed through the limited space between the giant metal props and pressed ourselves against the metal sides of the cage. Part of the roof had been removed to allow the props to fit; it was against safety regulations, but risks were necessary. It might even make my journey less stressful. *I was kidding myself.*

The floor of the skip was filthy and awash with muddy water, spilling across the detritus of discarded metal and rock from previous journeys. We stood on whatever we could, to avoid getting our feet wet. The gate slammed shut, and the winding gear let go. The skip began to drop with a familiar *whoosh* as it displaced the air in the confines of the shaft and blew through the perforated sides. My body was already stiffening as I looked at the locked gate. I tried breathing steadily but found myself gulping air into my lungs. Watching the shaft lights flash past, I avoided thinking of the confined space… and failed on all counts. My hands shook.

The skip clattered and screeched, accelerating under its weight. My ears popped, and my stomach turned over as my worst nightmare played out. I saw Steyn, looking down at his feet, doing his best to avoid the ebb and flow of the filthy water, steadying himself against the metal sides. As the cage closed in on me, the inside of my head was an explosion of illogical fears that I didn't understand and couldn't control. The more I tried to maintain perspective, the tighter the fear gripped my stomach with an icy claw.

The props were pressing against my body and shoulders, and I tensed, trying to force them away. I was losing the feeling in my legs. Pins and needles clawed up from my feet to the small of my back, while my body felt it was being compressed from above. I craved space, and my breathing became short as the air felt too thick to take in one mouthful.

The panic cycle had started, and I was helpless in its grip. My heart was racing and my body, hot and clammy. If I couldn't calm myself, I was afraid of what I might do. The nightmare of five years ago poured back into my

BREAKING POINT

consciousness, poisoning my resolve. *I wanted to die again.*

The cage was accelerating, and the noise increased, screaming in my ears. I tried to think pleasant thoughts, the hills and open spaces of my hometown, but all I could see and feel was the Brig Uchel mountain range. And a small boy... calling for me, from far away... just too far away.

Our father, who art in heaven... I couldn't close my eyes, and my heart was trying to body-punch its way out through my ribcage.

Hallowed be thy name... my irrational fears now had control, and their momentum was about to endanger those around me. The props weren't stable and leaned dangerously with the movement of the cage. Steyn was pressing his weight hard against them as though this alone would stop them moving. *Bloody fool, doesn't he realise we're all going to die.*

Thy kingdom come... I was burning up from the inside and turned to claw at the buttons of my boiler suit, desperate to cool down. In my frenzy, I'd forgotten about Embele. I looked around and there he was, watching me. Calm, expressionless. Judging me with unblinking eyes. It didn't matter now... nothing mattered.

Tears clouded my eyes. I wanted to cry out and punch my way from this confinement. *Look for a way out.* All reason had leaked away, sloshing around with the filthy water at my feet. I looked up. This had to be the best way out... to whatever relief was beyond.

Suddenly, Embele was at my side. He'd squeezed, unnoticed, through a gap between the props and frightened the shit out of me. Steyn was still in his own world dodging the sloppy water and saw nothing of my unfolding panic behind the metal cylinders.

'Let me help you with your belt, Boss.' Embele shouted above the noise.

'I'm okay!' I screamed, trying to catch my breath and angrily pushed his hand away. I was looking for a foothold to climb out. Big as he was, I was ready to kill him if he tried to stop me. 'I don't need your…'

He ignored my gestures and slammed me hard against the side of the cage. His left hand drove into my chest, smashing my head against the wall of the skip. The resulting *clang* from my helmet exploded through my eardrums. The force of the blow left me dizzy for a second and flashing stars appeared and disappeared across my eye line.

With his left hand pinning me back, Embele grabbed my belt with his right and pulled it so tight, it felt like a body punch. The air in my lungs expanded, painfully, and restricted my breathing. I thought I was going to swallow my tongue.

My instinctive reaction was to grab his arm and escape the grip, but it was impossible. I considered myself a match for most men, but his arms were bulging with muscle, and his hold was like a steel clamp, lifting me off my feet. I looked up at him, helpless. Not understanding. *Why is he attacking me?*

It wasn't uncommon for men to be assaulted underground, even murdered. *But why me? Why now?* And he was doing it with such relaxed strength that Steyn had barely noticed any of the commotion. I was about to be killed in front of my own Mine Captain, and there was nothing I could do.

Without warning, Embele's stern features suddenly collapsed and transformed into a broad smile. *What the hell is he doing now?* I thought.

I realised the restricted breathing had eased my anxiety. As brutal as it was, the physical pain overcame the psychological terror. I was less aware of the limited space, and my body temperature cooled. For the most ridiculous of reasons, I couldn't take my eyes off his teeth. Christ, they were perfect and reminded me of piano keys. I almost laughed in his face, and the paradox wasn't lost on me. One minute I'm about to climb out of a cage, hurtling toward

BREAKING POINT

the bowels of the earth. The next I'm ready to giggle at a stranger's dentistry. *Had I crossed the line?*

The background noise dulled and feeling came back into my legs and lower back, as though I'd been injected with cold fluid.

Embele's smile never faltered while the service skip reached Level 120, twelve thousand feet below ground. We bounced up and down with the cage, the wire ropes stretching and relaxing before finally settling, quiet and still. Embele released his grip, and his smile disappeared as if he'd pulled a switch. But he did manage to give me a wink as though I'd impressed him in some small way. *I was beginning to like him.*

Steyn opened the doors and let us out. No words passed between the three of us as we exited the skip. I tore at the constraints of my belt and breathed normally in the dust-filled air. Beyond, the passageway still had power and lighting, and I breathed a sigh. In the distance, urgent voices bounced off the walls, and I shivered, even though I wasn't cold. I was wondering what the hell I'd got myself into.

Inside a goldmine, everything is a thousand shades of black and white. The only contrast was our red safety helmets, backlit by our head lamps. A familiar smell caught the back of my throat; chalky and dry. Voices and sounds seemed compressed by the sheer weight of the rock above and gave the impression we had cotton wool in our ears. It was difficult to imagine how this tiny tunnel we were in, two miles below the surface of the earth, could withstand the weight of the rock above. I needed to put all those negative thoughts to the back of my head and move on.

The three of us settled into a jog, eastward; our clumsy movement casting uneven shadows along the tunnel. Three hundred yards into the passageway, we met two black men and two white, pushing a hopper toward us. The open cargo truck was on rails and filled with rock.

Steyn recognised one of the men. 'Erik?'

A middle-aged man lifted his head; he looked worn out. 'Here, Steyn… just about.'

'Is this from the collapse?' I asked, pointing at the rock. They all nodded.

'Ja, we were close by when we heard it go,' Erik said. 'Everyone just ran to help. Piet Reiss' team were there first and have already started digging people out. We're taking this lot back to the surface.'

'Good work boys,' said Steyn.

'There are three hydraulic props back there,' he pointed back to the service skip. 'Organise a team to winch them onto that hopper and get them to the fall as fast as you can. Hopefully, they'll stabilise the roof-wall and stop the bloody lot coming down again.'

The men nodded and pushed past us.

We continued into a much narrower opening, where the rail track ran through the centre. Unable to stand straight, our progress slowed. For another mile, we ducked below 12-inch and 18-inch pipes, suspended from the hanging-wall. These were the arteries of the mine and circulated high-pressure water throughout its many tunnels.

Embele was leading and moving quickly. Steyn and I were doing our best to keep up while avoiding the wooden sleepers, which ran between the tracks. Bent over like this, my lower back was aching like hell. Steyn had both his hands resting ungainly on his hips, and I knew he was feeling worse. Ahead of us, we saw two men, making their way back to the main shaft. They, too, were hunched, carrying a stretcher. Embele lifted the tarpaulin that barely concealed the broken, black body and studied the man's face.

'How far away is the fall?' He spoke to the two black workers in Fanakalo, the crude language of the goldmines.

'About half a mile.' One of the black miners replied in the same language. 'It's not good,' he said, shaking his head.

BREAKING POINT

'Where's the supervisor?' I shouted above the escalating noise coming from the darkness beyond the haulage.

'He's at the fall, Boss.'

Embele grabbed the man's arm, demanding his attention. 'Have you seen Andele, the Boss Boy?'

The man shook his head again.

Embele groaned and pushed past him, running even harder toward the clamour. Steyn and I followed as best we could. The dust and rock under our feet turned to mud, deep enough to hide the rail tracks we were following and further slowing our progress. With our feet slipping and sliding, our bodies bounced, painfully, against the sharp-edged sidewalls. Sections of the hanging-wall, above bulged like great blisters, as the rock threatened to rupture once more.

The further we travelled, the darker the space became. The emergency lights in this section were weak, and we had to rely on the beam from our lamps, flashing drunkenly from side to side. The air was thicker, and the temperature rising. We veered sharp left and heard the unmistakable sound of men singing. Low voices in pure harmony. We were close, and my heart beat faster. Squeezing past an abandoned pump, we were there, amongst the men, the noise… and total devastation.

I counted about twenty miners pulling away at the rock with their bare hands. All covered in the cloying mud, and their lamps darted indiscriminately, like spotlights searching for a target. Above them, fifty yards away, I could see three 18-inch pipes, fractured and spewing water. It was already up to the men's ankles. The support network, which held them, had been ripped apart. Steel mesh, once supporting the roof-wall, had ruptured and the rods holding it in place were splayed in all directions. Their safety function ineffectual against the force of nature.

A group of black workers were levering away at a huge rock, singing an African song; the rhythm harmonising their efforts to maximum effect. It was intense and soulful and added a surreal soundtrack to the chaos. The destruction, the noise and the pungent smell. I tried to make some sense of it all. Lamplights were flashing and strobing at all angles. *We'd discovered Hell.*

As the adrenaline rush receded, energy drained from my body like purging blood. I clenched my fists till my knuckles throbbed and damned myself for my weakness. I tried to spit the sour taste of bile from my mouth, but nothing came out. It was fear I tasted.

'Quiet everyone… Quiet!' Piet Reiss, the supervisor, shouted above the noise, his hand waving impatiently. The song died, and all the other voices fell silent.

He pushed his ear close to an excavated area and listened. Sweat dripped from his face, and his breathing was heavy and laboured. Everyone around me seemed to be holding their breath, trying to ignore the sound of the water above them.

I was doing the opposite. I couldn't take my eyes off the overhead pipes; the velocity of the water was unnatural. The fractured pipes were bent at odd angles and the metal clamps, holding them to the roof-wall, stood out from the rock like frenzied artwork. The water pressure was abnormal, but something else wasn't right. I couldn't put my finger on what… at least not yet.

After a minute of listening, Piet shook his head and wiped his brow.

'Nothing. Carry on digging.' He pulled himself up on weary legs as the rhythmical voices started again. The percussion of the hammers and picks striking in harmony.

I dragged my eyes from the pipes and shouted across. 'Piet, what's the news?'

He walked toward me, bare from the waist up; the top of his boiler suit was tied around his hips. It was rare to see Piet without a smile. He was always cracking jokes and taking the piss. Stained brown with the mud, he'd aged ten years.

BREAKING POINT

'Part of the main drive has collapsed, Danny. Looks like a pressure burst. Caught everyone cold.' He looked behind and pointed at the devastation. 'Enough to bring down everything along the haulage; supports, piping, jacks… everything.'

He barely had the energy to whisper, let alone shout above the background noise. *Now wasn't the time to bring up my concerns about the water from the fractured pipes.*

'Do we know how far the collapse stretches?' I shouted.

'Difficult to tell.' He turned back around. 'But I reckon it could be as much as half a mile.'

Jesus! I thought of how many men could be hurt along a collapse of that length.

'Is there another route to…' But I couldn't finish my question.

'Boss, I know the way.' It was Embele. He'd read my mind and was already doubling back from where we'd come from.

'Wait!' I shouted after him, but there was no response.

'We'd better stay with him, Danny.' Steyn turned up at my shoulder, gasping. 'He could try anything.'

'What do you mean?'

'The conversation back there.' Steyn nodded toward the passage. 'Andele is his brother.'

My brother is down there, Boss… I'd forgotten. I nodded and turned back to Piet. 'The rescue team should be with you in about fifteen minutes. Are you okay this end?'

'Ja, we'll manage, Danny. The guys on 130 are starting to bring their tools, so that'll help.'

'Is the First Aid Station organised?'

'Up to a point. With this amount of damage, I'm not sure how much they'll be able to do. We've asked for doctors to be sent down from the hospital.'

'Good work, Piet. We counted thirty-two men missing on Marius' shift, have you got the same number?'

'Ja.'

'How many accounted for?'

'Thirteen survivors so far; two fatalities.'

'Okay,' I said, working out the maths in my head and damning myself for sounding so clinical. Still, I needed everyone to know how many men we were trying to find.

'That's seventeen men unaccounted for. Any names for the dead?' I damned myself again, but time wasn't on our side.

'Not yet, only that we've got one black worker and one white worker. We haven't had time to identify…' His voice began to break.

'Jesus, Danny. This shouldn't have happened. I was talking to Marius only twenty minutes before. He walked away, laughing at one of my jokes and then…'

I grabbed his shoulder. 'Keep it together, Piet. Take a break if you need to, but I'm relying on you to keep control. Steyn and I will see if there's another access point beyond the collapse. Get someone to ring up to 110. Tell them to reduce the pressures on the Stabiliser supplying those fractured water pipes.' I pointed up. 'If it keeps pumping out at that pressure, we could end up drowning the bloody survivors!'

He smiled at my black humour and wiped his eyes with the back of his hand. 'Should we close them off completely?'

I shook my head. 'No, Piet, the back-pressure might create another problem.'

He looked at me with *Why?* hanging on his lips, but I was relieved he left it there.

I wasn't quite sure of the logic myself; it was a hunch.

'Okay, Danny. I'll get them to reduce the inlet pressure, and the flow velocity as well, as a precaution.'

The flow velocity… I'd forgotten about that and patted him on the shoulder. In the chaos, as tired as he was, he was still thinking clearly.

'There's a cross-cut chamber further back.' He pointed behind us. 'That should get you on the other side of the collapse. Hasn't been used for years but if you follow

BREAKING POINT

Embele, he'll know the approach. He doesn't give much away, but you can rely on him.'

I looked back toward the men clearing the rock, putting their own lives at risk to save their brothers. Then I caught sight of the empty fingers of a leather glove lying next to a hydraulic drill, half-buried in the wet rock and prayed that its owner was one of those rescued.

'Were they blasting down here, Piet?' I wondered if a charge had gone off by accident.

'No, the production team were drilling for the new sub-station, but blasting wasn't planned until tomorrow.'

'Were there any emergency supports along this section?' I was desperately searching for clues.

'None that I know of, Danny, no need. This area was given the all-clear weeks ago. Look, I need to go, and you need to find that other access point.' He turned, shouting encouragement to the other men.

Steyn pulled me away. 'Come on, Danny, or we'll lose Embele.'

We set off on his trail.

After ten minutes, we caught up, but only because he was waiting at the opening to the cross-cut chamber.

'Over here, Boss,' he shouted. This was a full-blown conversation from the *man of few words*, and before we had a chance to answer, he was gone.

Steyn sat, exhausted. 'You carry on, Danny. I'm going to rest a minute.'

He looked dreadful. 'You okay?' I asked.

'Ja, I'm fine, man. Say, what the hell went on in the skip with you and Embele? You have a falling out, or what?'

I tapped him on the helmet. 'He was telling me what a bastard you are to work for.' He laughed out loud.

'Now rest up, old man. Sit here and have a smoke.' I pointed to the pack in his overalls and headed into the cross-cut.

Ian Holland

There were no emergency lights now and progress was slow. As I semi-crawled in the restricted chamber, my head rang from the percussion of my helmet, ricocheting on the suspended piping. My feet twisted and tripped on the uneven foot-wall adding to my unease. Pulling my belt back in a few notches, I kept telling myself to breathe slowly and focus on the light.

The old rail tracks had been removed, and the ground was strewn with debris. The opening, long abandoned, was interspersed with timber packs supporting the hanging-wall. They'd been compressed into a dense, mass of wood, reduced to less than half their original height by the weight of the rock. It didn't fill me with confidence.

Eventually, I reached the end of the cross-cut and entered 120 East. Looking up, the hanging-wall and piping were secure, and the emergency lighting was operational. I was relieved to see Embele waiting for me and gave him a thumbs up. Together, we moved west, to find the other end of the collapse.

Compared with the chaos on the other side, it was like a graveyard. We ran into thick dust, a sign that our journey was ending. We covered our mouths with the collars of our boiler suits, and as we neared, the air cleared as the ground got wetter. The sound of water dominated the chamber when we reached the mass of fallen rock.

The collapse had exposed enormous splits in the chamber. The wire mesh, put there to reinforce the walls, had torn like gossamer webs. The length, affected by the fall, was mercifully shorter than the half-mile Piet had predicted and that meant more chance of survivors. I instinctively looked up at the 18-inch pipes. Only one had fractured, but already the water level was up to our ankles. I could hear the power of the water running through the other three pipes, flooding the other side of the fall.

We both started shouting into the mass of rock.

'Can anyone hear us? Is anyone there?'

An interminable silence.

BREAKING POINT

'Here, Boss.'

Startled by the voice, we spun around.

'Jesus Christ!' I screeched, as a group of black workers dragged themselves upright from a pump chamber cut into the sidewall. They were covered in mud and clearly in shock; some with deep cuts to their faces and arms. Embele went amongst them, looking for his brother. Satisfied he wasn't there, he turned back and started clearing the rocks.

'Are you okay?' I said to the nearest man. 'How many are you?'

'Ten, Boss.'

I moved amongst them but only counted nine. I recounted, still only nine.

He saw my confusion. 'One man's dead,' he said. His bloodied hand pointed to the space they'd emerged from. Embele froze and rushed to the pump chamber. I followed him and saw the body, crumpled on its side. He touched the coloured beads around the man's neck and removed the stained bandana covering the face. Andele's eyes were open, but he wouldn't see or feel his brother's embrace.

I left them alone. There were men still unaccounted for, and every second was precious.

'Okay,' I shouted to the group. 'We have seven men missing, relying on us to get them out. Split into two groups. First five, start clearing out the left side of the fall; you others, start clearing the right side.'

They were still dazed, so I grabbed the nearest man and pulled him toward the rocks.

'Understand?' I shouted, and the others finally reacted. 'Good, now let's save some lives.'

They bent their backs and set about the work while I went back to Embele.

'Your brother?' I asked, kneeling beside him.

The big man wiped away tears, carving through the mud on his cheeks. 'Yes, Boss... Andele.' His eyes never left his brothers face.

'Does he have a family?' I asked.

'A wife and child. Nkosi.'

I put my hand on his shoulder. 'There's nothing we can do for him now, Embele. We have to help find the others… your brother's friends.'

He nodded and wiped his eyes in silence. After carefully replacing the stained bandana, he raised himself and joined the others.

We were soon reunited with Steyn and a dozen more from the rescue team. Reinforcements came from 130, and the clearing work intensified with the help of power tools and hydraulic props. By then, Piet Reiss must have found the relevant Stabiliser because the clamour from the pipes above our head calmed and the flow from the ruptured pipe reduced dramatically.

Slow and dangerous work, it was physically and emotionally draining, and we took another twenty-four hours to meet up with Piet's team on the other side.

The euphoria of sending eleven survivors back to the surface was tempered by despair as another seven were delivered in body bags.

A total of nine had been killed, and *the suits* in Johannesburg would be sharpening their knives.

Chapter 3

I sat in my office, smoking a cigarette. The first since I'd given them up three years ago; the same day I'd taken over as Chief Engineer of Concorde IV. Drawing in the acrid smoke, I choked as it burned the back of my throat; but that wouldn't stop it from being the first of many.

I'd watched the last injured mineworkers brought to the surface and seen them taken to the mine hospital in a blaze of flashing lights and sirens.

My mind was full of unanswered questions. I hadn't slept for over twenty-four hours, and I wasn't about to get any soon. Draining the last of my black coffee, Steyn's comment was buzzing inside my head... *they were checking the seismic sensors in that area.*

In front of me was an aerial photograph of the Concorde site, dominated by the headgear and winding house. It was the only adornment on the white walls of my office. In the front-left corner was a drawing board where I reviewed drawings and documents. I liked the space and found it more convenient than the restriction of my desk.

Behind me was a bank of green filing cabinets, divided in the middle by a window that faced out toward the winding house and headgear. They contained technical documents and personnel files, allowing me access to information at any time of the day or night. The gap below the window was filled with a folding camp bed for the nights when I couldn't face going back to an empty flat.

In the far right-hand corner was a substantial computer taking up the space of two tabletops. I knew it intimately and had spent more hours than I cared to remember, punching out mathematical programmes onto the screen. This was where we'd started to develop a new underground safety system using statistics and probability. I say *we* because that's how it felt; a collaboration with an inanimate object, whose only warmth was generated by the electricity coursing through its circuits. I'd probably lavished more attention on this computer than any woman in my whole life. It was a sobering thought, and maybe I'd put too much faith in the relationship.

After an incident-free journey back to the surface, I'd arrived in my office at 2:30 in the afternoon. I was considering the possibility of closing the mine down until further notice, even though I had no authority to make such a unilateral decision. It would set off alarm bells within Rinto Gold, but I wasn't convinced it was a pressure burst. Head Office would give me some heat by the morning, but I felt I had no choice; I couldn't put others in danger. I'd asked Laura to look for any recent requests to check seismic sensors on Level 120, but there were none. *So why was Marius van der Merwe inspecting them independently?*

The last six months of seismic surveys were okay, and the readings for 120 East all equated to low-level risk. I'd had no concerns giving the area the green light for access and had resigned the clearance document only a week before the accident. Now I was doubting myself.

I'd instigated the *Seismic Sensor Scheme* or, *3S Initiative*, as it had become known, immediately following my own accident. I rang *the suits* at Head Office in Johannesburg, every day for weeks, nagging them to act on my report. I even broke ranks by sending a copy directly to Thys Van Heerden, the Rinto Gold President, ruffling a few feathers amongst the Board of Directors.

Yes, I'd exaggerated the cost savings, but I wasn't going to lose sleep. There were financial benefits attached to the Initiative, and I was cynical enough to know that none of these would reach any of the miners. They finally agreed to finance the scheme, probably to get me off their backs. Though rumour had it that Van Heerden had been impressed.

Once the funds were released, I'd arranged for seismic sensors to be positioned along the length of all the deep

BREAKING POINT

level haulage-ways on Concorde IV. Set into the walls, they electronically measured movement within the rock formation. The readings were captured on a handheld device, which the maintenance teams plugged in, as part of their daily routine. These were then passed to the Engineering Office and fed into the programme which I'd spent six months creating. The computer would take a couple of hours extrapolating the data before feeding the results onto a printout. The figures for each area would be classified as Green, Amber or Red, and became known as the *Traffic Light System*.

Green was an area with a low risk of pressure bursts and was given unrestricted access for all personnel.

Amber was a medium risk and was closed off until the engineering team carried out a visual inspection.

Red was an area with a high probability of collapse and was sealed off until a specialist maintenance team were sent in. They would assess and reinforce the *at risk* area or, in the worst case, seal off and reroute the entire chamber.

This last option was time-consuming and expensive, but it proved Rinto Gold was a progressive company. I set out knowing it was impossible to predetermine the Laws of Probability, and never suggested the system was perfect. What concerned me now was how *imperfect* it might be.

Nothing is ever foolproof in deep mining. But, for over two years, the *3S Initiative* had gained the confidence of the men; relying on it to keep them safe. After some initial scepticism, they'd begun to trust its capability to protect lives… their lives. We'd broken all safety records and almost reached one million shifts without a fatality… until nine men died in one terrible day. Right now, my feelings were numb on the Laws of Probability; the possible and impossible equally disturbing.

The phone on my desk rang.

'Hi Danny, it's me, Steyn. I need you to come over to the Mine Hospital right away. I'm with Marius van der

Merwe, Ward 2A.' His voice was a mixture of urgency and exhaustion, and before I could answer, he'd put the phone down.

I checked my watch, it was 5 o'clock, and the office had an eerie silence. I'd told everyone to go home early and be ready for a long day tomorrow.

Laura had popped in before she left and put a cup of coffee on my desk. 'Are you going to be okay, Mr Core?'

Coming up for retirement, she treated me like the son she never had and showed real concern. It helped more than she would know.

'I'll be fine, Laura, try and get as much rest as you can, tomorrow's going to be a busy day.'

'You're more than welcome to join us for supper tonight.'

There was always an open invitation to join her and her husband for some home cooking. She thought any man living on his own wasn't taking proper care of himself.

'Thanks,' I said. 'But I've got some things to do later, maybe another time.' Though I dearly wanted to forget this nightmare.

She left with the others, exhausted and emotional. There wouldn't be much sleep, especially for those who'd lost loved ones. I turned to look out of the open window and shivered. The headgear was operating again but only to transport the rescue teams, and still relying on the *3S Initiative* to keep them safe. I breathed in a whiff of fresh air. There was maybe another three hours of daylight left, but what day it was, I couldn't say.

BREAKING POINT

Chapter 4

I locked my car and walked toward the Mine Hospital. Passing a *Slegs Blankes*, Whites Only, sign at the front, I stiffened. No matter how much I believed otherwise, I'd become part of this injustice.

As I looked up at the azure sky, dusk blanched the setting sun. I caught sight of a plane tracking north leaving two condensation trails underlining the waxing moon. For the first time in five years, I realised how much I missed my home in Wales… and the enormity of abandoning the family I'd failed.

As I made my way to Ward 2A, my mind was still buzzing with unanswered questions. I couldn't face the confines of the lift and climbed the stairs to the second floor, my footsteps echoing in the clammy stairwell. Opening the ward doors, I was hit by the smell of warm food and disinfectant. The room resonated with the percussive clanging of dinner trolleys; rattling trays and plates of food, as they moved from one bed to the next. Whether it was this or the sight of Marius covered in bandages and connected to a tube, I don't know; but it was all I could do not to retch.

Dinner was being served by a large, black woman, who teased the patients as she delivered the plates loaded with some kind of meat curry and pap; a porridge made of white corn maise. As I approached, Marius acknowledged me with a thin smile and Steyn nodded from his chair.

'Hi, Marius, how are you feeling?' I asked. He looked worn out, and his bandaged hands were lifeless on the bed covers.

'Not bad Danny, not bad.'

'You've got to eat, Boss,' the black woman nagged at him. 'Try some tea; nice and strong.'

'No, thanks,' he answered wearily.

She shook her head and pursed her lips. 'No food, no good, Boss.'

I smiled as she moved on and turned to look at Steyn.

'You look like you need to get in with him,' I said. 'Why aren't you at home?' Like me, he was still in his dirty boiler suit.

'Plenty of time for that,' he answered. 'Thought I'd see, Marius before I made my way.'

He looked uncomfortable and didn't look me in the eye.

I turned to Marius. 'You've got to eat.'

'Haven't got the stomach for it. Doc says I was lucky, some damage to my hands and some cuts and bruises…' His voice trailed off.

'I'm sorry, it must have been terrible.' I clenched my fists at the banality of my words.

'I got out, Danny. Don and the others…'He couldn't finish.

'Do you remember how it happened; was there any warning?'

His eyes filled. 'It was all so sudden. We'd come down in the cage from 110 to 120 East to check out a report on *stress cracking* in the area. Within half an hour, we heard a terrible rumbling noise, then an explosion. Next thing I know, I'm waking up under tons of rock.'

'Was there any warning; any clue as to why the failure was so sudden?' I asked.

'None… it caught us cold. Christ, Danny, the whole area was designated Green. We didn't know why we were down there.'

I thought of the questions I wanted to ask but bided my time. Steyn was looking down at the floor. Something had been troubling him since the accident.

'Before I got here, Steyn, I looked for the request…' I stopped mid-sentence, realising he was close to tears.

'Dit is my skuld, ek is jammer Marius.' *This is my fault, I'm sorry Marius.* The words seemed to catch at the back of his throat, I'd never seen him like this.

BREAKING POINT

'What do you mean, *it's your fault?*' I said.

He wiped his eyes on his sleeve, but the emotion remained. 'Embele had seen signs of stress cracking at a pump station along 110 East.'

Marius looked at me, confused. 'I didn't see any signs of splintering.'

Steyn continued as though he hadn't heard him. 'He came to see me a couple of weeks ago, after his shift. His team were telling him the rock was, *talking;* you know the way they describe stress cracking.'

I kept my voice low and calm, trying not to make things worse. 'I didn't see that on the work log, Steyn?'

His hands were opening and closing.

'I know. Embele reported the problem on *110 East*, but I put *120 East* on Marius' work log. My mistake sent them into that area... and it's my fault that those men died.'

He hit out at the wall with his fist, and I heard a bone crack.

Marius tried to grab his arm, but the sudden movement made him flinch. 'Hey, man, ek is nie dood nie,' *I'm not dead yet.*

The gallows humour didn't help, and Steyn charged out. 'Ek het 'n sigaret nodig,' *I need a cigarette*, he muttered over his shoulder.

When he'd gone, Marius adjusted, to get closer. 'Don and I checked that stretch on 120 East a month ago, the whole bloody length. We did visuals with two surveyors and took photographs of all the sensitive areas.

'You've seen them, Danny, and you've run them through the programme. They showed movement, *ja,* and some splintering. But not to the point where there was the risk of a pressure burst. Christ, do you think we'd put our own lives at risk? The whole area was reinforced with *shotcrete* a year ago. It should have been as safe as houses.'

It was true that the phenomenon called *splintering*, was a sign of unstable conditions, but nothing was definitive. If every chamber had to be closed at the first sign of pressure on the rock, there wouldn't be a working mine in South Africa.

Marius took a breath; he was in more pain than he was saying.

'You don't need this right now,' I said, taking his arm.

'Forget it, Danny, I'm telling you, that chamber was safe. Whatever happened was catastrophic, but unless we had an earthquake above ground, something else caused that collapse. And that's why Steyn needs to stop blaming himself.' He brushed his bandaged palms over one another.

'You said you'd come down from 110. Why were you up there in the first place?' I asked.

'We decided to check the two new Recycling Stabilisers on the way down. We'd had a few complaints that they weren't performing properly, so we decided to have a look.'

'But those are brand new, we only installed them six months ago.'

'That's right, and they've been, sons of bitches from day one. The old ones are almost thirty years old, yet they perform much better.'

'So it was just a coincidence that Embele reported, *stress cracking* on that same level?'

'I suppose,' he replied. 'We were checking the Stabilisers, not the haulage-way.'

'And were they performing okay?'

He screwed his face. *'Nee, man*, something's not right. Nothing shows on the gauges, but they sound like shit. It's like they're trying to tear themselves apart. We were going to report back to engineering, and then this happened.' He raised his bandaged hands.

He was done in, but I needed to ask the questions that had been nagging me all day.

'When I was at the accident site, I noticed the water pipes had fractured.'

'Ja, that's all I could hear when I was down there. I thought we were going to drown.'

BREAKING POINT

'That's what's troubling me,' I said. 'How many drills did the production team have on 120 East?'

He closed his eyes, visualising the scene, his fingers counting. 'Four sets,' he replied. 'Three operators on each. Why do you ask?'

I ignored the question, afraid to break my train of thought. 'The drills were powered from one of the new Stabilisers on 110?'

'Ja,' he said. 'The gauge readings were high but okay.'

I looked out of the window, my mind frantically trying to join up the three-dimensional jigsaw. 'The water tracked from the Stabiliser on 110, down to the manifold on 120, and then on to the drills.'

'So what?' he snapped.

'So, after the collapse, the operators would have released the drills, automatically engaging the *Dead Man's Handle*.'

Now I was looking at him directly. 'And then what, Marius?'

He let out a groan. 'The back-pressure would trip the failsafe switches in the Stabiliser and cut off the water pressure. I don't need a bloody lecture on how the recycling system works, Danny.'

'So why were the pipes still pumping water, *after* the collapse?' I said.

Marius went quiet, playing out the scenario in his mind. Then I saw the logic crystallise into an inescapable fact as his eyes widened.

'Jesus Christ! How could I miss that... how could *we* miss that?'

He collapsed into his pillow, and I left him to sleep. I knew he was in for an unpleasant night. The deepest scars were the ones that lay hidden from view.

His confirmation had at least validated my suspicions. The failsafe switches within the Stabiliser should have detected the rise in back pressure and redirected the water away from the drills. It was a unique safety feature within the Stabiliser design… and it had failed.

I left quietly as Marius dozed and made a mental note to ask about the condition of the four sets of drills when they were recovered. I made my way down the stairs and out into the warm night.

There were lots of people milling around the entrance, relatives and friends of the injured. I spoke to a few, but couldn't tell them what they wanted to know… *what happened down there?* Everything was too raw for small talk, and I got the feeling my presence was only adding to their grief, so I edged away toward the car park.

The evening was filled with the sound of crickets chirping away in their secret places and kamikaze moths mobbed the security lights around the perimeter fence. I found Steyn leaning against my car, chewing on a cigarette.

'Any chance of one of *my* cigarettes?' I asked, settling down next to him.

He pulled out the crumpled pack without looking up and with the dextrous movement of a seasoned smoker, lit a match. As I leaned forward to take the flame, I saw his eyes wet and red, before the darkness overwhelmed us again.

'The accident is not your responsibility, Steyn. I've gone over all the figures, and 120 East should have been safe.'

He was looking at me now. 'That's the problem, *should have been,* isn't good enough. What if the *3S Initiative* is flawed?'

The comment stung, but I knew it was a real possibility. I'd often said, no system is foolproof, but I always had faith that this one was saving lives.

'We need to go back down, Steyn.' His eyes widened.

'What the hell for?' he replied, choking on a lungful of smoke.

'I need to check something.'
'Not tonight, Danny, surely?'

BREAKING POINT

I knew if I said yes, he would back me up, even with a broken hand. But we were both done in.

'No,' we'll get you back in there.' I nodded toward the hospital entrance. 'Get that hand seen to. Can you arrange for Embele to come with us tomorrow?'

'I'm not sure, he's pretty cut up about his brother. And anyway, why do you want to go back down to 120, haven't we seen all we want to see?'

I flicked my cigarette into the darkness, and the small explosion of sparks died in the dry earth.

'We're going to 110, Steyn. I want to look at those two new Recycling Stabilisers.'

Chapter 5

Thys Van Heerden looked out from the seventeenth floor of Rinto Gold's Head Office. Below, the intersecting streets of Johannesburg sprawled, snarled with pedestrians and rush hour traffic. It was familiar, but his mind was elsewhere.

As President of Rinto Gold, he was under more pressure than at any time in his five-year tenure. The mining industry had moved on. Gone were the days when fatalities were accepted as part of the industry. A disaster on the scale of Concorde IV was front-page news and on every news bulletin. His PR people were already putting together a response to present at a press conference later that afternoon.

Beneath thin, grey hair, his complexion was tanned and healthy, but the lean features were coursed with wrinkles. His wife used to call them *laughter lines*. But that was a long time ago before he'd been cursed with ambition.

The monitor buzzed on his desk. As he frowned, the lines etched deeper into his face, like chisel cuts fashioned in sixty-year-old wood. His six-foot frame stooped to press the intercom button, and he braced himself.

'Mr Van?' It was Jean Venter, his secretary.

Her shrill voice rang in his ears, like tinnitus, and he drew his head back, as though spittle had sprayed out. Everyone addressed him as Mr Van, and he was immensely grateful in the case of his secretary... anything that helped reduce the number of syllables she had to pronounce.

'I have Mr Schmidt and Mr Stomp ready to see you,' she screeched. The final word of every sentence was pitched like a question.

He unclamped his teeth, and the worry lines receded.
'Let them in, Jean.'

His voice was refined, with a smooth, South African lilt. He prided himself on being a *White South African*, tracing

BREAKING POINT

his lineage back three generations, to nineteenth-century Cornwall. No Boer blood in *his* veins.

Stylishly tailored, he'd never been down a mine in his life. He'd made his name on the Johannesburg Stock Exchange before joining Rinto Gold at the age of fifty-five. It had been a good match for both parties because the price of gold skyrocketed to an all-time high, thanks to Soviet problems in Afghanistan and the Iranian revolution. It was a slice of good fortune that his predecessor never enjoyed. But it augmented his credibility as a sound leader. Calm under pressure and ruthless.

He returned to the window, reaching to touch both edges. First with the tip of his left hand, then with the tip of his right, and repositioned precisely in the centre. He wiped the end of each finger with a tissue.

He'd led a privileged life and feared any amendments now would alter the serendipity of his existence. He wiped each finger three times, and if he miscounted, the process would have to be repeated for karma to return.

The door opened, and the Engineering Director, Joe Schmidt, walked in, followed by Karl Stomp, the financial controller. They stood at the desk, fidgeting like naughty schoolboys, looking awkwardly at Van Heerden's back. Stomp coughed quietly to attract his attention but was ignored, and a full minute passed in prickly silence.

Van Heerden observed their reflection in the feature window like a captain of industry on the bridge of his ship. He was angry, but anger was a weakness that needed to be contained.

Turning, and without looking at the two men, he took his seat behind a Stinkwood desk; an impressive monolith. Its dense, reddish, grain was highly polished, hard as teak and ludicrously expensive. Apart from a telephone, monitor and intercom, its only adornment was a Mont Blanc fountain pen, positioned dead centre and adjacent to the front edge. The lack of a writing pad was deliberate.

Secretaries wrote, and presidents spoke, leaving no visible trail.

No pictures decorated the white walls of the office and, in the mornings, the feature window offered magnificent views of Johannesburg until midday. After which, with the afternoon sun at its zenith, it would require welding goggles to see out. Vertical blinds provided some relief from the stifling heat but distorted the light with diagonal shadows. These conflicted with the perpendicular lines of the magnificent desk and often sent him home with a migraine.

'Good morning, gentlemen,' he said finally. 'Please sit down.' He looked up at them both for the first time.

'I hope you have good news about Concorde IV.'

They both looked at the single chair, polished to the same lustre as the desk, and declined to take the seat.

Van Heerden began gently polishing the edge of the desk with the soiled handkerchief. Three times clockwise; three times anti-clockwise. He looked up and gestured with his hands as they opened their prepared notes.

'Put those away gentlemen, this meeting is strictly off the record. I just want to understand what happened and how we can best…' He paused and looked over their heads at the blank wall, searching for an appropriate word. '*Avoid? Y*es, *avoid* any more adverse publicity about this tragedy.' He dropped the handkerchief in the waste paper bin and rested his chin on manicured fingers.

'And perhaps help me identify who is responsible.'

They ruffled their notes back in place and coughed nervously, each waiting for the other to begin.

'Well, Mr Van…' Karl Stomp was first to crack. 'I believe we need to nip this in the bud. If we agree to compensate the families, we can…'

Van Heerden interrupted. 'I understand that Stomp, but do we know *why* this tragedy happened?' He liked to call his people by their surnames; it avoided favouritism and emphasised his primacy.

BREAKING POINT

Joe Schmidt took his opportunity. 'Well, it's clear there was some sort of collapse on 120 East, Mr Van, but we're still investigating the accident site. It's too early to come up with any conclusions, particularly…'

A raised hand stopped him in mid-sentence. 'I'll be the judge of that, Schmidt. Two days have passed, and our shareholders are waiting for me to issue a statement.'

He turned to Karl Stomp. 'Can I ask you, as the financial man, how much we invested in the 3S Initiative for Concorde IV?'

Stomp thought for a moment. 'I think it was around half a million rand Mr…'

'You *think* it was, do you?' Van Heerden's tone was derisive. 'It was, in fact, six hundred and twenty-five thousand rand. And shall I tell you *why* I know the figure so well?'

The two men mumbled assent and nodded their heads, Stomp a little too vigorously, causing his glasses to bounce on his nose.

'Because, gentlemen, I made a promise to the shareholders that their investment would help protect the lives of the underground workers, and put Rinto Gold at the vanguard of underground safety.' He had an unsettling smile on his face.

'Absolutely, Mr Van, absolutely,' Stomp replied with a less energetic nod.

'Absolutely, *what*, Stomp?'

The smile disappeared. 'Well… erm… absolutely, *right*, Mr Van. Our goal is to keep the men safe?'

Van Heerden swung his chair back around to face the window as though he was addressing the whole metropolis. 'Wrong! Our goal is *not* to keep the men safe; our goal is to make money.'

Joe Schmidt agreed. 'Absolutely, Mr Van, and…' But before he could squeeze in another *absolutely*, Van Heerden repeated the question.

'Absolutely, *what*, Schmidt?' He watched their reflections; they were shaking their heads at one another.

'Uh... absolutely *right*, that our goal is... erm... to make money?' Van Heerden heard the enquiry at the end of the sentence and spun around to face them again.

'I asked you a question, Schmidt. Are you answering it with another question?'

'No sir, I just thought...'

'And I've just answered your question with my question. That's three unanswered questions, in one conversation. Aren't you here to give me answers?'

'Christ!' His voice rose uncharacteristically. 'I've just added a fourth unanswered question. Enough!'

Bang!

He hit the desk with a force that could have split a lesser timber... but not Stinkwood, and he immediately regretted his action.

Schmidt and Stomp simultaneously ducked, like boxers dodging a haymaker.

The blow hurt like hell, but Van Heerden was more distracted by the ugly smudge his palm had created on the polished surface.

As the room absorbed the noise and fell into another long silence, the Mont Blanc fountain pen rolled elegantly along the desk and teetered, off centre, in the centre of the smudge. He felt a migraine coming on, and it was only 9:30 in the morning.

Holding his hand under the desk, his features remained impassive as he waited for the throbbing to ease. He hadn't lost his temper like this since 1975.

'Gentlemen,' he continued. 'I don't want this to become a witch hunt, and this company is not in the business of pointing fingers. However, with an incident as serious as this I need to know, *who is responsible?*'

Schmidt was the first to regroup and step in. 'Mr Van, the Initiative was designed and set up by the Chief Engineer. His proposal was vetted, and the plan put to yourself and the Board of Directors to approve the funding. Since its inception, Concorde IV has not only out-performed all our other mines in the Free State, but it's done so with the best safety record.'

'Until two days ago.' Van Heerden's eyes flashed between the Engineering Director and the itinerant fountain pen; not sure which he wanted to grab first. It was time to give them a lesson in the facts of life... and death.

His voice was calm and controlled. 'Listen, Schmidt, for every collapse in every mine, there is a price to pay. True?'

'Yes, sir.'

'And that price is paid in lost production. Yes?'

'Yes, sir and, on occasions, in lives lost. Which is why we approved...'

'Quite. You've explained yourself fully on the safety Initiative, but let's develop my scenario further, shall we?'

Both men nodded as he continued.

'We know that lost production can be measured financially, in rand. Yes?'

'Yes.' Stomp took the lead.

'And for every day of lost production, Concorde IV loses approximately, 100,000 rand.'

'Yes, sir, that's about right.' Stomp was leaning into his financial comfort zone.

'And how do we measure lives lost?' Stomp almost choked, but Van Heerden ignored him.

'Difficult to answer? Then let me put it another way. If you were in charge of a mine and learnt of a serious collapse, what would your first question be?'

'Well, it would concern the fate of the men.'

'Of course it would, Stomp. So, I ask you both again. How do we measure lives lost?'

He watched them and again they were uncomfortable with the question, but he continued to probe.

'As I said, you are in charge of the mine, and thus, the security of *your job* relies on its productivity; achieving targets, meeting deadlines. But now the process is on stop and costing *you,* 100,000 rand for every lost day.

'And remember, gentlemen, this operation is seven days a week, fifty-two weeks a year. There is very little in the budget to recover any lost production.' His finger moved back and forth like a metronome.

'Meanwhile…' His lip curled, and the smile appeared again. 'That deafening noise you hear isn't your customers complaining. Nor is it the sound of your competitor's machinery, taking advantage of your difficulties and outstripping your production targets. No, that noise is coming from your own people…' He paused for effect.

'Not those injured in the collapse, but the Managers, Mine Captains, Foremen, Face Workers, all complaining about reduced wages and lost bonuses; their jobs put at risk. Then more noises from further down the production line. Those operating the crushers, the cyanide reservoirs, the filter processors and the emulsion tanks.

'Everyone of them, to a man, protesting they have no ore to process. *Their* jobs being put at risk.'

He was enjoying, showing off his knowledge, it took his mind off the mayhem on his desk.

'And onto the bigger picture.' He clasped his hands, the right one throbbing like a pulse. He saw both heads drop a fraction.

'Customers and shareholders, all demanding to know when your processes will be up and running.' Another pause.

'So, I ask you again…' His unblinking eyes were trained on both of them. 'What would your first question be?'

There was no fight left in either interlocuter, so Van Heerden filled the silence.

'We have to look at the wider picture and ask ourselves this. Will this incident close the mine, and if so, for how long? And before you think that I don't appreciate the suffering of those injured, I will remind you of the consequences of reduced productivity. Permanent job losses, gentlemen, *permanent*! This will not affect the dead, but those still living and dependant on Concorde IV for an income...' Another pause.

'So, when you say that I approved the *Initiative*, I did so to improve productivity, saving lives was simply a by-product.'

Both men seemed to shiver with the truth of it.

'We're not sure whether the mine will be closed, Mr Van. I'm going to visit...' Van Heerden's hand went up again, stopping Schmidt in his tracks.

'Swift action from me will limit the damage to our share price, but I need to be able to report *the possible cause.* I need to make them believe we have everything under control, that their investment is safe. Do you understand how difficult that will be?'

Both men nodded.

'So, either embrace your culpability and resign, gentlemen, or tell me now. Who is responsible?'

Chapter 6

My legs flexed with the movement of the cage as it bounced. A feeling of relief washed over me, as we waited for it to settle before the doors were allowed to open on Level 110.

My observations at the accident site had kept me awake all night, and I couldn't dismiss the possibility that the 3S Initiative *had* failed. If so, then I'd failed every one of the dead and injured, whose names were on the reports filling my in-tray.

When I doubted myself, I remembered that other time, that other place and resolved to trust my instincts. I was on my own again, and that would be enough. It had to be.

'Are you okay, Danny?' Steyn's voice broke the silence. I'd had my eyes shut for most of the descent, lost in my thoughts. When I opened them, Embele was staring at me.

Watching me all the way down, I thought. *Waiting to step in?*

He'd agreed to come with us, even though he was grieving for his brother. His face was the usual shade of *expressionless*, but despite misgivings, there was a lot I liked about him. I couldn't say what, or why, but in a short time, I'd found myself trusting him, even though he'd seen me at my most vulnerable.

'Ready when you are.' I replied.

Steyn led us out onto 110, his hand heavily strapped. Most would have used it as an excuse to drop out, but he wouldn't let me down. I'd been told that once you had an Afrikaner as a friend, it was for life, I was a fortunate man. Armed with a camera and notepad, I followed them along the chamber.

Walking for twenty minutes, we were still half a mile from the Stabilisers, and already I could hear them resonating in the distance. A deep bass throbbing in the

BREAKING POINT

atmosphere. With a quarter of a mile left, the sound was now uncomfortable, and we put on ear protectors. From then on, sign language would be our only way of communicating.

Ten minutes later, we entered the opening to the chamber. The noise was like someone hammering my ears with a shovel. The intensity of the low-pitched sound vibrated through my body, chattering my teeth.

I looked across at Steyn, his brow furrowed and eyes half-closed, as though he was walking against a force ten gale. Embele was more used to this, but even he looked uncomfortable... *this level of noise wasn't natural.*

In front of us, a trio of Recycling Stabilisers filled a cavity the size of an amphitheatre, the curved roof seemed to heighten the noise. Every inch of their design was familiar from my days with Mathers. I stood in front of the first Stabiliser; an older model that had been installed about thirty years ago, one of many throughout Concorde IV.

Fifty feet long, the Monel T20 alloy body looked like an enormous hourglass tipped on its side. 10-feet in diameter at both ends, and narrowing in the centre. The structure weighed over 25-tons and needed a steel frame, secured in concrete, to support the bulk, raising the centreline of the unit to almost 10-feet above the floor level.

Steyn had stayed a few steps behind, giving me space to take it all in. I moved around the safety fence toward the flat, rear-end, where two, 24-inch diameter pipes extended horizontally before being capped with two water pumps. There were various valves and gauges, but I couldn't see anything problematic from this distance.

Returning to the flat, front section, another four, 24-inch outlet pipes jutted like warship cannons. Again, nothing suspicious. I followed them for about a hundred paces, running my gloved hand on their surface. The temperatures were reasonable, and there was no excessive vibration as they disappeared westward, following the contours of the excavation.

So much could go wrong. Each change of direction, around and down the inclines, would be subjected to enormous side forces. I looked into the darkness; so much to see and so little time.

Moving back to the Stabiliser, the whole thing was like science fiction; an Armageddon bringer. But I knew within the vulgar exterior there was a unique arrangement of blades, deflectors and rubber diaphragms. By way of an ingenious design, these would transform the destructive energy of the water into a controlled force to drive the underground machinery.

The Stabiliser design changed the face of mining forever and remained unsurpassed by any new technology developed since. Usually, dams would be excavated to control the effects of water velocity. They were expensive, and the additional underground workings created a paradox; destabilising the environment they were built to protect. The Recycling Stabiliser changed all that.

Water rests upon the earth, benign and calm. But forced below ground and restrained by metal pipes, it pressurises to over four hundred pounds per square inch for every one thousand feet of vertical drop. Velocity increases exponentially, and linear forces multiply with every change of direction.

And all the time, the capricious flow searches for a weakness… for a way out.

I pulled my mind back to the present… *concentrate on what you can see.* I decided to inspect this one first; a benchmark to judge the others and scribbled *Stabiliser 1* on my notes.

Unlocking the gate, I breached the protective wire fence that surrounded it and climbed the metal ladder to stand on the mezzanine platform running along its length. Steyn stepped back, craning his neck. He was looking at the *smokestack,* rising from the centre. It was actually the input

BREAKING POINT

pipe, but the nickname had stuck because of the resemblance to the tapered chimney of a Wild West locomotive.

I looked up, following Steyn's gaze, and saw its ten-foot diameter pipe disappear through the multi-level excavations, toward the surface.

It was pointless trying to speak, the noise was malevolent at such close proximity. Fed by the water flowing through its manufactured organs, the whole structure vibrated like a living organism.

I put my gloved hand on the surface as I'd done many times during testing at Mathers, and felt the heat conducting through the metal body. This was normal and caused by the friction of the water channelling through its gut. Drawing my hand along its length, everything was as I remembered.

The horizontal unit was made up of three flanged sections, each held together with high tensile bolts. Rubber seals prevented leakage and maintained the internal water pressure; critical to its efficiency. Experience, instinct, call it what you will, but I knew this Stabiliser was working efficiently. Secure and dependable.

I'd been introduced to the product when I was an apprentice, and marvelled at the skills of its designer, Franklyn Mathers. Created in 1927, this technical masterpiece appeared to defy logic.

Checking the sensitive areas for signs of weakness, I noted down the pressure readings, water velocities and temperatures as a matter of rote. I took as many photographs as I dared, and another hour confirming what I already knew. Everything was as it should be.

Thirty years old, Marius had said, and he was right. It was still doing its job. As I descended the ladder, I turned to give Steyn a thumbs up; Embele was nowhere to be seen.

Moving on to the second Stabiliser, one of two recent installations, my stomach knotted, and a cold sweat formed

on my brow. I was dreading what I was about to discover...
or not discover. Steyn held back, as though he'd caught my apprehension, or maybe anticipating his comment... w*hat if the 3S Initiative, is flawed?*

Unlike *Stabiliser 1*, the four outlet pipes stretched east, along the sidewall of the chamber. They would veer off a different incline and eventually drop toward Level 140. In the same direction as the accident site, but another two hundred feet below.

I stopped in front of the enclosure and marked Stabiliser 2 on my notes. After taking a couple of photographs, I drew my eyes from the camera. This was different from Stabiliser 1, there'd been changes.

Unlocking the safety gate, I mounted the ladder onto the mezzanine floor. The vibrations beneath my feet were more severe and the noise, even with ear protectors, was considerably louder. I found myself squeezing the handrail to keep my balance. I put a gloved hand on the outer surface which felt much hotter; uncomfortably so. The vibrations were too intense, causing the unit to shudder. My initial thought was *water hammer*, which was a cancer to fluid engineering and maybe disturbing the flow. I drew my hand along its length for as long as I could bear the heat and saw Steyn watching me. He gave me a questioning thumbs up, but all I could do was grimace and shake my head. Embele was still missing.

I came back down the ladder to check the flange connections. Water was leaking onto the floor, not excessive, but the main seal had been breached and could be causing the water hammer. I noticed the flanges were held with only half the number of bolts used on *Stabiliser1*... it didn't look enough.

It was impossible to second guess the problems from the outside as the clues lay hidden beneath its metal skin. The condition of the failsafe switches, deflector plates and diaphragms would give me a complete picture, but were

BREAKING POINT

impossible to access without a partial strip down. Not only a huge task, but one which would invalidate the warranty and relinquish Mathers of responsibility. And I wasn't ready to do that until all my options had run out.

A brass plate attached to the side showed maximum pressures, velocities, etc., all the usual blurb. Checking my notes, there were some anomalies in the gauge readings but not enough to concern me. Another plate was inscribed *MK6*, in a large silver script; I made a note and circled it.

Further checks failed to ease the knot in my stomach. There were questions to be answered on the design changes, but nothing tangible. And not enough to be implicated in the collapse.

Steyn held the gate open for me, and we both moved wordlessly to the final Stabiliser; the most recent installation. This was the one that powered the drills at the accident site… *find nothing and Mathers has no case to answer.*

Steyn didn't look at me and unlocking the gate felt like accessing a prison cell. The floor was thick with ankle-deep mud. *The first indication of something wrong?*

I didn't bother with photographs and quickly climbed the ladder, onto the mezzanine floor; I wanted this over and done with as soon as possible. My confidence had been drained with the first two inspections, and I wasn't expecting anything different. I wrote *Stabiliser 3* on a fresh sheet and found the metal plate with the operating details. This was also a *MK6*, and I made a note.

The vibrations from the main body were, as severe as Stabiliser 2, and putting my gloved hand on the surface, it felt hotter. The temperature reading on the gauge confirmed my instincts. Again, I struggled to keep my balance, and the noise was painful and irregular; the whole thing seemed to be trying to tear itself apart. I was taking the pressure and velocity readings when the penny dropped. This Stabiliser was operating on lower operating conditions.

Ian Holland

I'll get them to reduce the inlet pressure and the flow velocity as a precaution... The words of Piet Reiss yesterday, and the gauges concurred. *If it was functioning this poorly now, what would it be like at normal levels?*

It was the first indication that there was a problem with the Stabiliser. I was energised and almost ran down the ladder to check the seals and bolts on the front section. Even with the reduced pressures, I could see the seal had been compromised, water was pouring out and flooding the floor.

One of the nuts had come loose, exposing the threads of the bolt and, given the amount of water leaking out, it was probable that others would be the same. I took deep breaths trying not to get ahead of myself.

Reverting to my checking regime, I followed the same procedures I'd carried out on Stabilisers *1* and *2*. Same observations and photographs, particularly around the flanges.

The incessant noise was making my head spin. My mouth was powder dry and sweat was stinging my eyes. I exited the safety fence and closed the gate e. Steyn gave another questioning thumbs up, but I just shrugged. Anything I said now could be construed as self-preservation, but this was the first sign that I might be on to something.

I traced a more optimistic path, following each of the four outlet pipes. Only yesterday they'd carried high-pressure water down to the devastation on 120 East. Today, with the reduced inlet pressure from the Stabiliser, they were relatively benign; at odds with the chaos inside the Stabiliser. They followed in the same easterly direction as *Stabiliser 2*, adding to the clamour bouncing off the walls of the chamber. *Eight pipes telling different stories.*

I followed the eight pipes as they continued along the side walls to a thirty-degree horizontal bend; the first vulnerable point. I took photographs of the pipe supports and the concrete plinths holding them. Such was their size,

BREAKING POINT

I had to take the pictures in stages and would join them up later.

The brackets were formed from heavy plate, cast into concrete plinths. The pipes snaked around the curve, and I soon noticed signs of damage. Shards of concrete were starting to break away, and cracks were developing on the sides of one of the plinths; another sign that something was wrong. I was convinced the nuts holding the brackets would be loose and made a note for the engineers to check the torques. I was starting to believe again.

Trying to take more photographs was difficult. The passageway was getting tighter the further I moved in, and the sensitive areas were hidden in shadow. I'd used up two of the three reels of film and needed to be frugal. The noise was relentless, and I was soaked in sweat; the conditions making it difficult to concentrate.

Out of the corner of my eye, I saw Embele approach from the darkness beyond the bend. He was shouting at me and pointing back from where we'd come from. Before I had a chance to ask where he'd been, he pulled me back toward *Stabiliser 3*. I'd never seen him so animated.

We went back through the unlocked gate and re-entered the wire cage; a tight fit for the two of us, especially with his shoulders taking up most of the space. Steyn was watching us, mesmerised.

Embele led me up onto the mezzanine floor and pointed to the *smokestack*. It should have been anchored securely but was flexing unnaturally. He dragged me back down the ladder and Steyn followed as we headed past the thirty-degree bend and beyond.

About a quarter of a mile further on, we reached the point where the pipes diverged. One set continued along the roof-wall, the others dipped down a 45-degree incline leading to 120 East and the scene of the collapse.

My heart was racing. I looked back at Steyn, who was crouched over, hands on knees, looking down the black hole of the incline, and then to Embele. He was pointing at something and shouting at me. The noise hadn't abated, still impossible to hear above the sound of the Stabilisers and water rushing through the pipes. The chamber was stifling and cramped, such was the size of the concrete plinths on the incline. They dwarfed those back at the thirty-degree bend and overwhelmed the free space and fresh air that we craved. I moved toward Embele, and he pushed me into a narrow corner, pointing his finger at something.

Then I saw it and held my breath. Steyn, looking over Embele's shoulder, saw it too. One of the plinths had shattered entirely, twisting the pipe brackets at a crazy angle. Three of the bolts had pulled away and were exposed like giant television aerials. Embele was shouting at me, getting more and more animated, but his words were futile in the cauldron of sound. He leaned across me, grabbing large shards of rock, shoving them at me with his eyes bulging.

'Rock Talking… rock talking.'

I could lip-read the words, but my head was being battered with the violent noise. I felt like a boxer being pummelled on the ropes. Calculations were running through my brain as I tried to give it a technical perspective.

Velocity equalled flow rate divided by the nominal bore of the pipe. If the pipe was 24 inches diameter? What was the multiplication factor… 0.55? No, it was 0.408… wasn't it? Or was the flow rate in metres cubed per hour or US gallons per minute?' Pressure increases with the vertical drop…

I was trying to visualise the piping system in three dimensions when it was impossible to think clearly in one. The noise was overpowering, the vibrations, everything. I was trying to work it out… should be working it out. But in the background…

'Rock splitting, Boss… rock splitting…'

BREAKING POINT

Embele was in my face again, I could smell his breath. My head spun, and my body was in a cold sweat.

What was the erosion factor on underground piping?
Had it been exceeded?
Was the pipework destroying itself from the inside?

I didn't know... couldn't focus. Everything was a jumbled mass of contradictions.

Was that why the Stabiliser was struggling?

He was hemming me in, blocking my exit. I felt sick, frustration turning to anger. My legs were going numb, my heart trying to hammer its way out of my chest... I had to get out!

I turned on him, grabbed his collar and tried to drag him out of my way.

I had more chance of moving the Stabiliser, and he just looked at me, confused.

'Get out of the fucking way, or so help me!' I shouted.

I put my forearm into his chest. He looked at me stupidly and then I lost it. I punched him on the shoulder, unaware of what I was doing, I just needed to get out.

'For fuck's sake, get out of the way!'

My second punch hurt him, and he retaliated with a left hook that felt like he'd removed my lower jaw. My mouth fell open as I took another swing at him. He ducked and took the full force on the top of his head. It was like hitting rock; big, black, shiny rock. I winced, and we ended up grappling on the floor, grunting and snorting at each other like a couple of drunks.

Steyn waded in to drag us apart, which locked all three of us against the broken plinth. I was crying to get away, but I couldn't move. My arms were pressed down with both their bodies on top of me. We were screaming like three deaf-mutes in the bowels of hell.

The last thing I remember was throwing up and wishing them both dead before I blacked out. When I came to, Steyn was dusting me down like a concerned father.

'You okay?' he asked.

At least I could hear him, and I could breathe properly. I put my thumb up and flinched with the pain in my hand as I raised myself on shaky legs. They'd dragged me from the incline to some sort of pump-room. It had the benefit of a door so the noise was muted and we could hear ourselves talk.

'What the hell got into you, man?' Steyn addressed me, coated in dust. 'You were like a wild animal.'

I was glad I didn't have to explain myself.

'Christ, Embele could have killed you. What's the matter with the pair of you?'

He looked across at Embele who was leaning against the wall and pointed.

'Jy is in groot moeilikheid.' *You're in big trouble.* Who the hell do you think you are, hitting the Chief Engineer, that's a sackable offence?'

I walked over, and Embele's eyes didn't flinch. He had good reason to be angry; I was the one who threw the first punch, and he was being threatened with the sack.

My eyes didn't falter either.

'He was lucky you stepped in,' I shouted over my shoulder. 'I was just getting into my stride.'

Steyn looked bewildered until Embele started laughing.

'Christ, he can laugh,' I shouted and would have laughed louder but for the pain in my jaw.

Steyn caught the bug. 'Stupid bastards,' he said. And the three of us relieved the pressure with manic laughter until we could hardly breathe.

I slapped Embele's shoulder and winced. *Shit, my hand hurt.* Then more laughter at my expense.

BREAKING POINT

Chapter 7

Putting our ear protectors back on, we stepped from the pump-room and back into the bedlam. I led them back to the incline and took photographs of the damage at the top. But I needed to see more and indicated to Steyn that I wanted to go further down. It would be tight, but the maintenance ladder, following the piping down, would help. Steyn handed me a small torch, and Embele found a length of rope he tied around my waist as a precaution. He winked at me and lifted my ear defenders.

'Any problem, Boss, pull on the rope and I'll get you back.'

I appreciated his concern and gave a thumbs up, wincing as the pain shot up my arm. The bastard laughed as he replaced the defenders.

I reverted to shallow breathing and ignored everything except the pipes above my head. I could feel the water vibrating inside them, conscious that they could collapse at any moment. Shining the torch down the incline, the foot-wall was covered with shards of rock, some big enough to crush bones. Pipe brackets were buckled, and bolts had disengaged entirely. Something had gone wrong down here, but there was no evidence of a pressure burst. *So why this much damage to the pipes?*

As I moved down, the damage increased tenfold. The majority of the brackets were bent and splayed, and the piping dangerously compromised. I struggled around the damaged metalwork to get a better look only to see more destruction. Flange bolts had stretched and sheared, causing the pipes to bend at odd angles, exposing the seals. Water, still being fed from the Stabiliser, was seeping out of the joints and flowed down the incline.

It was too dangerous to go any further, but I could see where the pipes tapered down to 18-inch diameter, and curved around onto 120 East. We were about half a mile from the collapse, and these were the same pipes that had set the alarm bells ringing in my head.

I'd seen enough. I finished off the reel of photographs and gave two tugs on the rope. Such was the force and speed that Embele pulled me back up, I thought he'd sprung a couple of my ribs. He looked as relieved as I was when I surfaced and I got the feeling he was looking out for me. I motioned him and Steyn back to the pump-room and closed the door behind us.

'I'm going to shut down Concorde IV until those MK6 Stabilisers have been checked out,' I said.

Steyn looked shocked. 'You can't shut down the whole works, Danny. You're putting yourself in the firing line from the top brass. What makes you think the shaft is at risk?'

I squeezed my eyes together with my fingers, thinking through the three-dimensional picture that was finally developing. 'Okay, tell me if I'm wrong. Once the repair work is completed, those two MK6 Stabilisers will continue to supply high-pressure water to 120 and 140 East.' They nodded in unison. 'And both Stabilisers have fail-safe switches which, when activated, should prevent extreme water pressure reaching those levels.'

'That's right,' said Steyn. 'The Stabiliser will automatically redirect the water to the exhaust system.'

I nodded and continued. 'So, in a perfect world, the pressure would be reduced, and the water circulated safely outside the main network.' I had them on board so far but was about to take them outside their comfort zone.

'Now let's assume the MK6 Stabilisers are not functioning correctly.'

Steyn shook his head. 'But we haven't found anything conclusive.'

'Stay with me, please,' I said.
'Okay, okay.'

BREAKING POINT

I continued. 'Let's assume the MK6 fail-safe switches didn't react to the *Dead Man's Handle on the drills*. Are we agreed it will continue supplying high-pressure water?'

'Ja, but that's never happened before,' said Steyn.

'No, not with the old Stabiliser's, but what if it did with the MK6?'

He thought for a moment and looked at Embele. 'Jesus Christ, water under that kind of pressure, with nowhere else to go, would try and rip the bloody pipes apart.'

'And, in the process, try to straighten out every bend in the system,' I added. 'Imagine the forces pulling at every support bracket, every fastening and every concrete plinth in its path.' In a court of law, I'd have been accused of *leading the witnesses*, but I was stating a fact.

'It would tear the bloody walls down,' Steyn said.

For the first time, I saw a chink of light, maybe the chance of a convert.

'Yes, it might, Steyn, and that's what we may have witnessed here. The result would be as catastrophic as a pressure burst.'

'I can see where you're going with this,' he said. 'But how do you prove it's one thing and not the other? Faulty Stabiliser or pressure burst?'

If I couldn't convince him now, I was ready to give up. 'The drills on 120 East were powered from Stabiliser 3, the MK6 clearly not functioning correctly.'

Embele nodded this time.

'Agreed,' said Steyn.

'So, if we assume the fail-safe switches *were* faulty, and the *dead man's handle* wasn't, then when the operators released the drills…'

'Yes, yes, I got that, Danny. The pressure could have burst the pipes, so get to the bloody point, man.' He was getting frustrated.

'The pipes *did* burst.' Embele's voice turned both our heads. He'd finally got it, and I could have hugged him.

'You noticed it too?' I said, controlling my excitement.

He nodded. 'I noticed it, Boss. I saw the water pouring out, but thought no more about it.' He seemed impressed.

Steyn looked shellshocked, so I filled in the blanks.

'If the water was unrestrained by a failure of the failsafe switches, yet restrained by the *dead man's handle*,' you'd have over a mile of piping trying to rip themselves apart under pressure.'

Steyn was nodding his head, then I saw the penny drop.

'Fuck!' He dropped his head into his hands. 'Which is what we're seeing,' he said, out loud. 'A massive whiplash effect. How the *fuck* did I miss that?'

I tapped him on the shoulder. 'It doesn't matter now, but are you agreed it could explain the collapse?'

'Maybe so, but how the hell do we prove it?'

That was the next hurdle, but I hadn't finished.

'So, if we're agreed that some sort of MK6 failure resulted in the collapse on the output side of the Stabiliser, the result of a failure on the input side would be ten times worse.'

It was Embele's turn to look puzzled. 'But how would that happen, Boss?'

Steyn understood and went on to explain. 'If the pressure backs up on the input side, above 110, then the forces would impact on the main shaft and every bit of conveyance that we use to bring men up and down. It could cause a failure of the lifting mechanisms, including all the man-cages and whoever was in them.'

'So why didn't that happen, Boss?'

'You're not going to like how I say this, Embele. But *luckily*...' I looked at him to show I wasn't making light of his brother's death. '*Luckily* the pipes burst on 120, relieving the pressure.

'Jesus, I still can't believe I missed those burst pipes.' Steyn was still berating himself, and I think Embele was starting to realise the implications as well.

'Pressure on the input side would kill hundreds,' I said. 'And until someone can prove otherwise, I'm closing the mine.' I looked at Embele. 'You work on these Stabilisers, have you seen this much vibration before?'

He thought for a moment. 'The MK6 Stabilisers were doing their job before the collapse, Boss. But the vibration is much worse than the old ones.'

I turned to Steyn. 'What's your opinion?'

He looked uncomfortable and pulled a cigarette from his top pocket. The bandage on his hand made his movements clumsy and slow. He offered me one, but I declined, so he lit his own and drew back the smoke.

'Look, Danny, you make a good case, but shutting down the mine. Are you sure you want to make that decision on your own?'

'No choice,' I said. 'Until we give these MK6 Stabilisers a clean bill of health, I can't risk it.'

Steyn took three more interminable drags on the cigarette before flicking it out and crushing it under his feet.

'I hope you're right,' he replied. 'But there are no reports of problems since commissioning. And without evidence, the damage we've seen, even the excessive vibrations within the Stabilisers, could still be attributed to the after-effects of a pressure burst.' He looked a bit embarrassed. 'I'm sorry, Danny, but that's how I see it.'

I understood what he meant, the theory was one thing, but it wouldn't stand up without proof.

'Then what made Embele report the *splintering* on 110, weeks before the collapse?' I wasn't giving up easily.

Steyn raised his eyebrows toward Embele. 'Well?'

Embele looked at me. 'I reported it because that's my job, Boss.'

Great, I thought, *another blind alley.* I couldn't get either man completely on-board. *Was I looking for excuses rather than admitting the failure of my 3S Initiative?*

I was knackered and told Steyn and Embele to close down the Recycling Stabilisers on 110 and return to the surface. At the same time, I made my way back to the man-cages, knowing I couldn't rest until I'd revisited the accident site.

Arriving at 120, things were a lot quieter, and the half-mile walk was less arduous with the chambers clear of rescue teams. When I approached, about ten fitters were putting the finishing touches to the new supports, bolstering the roof-walls. With the rock now cleared, I estimated the collapse had stretched over a quarter of a mile.

The men parted as I walked along its length, my eyes scanning the water pipes along the hanging-wall. I almost bumped into Piet Reiss.

'Danny,' he said, with no enthusiasm.

'Sorry, Piet, I didn't see you there.' He didn't look happy to see me.

'You struggling to see what happened?' he said. His eyes were lined and bloodshot. He was running on empty.

'You must be shattered?'

He waved his arm lazily, deflecting my concern. 'I'm just trying to get my head around it all.'

'Any ideas?'

He sucked on his cigarette and looked me straight in the eye. 'A pressure burst. That quick... that catastrophic. All the hallmarks.' His eyes wouldn't let me go as though looking for a reaction.

'And the *3S system*?' I asked, my mouth parched.

'Dit het misluk.' *It failed.* 'Simple and straightforward. Those men were in the wrong place at the wrong time. The haulage was dangerous.'

I stared into his eyes. He was an honest man, doing his best to conceal a wave of burning anger. 'Do you think the system let them down, Piet?'

He drew heavily on his cigarette again. 'I've worked underground for thirty years, and I've seen a lot of accidents. Not many fatalities, thank God. I know you think your fancy *3S System* has kept the men safe, but you've been lucky.'

BREAKING POINT

I nodded. I wanted to hear it straight. 'Could the system have been lucky for *so* long, Piet?'

I think he felt a challenge in my response and bristled.

'Listen, before you came along, yes, we had fatalities. But even *The Butcher* had his fair share of *luck*. Before they began giving prizes for this, *Fatality Free Shift* bullshit, no one gave a toss about the number of bodies we brought up. It was all hidden. The big bosses in Johannesburg couldn't care less about us, black or white.

'What did matter was bringing up the ore to make them more money. The men know the rules and accept the risk every time they go underground. And this won't stop them, it's all they know. It seems to me you got a bit carried away with your fancy Initiative.' He looked away, and I saw the cigarette shaking in his hand, the smoke spiralling up in a distorted pattern toward the roof-wall and the replacement pipes.

I grabbed his shoulder, and he whipped around as though he was about to take a swing at me. I stepped away and held up my hands.

'Piet, I appreciate your honesty, and I don't have any evidence to contradict what you're saying. But I think you're wrong. I'll investigate every aspect of this accident and determine what happened. And if the fault does lie with my *fancy* Initiative, then I'll scrap it, immediately. But I have one question?'

'What's that?' he said defiantly.

'What will you replace it with?'

His body deflated. All the energy holding him together over the last twenty-four hours compressed into a single moment of utter defeat. He stayed quiet for an eternity.

'I'm not trying to make things awkward for you, Danny, but I just can't see beyond a pressure burst. There must have been movement the seismic sensors didn't pick up, or maybe the computer just let us down.'

'I've got one last question, Piet, and then you need to go home.'

'What's that?'

'Have they recovered the drills from the collapse?'

He frowned. 'Ja, I saw all four of them myself before the engineers did their tests. Why?'

'Were the *dead man's handles* functioning?'

'Ja, we did a routine check, and they were all working okay. Why do you ask?'

'No reason,' I said. 'Just filling in the blanks.'

I was convinced, more than ever, that the collapse was caused by something other than a pressure burst. But now wasn't the time to garner support. I had nothing but gut instinct, and, without proof, that's no better than a lie. I looked up at the pipes, and Piet's eyes followed, trying to see what I was looking at.

'I think the answers up there, Piet, and I'm going to need all the help I can get to find them.'

'I hope you're right, Danny… I hope you're right, man.' I left him shaking his head.

BREAKING POINT

Chapter 8

It was six in the evening, and the temperature outside was still thirty degrees. Although exhausted, I'd decided to walk the mile and a half from my flat to the Rinto Gold Social Club. I'd had a shower and thought the time would allow me to put the last three days into perspective. It didn't.

After speaking with Piet Reiss, I'd checked out a few of the old-style Stabilisers operating on Concorde IV. Two on 80 West and another two on 90 East; both well away from the collapse. I'd looked at the records and found they were between ten and fifteen years old and still running efficiently. None of them suffered from the noise and vibrations I'd witnessed with the MK6. The pipework foundations were solid, and so were the seals. Zero leakage on as much of the system that I could drag my legs around.

I was keen to talk to Embele alone and had arranged for him to meet me outside the Rinto Gold Social Club at 6.15. It had been an eventful thirty-six hours, and by the time I'd made my way up the steps and onto the patio, I was bathed in sweat. I needed a drink and made my way to the bar. This was a male fortress; not that any woman would want to frequent the place.

Women and families kept to the lounge areas to avoid the risk of foul language, drunkenness and the occasional violent disagreement.

The function of this place was for employees to drink and it didn't pretend to be anything else. All levels of mine worker were welcome… as long as they were white and paid cash.

The room went quiet as I walked in; the sombre mood taking on a more disquieting element. I'd been so absorbed with my investigation; I hadn't realised how difficult this was for everyone else. A few men sat hunched at the bar, their stools straining under the weight. Most were filling the floor space, crowding my entry. A few acknowledged me with a nod and a grunt and parted to let me through, but most turned their eyes away. It was a long walk to the counter, but I was damned if I'd show them any weakness and I stared out anyone ready to make a point; hoping they wouldn't.

From inside the room, it could have been any time of day or night. Two revolving fans at both ends of the ceiling mixed the heat and cigarette smoke into an oppressive, humid cocktail. It was hot, sticky and dark; ideal conditions to keep everyone thirsty. All the fittings were varying shades of brown. They absorbed the meagre sunlight that peered through gaps in the closed blinds with no mirrors or slot machines to break the tension. A redundant pool table stood, lopsided in the corner, its green baize covered in empty bottles of Castle and Lion beer.

I licked my dry lips and ordered a bottle of Castle. As I made my way back outside, my footsteps were the only sound in the room. The hubbub returned as the door swung shut behind me, squeaking on its rusty springs.

The low sun was still warm, and perspiration continued to bubble on my brow. I brushed it off with the back of my hand, wiping the excess on my trousers, which left a damp smear. I closed my eyes and rolled the cold glass across my forehead, wishing I didn't have to open them again. I took a drink and looked out toward the bowling greens, in front of the Social Club; the manicured grass was stained with long shadows as dusk drew in. No one was playing today, the recent tragedy made games seem inappropriate.

I'd never experienced this before, and it shook me how deeply the community had been struck. We'd had tragic deaths before, but they were isolated, and part of the risk miners take. But the scale of this disaster was hurting everyone.

The last three days had brought my life into focus. I'd always been driven to be the best that I could be, but I

BREAKING POINT

wondered, *at what price*. If I was responsible for the men's deaths, then everything I'd believed in was built on a lie. And if that was the case, then what had been the point? My formulations were the bedrock of the *seismic sensor scheme.* I'd tested them again and again, leaving nothing to chance, believing that they were saving lives. I'd always maintained that a measurement of risk was better than a reliance on luck, and viewed my interventions as positive... until now. *Had I risked the lives of those men on a gambler's fallacy?*

I stared at my hands. The back, then the front, then the back again. The African climate had helped with my psoriasis, but it still burst out in times of stress, and now it was on fire. I scratched at a flaky patch of skin above my knuckles. Once strong and safe, they seemed large and clumsy; twisted veins bulging beneath the flecks of grey hair. I clenched them into fists; first the left, then the right. At each flexure, elastic skin stretched smoothly over the knuckles and returned, wrinkled and blemished with freckles. My fingernails were ugly and distorted, the scar tissue surrounding them never quite healing and still giving me discomfort. Penance for my sins, I thought.

Forty years old, and I was losing faith in everything that had gone on before. God, I was tired.

Chapter 9

'No problem, maybe another time.' Julie had refused me again. Eighteen years old and eight years younger.

'Maybe…' Hurried words, no time for excuses. It wasn't going to happen; way out of my league.

Another late night in work and tea left in the oven. No appetite.

'I'm going to the club, mum.'

She turns her head from the television. 'Enjoy yourself, son.'

Not tonight, just need to get out.

It's cold, and the wind cuts through my thin jacket. Shivering with the cold and about to enter, I'm suddenly pushed to one side by Julie, wrapped around a Mathers apprentice. They stumble through and giggle an apology before making their way up the road. Leaving me to my embarrassment. *He's more her age.*

It's quiet inside, then a voice breaks through.

'Pint, Danny?'

'Please, Mike.' An automatic response.

A couple of the regulars tap dominoes at one another. I nod in their direction then turn my attention to the barman as he pulls at the pump; drawing the beer and managing the froth with expert precision.

Behind me, the door opens, and a finger prods my shoulder. When I turn, Julie takes my face in her hands and kisses me, with lips I can still taste. Then disappears without a word. Mike looks at me, his eyebrows raised and the glass half full. It's all a blur.

The old men mutter in the corner, but I'm not listening. I close my eyes and linger on the moment, the seconds. It happened so fast I squeeze my hands together and wonder if it happened at all. Senses are heightened, and my cheeks tingle from her touch. I moisten my lips with my tongue and taste her once more, savouring the sweet perfume.

BREAKING POINT

The world has changed.

'Is she a good girl, Danny?' My mother, as excited as me.

'What sort of a question is that, mum?' My cheeks burn. Then the look.

'Your father would be very proud of his boy.'

And my smile falls away like broken glass. Why does she still miss him; the man who deserted us?

I hold on to her, surprised how soft she is and realise how rarely I touch her.

I'm shivering again. The cold gnaws at my bones and darkness closes in with the smell of wet earth. Wake up! Please, wake up!

My shoulders compress, and my arms lock in front of me. My fingers are clawing at the stony ground, shredding skin and ripping nails. Pushing forward, deeper; losing sight of the blonde hair... still and helpless.

Please wake up. Daddy's here... daddy's here.'

Chapter 10

A sharp tap on my shoulder pulled me back to the present, and I looked up at the black, shiny features of Embele.

'You okay, Boss?'

I was startled and relieved. I looked around and realised where I was.

'Where the hell did you come from?' I said, wiping drool from the side of my mouth. I had to squint into the low sun to look up at him. *Christ, he seemed even bigger above ground.*

'I had a message to meet you here.'

His voice seemed different, more resonant. Dressed in shabby shorts, his muscles bulged inside a torn tee-shirt. I looked down and noticed he was wearing wellingtons.

'Expecting rain?' I asked, trying to lighten the atmosphere.

He looked down and then back at me, as though I was from another planet.

'Wellies,' I repeated.

More confusion on his face before I realised my error.

'Gumboots,' I pointed to his feet. 'Expecting rain?'

A broad smile crossed his face. 'My evening shoes, Boss.'

He did have a sense of humour, after all.

Shadows were continuing to lengthen, and a welcome breeze had picked up. The pyrotechnics in my head were easing, and I was relieved to be back in the present.

'Have a sit-down,' I said. 'I'll get you a drink.'

'Boss?' The smile disappeared, and he looked at me strangely; until I realised his unease. This was unchartered territory, and it would have taken a lot of guts to come here on his own. The politics of this complicated country generally passed me by. But, when reality struck home, it was an uncomfortable feeling. I looked across at the bar and saw us being watched through a crack in the blinds.

BREAKING POINT

'Wait here, I'll get you a beer,' I said, and made my way back to the club.

It went quiet again, but I was feeling better in myself until a lump of a man stepped in front of me.

'You buying that kaffir a beer?'

His name was Jannie Burke, an underground blaster, and he had form for being a troublemaker. I'd suspended him for drinking on duty in the past; a heinous crime for someone dealing with explosives, and we should have got rid of him. His brother, Denis, had been caught up in the collapse and was recovering in hospital.

Jannie was drunk, and I didn't know if he was making a statement or asking a question. Either way, I wasn't going to answer, so I pushed him out of the way; no mean feat for someone built like a pit prop. He had huge sideburns racing down his broad, bovine face, which met up with a flamboyant handlebar moustache. His bloodshot eyes looked ten beers over the limit.

'Lager please, Fred,' I called out to the barman.

'Okay, Meneer.' he replied. 'Enige nuus oor die beseerde?' *Any news on the injured?*

I think he was trying to take the sting out of the situation and I was about to give an update when Jannie pushed his stomach into me.

'Ja, my brother's in a bad way, and now you bringing a kaffir to our club.' He was swaying, and his beer was spilling onto the floor.

'Kom nou Jannie, daar is geen behoefte vir dit.' *Come now, Jannie, there's no need for it.* I think Fred was afraid of potential breakages if this kicked off. By now, the bar had gone quiet, and all eyes were on me. I thought it through and decided I had two options.

The first was to try and punch Jannie's lights out, but that would anger the others. The second was to bite my tongue and let him have his say. With my hand still throbbing, I chose the latter.

'It's okay, Fred,' I said, raising my hand. 'Let's have it, Jannie. What have you got to say?'

Now that he was the centre of attention, he seemed taken aback. Draining his glass, he began speaking in Afrikaans, and he didn't hold back with his opinions. He blamed me for the failed system that had put his brother's life at risk. And took more than a few liberties with some personal insults; particularly about my heritage and ability to do the job.

Somewhere in there, he managed to lament the passing of *The Butcher's* tenure as Chief Engineer, which was particularly galling. He finished by telling me that I'd put all the men out of jobs.

My directive to close the mine had been implemented, and there was a lot of anger over the decision. Whether because of my rank or as a mark of respect, I don't know, but no one took sides as the tirade finally waned. Awash with spittle and sweat, he eventually ran out of steam. As a finale, he drew heavily from his glass before realising it was empty and belched in my face.

I glanced around at the faces for a long time, challenging each stare until, one by one, they turned away. An uncomfortable silence fell as my eyes rested on Jannie. 'Jy's dronk, Jannie. Gaan tuis voordat jy doen iets wat jy salspyt sê.!' *You're drunk, go home before you do something you'll regret!* I shouted into his face at the top of my voice, making everyone in the room jump.

I was in no mood for his stupidity and, against my better judgement, I closed in to apply option one with my good hand. It was unlikely he'd volunteered to help underground, judging by how drunk he was, and that only added to my anger. I stepped forward to emphasise the point that I'd understood every word he'd said and would take great pleasure in helping him sleep it off. He looked at me, stunned.

Whether it was the realisation that I could speak Afrikaans or just the fact that I was ready to take him on, I don't know. But it got a reaction from the crowd, and a couple of men pulled him out of my reach, while others held me back.

'Kry hom huis toe.' *Get him home.* Someone shouted, and Jannie was bundled out of the room. Me being around wasn't helping, so I took my beer and walked out the door; my whole body was shaking.

As I stepped outside, I heard the murmurings stir up again behind the squeaky door. Embele glanced up as I approached. He looked uncomfortable and stood ramrod straight, his eyes traversing between me and the entrance to the club.

'Don't worry about them,' I said, 'they're upset. Trust me, they won't lay a hand on you. Let's take a seat.'

'I'd rather stand, Boss.' His hands were locked behind his back, and his chest stuck out defiantly. He refused a cigarette as I placed his drink on the table. I needed to sit and stop my legs shaking.

'I think I should know your full name?' I said.

'Embele Ngozi.'

'How old are you?'

He frowned. 'Twenty-four, why?'

'No reason, it just seems young to be a Boss Boy.'

'I'm good at my job.'

'I can see that, Embele, and I also see how the other workers respect you. The supervisors have said good things about you.' Now he looked embarrassed, which wasn't the point of my conversation.

'How old was, Andele?'

He looked down at his feet. 'Twenty-two, the youngest.'

'I asked you here to say how sorry I was for his death, and to thank you for helping save the other men's lives.'

'We only saved one, Boss.'

'I know, but we wouldn't have got to him without your help.'

He shrugged his shoulders. 'I was one of many.'

I was getting exasperated. 'Look, it's obvious you don't like me, but I'm trying to tell you that I'm genuinely sorry for your loss.'

'It's not me who suffers, Boss. My brother's wife and child have little money. I will try to help, but I have my own family, and my money doesn't go far.'

A Boss Boy was one of the best paid black workers underground, but well below the average white worker's wage.

'Where does his family live?' I asked.

'Kwazulu.'

'I've been in touch with the personnel department, and your brother's wife will receive compensation to help deal with her loss; as will all the other families affected. I know it's not much against the death of a loved one, but it will help.' I rubbed the side of my jaw, which was tender, and saw him look away. Maybe he thought I was going to sack him for the assault.

'Your job is safe,' I said, quick to reassure him. 'I got what I deserved. And to avoid complications, it stays between the three of us.'

'Thanks, Boss.' He looked relieved.

'Just don't make a habit of it.' I grimaced, holding my jaw.

His mood began to thaw, and he sat to sip at his drink.

'How many children do you have?' I asked.

'One boy, Boss, nine months old. His name is Inyoni.'

'That means, *bird*, doesn't it?' I asked. He seemed impressed and nodded.

'His mother's choice,' he replied.

I began to ask the question that had been on my mind since the accident. 'That first day, going down in the skip…'

His eyes turned on me. 'I've seen fear like that before, Boss.'

I waved my hand dismissively. 'I don't want you to think…'

BREAKING POINT

He didn't allow me to finish. 'I've seen panic do bad things when men go down in the cage. I see it in their eyes before they realise what's happening. Like the darkness is suffocating them.'

'I've been down enough times to know...' He ignored my pathetic excuses.

'I saw the look in your eyes, Boss.'

I was embarrassed, and a shiver ran down my spine. I turned to pick up my drink; unable to admit my fear.

Embele's voice continued, deep and unemotional. 'I understand the fear, *ingebhe*.' He pulled a thick, elastic band from his wrist and handed it to me. 'When *ingebhe* comes, snap this on your wrist and breathe slowly.'

'You must know what it feels like,' I asked. But he didn't answer.

An awkward silence filled the space between us, and I tried hard to think of what to say next. I'd never had a weakness exposed so simply and eloquently and pulled the band over my wrist.

'Well you certainly got my attention down there,' I smiled. 'I'm grateful for what you did, and I hope...'

He nodded. 'It stays between us, Boss.'

I appreciated him finishing my sentence. We both stood, and I offered my hand. He seemed surprised and shook it self-consciously. Maybe he'd never shaken hands with a white man before; he'd certainly punched one. I could see he still had his reservations about me, but I didn't care. He'd done me a massive favour, and I respected him for it. We both gulped down our drinks and readied to go our separate ways.

'As soon as we know the cause of the accident, I'll let you know,' I said, resting my hand on his back.

He stopped and turned around. I almost walked into him.

'Do you want us to strip down the MK6 Stabiliser, Boss?' I was surprised at the comment. It hadn't occurred to me with everything else going on.

'Could your team do that?'

'We've stripped down the old models.'

'But this is a new design, would you know what you're looking for?'

'Maybe not… but you might.'

His idea hadn't occurred to me because the MK6 was still under warranty, but what he said made sense. If we got Mathers involved in the investigation, it would be in their interests *not* to find a fault. Conversely, if our investigation team tampered with the evidence, it would free Mathers of any responsibility and allow them to walk away. I was torn, but Embele had sown the seed.

'How long would it take?'

He thought about it. 'A week, Boss, maybe less. All the lifting equipment is down there.'

'It would be difficult to keep quiet, wouldn't it?'

He gave me a knowing look. 'Not if you talk to Boss, Broed.'

'You saw the damage to the pipes on 110, today,' I said. 'Was it as bad as that when you reported the problem to Boss, Van der Merwe?'

I liked the way he considered the question before answering. 'It was worse today…' he replied. 'Much worse.'

'You pointed up at the *smokestack*,' I said. 'Have you seen it moving like that, before?'

'No, only today.'

Now the million-dollar question. 'Do you believe the MK6 had anything to do with the collapse?'

'Maybe,' he said unenthusiastically. 'But there was pressure on the chamber, and the rock was splitting.'

'Enough to bring it down?'

He thought about saying something but stopped himself.

'What about the fractured pipes that we saw?' I was keen to find an ally.

He looked at me and hunched his shoulders.

BREAKING POINT

I would give it one last go. 'The seismic sensors we put down on 120 East didn't show up any critical weakness...' I was about to re-emphasise the safety Initiative, when he cut me short, again.

'The rock *talks*, Boss. The sensors don't.'

And with that withering statement, he turned and made his way back toward the hostels.

His gumboots slapping in the distance would have made me smile a moment ago. But now, with the light almost gone, I felt an overwhelming loneliness. *What had I done to those men?*

Chapter 11

It had been a long three days and, back in my flat, I had a chance to get a couple of hours rest. Only it didn't work out that way. Lying on my bed, questions filled my head, and my body stiffened with the effort of trying to answer them. Sleep wouldn't come tonight, and I returned to the office to try and understand what had happened.

It was futile, I couldn't keep my eyes open and collapsed, fully dressed, into my camp bed. When I did drop off, the nightmare of the accident seeped back into my brain and shook me awake again. I spent most of the night sitting up and adding to the scribbled notes I'd taken underground… afraid to close my eyes.

The rock talks, Boss, the sensors don't. Embele had summed up what I was afraid to accept; maybe they'd put it on my headstone in a Potters Field.

I turned to look at the clock and gasped as pain tore through my lower jaw. It was 6 am, my hand still hurt like hell, and my body felt as though I'd been trampled by a herd of wildebeest. If I didn't get up now, I might have to wait for someone to help me.

Everyone arrived at the offices around 7 o'clock, and the flow of information began not long after. Engineers and surveyors dropped in with reports and photographs at regular intervals. Their faces said it all. They wanted to know what was happening, but I had nothing to tell them.

I spent most of the morning putting the details into some kind of order before calling a meeting to explain the extent of the accident, and how we should deal with the fallout. I also put together a plan for the Engineering team to review the last three months of readings from the seismic sensors.

'I want you to put all the numbers back through the computer and look for any clues. Did we miss something?'

BREAKING POINT

They were shaking their heads; it was a considerable amount of work.

Then I asked the surveyors if they would go down and check all the seismic sensors on Levels 110 and 120. Another significant task, especially as I'd just closed the mine for safety reasons.

'The maintenance teams are busy securing the area, so we need all the help...'

One of the engineers put up his hand. 'What about the *Traffic Light System,* do we ignore it?'

I knew the question was coming but it didn't make the answer easier.

'It's one of the areas under investigation,' I said, swallowing hard. 'So, for now, we treat it as suspect.' I saw a few jaws drop and some shaking their heads. As I closed the meeting, whispered conversations filled the room.

I checked my watch, it was 1 o'clock. Laura had been fielding calls from Joe Schmidt, the Engineering Director, all the previous day and asked me to ring him urgently. I'd already got her to send out a directive to the senior management, informing them that I was closing Concorde IV until our investigations concluded. Joe would be pissed that I hadn't involved him in the decision, but it seemed a small consideration compared to risking more lives. He was going to rip my head off, and I wouldn't blame him.

In front of me was the surveyor's report of the accident. It had been on my desk when I arrived, and I'd read it three times. *Take photographs of every inch of the collapse area,* I'd told them. *And then assess the two MK6 Stabilisers on Level 110.* The second request had confused them, but I didn't want to give anything away. I needed their judgement to be unbiased, and I wasn't disappointed.

The section which summarised the condition of the Stabilisers was simple.

No reported problems and both Stabiliser units appeared to be working effectively before the accident.

Ian Holland

Visible damage and leakage on the outlet pipes likely to have been caused, post-collapse... cold and chilling.

It went on to detail most of what I'd already seen, but I couldn't read beyond, *post-collapse.* It conflicted with my suspicions and was at odds with my line of investigation. I was being pushed into an even tighter corner.

Photographs were strewn on my desk. I'd looked at them again and again, reliving the terror that the men had experienced. Pinned to the back wall was a surveyor's map of 120 East, including the disused cross-cut chamber that we'd clambered through to reach the other side of the fall. I'd looked at all the engineering drawings of the haulages to assess the strength of the supports, checked the pipework systems and their locations. Everything seemed in order.

I'd asked the Chief Draughtsman to double-check the calculations, and he'd assured me everything was as it should be. I saw nothing to disagree with his summary. A couple of the surveyors had gone through the most recent sensor results for 120 East, to see if we'd missed anything. Again, the outcome was negative. There was nothing to predict the collapse.

All the hydraulic drills had been recovered, and the reports confirmed what Piet Reiss had already told me. *All the Dead Man's Handles were working correctly.* It was another small piece to add to the jigsaw. I knew where it fitted, but there were still too many gaps to create an overall picture.

I was putting the finishing touches to my report; highlighting my concerns over the design modifications to the MK6 Stabilisers. *Did they have a link to the failure of the failsafe switches?*

The door burst open.

'Where the *fuck* have you been?' It was Joe Schmidt.

'Nice to see you too, Joe.' I said, trying to take the sting out of his anger, but it only added fuel.

'I've been trying to contact you since yesterday afternoon!' he shouted.

BREAKING POINT

I was stunned at his brevity as he ignored my outstretched hand. He turned to look out of my office window. His hands were on his hips, his shoulders heaving up and down. Judging by the creases in his suit, I guessed he'd just arrived on the company jet from Johannesburg.

'Laura, can you bring in some coffee?' I called through the open door.

Joe turned to face me, sweating and breathless. 'Jesus, we haven't got time for coffee. Van Heerden wants us back at head office *today*.' He stared at his watch. 'I won't lie, Danny, he wants a showdown.'

'A showdown, what for?' I asked.

'You've just closed down Rinto Gold's most productive mine, and you're asking, w*hat for?* Who the *fuck* authorised you to make that decision and how do you think it makes me look?' A rim of white foam frothed at the edges of his mouth. He looked like he was ready to jump on me.

'Three hours ago,' again he looked at his watch. 'Karl Stomp and I were roasted on Van Heerden's personal braii. Then just as we think he's had his fill, his secretary, the one with the screechy voice, comes in and passes him a fax.' He pulled out a handkerchief and wiped his mouth.

'As he's reading it, Karl and I can see his face colouring up like it's being heated with a blowtorch. He looks at me and asks why I've closed Concorde IV. And all I can do is stare at him with my mouth opening and closing like a fucking goldfish. He's looking me in the eyes and asking, *Why didn't you tell me about this decision, Schmidt?*

'Christ, even that bastard Stomp joined in the sport. *You didn't tell me any of this Joe?*

'What was I supposed to say, Danny? I'm the Engineering Director for God's sake, he pays me to know what's happening. Who do you think you are, P.W. *fucking* Botha?'

His mouth was buried in the handkerchief, and his shoulders started to shudder. *Was he crying?* He put it back in his pocket, looked up, and burst out laughing.

'P.W. *fucking* Botha, that's a good line, isn't it?' He took a moment to calm himself. 'Bloody hell, Danny, you should have seen his face, I've never seen him so worked up.'

He sat and took some deep breaths.

'I'm sorry, Joe, I never meant to…'

'Forget it,' he said. 'It's done now. I'd already been reamed for an hour, I was numb. He could have cut out my kidney, and I wouldn't have felt a thing.' He started giggling again. 'I made up some bullshit about getting our wires crossed in the chaos. We can argue about it another time, I think I've said enough, don't you?'

'Sorry again, Joe, I know I should have informed you first, but I've been underground for almost two days.'

'Found anything?'

'I've seen enough to know something's wrong, but as yet, no clear evidence.' I didn't want to mention the MK6 Stabiliser until I knew more.

'Well, I hope you find it, he's under pressure to make a statement, and right now all he's got is the *3S Initiative*. Which is why he wants us back there, pronto.'

'But I'm more valuable here,' I said.

'Forget it, Danny, Van Heerden's on the warpath, and he wants answers today.'

I pointed to the reports and photographs. 'This all has to be collated, Joe, it's not straightforward.'

He held his hand up. 'Listen, you and I have known each other for a long time. I persuaded you to take the Chief Engineers job, and I'm not turning my back on you now. God knows how many bodies we'd have brought up if, *The Butcher,* was still in charge. But the old man's got an emergency shareholders meeting scheduled for tomorrow morning, and he's ready to put you under a bus.'

BREAKING POINT

It was pointless trying to explain, so I pulled the reports and photographs together. Laura came in with two cups of coffee and laid them on my desk.

'I've been called up to Head Office,' I said. 'I'll be out for the rest of the day and probably tomorrow morning. Can you inform the engineers? Oh, and make sure Steyn Broed is informed; we had a meeting planned for this afternoon.'

'Okay, Mr Core,' she said, looking as perplexed as I was. 'Should I cancel your visit to the hospital?'

I nodded. It annoyed me that I hadn't spent nearly enough time with the families of the bereaved and injured. As Joe stepped out of the office, I turned back to Laura. 'I've left a report on my desk marked, *Recycling Stabiliser Concerns*. Can you type it up and fax a copy to Thys van Heerden at Head Office?'

She made a note in her pad.

'Send a copy to Mathers Engineering, in South Wales, for the attention of the Technical Director and another to the Heron Inc. Group, in Houston, Texas; for the attention of the CEO, Rik Last and the group financial controller, Luca Majori.' I knew them both from my days with Mathers. *Let them have a sleepless night*, I thought.

Another idea flashed through my head. It was unethical, but I needed all the help I could get, and some insider knowledge I could trust.

'Just between us, Laura, could you fax an unofficial copy to John Dread in South Wales. You'll find his personal fax number in my desk diary.'

She looked up from her notes. 'Is everything okay, Mr Core?'

'I hope so, Laura, I hope so.' Glancing back at my office, I wasn't sure I'd be coming back.

Chapter 12

Five thousand six hundred and sixty miles from Johannesburg stands the town of Crossways. Once a village it had become a town of repute, because of one man; a Scottish engineer named Franklyn Mathers.

In April 1939, Mathers decided to transfer his innovative business from a dilapidated factory in Glasgow to a custom-built development in South Wales. The move would help him take full advantage of the worldwide demand for his patented invention, the Mathers, Recycling Stabiliser; specially developed for the burgeoning deep mining industry.

In more recent times, the company had struggled to turn a profit and eventually succumbed to a takeover by the American industrial giant, Heron Inc. For the last five years, Mathers operated under the strict financial rules of its American owner.

Early morning sunshine in Crossways had turned dank and miserable. Now, a grey mist was rolling over the Brig Uchel mountain range and down the valley. At the entrance to the Mathers factory, a serious-looking man, wearing a blue, waterproof jacket, shrugged from the weather and stepped through the main gate.

John Dread's car had broken down, but that wasn't the only reason he was late. It had been a long time since he'd walked to work from his home at the top of the old village and he'd forgotten how exposed the old path had become.

Thirty-two years old, his stringy, athletic build, splashed through the doors of the Engineering Office; an uninspiring place, even after its recent upgrade. In the top corner of the ceiling was a dark brown stain seeping from a well-established leak in the roof. Beyond the office, through windowed panels, was the mechanical laboratory with its array of test benches and assembly equipment.

BREAKING POINT

John was greeted by Terry Socket sitting with his feet up on his desk, drawing on an un-tipped cigarette. He argued that they had a fuller flavour; as though smoke was synonymous with taste. Sitting next to him was Richie Tick, one of the young engineers.

Socket was forty-two years old. Stocky and physically strong. He demanded rather than earned respect as the Engineering Manager, by menacing those around him. Through years of missed opportunities, his objectivity had become distorted, and his outlook viewed through a flawed lens.

He lowered his newspaper. 'Hey, Dread, is it raining?' He peered through the smoke and nudged Tick.

John avoided eye contact while extricating himself from his sodden jacket, ensuring he splashed as much water over Socket. Like most of the other engineers, he found his arrogance tiresome.

'Very droll,' he said, pulling a lab coat from his locker. 'I didn't see you at the club last night?'

'Were you worried, my friend?' Socket replied, closing the newspaper and flicking it across the table.

'Unusual, that's all.'

'I was too busy pulling the best looking lady in Crossways.' Socket replied, sucking smoke deep into his lungs and exhaling unconvincing rings through pursed lips.

John could see him trying to draw Tick into the conversation. Richie, for his part, picked up the paper and pretended to read.

'Oh, right. Well good for you,' said John.

'Yes, my friend,' Socket exaggerated a yawn and stretched his arms out. Yes *ind-e-e-e-d*. And I expect you'd like to know who the lucky lady is?'

John watched him from the corner of his eye. *Pathetic,* he thought. Socket was ten years past his best as an engineer; an historical artefact.

'I expect you'll let me know when the time comes,' he replied, stirring his coffee. 'Maybe I should ask your wife?'

Socket swallowed one of his smoke rings and coughed for a full thirty seconds. Richie looked up with a sly grin.

'I don't think... *cough!*... *cough!*... that would... *cough!*... be a good idea, Dread, do you?' Socket's voice was three octaves higher, his vocal cords stretched by the coughing fit.

John saw his watery eyes and smirked. 'No, not from your wife's point of view.' He yawned and continued to stir.

'If I find out you've been talking to my missus...'

Before Socket could finish, John let loose.

'Listen, Terry,' he shouted. 'Cut the crap, will you? I might have some news you might be interested in.'

John saw him look at Tick. He didn't like being shown up in full view of the young engineer and would normally have responded, but curiosity got the better of him. He stubbed out his cigarette and released his legs from the top of the desk.

'What news then, *Johnnie boy?*'

John sat with his coffee, his eyes fixed on the steamy surface. 'I had a report faxed through to me this morning.'

Socket leaned forward. 'Who's sending you reports? Everything comes through me, you know that.'

'This was an unofficial copy from Danny Core,' replied John.

Socket couldn't hide his distaste and his features darkened. He'd always been jealous of their friendship.

'Danny, *bloody*, Core. Now there's a name I haven't heard for a long time. Is he still in *Fuzzy Wuzzy* land?'

'If you mean, South Africa, then yes,' said John.

Socket had the smirk back on his face.

Tick tried to join the conversation. 'He was the Engineering Manager before you, wasn't he, Terry?'

Socket ignored him. 'Does he know you're seeing his ex-wife, John?' He winked at Tick.

'Steady on, Terry,' Tick said. 'That's none of...'

BREAKING POINT

'Keep out of it, *Dick-tick*,' Socket blasted out, pointing his finger at the younger man.

John was caught off guard. 'What makes you think that?'

Socket laughed out loud. 'You must think I walk around with my eyes closed, Johnnie boy. You've been sniffing around her ever since she got divorced. Still call him your *best mate*?' He was blowing smoke rings again, and Tick had retreated to a neutral corner. 'Why else would you be taking his kid football training?'

'Because she needed help. Danny and I got on well, no more than that.' His voice faltered, and his face was heating up. He was already saying more than he wanted to.

'Oh, right,' Socket said. 'Well, maybe I should pop around and see if she needs any *extra* help. Know what I mean, Dread?'

John stood and stepped towards him. Physically he looked no match for the bigger man, but his build belied his toughness and Socket knew it too. If this escalated...

'Okay, okay, Dread, calm down. None of my business. I forgot you were Danny Core's little protégé... until he ran away.' The last words were spoken with another knowing look toward Tick. 'Anyway, what was in this report?'

John took a couple of deep breaths and sat back down, wrapping his hands around the coffee cup. 'He thinks one of our Stabilisers may be implicated in an accident.'

'Shit! What makes him think that?' said Socket, taking things more seriously.

John sipped from his cup. 'He doesn't say, but one thing's certain; Danny doesn't make rash statements for the sake of it. And the report does ask some awkward questions.'

'Does Billy Jones know about it?' All the sarcasm had disappeared from Socket's voice.

John shook his head. 'I'm not sure, but he soon will. The report said nine men have been killed.'

'Fucking hell!' Socket and Tick's eyes almost popped out of their heads.

'Anyway, nothing's proven yet,' said John, raising his hands to calm them down.

The room fell silent, as though all the air had been sucked out.

'I wouldn't like to be in Billy's shoes.' Socket's voice was almost a whisper. He lit up another cigarette and blew the smoke toward the ceiling. 'Is it anything to do with the MK6?' Smoke sputtered from his lips with each syllable.

'Is that just a lucky guess?' asked John. Curious that Socket's first response was so specific.

'What do you mean?' Socket.

John looked directly at him. 'Why do you think it's a MK6 issue, do you know something we don't?'

'Of course not, and anyway you should be asking Billy Jones that question?'

'Why Billy? You were managing the project.'

He'd hit the spot and Socket exploded. 'What're you trying to say, Dread? Billy Jones was directing that fucking project, not me.' He pointed his finger beyond the windows, toward Billy's office. 'The buck stops with him. And don't forget, you were part of the team too.'

'Calm down, *Terry boy*. You know I was removed because of my negative attitude.'

'You still saw enough in the monthly presentations,' said Socket evaporating into a panic.

'I saw enough to know it was run in line with Fred Stremsen's Project Management Tome,' said John. 'All the boxes got ticked, and the prototype passed all the required testing. I don't know why you're getting uptight?'

'Yeah, that's right, John, and we've got the data to back it all up, haven't we?'

It was John now, bosom buddies all of a sudden.

'I'm sure *you* do,' John replied. 'But even before I left the project, the proposed changes were beginning to impact on safety margins.'

BREAKING POINT

He'd exposed another nerve.

'Leave it there, Dread. You're getting ahead of yourself. Does Core point any fingers in this *secret* report?'

'No, it isn't detailed enough, so no point in jumping to conclusions. But there are some technical issues he brought up that may not have been considered at the time. And it's not a *secret* report, official copies have been sent to Billy Jones.'

'Anyone else?' Socket started to sound desperate.

John took a sip from his coffee, relishing the discomfort.

'Well?' Socket again.

John took another sip before returning the cup to the table. 'All the Heron top brass in Houston.'

'Shit! I need a copy of that report, Dread.' Socket stood and paced.

'You'll see it soon enough,' John replied.

'What do you mean?' He stopped.

'Don't you think it's unusual that Billy isn't in his office?' The other two instinctively looked across as though they could see Billy's office through the brick walls. 'Think of it, Stremsen flies in from Houston every first Wednesday of the month, ready for his monthly update meeting today, Friday afternoon.'

'So what?' said Socket.

'Well, he usually starts the process in Billy's office at eight sharp. But I've just passed there, and it's empty. Lights on, but deserted.'

'So?' Socket again, his voice rising.

'So my guess is they're already on a conference call with Houston.'

'But it's the early hours of the morning in Houston,' said Tick.

John looked at him. 'Nine men died, Richie. I don't think anyone will be sleeping soundly tonight.'

The telephone rang.

Socket picked it up. 'Terry Socket.' The voice on the other end of the line was loud but indistinct.

'Okay, I'll be there straight away.'

'Everything okay, Terry?' Tick's voice was a whisper.

Socket again ignored him, putting the phone down. 'Looks like you were right, Dread, I've just been summoned to the Conference Room.' He got up and started rifling through the project files.

'It's filed under *P*,' said John.

Socket spun round. 'What is?'

'The *Project Management Tome*. All the MK6 design changes are there. And remember it's Stremsen's baby, so make sure you don't contradict the great man's work.'

'Smart arse,' said Socket under his breath. Then he turned back with a sneer. 'I hope you've got your seat booked for the MK7 review this afternoon. Billy Jones is about to get reamed.'

He found the file and made his way to the Conference Room, slamming the door.

'You wound that bastard up, good and proper,' Richie said, tapping his fingers on the table. 'Seems like Terry has a problem with Danny Core. What was he like to work for?'

John shook his head and smiled. 'He could be a stubborn bastard, that's for sure, but he was fair. Socket had a bust-up with him years ago and never got over it. You can imagine what he was like when Danny was made Engineering Manager instead of him.'

'Did he deserve it?' Tick again.

'Without a doubt,' said John. 'He knew the Stabiliser design better than anyone. For the time they were together, he and Jack Smelt, the Technical Director, were good men to work for.'

'What made Jack leave?'

'You're asking a lot of questions today, Richie?'

Tick went red. 'Just asking; this is serious stuff.'

BREAKING POINT

John pushed his coffee cup to one side and nodded his head. 'Mmm, you're right. How long have you worked here?'

'Two years, why?'

'That would be three years after Heron took over, so you wouldn't have been involved in the MK5 Project?'

'No, I started in the middle of the MK6.'

'That's right, you filled in for me; lucky you.' They both smiled at the sarcasm as John continued.

'The MK5 Project had been very successful, but only because of the cost savings. We squeezed the suppliers to reduce their prices, speeded up the assembly times and even reduced the coats of paint. Any design changes were minimal. Even then it was three months overdue and we probably over-achieved.'

'Yeah, I missed out on all the bonuses that were going around at that time,' said Richie.

John smiled. 'Yeah, we *all* got carried away. Unfortunately, the achievements reflected well on Fred Stremsen's new PMT process.'

'Why, *unfortunately,* didn't everyone benefit?'

'Up to a point, but none more so than Stremsen,' John answered, pushing his cup away. 'He took all the plaudits and with his newly found credibility, decided to piggy-back a MK6 Development on the back of the successful MK5.'

'I remember that,' said Richie. 'That's where I came in. What a shit storm! I remember thinking... *welcome to Mathers, welcome to the PMT.*'

John got up and opened a filing cabinet. 'Stremsen wanted to enhance his reputation with crazy deadlines and even crazier cost savings. Jack told him what he thought of it, and I backed him up. We were immediately removed from the team; which was fine for me, but untenable for the Technical Director. Not long after they forced Jack into early retirement.'

'What about Danny Core?' asked Tick. 'Why did he leave?'

John was pulling three box files from the cabinet and stopped in his tracks. 'I think that's enough questions for now, Richie, we've got work to do.'

He laid the files in front of Tick, who looked at him confused. 'What are we doing with these?'

'Socket's right about one thing,' said John. 'We're all responsible for the changes on the MK6. And if there is a serious flaw, then we're all implicated. You and I are going to revisit the project files and check every detail until we're satisfied.'

As much as he liked Danny, he hoped his friend's suspicions were wrong, for all their sakes.

BREAKING POINT

Chapter 13

Heron Inc's CEO, Rik Last, came from a Merchant Banking background. He knew little about manufacturing and everything about sound investments. He picked up the framed photograph on his desk, surprised how heavy it was and his mind was taken back to that momentous day, nine months ago.

Heron Inc. had been voted the most profitable company in the United States, and he'd been invited to the White House. Part of a select group of high-powered executives, basking in shared glory. His hand tingled at the memory of the president's handshake, and he loved the way they both smiled toward the camera, like the best of friends. Pushing his glasses up the bridge of his nose, he drew the image closer and focused on the Heron badge set in his jacket. The camera had caught it in perfect profile; an outstanding endorsement of his company.

He reached for the ubiquitous badge in his buttonhole and pulled it off its magnetic hook. He polished the distinctive logo on his trouser leg and held it up to the light. Satisfied that it was pristine, he smiled and replaced it on the hook; it drew away from his fingers with a metallic *click*.

He brought his glasses back down and a broader smile cut across his face as he caught his reflection in the glass. *Damn good hair for a fifty-eight-year-old,* he thought and, as a matter of rote, reached for the comb inside his jacket pocket. After a few one-handed strokes, everything was as it should be. He put the comb back in his pocket and returned the frame to the desk. The memory put away for another time.

There was a knock at his office door and Mary, his secretary, stepped in. He looked up and caught the scent of lavender perfume.

'I wondered if you've finished reading the report I left on your desk, Mr Last.' In her late forties, she was *stouter* than her preferred dress size, which didn't do justice to her natural grace. Unfortunately, the mismatch caused her to generate an unhealthy amount of static electricity.

There was no sound, except the ticking of an antique clock on the windowsill behind him. A report entitled, *Recycling Stabiliser Concerns,* lay open in front of him. Some lines were highlighted in green, and some had notes squeezed between the lines in tightly constrained writing. His micro-management style could seem obsessive, but his approach had proved to be methodical and wise.

'When did this come in, Mary?'

'It arrived by fax, at 8 o'clock this morning,' she replied. Last was looking at the paperwork, gently stroking his hair.

'I thought you might want to know what time it is in Johannesburg,' she continued. 'Maybe I could find out where Fred Stremsen is.'

God, she was good, he thought.

'You've obviously read it,' he said.

'I read all the reports marked for your attention. But you know that already.'

Of course he did. He looked up, his eyes hooded by dark, bristly eyebrows, giving his gaze a hawk-like intensity. This could unsettle the most senior of his executives, but not Mary. She'd worked with him for almost twenty years and had become a trusted advisor.

'So, what do you make of it?' he said, leaning back.

'Whoever wrote it, seems to know what he's talking about. I don't understand the detail, but it's professional enough to warrant concern.' He was as uncomfortable with her pessimism as he was of his own as she continued.

'The tone of the report isn't accusatory, but the conclusions are enough to suggest misgivings about the recent design changes.

BREAKING POINT

'If you were in my position, Mary. What would you do?'

Her cheeks flushed as they always did when he asked her opinion. 'Well, considering your impending retirement, I think it's important to act with discretion.'

A good point, he thought. He hadn't considered his retirement in the deliberations.

'The financial risks to the company are obvious, but can be overcome,' she continued. 'And we both know who the best person is to talk about financial matters?'

'You think this could fall back on Mathers?' he enquired.

'No, Mr Last, I think this could fall back on *Heron*.'

Shit! The inner voice came from Likky Rast, Rik's psychological, coping mechanism.

Rik had taken an anger management course while working for *BancCity*, a prestigious New York bank. His volatile temper had threatened to derail his ambitions and render some of his clients unconscious. So on the advice of a lifestyle guru, a middle-aged hippy with *John Lennon* glasses and an annoying habit of calling him *Rikky*, he'd created a coping mechanism. This manifested itself in the form of an alter ego, whom he named *Likky... Likky Rast.*

Likky resided in Rik's sub-conscious and provided a release for his aggressive tendencies. The relationship seemed to work, and Rik trusted Likky implicitly. When pressure threatened his equilibrium, he could remain calm, while Likky ranted and raved in cranial isolation. They'd become good friends.

Last gently padded the back of his hair and remembered the value of self-restraint. He was stung by the thought of jeopardising his company's reputation.

Mary turned as her phone rang on the other side of the door, and Rik waved her away to answer it.

Heron's Head Office in Houston was a two-storey administration block just outside the central city; surprisingly modest for such a wealthy company. A reflection of the CEO's unpretentious character. Last's office was spare, with only a single framed picture on the wall. William Tecumsah Sherman, the Civil War General, sitting rigid and determined in a long coat, astride his military horse, Lexington. He was bold and masculine against the blue pastel shades, and Rik was staring directly at it.

'What would *you* do, Uncle Billy?' he whispered to himself as he thought back to the acquisition of Mathers, five years before.

He'd researched the birth of the company and the life of its founder, Franklyn Mathers. He loved the idea of someone building something armed with nothing but blood, sweat and *spunk*. The latter was a description he found stirring and used often; much to the amusement of his colleagues.

He looked up at his computer and consoled himself with the latest Wall Street trading figures. Heron was still climbing. Money wasn't blood and bone, but he rarely made a fiscal decision he regretted, and Mathers had been his first acquisition. Last believed in high standards and was ruthless with those who fell below the mark. He and the General were hard men. *They had spunk*!

'Mr Last?' He hadn't heard Mary come back into the room and arched his eyebrows towards the report.

'From South Africa, eh?' he said.

'Is that a question, Mr Last?'

He shook his head.

She placed a sheet of paper in front of him. 'Johannesburg is seven hours ahead of Houston, and the U.K. is five hours ahead. Here are the appropriate telephone numbers.'

He looked up at her in surprise. 'Why the UK, Mary?'

She was reaching across the desk to point out the phone numbers and accidentally touched the end of his finger. A blue spark arced painfully between the two of them, causing Rik to throw his head back and Likky Rast to shout. *Fuck!*

'Because that's where Fred Stremsen is.' Mary turned on her heels with a satisfied smile and *swished* out of the office. 'Sorry about that,' she called, over her shoulder. 'I've also arranged a meeting with Luca Majori for tomorrow morning to discuss those financial risks.'

Rik sucked on his finger and fumbled for a comb… *God, she was good.*

Inside his bony cell, Likky Rast damned Fred Stremsen to hell and back as Uncle Billy watched over them with a resolute gaze.

Chapter 14

'Go straight in gentlemen, Mr Van is expecting you.' Van Heerden's secretary pointed toward his office door. She was looking at me like I was something scraped off the bottom of her shoe.

'Is he in a good mood, Jean?' Joe asked. She rolled her eyes, and they spoke louder than words. I was pretty tense myself, and it wasn't all down to the roller coaster flight we'd just experienced.

We hadn't had much time to talk, not that we would have heard each other over the noise of the engines. It was only the second time I'd flown in the company jet, and I was already dreading the journey back. An ancient six-seater, it was used to transport officials back and forth to Johannesburg from the various mines throughout the goldfields. It took less than an hour to fly between the Free State and Johannesburg, but the turbulence made it feel like flying a sortie through enemy flak. I understood how my father must have felt flying Lancaster bombers over Germany, but at least he had a parachute. All I had was an elastic band.

I walked in behind Joe. Everyone I'd spoken to was looking no further than a failure of the *3S Initiative*, but if I could find time to review things properly… *there was no chance of that*. My only ally was Marius van der Merwe, and he was in a hospital bed, dealing with issues far worse than anything I was going through.

I'd never been in Van Heerden's office and was surprised how spartan it was. If a tidy desk was an indication of a tidy mind, then his intellect was pristine. He was looking out of a large picture window with his back toward us. Joe motioned me to resist taking the only seat, both of us knew I was in for my second rough ride of the day.

BREAKING POINT

Then Van Heerden spoke. 'Schmidt, would you leave us please, I wish to speak with Mr Core, alone.' He hadn't bothered to turn around.

Joe looked at me and shrugged his shoulders. He mimed *good luck* and gave me a thumbs-up as he left the room. The door clicked quietly behind me.

Van Heerden turned from the window and motioned for me to take a seat. I preferred to stay on my feet and declined the offer. He also remained standing. His hands were held together, as though in prayer, his fingertips resting on his lower lip.

The white cuffs of his shirt were clasped with gold cufflinks and extended perfectly from his dark grey suit. I noticed the company logo, *R.G.,* on both his cufflinks and tie-pin, and wondered how someone could look so immaculate. I felt like a stray dog.

He was more impressive in the flesh than in the many photographs I'd seen of him smiling and shaking hands in the mining publications that appeared on my desk. There was talk of a planned visit to Concorde IV once we reached the one million Fatality Free Shift target. But all that was history now, along with the lives of nine men. And he wasn't smiling.

'Well, Core, it seems we have a crisis.' I was about to reply, but he held up his hand, as though constructing the next sentence in his head.

'You've been involved with Concorde IV for three years, and under your management, it is outperforming every other mine in the Orange Free State.' I knew I wasn't here to be congratulated and remained silent and suspicious. 'Of course, you have me to thank for that.' He looked directly into my eyes.

'If you say so, Mr Van,' I said, grinding my teeth.

'Well, I *would* say so, Core. Let's examine the facts, shall we?'

'Yes, let's,' I replied with enough sarcasm for him to raise his eyebrows at me. I recognised the warning. 'Sorry, yes, let's go through the facts.'

He relaxed a little. 'Over two years ago, I was presented with the prospect of *wasting* six hundred and twenty-five thousand rand of Rinto Gold money on an unproved *3S Initiative*. Correct?'

I nodded.

'And since that time, it would appear my investment was a good one. Would you also agree?'

I was only going to nod until I knew where this was going.

'So, ipso-facto, I deserve the credit. Yes?'

'I suppose so,' I said, with no enthusiasm.

He turned his back on me again. 'Of course, that was until your *Initiative* failed.'

'I disagree,' I jumped in. 'It hasn't been proved that it failed.'

'I think we only have to count the bodies, Core, don't you?'

'I couldn't care less what you think of me, or the *3S*,' I said, my voice raised more than it should have been. 'I know it works and has done for two years. All I've heard for the last three days is everyone jumping on the same bandwagon. I can't say I can blame them, but…'

'Oh, I'm glad of that, Mr Core.' He turned around to face me with, what looked like, a little more interest. And I'd got a *Mr* out of him.

'I don't know what your background is, Mr Van, but I've been in engineering all my life, and I don't take anything for granted, especially when people's lives are at risk. I've never said the process was foolproof and you'll see that on the summary of my original proposal. But I believe it is fit for purpose, and I'll be the first to put my hands up if I'm proved wrong.'

BREAKING POINT

There was a look in his eye. I'd entered the room expecting to be given short shrift, but something had changed.

'So what do we do, Mr Core?'

We... was this a thaw in relations?

'You're telling me that you don't believe your system failed,' he continued to press. 'If that's so, then what other cause can there be?'

I cleared my throat. 'As you know, I worked for Mathers for many years before joining Rinto Gold...'

'Yes,' he interrupted. 'I'm aware of your CV.'

He leaned back against the window ledge and casually stretched his arms, touching each side of the frame before crossing them in front of his chest. It was a strange thing to do, and I was taken with the perfect symmetry of the image. He was framed by the window and dead centre of his immaculate desk. It reminded me of an Edward Hopper painting, or was it, Leonardo da Vinci?

'You were the Engineering Manager if I remember correctly?' He said it in such a way that I knew he'd done his homework; he probably knew my blood group.

'Yes, that's right,' I replied. 'And I worked exclusively on the Recycling Stabiliser.'

'Ah yes, the famous *Recycling Stabiliser*.' He arched his eyebrows, adding an almost comic quality to the last two words. 'The report I received from your secretary mentions it. You've asked a lot of questions.'

'That's right,' I continued. 'The original design is over sixty years old and was decades ahead of its time.'

Van Heerden nodded. '*Was?*'

I ignored the inference and pressed on. 'The two new Stabilisers on Level 110 have undergone significant design changes. They're identified as MK6 Stabilisers, whatever that means. My initial investigation leads me to believe that they're not functioning properly, certainly not as efficiently as the older models.' I looked into his eyes; he was still listening. 'I'm convinced one of them has contributed to the collapse on 120 East and the second is putting 140 at risk.'

'And that's why you've taken it upon yourself to close down Concorde IV.' His face reddened. The tone remained the same, but he was struggling to contain his anger.

'I've been down there,' I said. 'And in my opinion, something is seriously wrong. The Stabilisers are unbalanced and causing excessive vibration within the piping systems. I believe we need to investigate their performance, or we may have an even worse collapse on our hands.'

'I don't think you should be passing this disaster into *our* hands yet Mr Core, at least not until we've eliminated *your* 3S System from the investigation. Do you?'

'Point taken,' I answered. 'But I have real concerns about the safety of those MK6 Stabilisers.'

'You have proof of this?' His eyes widened in anticipation.

'No, not exactly. But examining the evidence over the last three days, there's enough doubt in my mind to warrant an official investigation and try to find out what changes have been made.'

He stood up straight and uncrossed his arms. 'And who do you think should lead this investigation?' His face screwed up.

'Well me, of course.' *Who else*, I thought.

'But I'm about to sack you.' There wasn't a trace of emotion on his face.

The statement shook me, and I moved to the edge of his desk, leaning on it with both hands to emphasise a point. He stepped forward to say something, but I continued before he had the chance.

'You can do whatever you want, you're in charge. But if you sack me, without acting on my report, you may be responsible for sanctioning the use of dangerous machinery on Concorde IV. Machinery that, without warning, could kill more workers and close down the mine, permanently.'

BREAKING POINT

He couldn't take his eyes off my hands, but my message was getting through.

'You sound very sure of yourself,' he said, finally looking up.

If I hadn't been holding onto his desk, I'm not sure my legs would keep me upright. I knew this was my last chance, and my knees were shaking. 'I'm not sure,' I said. 'But if you give me four weeks to carry out my investigation, I *will* find the cause.'

'How do I know your report will be impartial?' His voice was calm, but something was niggling him.

I stood upright and took my hands from the desk. 'If you doubt my integrity…' I noticed my sweaty palm prints on the immaculate wood and attempted to wipe them away with the sleeve of my shirt. I heard him gasp, and had a light bulb moment.

The desk, the furniture, his posture. It made sense. I'd upset the symmetry. As trivial as the handprints were, they'd disturbed some sort of equilibrium. I decided to emphasise the point by pulling the chair out from my side and sat down. This put it at an angle to the desk.

A muscle in his jaw twitched.

I was playing with fire, but I had nothing else to lose.

I'd only succeeded in smearing the stain on the desk which seemed to trouble him. I believed he wanted to do something about it, but would risk exposing his Achilles heel. *Knowledge is power,* so the saying goes, and I had him on the back foot for the first time. So I pressed on.

'We have a saying in the U.K., Mr Van. *If it looks like a chicken, smells like a chicken… it's a chicken.*'

He gave a thin smile… I was about to be undone.

Yes, I'd spoiled the symmetry and neatness he craved, and maybe exposed an obsessive flaw in his make-up. But a strong man's weakness can still overpower a weak man's strength. I'd left myself vulnerable, and Van Heerden was about to flex his muscles.

Ian Holland

He moved away from the desk, and walked around to the other side of the room, directly behind me. 'And you are convinced we have *a chicken,*' he said. It wasn't a question.

Seconds that felt like minutes of eerie stillness passed between us. I avoided turning and looked toward the window in front of me, trying to see his reflection, but the chair was too low. I could only imagine him observing me.

Each move I'd made he'd counteracted, effortlessly. Now I could feel his eyes watching me, out of view. I was snapping rhythmically on the elastic band around my wrist as sweat dripped from my armpits, the cold rivulets running down my ribcage felt like electric shocks. I was out of my comfort zone, and this whole thing felt like some sort of initiation test.

'Do you know anything about the laws of South Africa?' I wasn't ready for his question, nor the change in direction. But before I could answer, he pressed on. 'This is a very different country from the United Kingdom, especially concerning industrial law.'

All I could do was shake my head as he continued.

'Unfortunately, an accident of this magnitude cannot be judged within the confines of the Rinto Gold organisation…' Another long pause. The office was getting warm, and I pulled at the collar of my shirt to let some heat out. 'If it were, then those responsible would simply be sacked or reprimanded, and that would be the end of the matter.'

I uncrossed my legs and twisted around, I wanted to see his face. He was leaning back against the wall, looking down at me.

'I'm afraid this will become a matter for the John Vorster Square, Police Department.'

My heart banged against my chest, and I swallowed hard to avoid gasping. John Vorster Square was notorious for its treatment of detainees and human rights violations. I'd passed the blue cement facade on a couple of occasions

BREAKING POINT

when I was in Johannesburg and knew of its violent reputation. I couldn't believe the conversation had moved in this direction.

Van Heerden's face was implacable. 'You see, Mr Core because Rinto Gold has its Head Office in Johannesburg, any legal judgements, involving a subsidiary company, must be processed through the Central Johannesburg Police Station. Which in this case is situated in John Vorster Square.'

'Why would that be necessary in the case of an industrial accident?' I asked, my head was buzzing.

'You may already know the answer to that, but let me elucidate. We may be dealing with a case of *negligent manslaughter*.' I shook my head in disbelief. *I didn't know the answer to that!*

Van Heerden pushed himself off the wall and made his way back to the desk. He pulled out a tissue and, with his back toward me, rubbed my handprints from the surface. He turned his head a little as he spoke.

'I think you and I know each other a little better now, wouldn't you agree?' He walked around to his side of the desk and deposited the tissue in the waste paper bin. I squared the chair back around and faced him across the immaculately restored desk. The bastard was smiling.

'For all our differences, Mr Core, we are very similar to each other, deep down.

'I have my... let's call them idiosyncrasies, shall we? And you... well you have your elastic band.'

I pulled my hand away from my wrist in a futile gesture.

'We also share a similar loss in our lives.' His voice dimmed, losing some of its confidence in that one, brief sentence. It was more of a whisper, and I looked up in surprise. His eyes never lost their glint, but his face had sagged a fraction. He turned back to look out the window. The back of his head rose upward as though looking for something in the sky.

'I... I... don't understand.' I stammered like a fool. He was dissecting me.

'I'm sorry, Mr Core, that was indelicate of me, forgive me for bringing it up.' He turned back around to face me.

'It's none of your business.' I spat the words out.

He held out both hands in an open gesture, not quite an apology, but I could see for the first time he was feeling awkward. 'In a situation as serious as this, everything is my business.'

I closed my eyes and turned. My youngest son, Alex, came to me as he had done every day since he'd died. Then Paul, his older brother, who I hadn't seen for over five years. A familiar shame enveloped me; I'd let down the living and the dead. I rubbed at a raw patch of skin at the back of my neck. Irritation or embarrassment, I didn't know or care.

Then I looked back up, wiping away the weakness of my wet eyes. 'I owe it to the men who died, and their families, to find out exactly what happened,' I said. 'I want those responsible to be made accountable, and if the evidence points to me and the *3S Initiative,* then I'll hold my hands up and accept the consequences.' My voice was breaking up with emotion, I was barely holding things together.

Van Heerden picked up the telephone. 'Jean, would you bring in a glass of water for Mr Core?' As he replaced it, I experienced a wave of calm. The door opened, and his secretary came in and placed a glass in my hand. She looked genuinely concerned.

'Thanks,' I said, and her hand brushed my shoulder with a comforting smell of perfume.

'Is that all, Mr Van?' Her eyes were on me like a worried mother.

'Yes, thank you, Jean.' The door closed quietly behind her.

The pause had drawn the venom from my anger. 'I'm sorry you caught me unawares,' I said.

BREAKING POINT

'I didn't mean to.' He looked back out of the window as though afraid of showing too much of himself. 'A long time ago, my wife and I lost a daughter.'

'How old was she?' I asked.

He stiffened. 'As I say, it was a long time ago, and we both know life is never the same… in so many different ways.'

His hands joined behind his back, and he turned to face me once more. 'Your success in managing Concorde IV has been brought to my attention over the last twelve months. I've watched your progress more closely than you would know. Your career with Mathers appears to have been successful, and it surprised me that you made such a drastic move. But life… is transient and unpredictable.'

He walked around to my side of the desk and reached out to shake my hand. I stood, taken aback by the finality of the gesture.

'I'll give you one week to complete your investigations, Mr Core. That will coincide with the next shareholder meeting where, unless I hear otherwise, I will report the cause of the accident as the failure of your *3S Initiative*. I will then be obliged to terminate your contract and pass the details on to the Police Authorities. Until then, I will support the decision to close down the mine. All workers, other than a skeleton staff, will be sent home on half-pay.'

A week! I had a rough plan in my head and knew I wouldn't scratch the surface in that time.

'I shall expect to see you in precisely seven days. Please keep me posted on progress and let me know if I can help in any way.'

'I need more time, Mr Van,' I said. 'I'll need to visit Mathers in the U.K., and getting flights will take time.'

I was hanging onto his hand, trying desperately to think things through. I knew once I was out the door, there was no getting back. His eyes were burning into my face, straining to let go, but I was having none of it and continued to hold on.

He was thinking about it, and that gave me hope. Then he smiled and pulled his hand away. *Another bloody smile*, I thought. I had no idea whether that was a good sign or a bad one, my head was spinning.

'I will delay the meeting on your behalf, that will give you ten days to complete your investigations. That's a million rand's worth of lost production I am trusting you with.'

'Thank you, Mr Van, I appreciate it. And could I ask for one other thing?'

His smile froze.

'And?'

'I'll need some help; can I take someone along with me?'

His brow furrowed, and the smile disappeared. 'That is my last concession, Mr Core. We will continue to pay your wages and those of whoever you choose to go with you. But all sundry expenses will be your responsibility. Unless I hear otherwise, the mine will reopen in ten days, and the matter will be in the hands of the police.'

I had some *rainy day* money put away, and right now it was pissing down. I could just about cover short term travel and accommodation costs for the ten days, but that would be it.

Van Heerden led me toward the door and tapped me on the shoulder. 'Good luck,' he said and returned to his desk. I'm not sure why, but I think he meant it.

I snapped the elastic band on my wrist and thanked his secretary on the way out. I was already clearing my mind for the task ahead.

Ten days and counting.

BREAKING POINT

Chapter 15

It was ten minutes to two, and the ageing Research and Development Conference Room was filling up. In the corner, pinned to the wall, was a small black and white photograph of Franklyn Mathers, dated 1941. Wearing a double-breasted suit, he was staring confidently at the camera, nonchalantly leaning against a factory doorway. A cigarette hung from the fingers of his right hand; his left sunk into his jacket pocket. The photograph was slightly askew and coated in dust.

Voices blended in the room, creating a low hum, occasionally broken by nervous laughter. Everyone had loaded up with coffee. The running joke was that it would help keep them awake during another tedious presentation. Data was God in Fred Stremsen's PMT process, and the reviews were filled with minutiae which sapped energy from the room.

John and Richie were seated next to each other at the large, rectangular table, alongside three other engineers. Socket was at the far end. It was the first time they'd seen him since he'd been summoned from the office. Everyone was waiting for the entrance of the Senior Deputy Vice-President of Engineering, Fred Stremsen.

After five years of the PMT, they'd given up trying to explain the complexities of the Recycling Stabiliser to him.

I don't need to know the detail, the process will tell me everything of consequence, was his fallback position.

He divided opinion between those who *thought* he was an incompetent fool and those who *knew*. Few in the room understood why he had to make the trip in person when he could be just as ineffective on a conference call. The process would begin with an overview from Billy Jones, the Technical Director, on the progress of the MK7 Stabiliser Project.

Richie whispered across to John. 'Could some of Danny's concerns relate to work done on previous models?'

'Like what?' said John.

'Well, like the previous MK1s, 2s and 3s, etc.'

John smiled. 'They don't exist, mate.'

Tick looked confused, and John's smile turned to a snigger.

'Stremsen insisted that the first development to use his PMT scheme, shouldn't be designated MK1.'

'Where's the sense in that?' said Richie, doodling on a scrap of paper.

John blew his cheeks out. 'His idea was that if we marketed it as a MK1 model, our customers would wonder what our Development Department has been doing for the last sixty years. When it was pointed out that there was complete traceability on all previous Stabiliser developments, he said that was an old-fashioned way of doing things.'

'Wouldn't that have caused a lot of confusion?' said Richie, looking up from his squiggles.

'Just a bit,' replied John. 'When the MK5 was launched, nearly every customer was on the phone asking why they hadn't been offered the previous upgrades.'

'What happened?'

John shrugged his shoulders. 'He just walked away and left Sales to try and explain... you couldn't write it!'

At the end of the large table, was a smaller one positioned at right angles to form a *T*. On top this was a projector standing by to show the plethora of graphs and statistics that were part of the new *Cascade Briefing Process*, or *CBP*.

Confusion had reigned over the increasing number of acronyms developed during the birth of the PMT process. Stremsen had resolved this by introducing an *Acronym Dictionary* and had it designated appropriately; *A.D.* in the A.D.

BREAKING POINT

At 11 o'clock, a hush came over the room as Billy Jones, the Technical Director, walked in. Billy was Jack Smelt's replacement, much to the disgust of Socket who felt he'd been unfairly overlooked. Billy was a competent metallurgist, but it soon became apparent, from those who worked for him, that he lacked leadership skills and could barely read a technical drawing. Behind him, two other Board Members followed. Tony Peace, the Production Director and Bob Evans, the Financial Controller.

'Shit!' Richie covered his mouth. 'Who summoned the death squad?' John shrugged. It looked like word had spread about the accident report. Monthly briefings didn't typically get a high-profile audience like this. He looked along the line at Socket and wondered why he was so smug.

The Directors acknowledged the group and took their seats. The factory wasn't performing well, and Peace was under pressure to improve output.

New developments just get in the way, he would say to anyone who would listen.

He planted his bulky frame next to Bob Evans, arguably the most influential man in Mathers. Thin and gaunt, he was the antithesis of Peace and the alpha male on the Mathers Board.

Peace leaned over and spoke to him in a rasping whisper, as though he was sharing a secret. 'Do you think Billy's in trouble with this accident, Bob?'

Evans shook his head, his hand poised over his mouth to deflect Peace's notoriously bad breath. 'Why, should he be?'

'We all know the MK6 was plagued with difficulties. It was nine months late and just scraped past the cost-saving targets.'

'Mmm, that remains a mystery, but all the changes went through the process. According to Stremsen, that makes the development watertight.'

'Do you really believe that? Rumours were circulating that the amendments were starting to impact on the integrity of the MK6. The MK7 could be even worse, everyone's talking about it.'

Evans sighed and gulped in some fresh air. 'Well, I haven't heard *you* question the impact, Tony.'

'I'm not responsible for the calculations,' Peace sneered.

'No, but it's your signature that helps sign off each Stage-Gate. What bit of that don't you get?' Evans sensed the engineers picking up on the conversation.

'So is yours!' Peace answered, piqued and oblivious to the outside interest. 'Just remember I've got a memory like an elephant.' He pointed to his pink forehead.

'But I'm not questioning the MK6,' said Evans. 'And since we're so candid, you've also inherited the breath of an elephant.'

One of the engineers burst out laughing.

'Eh?' Peace grunted, but Evans had turned away. Fred Stremsen had just walked in.

Stremsen nodded at the Directors and took his seat at the head of the table. Billy switched on the projector, and the lights dimmed. The room fell silent. Shuffling his presentation papers, he looked nervous and subdued.

Fatal accident reports have a habit of doing that, thought John.

'Begin,' said Stremsen, not bothering to look up from his notebook.

The meeting commenced with Billy outlining some of the problems experienced during testing of the MK7. Never a good start with an audience craving good news. Armed with scores of acetate forms and graphs, he fumbled them onto the projector at various stages of the review. Socket, who'd confirmed only four weeks ago that the design changes were promising, was shaking his head in disbelief. Each failure that Billy reported had him *tutting* in surprise.

BREAKING POINT

He'd stood in for Billy at last month's meeting and talked of a breakthrough. This came as a pleasant surprise to those, *not* associated with the project. And a shock to those directly involved. Stremsen had seemed impressed with Socket's optimism.

'The MK7 design is failing and any breakthrough reported at last month's presentation was wide of the mark,' announced Billy. He made a point of staring at Socket before placing another acetate on the projector.

'On the left are the cost savings we were challenged with at the beginning of the project...'

'Design improvements!' Stremsen's voice called out, and Socket's head nodded.

'Yes, of course,' Billy said, with no enthusiasm. 'These are the cost savings *and* design improvement we were challenged with at the beginning of the project.'

He isn't letting go, thought John.

And so it went on for over an hour, a car crash. Inefficient and structurally weakened, there was little to be optimistic about the MK7. John watched Billy falter as the negativity formed in dark, heavy clouds. The deteriorating atmosphere choked his delivery, causing him to stutter and backtrack on previous statements. He frequently lost his place, shuffling back and forth through his notes. His tongue swept across his lips, trying to lubricate the faltering sentences. This was not the Billy Jones they'd come to expect.

Questions from the board members began to override the presentation and Socket's leg fidgeted as he, too, came under fire. Tony Peace enjoyed picking away at the project until its inadequacy finally spilt out.

'It's a heap of shit!' was one of his more eloquent comments. Terry used his vulpine tactics to defend his position and incriminated Billy as much as he could. Still, in the end, the result was carnage. Initial disbelief became anger, and their focus returned to Billy, who stood at the projector in a daze. John almost felt sorry for him.

'Billy, what the hell is going on here. You're in charge, aren't you?' Bob Evans called out in exasperation, causing the room to turn in his direction. *The numbers man rarely showed emotion.*

Gradually much of the anger flagged toward despondency as everyone realised that all the work and money invested so far, had come to nothing. John felt numb. If it wasn't so serious, it would be funny. He didn't rate Billy but was embarrassed for him. Only four weeks ago, Terry had told everyone that the project had turned a corner. Now Billy was telling them it had veered off a cliff, and taken the credibility of the development department with him.

Stremsen hadn't said a word since he began the meeting, but John noticed his eyes had not left Billy during the whole presentation. He showed no alarm at the failure, and his silence was unnerving everyone in the room. Surprisingly, he hadn't criticised Socket, but Bob Evans wasn't so forgiving.

'Terry, I understood from last month's presentation that you'd turned a corner. Can you explain what's happened in four weeks?'

Socket looked at Stremsen who lifted his hand. 'I suggest we take a ten-minute coffee break, gentlemen,' he said this with surprising calmness. As he got up, he gestured for Socket to join him at the other end of the room.

The stunned silence erupted into a babble of excitable voices, and John was reminded of school kids drawn to a playground fight. Billy took a seat on his own. Nothing was more repellent than failure.

Stremsen and Socket were in deep conversation; Terry scribbling copious notes in his book and nodding in such an exaggerated fashion that the other engineers began to mimic him. John saw something else.

BREAKING POINT

For all his outward calm, Stremsen seemed to have lost some of his confidence. There was impatience in the way his hands were gesturing.

A man under pressure, John thought.

After ten minutes, they were summoned to take their seats. The sombre mood was suffused with an air of expectancy; again, the *playground* mentality. All eyes were on Terry and Billy, who were now sitting together.

'Billy,' Stremsen's voice cut through a nervous cough from one of the engineers. 'Billy, are you happy with this presentation?'

Billy straightened up in his chair. 'Obviously, I'm not happy, Fred, but Terry…'

'I would hope not,' said Stremsen. 'And let's not bring Terry into it, he's got enough problems to solve at the moment.' He glanced toward John, then continued.

'I'll be reporting back to our CEO, Rik Last, following these latest set-backs and I'd like to know if you think I should recommend sacking you?'

Silence gripped the room, and everyone seemed to hold their breath. John saw Socket nudge an engineer next to him. Billy twisted in his seat, looking around at all the faces. An uncomfortable length of time passed before Stremsen continued.

'I won't ask you for an answer in front of your colleagues, but I'd like you and me to discuss, in private, a way out of this situation. Are you agreed?'

Billy's voice came back in a barely discernible whisper. 'Yes, Fred.'

Stremsen sighed and theatrically shook his head. 'Gentlemen,' he turned back to the group on the other side of the table. 'I think we'll take a rain check on the MK7 project until we have better news.' He gave Billy a sideways glance. 'Instead, I'll share some information we've received overnight from one of our customers.'

John braced himself.

'There's been an accident at Rinto Gold, one of our user sites in South Africa. None of you will be aware of this report we've received from the Chief Engineer of Rinto Gold,' he waved the sheets at the group. 'But in it, he implies that recent design changes to the MK6 Stabiliser may have contributed to a serious incident.' He looked around the room, allowing the words to settle, the drama to build.

'Nine men have died.'

There was a sharp intake of breath from most of the people around the table. John's eyes stayed steady, and Socket's smirk fell away as Stremsen continued.

'I want us to revisit the PMT process used to create the MK6 and ensure that the work was carried out to the highest Heron standards. In honour of those dead men.'

Brian Gladwyn, one of the young engineers, raised his hand. 'When did the accident occur?'

'Four days ago,' Stremsen answered abruptly. 'But trust me, as the architect of the PMT process, I have complete confidence that the results of your investigation will remove all suspicion from the MK6.'

That sounded like a veiled threat to John.

'So the accident involves the MK6 Stabiliser?' Brian was inquisitive.

He'll learn, thought John.

Stremsen looked across at Bob Evans, who shook his head. 'Not directly, it was only mentioned in the report.'

'Then it's implicated in some other way?' Gladwyn, again. Evans shook his head once more, his mouth looked too dry to speak.

Stremsen ignored the question. 'The Board and I have just been on a conference call with Rik Last, who is right behind us on this. He has total confidence in the PMT process and has asked me to return to the U.S. immediately to present to the Heron Board.

'Following what I expect to be a successful investigation, I will reassure Rinto Gold that the MK6

BREAKING POINT

Stabilisers are totally reliable. And that recent changes played no part in their tragic accident.'

He paused to take a sip of water, and John noticed his hand wasn't as steady as his voice. As he put the glass down, some liquid spilt onto the table.

'Now I'd like Terry Socket to give a brief presentation of the PMT for the MK6 Stabiliser, Terry.'

This was obviously pre-planned as Socket confidently got up from his seat and set to work, armed with the relevant information. The presentation was a master class of positivity. Even John was impressed by the way Socket set about detailing the successes of the project. It wasn't a surprise that he emphasised how the PMT had driven the MK6 to a positive conclusion.

By the end everyone was happy, and Terry even gained a round of applause from Stremsen, who rounded the meeting off by announcing that Socket would be taking charge of the accident investigation.

'He will add a, much needed, perspective and dynamism to the process,' he pronounced.

'Looks like Billy's going the same way as Jack Smelt?' whispered Richie.

He had a point. *But why, Billy?* Thought John.

The MK6 project hadn't been easy and missed almost every due date that was set. But every aspect of every change had been carried out within the detailed guidelines laid down in the process and, somehow, had achieved its cost reduction targets. It was the only part of the project in which they'd gained a bonus. Jack Smelt had been meticulous in following the guidelines and made sure the Stage-Gates were signed off by every Senior Manager and Director, right up to CEO level.

Billy hadn't fared any better when he took over and had followed the same guidelines. The launch dates continued to be extended, but all the calculations had been meticulously checked and double-checked. For all Socket's bluster, he was an experienced engineer, and with his name all over it, there was no way he would cut corners.

So, John asked himself again, *Why was Billy Jones being set up?*

Chapter 16

With daylight almost exhausted, I gazed out from the air-conditioned terminal of Jan Smuts Airport, Johannesburg. Outside, yellow suited ground-staff loaded the conveyors, force-feeding the static Boeing 747 bound for London.

Steyn was getting coffee and had left me alone with my thoughts. His reaction wasn't unexpected when I said I wanted him to come with me... *The UK, what the hell do you expect to find over there?*

I didn't know myself, but I needed his support to have any chance. His protest was half-hearted, and I knew he would help. I'd already booked the tickets.

Embele's suggestion to strip down the MK6 had intrigued me, and the more I thought about it, the more the risk seemed worthwhile. After flying back from the meeting with Van Heerden, I broached the subject with Steyn. His reaction was predictable.

'You're crazy, man! Once we start meddling, we lose any warranty we have. It could cost us thousands of rand in the future; plus no one will believe us if we do find something. They'd say we tampered with the evidence.'

'I need it done,' I said. 'But I don't want anyone to know what's going on. Something's not right, and I've been given ten days to find out what. I'm already down to eight.'

'But you're destroying all the evidence, man. This site will need a proper investigation with independent witnesses; you're risking everything on a hunch.'

I couldn't disagree with his logic; I would have said the same things in his shoes. 'Trust me, Steyn, I need your support.'

I knew it was unreasonable. Steyn liked order and control. If he was travelling from A to Z, he needed to visit every letter in between. It was in his DNA, and this other stuff I was throwing his way was confusing the hell out of him.

'Any suggestions who we get to do it?' he asked. He was angry with me, but I don't think he'd lost faith... yet.

'Embele has volunteered,' I said. 'And I thought we could get Piet Reiss to lead the team.'

He raised his eyebrows. 'You know Piet's not enthusiastic about your theory.'

'I'm not looking for supporters,' I replied. 'I'm looking for evidence, and I know he's a good man. Plus, as the maintenance team leader, he won't raise any suspicions.'

'How do we get them down there, you've shut down the headgear?'

I'd thought of that. 'They can go down the new ventilation shaft,' I replied.

Steyn raised his eyebrows again. 'It's not finished yet; they'll have to go down in the *kibble.*'

'That's right. A bit uncomfortable, but it'll be away from prying eyes.'

The new ventilation shaft wasn't complete yet, but it would get Piet and his team down far enough to reach a cross-cut where they could access the Stabilisers on 110.

The only transport, up and down the narrow shaft, would be via a *kibble*. This was a large steel bucket hung from cables running from a small, temporary headgear. Everything that required taking down or bringing back up was transported in the *kibble.* Men, tools, mud and rock, they all shared the same space. It would only take four men at a time, gripping onto whatever they could find in the confined space, but experienced miners were used to it.

He'd relented and arranged for Piet to secure the area and organise Embele and two others to carry out the strip down while we were away. *Only the front section,* I'd told him. It was the area worst affected and would provide most of the answers.

BREAKING POINT

They wouldn't be able to make a start until Monday morning because the maintenance teams were still securing the collapse on 120. It wasn't ideal, but I was desperate for answers. He provided cameras to take down with instructions to photograph anything of interest. All information would be sent exclusively to us in the UK.

'You need to impress on him, that on no account must he start-up the other MK6 Stabiliser,' I said.

'You think it'll be *that* dangerous, Danny?'

'I don't want anyone taking risks down there until we have some answers,' I replied. I knew Steyn was sceptical, but he was doing his best to agree with me.

I'd contacted Billy Jones at Mathers to tell him when we'd be coming to the UK and, without going into too much detail, the purpose of our visit. He was reluctant at first, but when I suggested the alternative was for them to come to South Africa in the next two days, he relented. He said he'd arrange for me to be given access to their mechanical laboratory and any relevant information.

As short as my time would be in the UK, I needed to make contact with my ex-wife, Julie and my son, Paul. Assuming she agreed, it was time to face up to my responsibilities and put things right, regardless of my future.

I'd phoned my old friend, John Dread, who would arrange to get me Julie's phone number. And here we were, getting ready to fly to the UK, with eight days to go.

Chapter 17

Luca Majori collected his presentation and made his way to Rik Last's office. On the way, he stopped to chat with Mary, Last's secretary.

Luca was the group's Financial Controller, a man with his hands on the Heron purse strings and a close confidante of Last... *A good man to have on your side*, was how Last referred to him.

'How is he, Mary?'

'A bit grumpy, he bumped his car on the way in, so tread carefully.'

'What's all this about?' He waved Danny Core's report at her. 'And calling us in on a Saturday!'

'He's nervous about the accident in South Africa and wants to look at the financial risks. I suggested he talk it over with you.'

'Mmm, normally I'd be comfortable with it all, but Stremsen's involved and that always worries me.'

She began to probe. 'Do you think Mathers *could* be responsible?'

'Say, I like that perfume you're wearing, Mary. What's it called?'

She pulled a small scent bottle from her drawer and offered it to him. As Majori stretched out his hand to take it, a blue spark arced across their fingers.

'Ow!' He squealed, shaking his hand in the air. Mary didn't flinch.

'It's called *Evasion*,' she said, with a wicked smile.

'You're a hard woman, Mary. If I didn't know better, I'd say you were going off me.' They both laughed.

'You'd better get in there; you know how he is with punctuality.'

He gave her a wink. 'Thanks a lot for the invitation,' and opened the door into the office.

BREAKING POINT

'Luca,' Rik Last motioned for him to sit down on the chair opposite his own, and just beneath *Uncle Billy*. 'Thanks for coming at such short notice.'

As if I had a choice, Luca thought.

Last leaned back, stroking his hair. His lean, six-foot two frame was casually dressed in a polo shirt and chinos.

'As you know, five years ago, Fred Stremsen was promoted to Senior Deputy Vice President of Engineering,' Majori couldn't help making a face. Last ignored the inference and continued. 'As part of Fred's brief, I asked him to come up with a step by step process on how to develop and introduce new products into the Heron portfolio.' He spread his arms as though encompassing the whole group inside his reach.

'I aimed to encourage all our development facilities to apply a systematic approach when undertaking large scale projects. You're familiar with all this?' He looked directly at Luca and received a nod.

'I am, Rik, but almost four years on and he hasn't rolled the process outside of Mathers!'

Last sighed and waved the comment aside. 'We know the PMT title gave everyone cause to smile, but we're not here to crack jokes today. Fred is over in the UK on his monthly visit to Mathers and is about to meet with Rinto Gold's Chief Engineer, Danny Core. You and I met him when we were in the process of buying Mathers, back in eighty-four?'

'I remember him,' Luca replied. 'He was the Engineering Manager at the time, and I was involved with the due diligence.'

'What did you think of him?' Last squinted his eyes.

'Struck me as someone who knew what he was talking about; I'm not sure he'll have that much in common with Fred.'

Cheap shot, Likky.

'Yes, okay,' said Rik, ignoring the smirk on Luca's face. 'He's got spunk from what I remember, but I'm not sure that's a good thing in this case.'

'What do you mean?' said Luca.

Last pointed to the report on his desk. 'You've read this. He strikes me as the sort of guy who could cause us a lot of trouble.'

Majori narrowed his eyes. 'It's been a while, but I do remember having a couple of days with him discussing the potential for new projects. He was excited at the prospect of a big company like Heron getting on board and had some impressive ideas. I was surprised when I heard he'd left, I thought he was lined up as the next Technical Director.'

'We'll never know,' said Last. 'Now, this Recycling Stabiliser is on its third generation in four years of the PMT process.'

Luca nodded. 'It's the MK7 version.'

'Mmm, do you think Stremsen's obsession has put the product at risk?'

Luca referred to his notes. 'The PMT process should have been about developing the product...'

'There's a *but* coming,' Last leaned forward.

'Yes, there is,' said Luca. 'The focus appears to have changed, and it's become all about cost reduction.'

'Is there a problem with that?' There was a threatening tone to Last's comment.

'Of course not, as long as the targets are achievable,' said Luca.

'And you don't think they are?' Last could see that Majori was choosing his words carefully.

'Not in the case of the Stabiliser; they've squeezed the life out of it.'

Seconds passed as Last absorbed the words one by one. 'I was afraid you were going to say that,' he finally said.

The tension in the room seemed to release, as though they'd found common ground.

BREAKING POINT

'I'm not saying there's anything wrong with cutting costs,' Luca continued. 'It's a competitive industry, but it needs to be done carefully. If it steps over health and safety boundaries, we need to have the courage to stop.'

Last's eyebrows closed in a frown. 'Do you think safety has been paramount in the minds of those setting the targets?'

'I'm not qualified to answer that, Rik. You know he's not my favourite person, but that doesn't mean he's not doing a good job.'

A weak smile washed across Last's face. 'I think you're holding back, Luca, let's have it straight.'

'Okay, but you're not going to like what I'm going to say.'

Likky perked up, as Luca took a deep breath.

'Stremsen's, Project Management Tome, plagiarised every tried and tested technique used in the automotive industry. He stitched them together and sold the resultant *PMT* as *his* creation. It suited his needs and Herons. To be honest, he was the only one with enough time to put the package together, but it didn't fool anyone outside of the Board of Directors.'

Easy, boy. Don't get ahead of yourself, Likky.

Last shuffled uncomfortably in his seat.

Luca continued. 'He presented the package as a *Next Generation*, development tool, which it clearly wasn't.'

'What was it then?'

Majori had to choose his words carefully. 'No more than an elaborate *to-do* list.

Last pulled his comb out and ran it through his hair a couple of times. 'Fred guaranteed it would reduce risk,' he said.

Luca blew his cheeks out. 'It requires a huge amount of data before each stage has to be signed off by every Tom, Dick and Harry in the organisation. It's no wonder every project has been late.'

Last nodded and returned the comb to his pocket. 'Doesn't that reduce risk?'

'Not in my opinion, it merely spreads the responsibility for failure. You gave Fred the title he craved and an opportunity to sit at the *big table*.'

Shit! Likky.

'Do you think that was a mistake?' Last's tone was measured.

'It helped Heron to be seen as progressive, but...' Majori held back.

'But what, Luca?'

Spit it out! Likky was getting personal.

Majori cleared his throat. 'The measure of success changed somewhere along the way. It became *how much money can we save?* This lack of focus moved it away from a risk-averse scheme to something...'

Last was waiting for a commitment. 'Something what?'

'Well... something more difficult to quantify.' Luca was looking uncomfortable.

A numbers man who can't quantify. What the fuck are we paying you for? Likky

'I'd like *you* to quantify it, Luca. How has a cost-cutting scheme increased risk?'

Luca threw his arms in the air. 'Okay, Rik, I'll give it you straight. If you carry it out on the same product, *MK5*, *MK6*, *MK7*...' he counted each iteration on his fingers. 'On sophisticated products like the Recycling Stabiliser, then you're going to increase the risk of failure.'

Failure? Likky.

'Has Fred overstepped the mark?' Last was impassive.

'Examine the evidence, Rik. There were some demanding targets set on the MK5 project, and all the product improvement were achieved. But the major accomplishment was in cost-saving.

'Then the MK6 followed immediately, with hardly any product improvements. The emphasis this time was on cost savings and the time scales were compressed. It didn't make sense because the MK5 had been three months late.

'We all know the MK6 hit difficulties, and Stremsen's solution was to remove Jack Smelt from the team. Not only that, but he allowed him to take early retirement; a decision which I disagreed with, but got overruled.'

'You won't let me forget that, will you, Luca? I told you at the time, Fred was in charge. He felt he needed fresh faces, and it was his responsibility to run the team, not ours.'

'It was only my opinion, Rik, but we jettisoned thirty years of experience in the middle of a critical project. We were reliant on experienced Mathers people to manage the technical changes because we didn't have any expertise of our own. Only Fred Stremsen and his PMT process.'

Fuck you! Likky was bouncing.

'Carry on, Luca,' Last remained calm.

'We took on Billy Jones as Jack's replacement, but not before another two engineers resigned; it didn't sound like a happy band of brothers. Finally, against all the odds, and nine months late, it was reported that the cost targets had been met. It went against all previous predictions and surprised everyone, except Fred.

'And now we're in the process of carrying out a MK7 development, with cost-saving targets the top priority. There's a dangerous pattern forming, Rik, and we've overlooked it.'

Last had taken his glasses off and was cleaning them with a handkerchief. His eyes were on Luca, but his mind was elsewhere.

'Something Danny Core once said has always stuck with me,' Luca continued. '*If it looks like a chicken, smells like a chicken...*

'...It's a chicken,' said Last, finishing the sentence. 'I remember him using the expression.'

'Mathers was a good acquisition,' Luca continued. 'And I understand why we thought it would be a good test for the

PMT, but maybe we should have tested the process on some of our other companies sooner. Allowed Stremsen to take a step back.'

Last replaced his glasses and sat upright, rubbing his hands as though he was cold. 'You said... *it was reported that the cost targets had been met,* as though you've got some doubts?'

'Well we all signed off the Stage-Gate process because all the *I's* were dotted and the *T's* crossed,' said Luca. 'But Core's report does ask some awkward questions. One in particular.'

'Which one?' said Last.

'Why did the Stabiliser continue to pump out water after the accident? The failsafe switches should prevent that happening. If we can't explain that, then Rinto Gold won't let go.'

'And if we can't?' asked Last.

Luca thought for a moment. 'Then we need to get our lawyers involved.'

That bastard, Stremsen, said Likky

'Okay, Luca, what do you suggest?'

Majori seemed to be expecting the question. 'Firstly, we admit nothing, but carry out a full investigation ourselves.'

'Stremsen to lead?' asked Last.

'Damn right,' replied Luca.

Fucking right, Likky concurred.

'And?' Last.

'We stop work on the MK7 Stabiliser.'

'And?'

'We give full cooperation to Rinto Gold and Danny Core in particular. We need to be open and honest.'

'Squeaky clean.'

'Yes.'

'And?'

'Visit the site as quickly as possible. If there is a problem, we need to understand what it is and be seen reacting to it.'

BREAKING POINT

'Is there a problem, Luca?'

Fred, fucking, Stremsen is the problem. Likky again.

'I don't know, Rik, I honestly don't know.'

'Okay, Luca I'm going to take on board all your suggestions, and I have one more of my own.'

'What's that?'

'You will shadow Stremsen and oversee the investigation.'

Majori gasped. 'Rik, I can't manage an engineering project like this, I'm a Financial Controller. Besides, how suspicious would it look from Rinto Gold's perspective.'

'I'm not asking you to manage an engineering project, Luca. I'm telling you to oversee an accident investigation.'

'And to babysit Stremsen.'

Hang the bastard if you have to, Likky.

'I need to know if Heron is implicated,' said Last.

'You mean you don't trust Stremsen.'

'I want an independent opinion,' Last replied. 'I want to know if his process is secure, and I want to hear it from someone I can trust.

'Someone with a bit of spunk.'

Chapter 18

The fourteen-hour flight had gone well with no delays. We were picked up by one of the Mathers engineers and shipped to The Lion Hotel in Crossways. After dinner, we'd gone to bed knackered. Steyn blamed jet lag. When I told him there was only an hour's difference between South African time and the UK, he wouldn't believe me.

We're on a different bloody Continent, man, there must be more than that. Why else am I feeling like shit? Even when I showed him the clocks in the hotel room, he refused to accept it. He'd never ventured outside South Africa, and I was humbled to think of the sacrifice he was making for me when my name was so toxic.

My mind was too busy for sleep, and I was glad when daylight leaked through the curtains. I showered and dressed, keen to take a walk around the outskirts of my old town, on my own. This trip was a significant battle in my ten-day war, and I was armed with nothing more than a stubborn belief that I was right. Thys van Heerden had taken a more significant risk than he imagined.

The sky was starting to clear, but the cold wind made me shiver; I zipped my jacket up to my neck. The roads and pavements filled with commuters, and a red bus passed me with the roar of a fractured exhaust, a cloud of diesel smoke catching the back of my throat. I recognised some of the faces staring out of its windows but kept my head down. I had enough on my plate without advertising my presence.

It amazed me how two countries, on different Continents, could feel so familiar on a working morning. The smell and taste of the place seeped back into my bones, releasing latent memories.

I cut across the canal bridge and took a footpath toward the old village. Overshadowed by the new town, many of the small shops were now boarded up, the rest fading with neglect.

As I meandered along the canal, toward the new shopping centre, I realised how close I was to my old house; Julie's home. Curiosity got the better of me, so I cut across a small woodland and came at it from the rear. Backed by trees and bushes, I stood on the edge of a concrete footpath that ran behind the row of houses and lifted the collar on my jacket. From here I could see over the hedge and into the kitchen window, without looking too conspicuous.

As I lit a cigarette, two boys in school uniform ran by, and I realised how ridiculous I looked. I turned to make my way back to the hotel when the kitchen door opened and a young boy ran out, carrying a football. I felt numb, it was my son, Paul. So tall... so different.

'You forgot your homework.' A woman's voice called from the kitchen, then appeared at the door holding out a blue holdall... it was Julie. Paul skidded on his heels with his shirt-tail flapping and turned back to snatch the bag, but she didn't let go. As he stalled, she grabbed him roughly and pulled him to her.

'You be a good boy.' She planted a kiss on top of his wheat coloured hair before he escaped with an, *okay mum*, and a cursory wave. He hurdled the low gate and ran past me with the pace of a young athlete. A loose lace slapped against the side of his shoe as he dribbled the football along the path toward the two other boys... *he looked like he could play a bit*.

I turned to look back at Julie, but she'd closed the door, and I was left watching the space between the open curtains of the dining room. A figure passed fleetingly across the gap, but it wasn't her. She returned to the window to straighten the curtains, and as she turned away, a man filled the space and snatched a kiss on her cheek before both disappeared. I saw nothing of his face, only a pink shirt. I wanted to walk away, but my legs felt like lead. Stunned and embarrassed, it felt as though I'd witnessed something indecent.

I couldn't remember anything of the journey back to the hotel, I was busy trying to put what I'd seen in perspective. I'd been away for almost five years and divorced for nearly the same amount of time. How could I be so naive to think that there wouldn't be other men; that I'd been long forgotten. Apart from my monthly cheques and Paul's Christmas and birthday cards, I didn't exist.

That could have been her husband for all I knew! The thought saddened me, which made no sense.

On my way back to the hotel, I remembered how well she looked. The black, tracksuit bottoms and grey jumper, made her look younger and more vibrant than I remembered. Her damp hair was greyer, but that had only enhanced... I stopped myself. *Christ, I took in a lot of detail.*

And Paul, so much bigger, now a young man. My five years away was half his lifetime. Why should he remember anything of me? On the flight over I'd been having doubts about seeing them again. But now I wanted nothing else in the world.

I looked up at the Brig Uchel Mountain range and shivered. Though the morning had warmed up, the peak was still covered in mist, and I could see it swirling in the wind that always stalked the high ground. Even in summer, it could cut you in half. I turned and released my clenched fists to concentrate on the road ahead.

When I reached the hotel, I made a phone call to Mathers and asked to speak to John Dread. He was in work and alone, it was safe to talk.

'Am I okay to pick you up at eleven?'

'That's fine,' I answered. 'I'll be bringing Steyn Broed along. You'll like him, he's a good engineer and doesn't suffer fools.'

BREAKING POINT

'He'll have a hard time making friends here, then.' He laughed, and I realised how much I'd missed his humour. 'How was the trip?'

I told him I hadn't slept much, and Steyn might be a bit grumpy. 'Who will we be meeting?'

He said they'd arranged a reception committee led by Terry Socket and Billy Jones.

'Socket?' I said a little surprised. 'What happened to Jack Smelt?'

'Jack took early retirement about 18 months ago; he got fed up being kicked around.'

'I can't believe it,' I said. 'Jack was Mather's through and through. I thought they'd need a crowbar to prise him out.'

'We did too, but he left with a lot of bad feeling, and right in the middle of a big project.'

'That doesn't seem like Jack's style,' I said. 'He'd never been one to leave anything unfinished. What project was that?'

His answer was hesitant. 'Well… it was the MK6 Stabiliser.'

I felt a cold shiver run through my body. 'That's a coincidence, did that have anything to do with Jack leaving?' I knew I was crossing a boundary.

'Erm, I wouldn't say that, Danny. He was more frustrated about the way he was being asked to run the project.'

'So it was nothing to do with the proposed changes?'

Another pause.

'Sorry, John, I said, 'I'm putting you in an awkward spot. Let's talk more when we get together.' I could feel his relief on the other end of the phone. 'Anyway, who's this Billy Jones?'

'Billy is Jack's replacement.'

'Sounds like musical chairs. And what about you in all this, why didn't *you* get my old job?'

It went quiet again.

'Jesus Christ!' I gasped. 'They didn't make Socket the Engineering Manager, did they?'

'Yes.'

I'd touched a nerve and changed the subject once again. 'Is this Billy Jones up to the job?'

'Not particularly,' said John, 'but to be fair, it would be difficult for anyone to look good at the moment. He's a decent enough metallurgist, but not the sharpest tack in terms of design.'

'So why did they choose him?'

'He sold himself as a good Project Manager, but I haven't seen too much of that, either. I think he may be on borrowed time… like Jack. Everyone thinks Socket is being groomed to fill the role. He's so far up Stremsen's arse, you can just make out the soles of his feet these days.'

'What's Fred Stremsen like?'

'He's the Senior Deputy Vice President of Engineering from Houston. He set up the new development process. It's called the PMT.'

I heard him giggle.

'I hope that doesn't mean what I think it does?' I said.

'No, it stands for Product Management Tome.'

'Thank goodness for that, but it's still a bloody mouthful.'

'Yeah, like his title. You should see it, Danny, it's the process we have to follow for every project that goes through the department. A control freaks delight and a tangle of red tape.'

'Is *he* any good?' I asked.

'No.' John's answer left no room for doubt. 'He's a waste of space. Knows nothing about engineering and professes he doesn't need to know. As long as the *PMT* is followed, all will be well in the world.'

'It would be a big step up for Socket to become Technical Director. Is he up to it?'

'You know that better than I do, Danny, but he hasn't got much to follow.'

BREAKING POINT

'He'd never admit he wasn't up to it, that's for sure,' I said. 'But maybe we're all guilty of arrogance.'

There was another awkward silence before he spoke again. 'I saw Julie yesterday, and she gave me her phone number for you to ring.'

My mind went back to her hugging our son. 'Was she surprised?'

'You could say that. Anyway, she asked that you ring this evening after Paul gets back from school.'

Shirt-tails and loose-laces. I really wanted to see my son again, talk to him. There was yet another awkward silence.

'Danny, you and I need to speak.'

'Of course,' I said. 'We'll be seeing each other in a couple of hours.'

'No, I mean we need to talk about what's been happening, regarding Julie. Things have changed recently and…' His voice trailed off.

'What do you mean, is she in trouble?'

'No, nothing like that. I can explain it better when I pick you up. It's a bit awkward on the phone.'

I was puzzled and put it down to my lack of sleep. 'Okay,' I said, 'I'll see you soon.' And put the phone down.

After a short while, Steyn joined me for breakfast. It was 10 am, and he looked knackered.

'How's the hand?' I asked.

He pulled it up as though seeing it for the first time. 'No problem, aches a bit but nothing the painkillers won't fix. And plenty of these.' He drew out a couple of cigarettes and passed one over. 'How's yours?' he asked with a giggle.

I made a fist and feigned a punch.

'Impressive,' he said.

I squinted my eyes as I lit up from the flame he offered and between us, we managed to envelop the table in smoke. I checked we were in the smoking section; it would be a shame to get kicked out on our first day.

'Anyway,' he said. 'What's the plan for today. The quicker we get started, the quicker we get out of this place; and back home.'

I smiled. 'I am back home, Steyn.'

'You know what I mean,' he said.

I did, but something had changed since the accident.

'You think this is a waste of time, don't you?' I asked.

'I wouldn't say that.' He fiddled with his bandage.

'What *would* you say then?'

'Look, Danny, I'll do all I can to help you, but I don't know what I'm looking for. I told you before, I still can't see how we can prove that the Stabiliser caused the collapse, but I'm relying on you to do that.'

I smiled and looked out of the window toward the mountains and the swirling mist. South Africa had been my address for five years and, like Steyn, I referred to it as home. But the sentiment wasn't heartfelt.

My home would always be here, the place where I was born, married and divorced. Where once I had a family, and my sons had a father, worthy of the name.

'You're a good man, Steyn,' I said, turning to face him. 'I used to know the Stabiliser well enough, but that's in the past. It's all got confusing, like everything else. Maybe I'm just scared it *was* my fault.'

'Stop blaming yourself,' he said, grabbing my shoulder. 'No one can predict a collapse.'

I looked back out the window, lost in my thoughts. *I'd given those dead men the belief that I could.*

Chapter 19

John picked us up at ten thirty wearing a blue, waterproof jacket complete with the Heron logo. *All very professional*, I thought. We exchanged handshakes with the usual banter, it was good to see him again. After a ten-minute journey, he was driving us through the factory gates where time seemed to have stood still. *Was it twenty-four years ago that I'd walked through here as an apprentice?*

I looked up at the morning sun as it reflected unfavourably on the chipped paint and rust sores blemishing the main warehouse. The maroon building dominated the view from the main road. Beyond its crooked shadow was a shabby car park where potholes and weeds had distributed themselves amongst the faded white lines.

Behind the warehouse was a large brick building crowned with an asbestos roof. It was interspersed with skylight windows that once allowed natural light to play on the workers below, but were now blinded by flaking paint.

This was the production department where the noisy machines of industry shaped, cut and joined all the multi-various parts of the Mathers Recycling Stabiliser into a whole.

Beyond the production department, and bisected by a narrow road, was another brick building fronted by two storeys of slender paned windows. The entrance to the reception and administration departments. A square of grass at the front of the building, no bigger than a five-a-side football pitch, seemed out of place. Its purpose lost in the various rebirths of the company.

'Christ, this isn't what I was expecting,' said Steyn, craning his neck left and right.

'In what way?' said John as he reversed into one of the parking bays.

'Well, something bigger. No disrespect, man, but it looks like its seen better days.'

John gave me a wry smile. 'You said he was very observant, Danny.'

We walked into the reception area to sign in, and I was hit by the familiar smell of the place; it was like putting on a favourite coat.

Then a slice of reality hit home.

'Hello, Danny, what a lovely surprise.'

I looked toward the familiar voice and tensed. Dawn came around from her desk and kissed me on the cheek. She'd put on a bit of weight since the last time I'd seen her, but she could still turn heads.

'I thought you'd left Mathers?' I said, surprised to see her again.

She glanced at John and Steyn, who looked on awkwardly, then turned back to me, still holding my arm.

'I did for a while, but I missed the place. A lot of good memories.' I turned away from her eyes and stared at the *Heron* sign above her desk. She saw me looking. 'We're part of Heron now, Danny, *all American,'* she said the last words in a mock accent.

'You'll still see some Mathers signs around, but they're gradually disappearing,' said John. 'That's progress, I suppose.'

He introduced Steyn to Dawn and asked if she could look after him while we went to get some coffees.

'I'll have mine black,' Steyn said as he took a seat. I was concerned all this unfamiliar attention was affecting his mood.

As we approached the coffee machine, I nodded at John's blue jacket. 'Nice touch,' I said, pointing to the *Heron* logo on the breast pocket.

He looked down at the black lettering, as though seeing it for the first time. 'Everyone gets one of these now; work shirts as well. It's supposed to prevent elitism. Proof that everyone, from the lowliest shop floor worker, right up to the CEO, is just as important to Heron.'

'Sounds reasonable.'

He smiled back at me. 'Yeah, it was at first, until two years ago when Stremsen made a change. The shop floor workers were reissued with black shirts, office workers with blue and senior management with white.'

'But they all have the same logo.' I smiled back.

'Of course,' he said. 'It's more elitist than ever. But everyone's happy because they still get free shirts.'

I sensed there was tension, perhaps the years apart had changed our relationship. John opened his jacket and reached into the top pocket of his shirt to pull out a piece of paper.

'How come you're wearing a pink shirt, still a non-conformist?' I said, hoping to break the ice.

'Oh, this,' he replied. 'Yeah, I got caught short this morning.' He passed me the note. 'That's Julie's number on there.'

I folded it into my pocket and punched some numbers on the coffee dispenser. It hissed and sputtered as it dispensed its steaming brew. I handed one to John, but he declined. I could see something was troubling him.

'Everything okay?' I asked.

'I'm not sure, Danny.'

I immediately thought of my report... *what wasn't he sure of?*

'Do you need me to go through it with you?' I said, knowing he was unlikely to ask me anything I hadn't already asked myself a hundred times.

He looked back at me, confused. 'Go through what?'

'The report. Do you want me to go through it with you?'

'I've been seeing Julie, Danny.'

My face went rigid, and my legs turned to jelly. The words were like a kick in the stomach, and then I realised the significance of the pink shirt... *it was John at Julie's house this morning.*

'I know this isn't a great time to be telling you, but I'd rather you heard it from me.'

I was numb and couldn't get rid of the stupid look on my face. I gulped at the coffee and nearly choked.

'Jesus Christ!' I said, louder than I'd intended. He took a step back as though I was about to hit him.

'I'm sorry, I would have told you before but...'

'No, no,' I coughed and spluttered for breath. 'Shit! This coffee's hot.' My eyes were watering. We both stared at one another speechless for a long time. I was reeling from a knockout blow, pretending it hadn't hurt.

'Wow, I just wasn't expecting that,' I whispered. My eyes refocused, and my brain emerged from the jolt of electricity.

'And Paul?'... *shirt-tails and loose-laces.* My hands were trembling, desperately holding onto the cup.

'What about him?' he said.

His tone annoyed me, and a surge of anger rose in my chest... *what about him? He's still my bloody son.*

I was about to get unreasonable but held back. 'I'm not ready for this at the moment,' I said and set off back toward reception.

'Danny...' His voice faded in my wake.

'Are you feeling alright?' asked Dawn as I approached.

I ignored her enquiry and passed the steaming cup to Steyn,

'Christ, you look like you've been in a sauna,' he said. 'Why you looking so flushed?'

'Coffee's hot,' I lied.

'You not having one?'

I didn't answer, couldn't answer. And Steyn, like all good friends, let me sulk in a prickly silence.

'Danny Core, nice to meet you at last.'

BREAKING POINT

My bubble *popped* with the unfamiliar voice, as a small, wiry man extended his hand toward me. Behind him were two men I recognised and one that I didn't.

'I'm Billy Jones, Technical Director,' he said. Terry Socket was behind him, looking daggers at me.

'Hello,' I said, with no enthusiasm and stood up to shake his hand. 'You received a copy of my report?'

'Yes, I did,' he said. 'Very interesting.'

He looked nervous as he continued. 'Erm, I've passed copies to everyone here on the Executive and Senior Management teams, but you've muddied the waters a bit by sending copies directly to the CEO in Houston?'

'What waters are they?' I said. 'I've met Rik Last and Luca Majori previously, and thought it only appropriate to…'

Socket broke in. 'You should have sent it here first, and then we would have distributed the conclusions to Houston. It's broken the normal lines of communication. I'm surprised you weren't aware of the company protocol after so many years.'

He was showing off, so I put my hand up to stop him. 'I work for Rinto Gold now, Terry. I'm *your* customer. I'm sure if I was any other client, you wouldn't be using that tone.'

It went quiet as I continued.

'In fact, *I'm* the one who's surprised at *your* attitude. You do know the Mathers code of conduct for dealing with customer complaints, or has it changed?'

Socket went red in the face. 'No, it hasn't changed, but…'

Billy Jones intervened to save his blushes.

'Sorry, Mr Core. Terry didn't mean to upset you with his comments, it's just that we're all a little taken aback with the report. Let's start again, shall we?'

He was doing his best.

'You've already met, John Dread…' John couldn't lift his eyes from the floor. 'And, it seems you know Terry

Socket... only too well.' The pause was for effect, and it resounded like a klaxon.

No love lost between these two, I thought. Socket nodded at me as though he was sucking a lemon. I noticed he was wearing a white Heron shirt... *Senior Management.*

Billy Jones finished his introductions. 'And this is our Senior Deputy Vice President of Engineering, Fred Stremsen.'

Steyn raised his eyebrows at me, impressed with the title.

Stremsen pushed himself to the front and shook my hand. The first thing I noticed was how short he was, five-seven at the most. The second was how delicate his hand felt. Whether he was conscious of this himself, I don't know, but he seemed to be over-emphasising his grip. My hand still hurt from punching Embele's forehead, and I winced.

Maybe I was already wound up, but I'm sure he smiled at my discomfort, so I adjusted my grip and tried to squeeze the blood from his knuckles. Maybe longer than necessary.

'Nice to meet you, Mr Stremsen,' I said with a tight smile. I heard him squeak and let go, I was still angry after the revelation from Dread.

He backed off and buried his whitened fingers in his trouser pocket. 'Glad to meet you, Mr Core,' he said through clenched teeth. 'You've quite a reputation here.' His smile vanished, and I sensed we weren't going to be the best of friends.

'Yes, Danny was the Engineering...'

'I'm aware of what he *was*,' Stremsen cut Jones off without breaking step. That made three of us angry.

I introduced Steyn as the Mine Captain of Concorde IV, and he set off on another round of handshakes.

'Mine Captain, eh?' Socket took Steyn's bandaged hand. 'Do you have a cap with an anchor on it?' he said with a cocky smile aimed toward Stremsen.

BREAKING POINT

Steyn tugged his hand, causing Socket to stumble closer. 'We wear helmets, not caps,' he said. 'Stops your head getting crushed.' Then he rapped his knuckles three times on top of Socket's head with his free hand. 'But even helmets didn't help those poor bastards last week.'

That made two aggravated assaults and five angry men. I'd had better introductions in my career.

Now it was Stremsen's turn to relieve the tension. 'We're going to leave you in the capable hands of Terry Socket, Mr Core. He'll give you, and your *Captain*, a tour of the factory. Show you some of the improvements we've made since you left. After that, I'd like you to join a presentation I'm giving this afternoon on the Product Management Tome. I'm sure it will help with future discussions.'

I noticed Stremsen was wearing a white shirt. But beneath his logo, he had his name embroidered in blue letters... *shirts were a serious status symbol in the Heron hierarchy.*

'About those discussions, Mr Stremsen...' I said.

'Call me Fred, let's not make this too formal.'

'Okay, Fred. I just wanted to say that I don't have a great deal of time and there are many things I'd like to examine and talk about, while I'm here.'

'Of course, and we will all be available.' He spread his short arms wide. 'All our documentation is ready and waiting for you to look at, as I'm sure yours will be for us.' He emphasised the last part of the sentence.

'No problem,' I said.

The group broke up, and we were led away by Socket, rubbing the top of his head.

Chapter 20

An excruciating hour was wasted as Socket took us around the factory, scowling at Steyn whenever he could. The plant looked clean and smarter than I remembered. There'd been some reorganisation which Socket explained was a blueprint for all Heron factories worldwide.

'We call them, *Manufacturing Pods*,' he said.

'So what other businesses do Heron own?' Steyn was enjoying winding him up.

'We have plants all over the world, we're a cash-rich company and can afford to buy whatever businesses we want.'

I'd forgotten what a pompous idiot he could be. 'Only if they fit into the portfolio,' I said for devilment.

'What do you mean?'

I was feeling prickly, and his *glaring* was annoying me. 'They bought Mathers because it fitted in with the mining side of their organisation. If they were in construction, they wouldn't buy a company making Recycling Stabilisers, would they?'

'Maybe the MK6 would be a better fit in the *demolition* side of their business.' Steyn directed his comment to me, but Terry was meant to overhear.

'We don't have a demolition…' Socket began, then realised the implication. It was uncalled for, from Steyn, but I looked on the positive side. Maybe he was questioning the same things I was. Socket quickly moved us on.

Passing through the assembly department, I noticed that repainting was a significant part of the factory makeover. Below the skin, very little had changed. It was the same equipment repositioned into the new *manufacturing pods*; the shape of which didn't seem to make sense.

This was wasting time, and I was keen to get on with the real business of discussing the MK6 Stabiliser.

BREAKING POINT

'Terry, I think we've seen enough of the factory for now. Can you show us around the development lab?' I wanted to see evidence of the work carried out on the MK6.

'Okay,' he said. 'You'll see we've made some positive changes since the dark, old days when *you* ran the show.' I didn't miss the intended slight and Steyn gave me a smile.

The laboratory was detached from the main factory, and I looked up at the new sign above the entrance, *Heron Centre of Excellence.*

'Nice sign,' I said ironically. Though when we stepped into the main building, Socket saw the look on my face.

'You look impressed,' he said as I turned three-hundred and sixty degrees to take it all in.

'I am,' I replied. And I wasn't lying.

In my day, very little money was invested in the infrastructure. The building was nestled so close to the railway track that passing trains would rattle the upper windows that had loosened with age. Now they were double glazed with white plastic frames. The dislocated venetian blinds of my era had been replaced with vertical blinds, fit for an executive office.

Around the brightly painted walls were glossy posters of the Stabiliser; tracking its evolution from the days of Franklyn Mathers to the present incarnation with Heron. I noticed the last poster was entitled *MK6 Regeneration*, and showed how the overall shape had changed significantly from previous models. Something I hadn't fully absorbed on Level 110.

I looked around the building again; it had undergone an impressive makeover. There were fewer workbenches, and they'd all had the customary paint job. At the rear of each workbench were the same metal panels, strewn with pneumatic and hydraulic valves, each linked with umbilical pipes to gauges on the front. I noticed all the calibration stickers were up to date and the ubiquitous oil leaks of my day seemed non-existent.

At the epicentre was a half-scale replica of a Recycling Stabiliser. About five feet in diameter and maybe twenty-five feet long, it was impressive. The *smokestack* rose toward the ceiling and was blanked off at the top. The inlet and outlet pipe were scaled to suit and enhanced the engineering beauty of the product. *MK5* had been hand-painted in red letters along its base.

'This was another innovation carried out since you left, Danny.' Socket was enjoying himself. 'We now prototype half-scale models for any new Stabiliser developments. It's more efficient and user-friendly.'

'What happened to *The Ballbreaker*?' I asked.

'Outdated,' he brushed the comment aside. 'We've moved on.'

The Ballbreaker was a nickname given to the test equipment, which once stood in the middle of the laboratory. It was colossal and designed to hold a full-size Recycling Stabiliser and subject it to the most extreme conditions. The bespoke equipment could replicate the intense forces that the Stabiliser would have to withstand underground. During testing, it would be impossible to hear anyone talk, and the vibrations were so fierce they transmitted through the reinforced concrete floor, to the fitter's workshop next door. *We used to joke it kept them awake.* But we were confident that any new Stabiliser development that passed *The Ballbreaker* test was more than capable of dealing with the extremes of life in service.

It also explained why the laboratory looked so spacious.

'And anyway,' Terry continued. 'This compact test equipment is a lot quieter.'

And a lot cheaper, I thought. Everything seemed to centre on saving money, and alarm bells were going off in my head.

'Are you sure it will react in the same way as a full-sized Stabiliser?' I queried. 'I notice you've fabricated the bodywork on the prototype. Are you sure it will replicate the same characteristics as a cast body?'

He probably thought I was *picky*, but it was a reasonable question.

'We've thought of that,' he said. 'Come into the office, and I'll show you something.'

I could see he was getting excited, and we followed him around the perimeter of the safety rail toward the office. My initial surprise at the lab had waned, and I became aware of the lack of activity around the place. Only one technician was working in the area. I thought back to the noise and vitality of the site five years ago, engineers and technicians vying for tools and space. There was a constant soundtrack of machines and compressed air; voices and laughter. This was sterile by comparison.

A gentle *thrum* from a generator hung in the air, coupled with the pulsing beat from a pneumatic test. But apart from that, nothing. The lack of people out here was at odds with those inside the office, which was partitioned from the central laboratory with full length, glass panels. Steyn had gone quiet; his eyes were scanning everything around him.

As we entered the office, the hubbub of voices died quickly, and everyone turned our way. I wasn't sure how my return would be viewed; so far, most people I knew were reserved. I put that down to my own problems, my last few months at Mathers hadn't been my finest.

I shook hands with a couple of familiar faces, but there was no warmth coming back. I was an outsider now, questioning their product and threatening their jobs. I'd probably react in the same way, given the circumstances.

Instinctively I looked toward the corner where my office used to be. It was the same desk, but a new chair. On the wall behind was the same framed picture; an original design sketch by Franklyn Mathers. I'd been tempted to take it with me, but it would have felt like stealing an artefact from a museum. The ceiling had a brown stain, weeping water down the freshly painted wall into a red bucket. Some things never change.

Terry drew me over to a large computer in the opposite corner. John was punching out some numbers, and I sensed this had all been pre-planned.

'This is our new software programme.' Socket tapped the monitor. 'This will give us enough accurate data to completely eliminate the need for prototypes. Particularly with our "*state-of-the-art*" designs.' He created punctuation marks with his fingers. John looked embarrassed.

'What do *you* think, John?' I knew my question would create an awkward situation, but I was still pissed off with him. The room went quiet as he coughed and fidgeted as though sitting on an ant's nest.

'Well… personally, I'm used to testing with full-sized prototypes, but this software appears fairly accurate in comparison.'

'In comparison to what?' I asked before the last syllable left his mouth.

'Erm… in comparison to the legacy data that we have on record.'

The right answer, I thought, *but the wrong context.*

John would know that I'd been part of the team collating that legacy data… and I'd spotted the flaw.

'The legacy data only accounts for past designs,' I said. 'All validated with *actual* results, using full-sized prototypes on *The Ballbreaker*. Why do you trust the software on "*state-of-the-art*" designs without that same validation?'

I'd created my own punctuation marks for effect and immediately felt foolish, but I had everyone's attention. The only other sound came from the pneumatic test pulsing beyond the panelled walls.

Socket was twitching, his eyes flashing across from John to me. 'We're still developing the software,' John said, unconvincingly. 'We now rely on the half-scale models to authenticate the results.'

BREAKING POINT

I turned to face him directly. 'So, where's the model for the MK6 Stabiliser?'

Socket butted in. 'That's it in the workshop.'

John's eyes sought refuge on the computer screen.

'Hmm, but that's got MK5 written on it,' I said with exaggerated curiosity. 'Is that a mistake?'

Socket's mouth opened and closed a couple of times, as though his teeth had become too heavy for his lower jaw. Nothing came out except a couple of grunts. I glanced at Steyn, who winked back at me. He wouldn't know where I was going with this, but he was enjoying himself all the same.

I turned back to Socket, his jaw had reconnected, but his face was bright red. His eyes flashed across the faces of the watching engineers, the air crackling with tension.

'Cat got your tongue, Terry?' I raised my voice. 'It's a simple question... *is that a mistake?*'

'Erm, hang on now Danny.' He cleared his throat, buying time. 'We weren't supposed to get into this detail until later in the day.'

I'd knocked him off-course.

'What do you mean?' I said. 'Now, tomorrow... next bloody year! It doesn't affect the answer, does it?'

'No... no, of course not.' He'd had time to think and came up with the wrong response. 'The answer is *yes*.'

'*Yes*, it's a mistake?' I asked, perplexed.

Another pause, I could almost hear the wheels turning in his head.

'No', he said, and there was a giggle from one of the engineers.

'No, it's *not* a mistake?' I countered.

'No... I mean, yes!' He finally spat it out. 'Yes, it is the MK6 prototype, we just haven't changed the label.'

John became intrigued with some detail on the screen and pushed his face up closer. I got the impression he wanted to disappear inside it.

The hairs on the back of my neck felt charged with static. I turned to face the others in the room and stared them out. One by one, they looked away. It confirmed my suspicions... *they knew Socket was lying.* He'd made his first big mistake, and there was a room full of unwilling, partisan witnesses.

An uncomfortable length of time passed in silence. An excruciatingly long time for someone who'd just lied. It was another glimmer of hope that my suspicions had foundation. I turned back around to face Socket and licked my dry lips.

I looked him in the eye.

'The MK6 Stabiliser, now under investigation, has significantly fewer bolts than the MK5. The prototype out there doesn't reflect that change, nor does it match the *MK6 Regeneration* poster on your walls.'

Everyone, except Socket, looked across at the poster as if seeing it for the first time.

'Do you expect me to believe that that out there,' I pointed, and once more everyone's eyes followed my finger. 'Is a replica of the MK6 design?'

'No... no, Danny, of course not. And... okay... yes, the prototype you see in the workshop *was* used for the MK5 *and* MK6 models. It made sense to keep the costs down.'

I was starting to feel my collar getting hot. 'You reduced the number of bolts on the MK6 by at least half, but that isn't reflected on the prototype out there. So, you haven't fully tested your "*state-of-the-art...*"' I did my stupid punctuation marks again, '... design change on a half-scale model. Let alone a full-sized prototype?'

'Well... erm... we used the... erm...'

I decided to risk my hard-earned advantage by revealing my suspicions. 'You didn't have a prototype made to reflect the MK6 design because of the cost, and instead used *unproved* software in the hope that it gave you a favourable result. That sums it up, doesn't it?' I'd raised my voice again and banged the top of the screen for emphasis.

Terry looked at John for something, anything; but nothing was forthcoming. The atmosphere in the office was intense, no one seemed to be breathing... and I knew I'd got it right.

Socket attempted to close the discussion down. 'Well, as I said, we need to discuss this in a more formal setting. Maybe after Fred Stremsen's presentation, this afternoon.'

I ignored his waffle and poked John's back. 'We used to say, *fairly accurate*, wasn't accurate enough, John. Has that criteria changed?'

His eyes swivelled between Socket and me until he finally sighed like a deflating tyre. 'No, Danny, it hasn't changed, but it's early days and, in my opinion...'

'Hang on, Dread,' Socket broke in. 'You don't have an opinion on this. That's why you were taken off the MK6 team. You have no say in this!' His voice was louder than it needed to be and unprofessional. I'd poked the nest and Socket was getting stung. Steyn raised his eyebrows and made a mock wince in my direction.

'Okay, you lot,' Socket's voice was less assured now as he looked over his shoulder at the audience of engineers. 'Show's over, get back to bloody work.'

The room began to rumble with the movement of people and chairs scraping across the floor as they pretended to settled back into their work.

Socket ushered Steyn and I toward the door, still trying to explain himself.

'Part of the PMT strategy is to replace non-essential prototype costs with computer software. It makes economic sense.'

If he was hoping to convince me, he was way off the mark. And Steyn wasn't about to make his life any easier.

'Ja, man, but not until the software's proven, surely.'

Socket was still fidgeting as we stood at the open door. 'Of course not, but this *is* proven, believe me.'

'And who decides when prototypes are *non-essential?*' This had legs, and I wasn't letting go.

'What do you mean?' he was glaring again.

'Well, you're starting to sound like a salesman. The more you say something, the more you think I'll be convinced. It doesn't work that way. I want answers, and I want proof of those answers.'

'I'm telling you, Core…' His words puttered and puffed. He couldn't get them out quickly enough, *and* he was back to surnames. It wouldn't take long for this conversation to deteriorate further. But I wanted to re-emphasise my point in earshot of all the engineers.

I held up my hands. 'Okay, Socket, let's agree to disagree. But we've been here long enough to know that engineering is driven by facts, and that's what I'm here to verify. So cut the bullshit and…'

'Yeah, but you're not here anymore, are you?' He pushed his finger into my chest.

I was about to lose it when Steyn grabbed my arm. 'Let's move on, Danny, we don't have that much time.' I nodded reluctantly.

Socket and I didn't have much to say after that.

BREAKING POINT

Chapter 21

The phone was ringing four thousand seven hundred miles away. With a time difference of six hours ahead, Luca Majori was guessing it would be mid-afternoon in the UK. He was phoning Stremsen's office number, and while he knew he needed to speak with him, there was a part of him that hoped he wouldn't answer.

Already burdened with babysitting Stremsen, he was being asked to oversee an accident investigation with very little engineering expertise. He needed to find a way of imposing himself.

There was a click on the other end of the line. 'Hello, Fred Stremsen's office.'

It wasn't Fred, but the voice was familiar.

'Hi, is Fred Stremsen there?' A pause. Majori imagined the man behind the voice looking around.

'No, he left early.'

'Oh, right. My name's Luca Majori, phoning from Houston. Who am I speaking to?'

'John Dread.' *No embellishments,* Majori immediately put a face to the voice.

'Hi, John, we met last time I was over. Any idea how I can get hold of Fred?'

'Preferably by the throat.' The voice was deadpan. 'Only joking, you'll get him at his hotel, the King's Head.'

Majori sensed he wasn't joking. 'Thanks. Sounds like Fred's making an impression?'

'As I said, I was only joking.'

'Are you involved with the team looking at the incident in South Africa, John?' *No harm in making enquiries,* thought Luca.

'You'll need to speak to Stre... Fred Stremsen about that. It's still being evaluated.'

'Sounds like a politicians answer?' Luca replied.

'As I say, you need to speak with Fred.'

'Okay, thanks. Say, we might bump into each other in the next few days...'

The phone went dead.

That went well, Majori thought. He looked up the number for the King's Head Hotel in Crossways, and his call was answered by the hotel receptionist. She transferred to Stremsen's room, and he answered on the third ring.

'Stremsen.'

After a round of niceties, Luca got to business. 'Fred, I've just come out of a meeting with Rik Last, and he wants me to oversee the investigation concerning the Rinto Gold accident.'

There was silence at the other end.

'Fred, are you still there?'

Static crackled through the earpiece, then an exasperated voice.

'I'm still here, but I don't understand why you're getting involved. I've got everything under control this end.'

'I'm sure you have, but Rik wants another pair of eyes and ears on the case, I hope we can work together on this?'

'Sure, whatever Rik wants.'

Rik gets, thought Majori.

'I was about to call a meeting with Core and his Mine Captain,' Stremsen continued. 'Give them confidence in the process before we tackle the issues surrounding the accident.'

'That's fine, but at this stage we admit nothing.'

'Of course not, we've nothing to hide.'

'Good, I hope that's true. Have you made arrangements to investigate the accident site?'

'Not yet, but I'll arrange to send out some engineers from Mathers...'

'Hold it there, Fred,' Majori stopped him in his tracks. *'You're* leading the team, and *you* need to visit the accident site. Drive it from the front!' The line hissed again. 'Are you still there?'

BREAKING POINT

'Yes, I'm here. Luca. I've never been underground before, it would probably break some health and safety rules.'

'How do you make that out, Fred?'

'Well, I'm not really the right shape to be crawling around...'

'Nothing is outside your remit on this one,' Luca stopped him finishing. 'Not until this mess is put to bed. And if that means I have to crawl around with you, then so be it. Rik Last's orders!'

'Sure, sure, I get the message.' Stremsen sounded touchy.

'We'll both do whatever it takes and nothing less,' said Luca covering the receiver and taking some deep breaths.

'Is that it?' Stremsen.

'No, two other things. Firstly, stop any work being carried out on the MK7 Stabiliser; with immediate effect.'

'What's that got to do with the accident...' Majori sensed the penny dropping. 'This is about the PMT process, isn't it?' Stremsen added.

'Damn right it is,' said Luca, 'and until it's fully exonerated in this investigation, it remains in cold storage. Got that?'

'This is crazy...'

'People have died here, Fred.'

'I know that!'

'I'm not sure you know it enough. This is not a straightforward industrial accident and could become a criminal investigation. Stand the MK7 team down until further notice, and keep the reasons below the radar.'

'What's the other thing?' Stremsen sounded impatient.

'Danny Core's report asks why the failsafe switches didn't operate after the accident.'

'What do you mean?' asked Stremsen.

'The Stabiliser was still pumping out water, Fred, haven't you read the report?'

There was a pause. 'Of course I have, the severity of the collapse must have damaged the unit and stopped the switches functioning.'

'Do we know that for sure?'

'Only Danny Core is questioning the MK6 Stabiliser, and that's all about self-preservation. Everything he's put forward is subjective, there's no evidence to back it up,' said Stremsen.

'Will he find any?'

Another pause. 'There's nothing to find. It's foolish to argue that a collapse, destructive enough to kill nine men, wouldn't affect the efficiency of the Stabiliser.'

'That's why you need to see it for yourself, Fred.'

'It's under control,' said Stremsen.

'Have you spoken with Danny Core yet?'

'We've just been introduced.'

'What do you think of him?'

'Nothing I can't handle, tell Rik not to worry.'

Majori could sense the sneer behind the comment and dropped his head in his hands. 'Listen very carefully, Fred. I met Danny Core when he was at Mathers. I had enough dealings to know that he's nobody's fool. I suggest you don't take him lightly.'

'No worries, Luca. I've handled bigger fish than him.'

'Don't underestimate this guy.' Majori felt an uncomfortable sensation in his stomach. 'He knows more about the Stabiliser than we know about mining, and that's a big advantage.'

'I won't underestimate anyone,' Stremsen replied, icily. 'I've planned to present the MK6 PMT this afternoon and show Core how meticulous the process has been.'

'Have you listened to a word I've said? Cancel it!'

'Listen, Luca. I don't know why Rik's given you this role, but I'm still in charge of engineering at Mathers. A presentation like this will scare Core off. He'll see how all changes have been checked and rechecked.'

BREAKING POINT

'It was Rik's call,' Majori lied. 'He believes it's too early for that kind of transparency. Give him as much as he asks for, but no more.

'You need to get him out of Mathers as soon as possible. He could turn up anything, wandering around there on his own. Invite him to our facility in Houston, we'll give him the red-carpet treatment, and maybe you can give him your PMT *show* over here.' There was a pause, and he sensed Stremsen grimacing at his derogatory reference.

'You've never believed in it, have you, Luca?'

'I'm not getting into that with you, Fred. All I know is that Rik's getting jumpy and wants this closed off without collateral damage to Heron.'

Another pause from Stremsen. 'I'm not happy about it, but I'll fall in line with the CEO's wishes and keep you posted.'

'Just one last thing, Fred.'

'What now?'

'How come you finished early today?'

'Oh, I had a bit of a headache after the journey, decided I'd work from my hotel room, then an early night.'

'Oh, okay, I hope you feel better in the morning.'

Stremsen put the phone down and looked across at Socket sitting on the sofa, surrounded by paperwork.

'Change of plan, Terry... change of plan.'

Chapter 22

Another day was disappearing fast. Stremsen's PMT presentation had been cancelled at the last minute, leaving Steyn and myself on our own for the rest of the afternoon. We'd been given a small office next to reception and Dawn had linked us up with our own phone.

I asked Steyn to try and make contact with Piet Reiss to find out how the MK6 strip-down was progressing. I think Dawn had taken a shine to him, so he had a plentiful supply of coffee and biscuits.

I needed some time on my own to make a private phone call and said I'd see him back at the hotel. Seven days to go, and I was still no further forward,

Dawn had pointed me in the direction of an empty office down the corridor where I wouldn't be disturbed. I sat at the desk and pulled out the piece of paper that John had given me. It took a while to summon up the courage to dial the number.

Fifteen minutes later, I put the phone back down. The conversation had been the hardest of my life, but I deserved everything I got. Julie had sounded as distressed as I felt, and I was already questioning my motives.

It hadn't gone well, and why should it. She'd refused my request to come around and see Paul, which was understandable. To be confronted with a father who'd disappeared five years ago would be impossible for any child to understand. She made it clear what she thought of me, but after a lot of pleading, I got her to agree to meet me at the hotel, later in the evening.

Every guilty bone in my body was aching after I put the phone down. I didn't warrant it, but I had a chance to meet my son and try to explain my mistakes. It rang back almost immediately, and I picked it up, hoping it was Julie with a last-minute change of heart.

BREAKING POINT

'I've got Fred Stremsen on the line for you, Danny.' My heart sank.

'Okay, thanks, Dawn.'

I heard the click as she transferred the call.

'Fred Stremsen here,' His Texan drawl was already getting on my nerves. 'I've got Terry Socket with me. We'd like you and your Mine Captain to come down to the conference room tomorrow morning and go through your report. How about nine-thirty?'

'That's fine, Fred, but disappointed you cancelled the presentation. I really need to discuss the MK6 in detail.'

'Yes, apologies for that, something came up,' said Stremsen. 'But tomorrow should provide you with that opportunity.'

At last, a chance to get some answers.

I said that would be fine and lied that Steyn wouldn't be able to make it. I needed him to get some feedback from Piet and Embele. As soon as I put the phone down, I remembered Jack Smelt's old motto; fail to prepare, prepare to fail, and began to evaluate the scale of the task in hand.

In Mathers corner, Stremsen and Socket, defending the moral high ground with the resources of a multi-national company backing them to the hilt.

Opposite, me. With no evidence, and a hunch that hadn't convinced anyone in Rinto Gold. Not a promising start.

I focused on the personnel. One known quantity and two unknowns.

First Socket, *the known*. Technically competent, but no more than that. Ambitious and outwardly confident, but his inflated ego was at odds with low self-esteem. He gained respect from his peers by physically menacing them, but that wouldn't work with his superiors. His shortcomings had always hampered his progress into senior management... until now. If what John had told me was correct, the prospect of him becoming the Technical

Director was more than a pipe dream. *What had changed in the eyes of Heron?*

We'd played rugby together as teenagers and Terry had been the star player, until the day he'd reported that the player's savings had mysteriously gone missing. No one was in any doubt as to what had happened and whose pocket they'd slipped into. But there was no proof.

Retribution was inevitable and took place during a particularly nasty training session. No one owned up to the final stamp that shattered Socket's knee, but mine was the face he remembered seeing and he'd held a grudge ever since. Everyone knew who was responsible because there'd been lots drawn the night before, and to this day, no one revealed who pulled the short straw.

It didn't help, as time went on, that my engineering career continued to outstrip his, despite me being two years younger. But now it looked like he was in touching distance of the opportunity he craved.

Heron hadn't found him out… yet.

Stremsen, the first *unknown*. Senior Deputy Vice President of Engineering. I looked at his business card, it was more of a sentence than a job title, and he obviously liked the limelight. So far, he hadn't impressed me, but it was early days, and maybe I was missing something. *Judging by John's comments, I didn't think so.* He seemed all fired up with his PMT presentation, yet cancelled it at short notice. Was the process flawed and they didn't want me to see it? *All documentation will be available to you…* I was going to hold him to that. There wasn't much else to go on, and that made me nervous.

Billy Jones, the second *unknown*. Where was he in all this? He was the Technical Director, yet wasn't involved in tomorrow mornings meeting. Maybe John was right, and he was being squeezed out. He may be a good metallurgist, but he didn't strike me as having the experience to handle a

BREAKING POINT

director's role. The job demanded expertise, so when things went wrong, there was know-how at the front end; which begged another question. Why did Jack take early retirement in the middle of the MK6 project? I'd known him for twenty years; it was something he'd never do willingly. Had he been pushed, and why?

Seven days ago, I'd have backed myself against any of them. But now I found myself unconsciously snapping an elastic band around my wrist.

Chapter 23

After failing to contact Piet Reiss, it had taken three phone calls, two cups of coffee and half a dozen biscuits, before Steyn eventually got Embele on the line.

It was 5pm in South Africa, and he'd finally tracked him down at the Zulu hostel. With only one telephone, it was zealously guarded by the hostel manager, but no one turned down a request from the Mine Captain.

'Boss?' Embele's voice was deadpan.

Steyn smiled to himself. Embele was his usual talkative self.

'Relax, man,' Steyn kept his tone matter-of-fact. 'I'm just ringing to ask how the strip down is going. How much have you done, have you seen anything suspicious?'

He was strangling the phone with sweaty palms, as though it was about to jump out of his hand. He realised he was starting to shout and lowered his voice. On the other end, all he could hear was heavy breathing.

'Embele, are you still there?' His voice rose again with agitation.

'Boss?' Embele again. 'I can't hear you.'

Steyn sighed and readied to repeat himself.

'Wait, I can hear you now,' Embele answered.

Steyn remembered the phone delay; he would need to be patient. He waited ten seconds, listening to more heavy breathing and was rewarded.

'The strip down is going well,' Embele answered. 'We have maybe another day's work before we can split the flanges and see inside the Stabiliser.'

'Have you seen anything unusual?' Steyn counted to ten.

'Some damage to the bolts and seals.' *Ten seconds passed... twenty seconds.* Embele had said all he wanted.

'The area's sealed off?' Steyn asked. *Ten seconds.*

'Yes, Boss.'

BREAKING POINT

'Okay, I'm not going to chase after you tomorrow.' Steyn decided to give up, it was pointless asking too many questions until the strip down was complete. 'Once you've completed the work and carried out your checks, get Piet Reiss to ring this number.' *Ten seconds.*

'Okay, Boss.' And the phone clicked off.

Steyn lit a cigarette and stared at the door. He hadn't seen or heard enough to convince him that the collapse wasn't caused by a pressure burst; as much as he wanted to believe differently.

His mind went back to Danny's spat in the office with Socket. He didn't trust the Mathers man and couldn't figure out why he'd tried to lie about the MK6 prototype. He took a final pull from his cigarette before crushing it into the ashtray and made his way into the reception area. Dawn was just finishing a call, so he leaned on her desk with his arms folded.

'Hello, Steyn,' she said, putting the phone down. 'Do you want me to make you a coffee?'

'No thanks,' he answered. 'I'll be high as a kite on caffeine.'

She giggled. Steyn liked her accent and the way her dimples showed when she smiled.

'Are you enjoying your trip so far?' she asked.

'Ja, good thanks, just a pity it's under such tragic circumstances.'

Dawn's dimples evaporated. 'Yes, the news is all around the factory; everyone's so sorry for those poor men who were killed. Did you know them well?'

'Pretty well,' he replied. 'Most had families who'll be left without a breadwinner now.'

'Oh dear, what about compensation?'

'They'll get something, Danny will make sure of that. But Africa's not like here, things work differently.'

'Yes, we read about it in the newspapers and see it on the television. It's terrible how they treat the black people over there.'

He didn't want to debate politics and changed the subject.

'Say, I was wondering about some things, and maybe you could help.'

'If I can,' she replied.

Steyn rubbed his chin and moved in closer, his voice low. 'It seems like there's a disagreement brewing in the development lab. We just came out of a meeting,' he lied. 'And there was an unholy row between a couple of the guys. Seems like a bit of tension around the place.'

Dawn gave a knowing look. 'I expect Terry Socket's at it again.'

'He was certainly in the middle of it,' Steyn stoked the embers. 'He seemed a bit jittery when we asked a few direct questions.'

She looked around, making sure no one was close by.

'Doesn't surprise me, he's a bit of a bully if you ask most people here. Rumour has it that he's in line for Billy Jones' job, and that's made him ten times worse.'

'What about this, Jack Smelt guy?'

She raised her eyebrows. 'Jack was never the flavour of the month with the new American owners.'

'Was he good at his job?'

'He had an outstanding reputation, not only here, but with our customers. The Heron people just didn't seem to take to him.'

'Anyone in particular?' asked Steyn.

'Fred Stremsen. They had some terrible rows.'

'Over what?' he was warming to his interrogation.

'He didn't think he was dynamic enough, too stuck in his ways. They put him under a lot of pressure.'

'What's Stremsen like?'

She rolled her eyes. 'Horrible man, he flies in once a month just to tell us how bad we are. He intimidates everyone and threatens to close the factory. He's another bully, but it looks like he's grooming someone else to do his dirty work.'

BREAKING POINT

'Socket?'

'Yes. Since the accident, the two of them have been as thick as thieves. It wouldn't surprise me if they...' She seemed to realise she was getting carried away and changed tack. 'Listen to me, talking as though I know what's going on, take no notice of what I'm saying.'

Steyn smiled as her dimples reappeared.

'Anyway, enough about work,' she took a deep breath. 'What about you, Steyn. Have you any family?'

He'd probed enough for one day. 'Yes, I've got a couple of grown-up daughters, how about yourself?'

'One son, grown up and left the nest. How about Danny, has he remarried?'

Steyn's features froze, and his mouth hung open. He felt the room turn in on itself and the background noise buzzed inside his head.

'What's the matter?' she asked.

He couldn't think of a reply and blew his nose to try and clear his ears.

Dawn squinted. 'You didn't know he'd been married?'

'Erm...' He couldn't think of an answer.

'Or that he's got a family here in South Wales?' she added.

He didn't know whether he was smiling or grimacing; his face muscles were in spasm.

'You've caught me cold,' he eventually replied. 'Danny's never mentioned a wife or a family.' He fumbled in his pockets for a cigarette he didn't want, racking his memory for a past conversation.

'Okay if I light up?' he asked, still distracted.

'Yes, of course.' She passed an ashtray.

He sucked the smoke deep into his lungs and exhaled away from her. Then immediately extinguished it in the ashtray.

'Sorry, I can't get used to your cigarettes. How many kids has he got?'

'He had two boys, Paul and Alex,' she replied.

'How old are they?'

Dawn looked uncomfortable. 'Paul is ten now, so Alex would have been eight.'

'Would have been?'

'Alex died when he was three years old.'

Steyn slowed his breathing, trying not to get emotional, but his eyes were wet as he turned away from her.

He felt her hand on his shoulder. 'I'm sorry, I thought you'd have known?'

He gently moved her hand away and rubbed his eyes with the back of his bandaged hand.

'Ja, me too.' He recovered his composure and tried to make some sense of it all. 'Was that why Danny left here?'

'It's complicated,' she said, looking uncomfortable.

'You and Danny, you seem… quite close.' Steyn had noticed her reaction when they first arrived. 'Sorry, you don't have to explain anything to me, it's none of my business. The death of a child must be…' He ran out of words.

She didn't seem to be listening, her thoughts elsewhere.

He tried to change tack. 'Danny never spoke of his life back here; he always changed the subject. Everyone back at Harmonie assumed he'd always been single, always on his own.'

'I think he's been on his own ever since the accident.' The sorrow in her eyes was unambiguous, the words barely a whisper.

'Accident?' Steyn's voice was hushed as though in church. 'What happened?'

She looked down at her hands, her thumb rubbing the varnished fingernails. 'It's not my place… and it was such a long time ago.'

'I don't mean to pry,' he said. 'But I've known Danny for almost five years, and this has come as a real shock.'

She looked up. 'It was a tragedy that tore the family apart.'

'Listen, Dawn, I don't want to upset you over this.'

BREAKING POINT

She composed herself, as though preparing for an ordeal, and took another deep breath. 'It happened in the spring, during one of the loveliest weeks of the year. We don't get many like that, which is why everyone remembers it so well. Crossways isn't the prettiest of towns, but after enduring one of the coldest winters on record, it was something special. And to cap it all, it was the fiftieth anniversary of Mathers, so it seemed a bit unique for the town itself; a good omen.'

Another deep breath. 'Everyone was outdoors, enjoying the weather and Danny was no different. He'd taken the day off work to take his youngest, Alex, walking in the hills while Julie, his wife, took Paul for a doctor's appointment...' She began to falter.

'It's okay, take your time,' said Steyn.

'It's been a long time since I talked about it.' She seemed to be looking right through him.

'The first we heard was when Julie phoned up asking if Danny had popped into work with Alex. I told her that we hadn't seen him all day and that's when she started to get agitated. He'd been out since mid-morning and planned to be back for lunch. But when Julie returned from the doctor's, the house was empty, and it was getting late.

'She knew something was wrong. Danny would have let her know if he was going to be late; especially with a three-year-old in tow. She'd tried everywhere else; Mathers was the last resort.'

'Was it getting dark?' asked Steyn.

'Yes, the nights were still drawing in early, and it was bitterly cold. I said I'd ring around a few places and let her know as soon as I had any news. I tried John Dread's home number, and he said he'd bumped into them while walking home from his morning shift. They were taking a short cut along the eastern ridge of the Brig Uchel mountains, past the old mine workings. John said they were fine.'

'Don't make this hard on yourself,' said Steyn.

She wasn't listening and seemed caught up in the memory.

'I wasn't concerned until I tried to ring Julie back, to tell her what John had said, but there was no answer. I tried again when I got home from work, still no response. That's when I knew something was seriously wrong. I tried phoning John back, but he wasn't there.

'About 2 am, I had a phone call from John. It isn't difficult to think the worst when you get a call that late at night is it?' She looked at Steyn, her eyes were streaming, and he offered his handkerchief.

'What happened?' His voice catching the back of his throat.

'Alex had fallen down a narrow opening, hidden in the mountain grass. All the reports and news bulletins called it a *rogue mine*.'

'What's that?' Steyn asked.

'Years ago, people would scavenge coal from the mountains. If they found an exposed seam, they'd follow it down.' Her mouth tightened. 'When the coal was exhausted, the men moved on, and nature concealed the openings.'

'Until Danny's son…' Steyn couldn't finish the sentence and shook his head.

Dawn continued. 'They'd been playing, and Alex was running ahead. He was no more than ten-feet away from his father when the ground just swallowed him.

'He'd fallen about twenty-feet and was badly injured. Danny tried desperately to get down to him but got himself trapped. I remember how cold it was that night, freezing cold.'

Steyn walked around the desk to take her hand, but she resisted and continued.

'When the Mountain Rescue team found them, they had to dig them both out. The little boy was dead… he was three years old.'

BREAKING POINT

She was sobbing uncontrollably. When someone walked into the Reception, Steyn shooed them away.

'Let's get you a drink,' he said.

'No, no, I'm fine, really. I just need to freshen up.' And she disappeared into the toilet. The phone rang a couple of times, but Steyn cut the calls off.

After ten minutes, Dawn returned. 'Sorry about that.' And wiped her eyes with a handkerchief.

'Nothing to be sorry about,' he said.

'I heard the telephone ring; did you manage to transfer them?'

'Sure,' Steyn lied, and she smiled again. He was relieved.

'It's a terrible thing to live with the death of a child,' he said. 'Was Danny badly injured?'

'He had hypothermia, and his hands and fingers were severely damaged where he'd tried to claw his way down, but he wouldn't stay in hospital. I went around their house a couple of times. Danny was never there. Julie made excuses, but I knew something was wrong. She told me he was having panic attacks in the middle of the night and couldn't sleep with the doors closed. She worried he might do something silly.

'Paul, their eldest, was nearly five at the time and had just lost his brother. Before his sixth birthday, he'd lose his father as well.'

'What made him leave like that?' Steyn asked. 'Danny loved his other son, didn't he?'

She looked embarrassed. 'The funeral was the saddest I've ever known. Mathers closed for the day because so many people wanted to attend. The whole town was affected. After the funeral, Danny threw himself into his work, weekdays and weekends. He began pushing his engineers harder and eventually got reported.'

Steyn's ears pricked up.

'Julie was convinced he was trying to work himself to death.'

'A form of punishment,' said Steyn.

'Yes, exactly, *a penance,* was how she described it.'

She looked at Steyn directly. 'You've seen his skin condition?'

Steyn nodded.

'That appeared after the accident. Danny's body was covered in dry, scaly patches.'

'Must have felt like a curse.'

'Maybe, but he began pushing people away. His friends, work colleagues; even his family. It was happening in front of our eyes.'

'That must have been hard to watch,' said Steyn.

There was a long silence as she looked from him toward the entrance and back. Then she whispered.

'You were right when you said Danny and I are... I mean... *were* close. He would talk to me for hours about his problems, I seemed to be the only person he trusted. We were both vulnerable and... one thing led to another... we...'

'You don't need to put yourself through this, Dawn.' Steyn was uncomfortable.

'No, I need to tell you in my own words, there were enough rumours. It only happened once, but that's all it takes, doesn't it? I knew it meant more to me than Danny, but it doesn't make me feel less guilty. He couldn't live with the secret, and when he admitted his failings to Julie, it was the final straw.

'Before we had any idea of what he was going to do next, he'd handed in his notice and left the company. I left Mathers for a time, and when I returned a couple of years later, I found out Danny was divorced and living in South Africa.'

'Does he keep in touch with his son?' Steyn asked, stunned by the revelations.

Dawn looked guarded. 'I know he sends Julie money every month, Christmas and birthday cards. She's told me that. But whether you would call that, *keeping in touch,* I'm not sure.'

'And Julie's okay with you, now?'

'It took a while, but I think she knew it was over between her and Danny, long before I messed things up.'

'You mentioned Danny got reported, what was that about?'

'I shouldn't be talking so much.'

'Look, Dawn, I've known him for a long time, and this has come as a shock. I need to know as much as I can, for his sake.'

'I hope he's not in trouble, Steyn.'

'Who reported him?'

'Danny's mental state was deteriorating toward the end, and it was suggested he was drinking.'

'You mean in work?'

'I don't really know.' She'd become defensive again. 'But it's something that was doing the rounds at the time.'

'So who reported him?'

'I shouldn't be saying any more, I'll get into trouble.'

'Was it Terry Socket?'

She looked at her hands. It was as good as a confirmation.

Steyn apologised and thanked her for being frank.

'I'm glad he's better now,' she said.

If only that were true, Steyn thought.

Chapter 24

Billy Jones stared out of the dirty office window to the hills rising and falling on the horizon. His thoughts were as far from Mathers as the trees receding in the distance.

At thirty-six, he'd outstripped his career expectations, and this new role rested uncomfortably on his shoulders. Billy wanted to be liked, but since coming to Mathers that hadn't been possible. He'd become part of the *new* management team; responsible for tearing down the Mathers's legacy. Laying people off, freezing wages, reducing overtime; all these had become the Heron mantra. No one stopped to talk to Billy when he went onto the shop floor. He was an outsider.

His office wasn't ostentatious, which suited him, and was situated down the corridor from reception. It isolated him from the engineering departments, which benefited him even more, as engineering wasn't his strong point. His title could demand attention from the engineers, but he knew there was little respect. He had once believed he was being shunned because of his status but now recognised the truth… they knew he wasn't up to the job.

'Billy.' The voice formed part of his thoughts as he scanned the hills. *How he wished…*

'Billy!'

He turned, surprised at the intrusion. Stremsen had walked in with Terry Socket in tandem.

'I wasn't expecting you this morning, Fred.' He looked at his watch, it was 9 o'clock… e*ight hours to go*.

Stremsen shook his head in annoyance. 'You do realise the seriousness of this incident, do you?'

'Yes, of course,' said Billy. 'Why would you think otherwise.' He tried to bite the words back, but it was too late.

Stremsen drew a deep breath. 'I'll tell you exactly why. Terry, here…' he put his hand on Socket's shoulder, 'appears to be the only person in this organisation who seems to give a damn about Core's accusation.'

Billy put his hand up to protest. 'I'm not sure I agree with that.' He looked at Socket but received nothing in return. 'I've been giving it a great deal of thought, and I've got a suggestion.'

'What's that?' asked Socket.

Stremsen crossed his arms and nodded to Billy.

Now Billy took a deep breath. 'With the MK6 development at the heart of Danny Core's investigation, we should consider bringing Jack Smelt back in. Let's get his opinion.'

'You realise what you're suggesting?' said Socket. He looked like he'd been slapped in the face. 'Core was Smelt's protégé, it would play right into his hands to get him involved.'

Billy was determined to get his point across. 'What harm would it do? Jack Smelt had been directing the project. His input could be crucial.'

Stremsen rocked on his toes. 'Don't you think that would make us all look incompetent. Particularly you, as Smelt's replacement?'

Billy ignored the put-down. 'Jack was there at the very beginning; he could shed light on…'

Stremsen put his hand up. 'No, not a good idea, but things need to change. We're starting with a restructure of the Centre of Excellence group.' Stremsen glanced over at Socket.

'It's time to bring in fresh ideas, a fresh face. Mathers has been linked with a serious incident, and Danny Core is looking to incriminate us all. I will not allow that to happen.'

Billy shook his head. 'I'm not sure *incriminate* is the right word. As I see it, Core is looking to clarify…'

Stremsen held up his hand again. 'There you go again, not taking his threat seriously enough. Core is looking for a way out. He's trying to deflect attention for his incompetence and blame the MK6 for the accident, and you're defending him. I need to make sure we don't give him any opportunities.'

'I'm not defending him, Fred,' Billy was as close to angry as he could get. 'What I'm saying is that everything *is* covered. All the data recorded in the PMT documents are fireproof, and there's nothing to fear in giving Core full access.'

Stremsen again looked at Socket, who nodded.

'I will be announcing, Terry as the WQD very shortly, but for now, I need him to be on the front line of this investigation… a technical observer.'

'WQD?' It was a term Billy hadn't heard before.

'Worldwide Quality Director,' said Stremsen.

'But quality is part of my responsibility,' said Billy.

'And so it will remain until this Rinto Gold problem has been resolved,' said Stremsen. 'After that, we will set out a formal structure where the Centre of Excellence will come under the umbrella of the WQD.'

'So my development team will be responsible to Terry Socket?' Billy couldn't hide his scorn.

'I see it more as a dotted line connecting the engineering and quality teams. But yes, *you* and your team will be accountable to Terry.'

'But that doesn't make sense…'

'Only as far as you're concerned,' interrupted Stremsen. 'It *will* work with or without you, and it *will* help in future situations like this.'

'Are we expecting *more* situations like this?' said Billy. 'What about the invulnerability of the PMT process?'

Stremsen stiffened. 'Of course, we're not expecting more, and we're not hiding anything. But I need someone I can trust to face up to Core and, so far, your performance has been sub-standard.'

'What do you mean *so far*?' Billy's face was heating up. 'I've only just met Danny Core, and the accident report has been in my hands for less than three days. Isn't it a bit early to question my performance and talk about restructuring?'

Stremsen ignored him. 'Terry and I will be meeting Core at 9.30 this morning and asking him to go through his report, in detail. Terry will also manage the amount of information we allow Core to access. Just because Rinto Gold has blood on their hands, it doesn't mean we have to give them free rein with our more sensitive records.'

'But we said, *full access.*' Billy's shock was turning into incredulity.

'And he'll have it…' said Stremsen. 'As far as he is aware. But I will not allow him access to the more sensitive aspects of the MK6 project.'

'There are no sensitive aspects,' said Billy. 'It was product development and, as I understand it, Danny Core has more knowledge of the Stabiliser than any of us. Who are we trying to kid?' He saw Socket grimace.

'The subject is closed,' said Stremsen. 'I'd prefer to announce the restructure immediately, but reorganising like this in the middle of an investigation would look suspicious. You will continue as normal until the investigation is concluded. But I can assure you, if you fail at the task, I will have no alternative but to ask you to stand down permanently. Do you understand?'

Billy nodded lamely. *Fail at what? Mathers had nothing to hide.*

'Do you want me to attend this morning's meeting?' he asked with no enthusiasm.

'No, we'll deal with Core. The fewer people involved, the less chance he has of intimidation.' Stremsen readied himself to leave.

'Isn't he going to find it odd that I'm not there?' asked Billy.

Again, Stremsen ignored the question. 'I'm going to invite Core to our facility in Texas and introduce him to Luca Majori and Rik Last. Majori is the group Financial

Controller and has been asked to take a minor role in this investigation. I'm taking him under my wing.'

Billy thought his grin looked a bit forced.

'As you can see, this whole process is being run from the very top,' Stremsen continued. 'Mathers has built a great reputation for its Recycling Stabilisers and has a loyal customer base. We cannot allow its good name and subsequently, Herons, to be dragged into messy litigation. Are you with me, Jones?'

Billy's eyes had glazed over. 'Yes, yes, of course.' Stremsen sneered.

'Now, for this process to work in our favour we need to show Mathers off in the best light. We must show absolute competency to Danny Core and make no mention of the imminent changes to the organisation. And I repeat, all documentation needs to be vetted by Terry before it is passed to Core. Okay?'

Billy was sweating, and his mouth was dry. He gulped water from a glass and choked as it went down the wrong way.

Stremsen rolled his eyes.

'Sorry... *cough!*... yes I do see,' said Billy.

Stremsen looked across at the green, four-drawer filing cabinet behind Billy's desk. The top one was marked, *Quality Control*, in bold white letters. The second, *MK5 PMT*. The third, *MK6 PMT* and the bottom drawer, *MK7 PMT*.

He pointed to the third drawer. 'We'll take the MK6 documentation to my office. Terry and I will go through a redaction process of the more sensitive sections, before passing copies to Core.' Stremsen nodded to Socket who got up and pulled three large box files from the drawer.

They were heavy, but Billy wasn't sure that was the reason Socket looked uncomfortable.

Stremsen continued. 'I won't have this investigation derailed by the incompetence of the engineering department. Discretion is the key at this delicate stage, and *everything* is classified information.'

It sounded to Billy like he'd finally run out of steam. 'Leave it to me, Fred, I've got it covered,' he answered.

Stremsen and Socket left the office in silence.

Billy opened his drawer and pulled out a concise dictionary, but before he could look up, *Redaction,* the door burst open and Steyn Broed walked in.

Chapter 25

'**I can understand** why you want to question the changes we've carried out on the MK6, Danny. After all, you wouldn't have experienced this degree of innovation during your time in charge.'

I'd just finished presenting my report, and already Stremsen was doing his best to taunt me. He and Terry were sitting opposite, though Socket was surprisingly restrained. At the head of the table was an overhead projector with some slides lying next to it.

They explained that Billy Jones had been called away on urgent business. *What's more critical than a fatal accident?* I'd asked. Only to be told that they were not implicated and were simply helping my enquiries.

'I thought the PMT presentation had been cancelled?' I said, nodding my head toward the projector.

'I thought I'd just go through a few slides,' Stremsen said with barely disguised excitement. 'And then maybe we could throw a few questions at one another?'

I nodded. The room was dimly lit, and for the first time, I was able to take stock of Stremsen as he strode up to the projector. I had him about mid-forties, and he was a cocky so and so. From the top of his square-headed crew cut to the bottom of his slip-on brogues was no more than five and a half feet.

His short legs and long body accentuated the width of his shoulders, which he seemed keen to exaggerate by swinging his arms away from his body whenever he walked.

His face was doughy and shapeless and looked surprisingly vulnerable. But even in the reduced light, his eyes, topped with bushy eyebrows, were sharp and uncompromising. He carried excess weight that amplified his bowed legs and, remembering his soft hands, he was obviously an office animal.

BREAKING POINT

He put on his reading glasses and switched on the projector.

His talk involved Value Propositions, Key Features, DFMEA's, QFD's, Brainstorming Techniques. It was impressive, and he carried himself with confidence. The presentation was professional, and his body language persuasive. I could see where his strengths lay, though he couldn't stop himself showing off. If he'd had all the roles and experiences he talked about, he would have been in his eighties. Still, it was easy to see how someone could be fooled.

It reminded me of a presentation I'd given Jack Smelt, years ago. I thought I'd done a pretty good job, but I never forgot his comment when I asked him what he thought. *You left me none the wiser, but better informed,* he said. He had a big smile, but I took the *faint praise* on board and measured others by the same standard.

The more questions I asked about the MK6, the more clichéd the answers became. No substance. This absence of engineering knowledge, even on fundamental issues, was a startling contrast to what had gone before.

Toward the end of a long hour, I switched off. My attention was drawn to Socket, who'd been unusually quiet throughout the presentation. His mind, like mine, seemed elsewhere.

'I understand you carried out some major changes in your time as Engineering Manager, Danny.' I was caught unawares for a second and hadn't noticed Stremsen had finished and was sitting back down. He was looking at me directly.

'Yes, we did carry out a few improvements along the way,' I said. 'Mathers was always trying to stay relevant in the industry.'

He looked at Terry, drawing him into the conversation. 'And all these changes are on record?' he leaned back in his chair; hands clasped.

'Yes, of course. Any changes were categorised, and the drawings and calculations put into the development database.'

'And who signed off those changes?'

I sensed a trap. 'The drawings have all got my signature, as do the calculation sheets; it was standard procedure.' I looked at Socket. 'Do you still keep those documents, Terry?'

He switched his attention to Stremsen. 'We kept a few, Fred, but most have been thrown away.'

'Thrown away!' I was genuinely shocked. 'Are you sure that's a good idea?'

Socket looked surprised. 'Yeah, why not?'

I couldn't believe he was so naive.

'Documentation for all new developments has to be kept for a minimum of twenty years to comply with the International Mining Standards. I'm surprised you still conform if you've thrown them away?'

Stremsen came back quickly, as though I'd hit a nerve.

'All part of our *housekeeping* exercises to keep the department lean and focused. The Process Management Tome has replaced all those antiquated systems. We now have processes that are *fail-safe*.'

I shook my head. 'I'm sure you think you do, but Terry and I have enough experience between us to know that nothing is completely *fail-safe* in this industry. Wouldn't you agree, Terry?' I looked him in the eye.

'Things have changed,' he replied. 'The PMT process has enough checks and balances to ensure any changes we make are virtually foolproof.'

'Sorry to pull you up again, Terry,' I said, not meaning a word of it. 'But *virtually*, destroys your argument. It's like saying your wife is virtually pregnant.' He didn't like that, but I didn't care and carried on goading. 'So are the auditors aware that you've destroyed documentation less than twenty years old?'

BREAKING POINT

'What do you mean?' He was caught in the headlights again.

'You know you can lose your trading license for that?'

Socket wanted to spit back, but Stremsen jumped in again to change the subject.

'I'm glad you brought that up, Danny. In your report, you talk about the safety system you introduced underground. Was it called the 3S Initiative?'

I realised the crafty bastard was manoeuvring me into a corner. 'Yes,' I said. 'And before you ask me, the answer is, *No*.'

Stremsen feigned confusion.

'*No*, I never pretended it was fail-safe,' I said.

He smiled at me and winked at Socket who looked increasingly uneasy. My hands gripped the side of my chair, I didn't want to lose my temper this early.

'Obviously, your Initiative was an important part of the safety culture at your mine,' he continued. But it's accuracy in predicting a fall should be questioned as much as the MK6 Stabiliser, shouldn't it?'

I nodded. This meeting was achieving nothing; just a game of who could piss the highest.

'Okay, Fred,' I said. 'I take your point, and I'll gladly supply you with any details of the 3S Initiative...'

'No, no,' he said. Again, that smile, those sharp eyes and that annoying Texas drawl. He pulled two box files from the floor and handed them over to me.

'What are these?' I asked.

'These are copies of the files we promised, Stremsen replied. 'I'm sure they'll clear up any doubts you have concerning the MK6 Development. As far as your 3S Initiative. Well, that's for you to try and *defend*.'

The last word was said with malice. My grip on the chair relaxed, and I took the files. At last, I had some technical data.

'Oh, by the way,' he said. 'I'd like to invite you over to the Heron facility in Houston and meet with some of the Board. We'd like to show you around the facility.'

'Very kind, Fred, but I'm short on time and…'

'Nonsense, you have a personal invitation from our CEO, Rik Last, someone you've already met.'

I could just about put a face to the name.

Stremsen carried on. 'I've told my secretary to get us flights for tomorrow night, I hope that suits you?'

'And Steyn?' I said.

I thought he'd swallowed a fly. 'No, no, I think just the two of us. It'll help keep costs down.'

Costs again, I thought.

'We'll spend a day together in Houston and get you straight back on an evening flight.'

I only had six days left, and the journey would eke valuable time from Van Heerden's deadline. *Was there anything more I could learn here or had I become distracted with personal issues?*

I felt the box files in my hands, these were what I wanted most.

'I'll need to confirm things with my boss,' I said, 'and give you a ring later tonight.'

I took the phone number of his hotel and left the room cradling the two sets of files; I couldn't wait to start analysing them. Looking at my watch, it was 12:30, and I'd arranged to meet Julie at eight.

I needed to find Steyn and get back to the hotel as soon as possible.

BREAKING POINT

Chapter 26

'**Hi, Billy, you** don't mind if I ask you a few things while Danny's tied up, do you?' The fact that Steyn had already taken a seat and was lighting a cigarette seemed to make the question superfluous.

'Er, no... no of course not. It's Steyn, isn't it?'

'Ja, that's right.' He reached over to shake hands, and there was sufficient eye contact to let Billy know this wasn't a social call.

'Just saw Fred and Terry come out, they looked a bit serious. You boy's had a falling out?' asked Steyn.

'So, what do you think of Mathers so far?' Billy said, clumsily changing the subject. He didn't have a clue what a Mine Captain did, but judging by Steyn's physique, it looked more physical than intellectual.

'I didn't know what to expect,' said Steyn. 'The trip was arranged at such short notice.'

'Yes,' Billy nodded. 'I can understand why you'd want to come over and check everything for yourselves. After such a tragic accident.' He lit his pipe and gathered his thoughts in the comforting smog. Tactics ran through his mind and straight back out again. After the warning he was given by Stremsen he was on edge but determined not to be intimidated by the Afrikaner.

'Now what can I do for you?' he said, crossing his legs casually.

'I just thought I'd get some background on the MK6 development,' Steyn said, creating his own smoke signals. 'I understand you took over about 18 months ago?'

'That's right, I took over from Jack Smelt,' said Billy.

'So, what made Jack leave in the middle of the project?' From what I hear, he wasn't the type of person who gave up on anything.'

Stay calm, Billy. 'Well, he'd been here for a long time and had been thinking about retirement for a while. It just coincided with that particular timeline.'

'No pressure then?'

'No more than the everyday pressure of a stressful job,' Billy smiled, but nothing came back.

Steyn continued. 'Danny told me he was a top bloke, knew his stuff. He was surprised Jack would leave without wrapping everything up.'

Billy casually brushed the knee of his trousers. Broed mentioning his predecessor by his first name was strangely disquieting.

'I only met him the week before he left, so I can't answer that,' Billy replied. 'Maybe the dynamics of managing the new PMT process were proving a bit daunting. I certainly had my work cut out, and I'm a lot younger than Jack.' He drew quietly on his pipe, inhaling the acrid smoke and exhausting it from his nostrils.

'More experienced than Jack?' The directness of Steyn's enquiry was threatening, and he was referring to him like a friend.

'Well, that's for others to decide, but I got the MK6 past the final stage gate. Something which Jack failed to do.'

'Maybe he was too cautious,' said Steyn.

Billy nodded his head. 'Could be.'

'So how do you feel about the MK6 development, are you satisfied that it was a secure process; *fit for purpose* and all that?'

Discretion is the key at this delicate stage... With Stremsen's words still ringing in his ears, Billy tried opting for one syllable answers and failed at the second hurdle.

'Yes,' he said.

'Yes, what?' asked Steyn.

'Erm... well... Jack did the preliminary work, but it was going nowhere until I came in. It was one of the reasons they got rid of him. They needed someone with the skills to lead a modern development process, and I fitted the bill.'

He relaxed back into his chair.

'But I thought Jack had retired voluntarily?' said Steyn.

'Yes... yes, he did,' Billy bit down on his pipe.

'But you just said... *It was one of the reasons they got rid of him.* Who are *they,* and why did they want rid of Jack?'

Billy tried to recover. 'What I meant to say was that Jack had been planning his retirement for a long time, Mathers just brought it forward. Hypothetically speaking.'

'What do you mean, *hypothetically speaking*, man? Either Jack retired voluntarily, or he was pushed. Which one was it?'

'No... no, forget the previous comment, my mistake.'

The sound of a train passing sent a gentle tremor through the floor of the office and Billy wished he was on it.

'Now, are there any concerns about the MK6 project I can help dispel?' he continued.

'Like, *why did they get rid of Jack Smelt*, you mean?'

'No... no, that was a slip of the tongue. I meant anything else.'

Billy was aware he was saying *no* an awful lot, which was causing him to draw hard on his pipe, despite his lungs already burning.

Steyn leaned over and screwed his cigarette into the ashtray, his face no more than twelve inches from Billy's. He leaned back and looked Billy up and down for several seconds.

'I've just done a factory tour with Terry Socket; did he have much to do with the MK6 project?'

'Well, of course,' Billy was going over each answer in his mind making his delivery painfully slow. 'He was the Engineering Manager at the time, so...'

'Isn't that his title now?' Steyn cut in.

'What do you mean?' asked Billy. Aware that Broed hadn't blinked for a long time.

'You said, he *was* the Engineering Manager, *past tense*. Has Terry's role changed?'

Billy felt a hot flush and realised that tobacco ash had spilt from his pipe and was burning a hole in the front of his trousers.

'Not yet,' Billy was distracted and stood to damp down the embers.

'Not yet?' Steyn appeared startled. 'So there are going to be changes made soon?'

'No, I didn't mean that,' Billy was poking and pulling at his groin.

'Well, what do you mean? Were these changes planned before or after the accident?'

Billy was distracted, but Steyn was relentless with his questioning. 'Well no, not really,' said Billy.

'What do you mean, *not really*? Either they were, or they weren't.' Steyn's voice was getting louder, the more frustrated he became.

'It's not that easy, I wish it were,' Billy's voice had also moved a couple of octaves higher. 'There are some things I'm not at liberty to disclose. You understand that, don't you?'

'Not really, Steyn answered brutally. 'Fred Stremsen promised full cooperation and access to all documentation and information. Are you implying that isn't the case?'

'All documentation relating to the MK6 PMT process will be available to you whenever you want, you have my promise,' said Billy, finally in control of the fire down below.

'Okay,' Steyn replied. 'I'll have that documentation to get on with. Do you have it to hand?'

Billy felt ill. 'What, right now?'

'Ja, I can wait here for them.'

Billy noticed Steyn had stopped blinking again. 'Listen, Steyn, can I trust you?'

BREAKING POINT

'Maybe?'

Billy wasn't sure what to make of the answer. '*Maybe*, isn't good enough,' he replied. He was becoming defensive and chided himself.

Folding his arms, he straightened his back and stuck out his chest. He wasn't going to be intimidated. Unfortunately, his teeth had to work overtime to hold his pipe in place, and it hung precariously to the corner of his mouth, below a rictus grin.

'Well, what would you like to *trust me* with?' asked Steyn.

'That depends on how *much* I can trust you. You see that, don't you?' The pipe was bobbling up and down in front of his eyes.

Steyn exploded. 'I've just asked you for the MK6 documentation, and you're asking me if I can trust you. What the hell's going on here? Just get me the damned documentation, as promised, and I'll be out of your hair.'

Sweat dripped from Billy's armpits onto his ribs; the resulting shiver caused his pipe to dislodge and clatter to the floor.

'I haven't got them to hand just yet,' he said, ignoring the smoke rising from the embers at his feet.

'*All our documentation is ready and waiting...* is what Fred Stremsen told us this morning. Isn't that them in the green cabinet behind you?' Steyn pointed beyond Billy's shoulder. 'The drawer with *MK6 PMT* on it?'

Billy craned his neck as though he was seeing it for the first time. 'They're with Fred and Terry at the moment; tidying them up for you.'

'Tidying them up?' said Steyn. 'I thought the PMT process was all about thoroughness. How come they need tidying up?'

'It's part of a redaction process,' said Billy. 'They won't have them for long and then they'll...' He didn't like the look on Steyn's face.

'Redaction process!' Steyn got up to look out of the window as another train passed. The same gentle tremor following the sound of the engine, until everything was quiet again.

Billy felt he should say something but didn't know what.

Steyn returned to his seat and blew his cheeks out.

'One minute you're telling me Jack retired willingly and the next that *they* got rid of him…' Billy started to speak, but Steyn wouldn't let him. 'Then you imply that there's going to be a reorganisation and start backtracking when I ask for details.'

Billy watched Steyn's face getting redder.

'And now you say we can't have the documentation we were promised until Fred Stremsen and Terry Socket *doctor* them. Don't you think this all sounds a bit suspicious, Billy?'

'I never said they were *doctoring* them, Steyn. You're putting words into my mouth,'

'Redacting! You know what that bloody means as well as I do?'

Billy looked at the open dictionary on his desk.

'You misunderstand me,' he said. His hands were fists below the desk.

'Then how come we're talking about these things now… eh?' Steyn was staring him down.

'Because you brought them up, that's why,' said Billy exasperated.

'And why do you think that is Billy? Think hard before you answer because I'll get angry if you try and bullshit me again.' Steyn crossed his legs and leaned back into his seat.

Billy didn't want to think hard, in fact, he didn't want to think at all. *How the hell had the conversation got here?* He thought.

'Because Danny thinks the MK6 Stabiliser is implicated in the accident at your mine?' Billy said, clearing his throat.

BREAKING POINT

'And from what you've been saying, I'm starting to agree.'

'What do you mean, *from what I've been saying?* I haven't said anything to question the integrity of the MK6.'

'No?' Steyn leaned over and almost whispered. 'Then why all the secrecy around the documentation. Redaction is censoring, and the question I'm asking is *why*?'

Billy turned ashen, he felt sick. 'Erm... we're just keen to make sure the information doesn't get misinterpreted.'

He'd tried to retain some poise, but his tongue was sticking to the roof of his mouth.

'So you believe the Stabiliser *might* be implicated?' He could feel Steyn drawing him in.

'No,' his voice began to rise... again.

'A definite *no* then. And you'll sign off on that?'

'Well not categorically no. You know as well as I do that nothing is *completely* foolproof.'

'So that's a *yes*, then?'

'Well not categorically *yes*... all mechanical components have their limitations, but... *maybe*.' Billy was completely dishevelled.

'So you're saying the Stabiliser could be implicated... *maybe*?' Steyn concluded.

'Well... *yes*, if you put it like that.'

'Like what, Billy, it's a simple yes or no, isn't it?'

'Well, put that simplistically, *yes*!'

As the silence grew between them, Billy grabbed for the glass of water and took long gulps.

'Well, it's been a fascinating conversation,' Steyn said, standing and preparing to leave. 'I'm going to...'

It was Billy's turn to jump in. 'Talk it over with Danny Core?'

Steyn glared back at him, and Billy felt he needed to act quickly, make amends.

'Before you suggest there's a fault with the new Stabiliser, let me show you some documentation.'

He swivelled in his chair and pulled out the top drawer of the green filing cabinet marked *Quality Control*. Reaching in, he extracted two files from the section labelled *MK6* and handed the thinner one, *Material Certificates*, to Steyn.

'These are all the quality control, material certificates for every redesigned component on the MK6 Stabiliser. They confirm that all the components were made using the correct material, to the correct, worldwide standard. And all passed the stringent mechanical testing criteria. In essence, the DNA of each new product can be traced back to the base metal it was made from.'

'Impressive,' said Steyn, smiling. 'And the other folder?'

Billy passed it across. It was thicker and marked, *MK6 Calculation Database*.

'This folder contains all the calculations used to ensure any new products were designed correctly and with the appropriate safety factors.'

'Thanks,' said Steyn. 'I'll let you have them back when we've looked them over.'

Billy's newfound confidence dissolved. 'I can't let you have those!'

'Why, do you need to carry out a *redaction process*?'

Billy saw the sneer cross Steyn's face. 'No, it's just…'

'I'll bring them back tomorrow, Billy. And don't worry, I won't mention it to anyone.'

'No, I didn't mean…'

Steyn shook his hand before he could finish and walked out the door with the files under his arm.

Billy stepped around his desk to plead with him when something cracked under his foot. He groaned out loud and picked up the two halves of his pipe. *Oh, fuck!* He thought.

BREAKING POINT

Chapter 27

The journey back to the hotel was surreal as Steyn told me about his meeting with Billy Jones. When I told him I hadn't realised he'd scheduled one, he said it had slipped Billy's mind as well. Whatever went on between them, he'd surprised me by producing two more files.

They need to be back with him, by tomorrow morning, he told me; adding that the files Stremsen and Socket had given me had been edited. Now my head was spinning with conspiracy theories. I had a pair of *censored* files and a pair of *prohibited* files. My workload had doubled, and my trip to Houston was looking less likely, which suited me anyway.

John had picked us up outside reception, and we hadn't said two words to each other since this morning. I had no justification for being so angry with him, but I was still in shock.

I've been seeing Julie, Danny…

I could barely look at him as he dropped us off at the hotel.

'If I can do anything, Danny, just give me a ring,' he said.

I nodded. 'I think you've done enough, John, don't you?' It was uncalled for, and I could have ripped my tongue out the minute the words escaped. 'Actually,' I said, trying to make clumsy amends. 'There is something you could do. Have you got time to take Steyn tonight?'

Steyn looked back at me, surprised.

'It's just that I'm going to have an early night to sort through this paperwork and I won't be much company.'

'That's okay,' Steyn replied. 'I'll give you a hand.'

'Thanks, but I won't be much company.'

I appreciated the offer, but he deserved a night off.

'How about he picks you up about 6:30. Is that okay with you, John?' I looked across at him.

'No problem,' he replied. 'I've got no other plans.'

'Maybe take him to the rugby club for a few beers, make a night of it?' I tried to be light-hearted, but my insides were churning.

He turned to Steyn. 'There's a game on tonight, do you like rugby?'

Steyn bristled. 'I'm South African, man. You may have invented the bloody game, but we show you how to play it.' The banter broke the ice.

'5 o'clock, sharp then,' John replied and left us.

As we made our way back to the rooms, I stopped him in the corridor.

'John can get a bit…' I was struggling to find the right word. 'Headstrong after a few beers.'

He looked at me and smiled. 'You mean, *punchy*?'

'He's good as gold normally,' I replied. 'But can be a pain in the arse when he's had a few.'

Steyn bunched his fist; it looked like a lump of knotted wood. 'If he steps out of line, he'll wake up with more than a sore head.'

I smiled, and a thought crossed my mind. *I wondered if John knew I was planning to see Julie.*

I got back to my room and put the four sets of files on the bed. I cleared the writing desk, and from my suitcase pulled out a calculator, pencil and pad. At the bottom of the case was a shabby A4 file. I picked it up and shuffled through the pages of calculations inside, each section categorised with the Stabiliser component they were aligned with.

This was my *bible* and contained all the information I'd gleaned over the years with Mathers. It was based on the original work carried out by Franklyn Mathers with some of my own computations. I'd kept it as a keepsake, never thinking I'd need it again.

I was the tortoise in this race, and new technology was superseding my scribbled notes. Still, I'd invested twenty years of trust in them and never been let down.

BREAKING POINT

I started immediately, testing the calculations in the Heron documents with my handwritten notes. Perversely, I was enjoying myself. The notion of checking work wasn't new, although I'd never done it *hoping* to find a flaw.

Working on the numbers, I'd lost track of time and jumped at the sound of someone knocking. At the same time, the telephone rang. I instinctively looked at my watch, it was 8:20 pm.

Jesus Christ! I thought and lunged toward the door, scattering sheets across the floor. I held my breath as I opened it, and there was Julie, standing there with a resigned look.

'You'd better answer that?' She nodded at the phone, ringing on the bedside table. I tripped as I turned back to pick it up.

'Hello, Mr Core, this is the reception desk. There's a Mrs Julie Core on her way up to your room.'

'Thank you,' I said and slammed it down.

'No need to take it out on the phone.' Julie's features were unnervingly calm.

I was embarrassed. I'd had this all planned, and here I was a shambling wreck. I put on the best smile I could, but it never reached my eyes. 'I'm so sorry, Julie, I got caught up in some work.'

She walked past me, stopping to stare at the sheets of paper strewn across the bed and spilling onto the floor, as I began to clear the desk. 'Have you been burgled?'

I tried to smile again, but it must have looked grotesque. My mouth was numb, and I didn't know where to put my hands.

'I'm sorry, I just lost track of time.'

She gave me a cold stare. 'Just like old times.' Her voice was steady and far too reasonable.

She was wearing a dark blue, polo neck jumper and denim jeans. A brown leather bag was slung over her left shoulder and hung on her right hip; the strap running diagonally across her chest, dividing her breasts. She had on black, knee-length boots and a tartan scarf that looked familiar.

'Are you having a good look?' she said, not bothering to make eye contact.

'I'm sorry, it's just been so long since…' She didn't let me finish.

'Since you saw your son? Is that what you were going to say?'

I turned my gaze to the papers on the floor as she walked around the room.

'You never could prioritise your family, could you?' She kicked at the sheets; the first sign of temper.

'What's all this?' she was shouting. Grabbing at more notes on the bed and throwing them to the floor.

'Five years on and you're still putting work before your family.'

Her face was flushed, and tears were welling. 'You'll never change, will you?'

'No,' I said as quietly as I could. 'Not when you put it like that. I've got no excuses left, other than those you've heard before. I'm sorry.'

'How many times have I heard, *sorry*? Sorry about this, sorry about that. Always sorry, until the next time.'

She wiped the sleeve of her jumper across her eyes, and I saw the tears sparkle on the black fabric.

'I thought I'd heard the last of them. I got sick of it, sick of making excuses for you. After five years I'd almost forgotten how selfish you were and yet it's only taken a minute to remember.'

'I'm sorry,' I whispered again, I had nothing left to offer.

She started to calm, and I expected her to walk out and never see her again.

'I'm going down to the restaurant,' she finally said. 'If you prefer to stay and finish your precious work, that's up to you. I'm only doing this for my son… for *our* son. This

BREAKING POINT

will be your last chance to see him. After tonight, I don't expect to see you again.' And with that, she left the room.

'I'll be down in five minutes,' I shouted. But the words fell against the slammed door.

Chapter 28

The rugby club was a cacophony as both teams refreshed their bruised bodies with free jugs of beer passed down the lines of their respective tables.

Steyn and John were sat amongst them and had benefitted from the flow for the last two hours. The match had been hard-fought, but Crossways had won, and all was well with the world. The building was small and crammed with so many people that the voices parried to and fro; rising and falling as people tried to make themselves heard.

Steyn's accent had captured everyone's attention, and he'd become a bit of a celebrity.

'You'd swear I'd played for the bloody Springboks,' he shouted to John over the din, as their beer glasses got filled once more.

'They seem to like you,' he answered. 'I don't know why, no one likes South Africans these days.' He laughed, but there was no humour in his eyes.

Steyn had eased back on the free-flowing beer, but John had no such inhibitions. Danny's warning was becoming a reality, and Steyn noticed the change in John's demeanour with each emptied glass. He was about to challenge him when a voice boomed out over his shoulder.

'She's let you out tonight, has she?'

He turned around to see Terry Socket smirking at John, his hand wrapped around a pint glass and a cigarette hanging from his lips.

John looked up at him. 'Fuck off, Socket,' he said, taking another gulp of beer.

'Steady on, Johnny, boy. Just remember who's your boss.'

John got up on unsteady legs. 'We're not in work now you piece of shit.'

As he made to get nearer Socket, Steyn stood between them. 'Alright, you two.' He pushed them apart and turned

BREAKING POINT

to Socket. 'I suggest you find somewhere else to drink; otherwise, we all might have regrets in the morning.'

Socket looked down his nose at Steyn, then at John who was struggling to stand up straight.

'Has she kicked you out, now she's got her old man back?'

John lunged, but Steyn managed to hold him back with the help of two of the rugby players. Socket disappeared into the crowd as the excitement died down. With so much noise filling the room, only those nearby had noticed the altercation.

'I think he needs a bit of fresh air?' said one of the players, pushing John toward the door.

Steyn took him outside. There had been some rain since the end of the game, and the night had turned cold. They both shivered as Steyn pulled out a cigarette and lit up. Two drags later he realised it had no taste; he'd had too much to drink.

'He likes winding people up, doesn't he?' he said to John, who was swaying in the breeze.

John gave a derisory laugh and shook his head. 'I'll have one of those,' he said, pointing at the cigarette.

'I didn't think you smoked,' said Steyn, pulling out the packet.

'Mmm, gave them up a year ago. But fuck it, why not.'

Steyn lit it up for him and tried to reduce the tension. 'Are you married?'

John coughed as he inhaled, then turned and sneered.

'Didn't you understand what Socket was saying?'

'Understand what?' said Steyn.

'Danny caused all this.' John's reply was slurred and laced with contempt. He took another draw on the cigarette and released another coughing fit.

'Danny?' Steyn looked bemused. 'What the hell has Danny got to do with this?'

'You don't know, do you?'

'Know what? Stop speaking in riddles, man.'

John looked up at the sky and gave out an empty laugh.

'She's let you out… Socket was referring to Danny Core's ex-wife.'

Now she's got her old man back… Steyn got it.

'That makes things awkward, does Danny know about you and her?'

John picked at his nails. 'I told him today, we've got nothing to hide.'

'Mmm, maybe not, but how did he take it?'

'Not great, but I couldn't care less. Not my bloody problem.'

'Doesn't look like that from where I'm standing.' Steyn could see he was getting worked up again.

'Christ, he's been away for five years and then turns up out of the blue to investigate a bloody accident. What the fuck's that got to do with him?'

'More than you think,' answered Steyn. 'Are you and this Julie, serious?'

'*This* Julie,' John sneered. 'We've been together for over a year, and it's been good… until now.'

'What do you mean, *until now*?'

'Well, it's obvious, isn't it? He's trying to get her back. Why else would he make up an excuse to come over here.'

'You think he used this accident as an excuse to get together with his ex-wife?'

John sneered again. 'You're his mate, you'd say anything to cover for him.'

Steyn had an uncomfortable feeling in the pit of his stomach. He was starting to dislike John Dread.

'Aren't you his mate?' he asked, tempted to give him a shake, but realised there was no point. 'I think you need to go home before I say something I'll regret.'

He looked out at the car park and saw John's car. 'I don't think you're in any condition to drive, I'll organise a taxi.'

'I'm alright,' John complained.

BREAKING POINT

'Wait here!' Steyn poked him in the chest before returning to the clubhouse to make arrangements.

By the time he returned, John and his car had disappeared.

Chapter 29

The plates arrived steaming hot and tumbling with chicken curry, rice and chips. As I cut into it, the sauce seeped from the edge of my plate onto the white tablecloth. I moved it over to cover the stain but wasn't quick enough.

'You always were a messy eater.' It was the first words Julie had uttered since ordering. We'd become strangers, with nothing in common apart from a failed marriage.

I smiled in embarrassment.

'And you've got sauce on your chin,' she added.

I wiped it away, putting another ugly stain on the serviette.

'I'm not doing very well, am I?'

Here I was, sitting with a woman I knew more intimately than any other person in the world, and I couldn't string two sentences together.

'What are we doing here, Danny?' She seemed to deflate as the words came out. Her face was pale and drawn and the vibrancy I'd seen earlier that morning had evaporated. And I'd caused this.

She put down her knife and fork, and I saw the resentment building behind her eyes.

'I just wanted to try and see Paul again, apologise for my behaviour,' I replied, desperate for her to listen. 'Find a way to explain what was going on in my head and try to put things right between us.'

Listening to the words out loud, made me realise how naive I'd been to think I could turn up like this and expect her to open up to me.

'We have two children,' her eyes narrowed. 'Alex is gone, but I still need to think of him as though he's still here. I talk to him all the time, involve him in everything I do. I can't think of him on his own… somewhere else.' Her eyes were filling, and she dabbed them with a tissue.

'I'm sorry.' I said.

BREAKING POINT

'Stop using that word.' Her jaw muscles tightened as she struggled to keep her voice even, she was ready to spit in my face.

'I've heard enough of it to last me a lifetime. It's not sufficient and never was.'

I looked at my hands. The scars and deformed nails that had refused to grow properly since that night on Brig Uchel.

She got up, her chair grating across the floor, drawing glances from other diners. 'I can't do this... I can't.' She turned and walked out without a second glance.

I was going to let her go, but saw sense and followed. She disappeared into the toilets, and I followed her in. I hadn't travelled this far to lose my nerve. She was holding onto the basin, crying openly and spun around as I entered.

'You can't come in here!' she shouted. Her eyes flashed left and right, but we were alone. Not that I cared.

My heart was racing, and my eyes wet. 'I made all my excuses a long time ago,' I said, struggling to form the words. 'And you know what? They were never enough for me, either. I got sick to death of people sympathising about what happened. I tried living with it and getting on with life, but in the end, all I had left was *sorry,* and it sickened me.'

We were both sobbing uncontrollably. 'It will never be enough, but what else do I have? I can't bring him back!'

She moved toward me, and I gathered her into my arms and held her. Everything that needed to be said was a distant echo from a time I had tried to forget. Now there was only silence and sadness.

I turned my head as a woman came into the toilet.

'Sorry...' she said, turning on her heels. 'I thought this was the ladies?'

I could feel Julie's sobs mix with suppressed laughter. *Funny how conflicting sensations can spring from similar depths.*

We let each other go with embarrassed smiles, and I left her alone.

'I'll wait for you outside,' I said.

I wasn't sure what would happen next and was surprised when she came out and suggested we go back to the lounge and try to talk.

I brought two glasses of wine back to the table, and she gave me a weak smile. Neither of us seemed to know where to start, so I just came out with it.

'I'm surprised you're still willing to talk, I thought I'd blown my chance of seeing Paul again.'

'He deserves a better father than you.' The words cut.

'I'm not going to disagree,' I replied. 'And even if I did, I haven't time to argue.' I tapped my fingers on a beer mat.

'How long are you staying?' She took a long drink from her glass.

'I'm supposed to be flying to America tomorrow night,' I said, 'but I'm going to cancel.'

Her hands surrounded the wine glass, and she gazed through the liquid.

'What's going on, Danny?'

'What do you mean? Nothing's going on.'

She looked up at me and shook her head. 'I can read you like a book. You've come over here after five years, without warning, and now you're saying, *I'm off to America.*'

'I'm going to cancel,' I said, but her eyes wouldn't let go. 'I'm part of an accident investigation team, nothing more.'

She emptied her glass and passed it over to me. 'I'll have another one, please.'

I took it and leaned in close. 'I'm just going to make a phone call.' Her hair smelled of fresh flowers, and I saw the familiar birthmark on the side of her neck; my legs went weak.

She turned to look at me, and our lips almost touched. 'You're not going to stand me up, are you?' She rewarded me with a smile. I returned it, not sure if she was being serious, and made my way to the payphone.

I managed to get through to Stremsen's hotel room, and he wasn't best pleased when I declined his offer to visit the Heron factory. Initially, he took an aggressive tone, telling me that my time in Mathers was causing problems. I was undermining Terry and Billy and creating unrest amongst the other engineers. When that didn't work, he pleaded that Rik Last was looking forward to meeting me again. *I'll arrange first-class travel, and you can bring your Mine Captain along.*

The more insistent he became to get me out of Mathers, the more convinced I was to stay.

I returned to the lounge and ordered another two glasses of wine.

'It's Danny Core, isn't it?'

The voice came from along the bar. I looked across and recognised Diane Stott, one of Julie's friends, sitting next to her husband, Bryn.

'Hi,' I said, not taking too much notice.

'You've got a nerve coming back after all this time.' Her comment was laced with bitterness. I noticed the barman fumbling with the corkscrew as his attention was drawn to the outburst.

'Sorry,' I said. 'Are you talking to me?'

By this time, Bryn was trying to shut her up.

'Leave it there, love.'

But she was having none of it. 'Running off and leaving your wife and child like that.'

It came as such a shock that I didn't have time to get annoyed. Everyone else's conversation stalled as we became the focus of attention.

My anger built, *what gave her the right*... I stepped toward her and was disturbed to see her draw backwards; *I wasn't here to scare anyone.*

I took a couple of deep breaths.

'We both lost a child,' I said. 'And what went on between...' But before the anger kicked in, Julie was at my side.

I don't know who was more surprised, me or Diane Stott.

'Oh, Julie, I didn't realise,' she said. Bryn was looking embarrassed for all of us.

'No, you didn't, Diane, and you didn't think either.' Julie turned to acknowledge everyone in the lounge. 'And those of you who feel you have the right to voice an opinion about me or my husband... *ex-husband*, lost that privilege five years ago.'

She was holding my arm, and I instinctively rested my hand on hers.

'I'm sorry, Julie, Danny,' Bryn broke the silence. 'Diane was out of order; one too many.' He took her arm. 'Come on, love, let's get you home.' And led her out.

Gradually the atmosphere normalised.

Julie took her hand away from me. 'That'll keep the jungle drums going for a while,' she said.

For all her bravado, I could see was upset.

'Shall we go?' I whispered, feeling exposed standing at the bar.

'No, I'm not wasting my drink for them.'

I followed her back to our table, and we both took a while to recover, sipping our wine in silence. Our eyes met, and I was about to say something when she grabbed my arm.

'For Christ's sake, don't say sorry again.'

I smiled. 'No, I was about to say I've cancelled the American trip.'

She ignored the statement. 'Have you seen Dawn since you've been back?' I knew the question would come.

'I saw her briefly when we arrived,' I answered, feeling the tension rise again.

She was turning the wine glass in her fingers; the silence was drawing me into another apology.

BREAKING POINT

'It was a mistake, and I know the harm it did, but... it was a difficult time.'

She shook her head. 'She probably did us a favour.'

I nodded. I'd pushed the memory into the background, but now it was exposed, I remembered the hurt inflicted.

'Have you met anyone else?' she asked, peering up from her glass. Her eyes were a beautiful emerald green. I looked away, embarrassed.

'You've gone red,' she said, smiling at my discomfort.

'No, I haven't met anyone,' I answered. 'And you?' I braced myself.

'I haven't locked myself away with grief if that's what you mean,' she said with a twinkle in her eye. 'But the boys...' her face dropped as she corrected herself. 'Paul keeps me busy.'

The stilted conversation meant we drank more than we talked, and three glasses of wine later, she looked at her watch. It surprised us both that it was 10 o'clock.

'I'll need to leave my car here tonight. Can you order me a taxi?'

I was halfway to the telephone when I thought of something and turned back. 'Why don't I walk you home,' I said. 'It's not that far.'

She looked out the window. 'Fine by me,' and we made our way to the exit. It was a chilly night, the air was fresh after the rain, but felt good after the stuffy atmosphere in the lounge. I automatically pulled out a cigarette.

'Since when have you started smoking?' she asked.

'A while,' I replied, forgetting she hated the habit, and replaced it back in the pack.

The alcohol was doing its job and helped relieve some tension between us. We talked about Paul and Alex without inhibitions, reminiscing as though they were tucked in bed together. The sky was clear, and the streets empty of sound except our busy voices and exaggerated memories.

When a light breeze teased through her hair, I caught her scent on the wind and felt my chest heave with nostalgia. She reminded me of so much that I'd chosen to forget.

I listened as she opened about her life, past and present, she remained guarded but seemed unchanged. The passing of time had been subtle, and what differences there were appeared for the better. As we talked of our previous lives, I moved closer, and we linked arms. I squeezed hers gently and thought she reciprocated while daring confidences seemed to grow.

We let go of one another at the front gate of the house, a light was glowing behind the closed curtains.

'Who's the babysitter?' I asked.

She looked toward the window. 'That's Steph, the next-door neighbour, she often sits for me. I'd invite you in, but it would take a bit of explaining, and Paul will be asleep.' Her eyes crinkled together in apology.

'No, that's okay,' I said, hiding my disappointment. 'I need to get back. I've got an early start in the morning.'

She looked up at the bedroom window. 'Paul's got a football match after school tomorrow. You can come and watch him play if you like?'

'Will you be there?'

Her mouth tensed a fraction. 'I'm always there.'

With the work I had in front of me, it would be tight, but I would find a way. 'That would be great.'

She looked into my eyes. 'Are you in some sort of trouble, Danny?'

I wondered whether John had spoken to her.

'Nothing I can't handle,' I said, lying through my teeth.

'Fine, then I'll see you at the school playing fields, it's a 4 o'clock, kick-off. She leaned towards me, and I took her shoulders, ready to kiss her on the cheek, but she turned to face me and met my lips. Her mouth opened and held me fractionally longer than necessary, or was I deluding myself. Before I could react, she gently pushed me away.

'I was dreading tonight, more than you could ever know.' As she spoke, her eyes turned to the sky, and I noticed the small scar on her chin from a childhood accident. Then she looked back at me. 'But it's been a nice evening.'

I absorbed her smiling eyes, and for a moment was taken back to another place and time... wishing I could tell my mother.

With Paul tucked up in bed and the babysitter long gone, Julie prepared for bed. She took off her dress ring and put it in the jewellery box. Her hand hovered and pulled out another ring. It was tarnished, and a stone was missing from the cluster of three. Danny had bought it not long after they'd first met.

She removed the tartan scarf from around her neck and wondered if he'd remembered when he bought it for her. In a different time, too long ago.

Desperate not to care, she found she couldn't and the realisation became too much to bear. Holding the fabric to her face, her shoulders began convulsing, and from a place deep within, she sobbed in silent despair... afraid she might wake their son.

Chapter 30

As I walked home, I intuitively licked my lips and sensed the dry taste of perfume on my tongue. I was on auto-pilot as my mind continued to flashback to the events of the last few hours. Each time I thought of the negatives, I couldn't help reflecting on the more positive aspects.

The streets were silent but for my footsteps following the steep incline towards the hotel. I was smiling, feeling happy for the first time in a while. In the distance, above the sparkling lights of Crossways, I saw the profile of the Bryn Uchel mountains silhouetted across the moonlit horizon. Black and lifeless, they seemed to be watching me, judging me.

How could I be happy near that monster? Reality doused me like a cold shower, and any good feelings I had were washed away. I lowered my eyes and picked up the pace, instinctively snapping at the band on my wrist.

I didn't feel the blow to the back of my head immediately, just the all-encompassing sound of my brain ricocheting inside my skull. A burst of bright light and stars flashed across my eyes, and I fell heavily to my knees. And then the pain hit.

Starting at the point of the blow, just behind my ear, it lit up every nerve ending like thousands of electric shocks. As it reached the pit of my stomach, it intensified and returned to the wound with a nauseous, sickening taste that soured my throat and made me gag for breath.

Before I could take in what was happening, I glimpsed a golf club swirling in an exaggerated backswing, ready for another blow to my body. I could barely breathe but knew I had to defend the next strike. As it swung down, I heard my attacker grunt, and the exertion gave away his gender. I twisted from its trajectory, using all the strength I had left in my legs and arms, and fell from the pavement onto the

BREAKING POINT

road. It didn't stop the blow but minimised the force, as it deflected off my shoulder. Painful but not debilitating.

I heard another groan, this time disappointment, and tried to catch a glimpse of his face. I'd assumed the onslaught was over, but I was wrong.

There was no time for recognition as he set his right leg down onto the road, settling into position before swinging the club back again. *The bastard was trying to kill me!*

I looked around for something to defend myself when a glint of reflected light, near my right arm, caught my eye. Tucked between the road and the kerb was a piece of metal; a discarded windscreen wiper.

As he started his downswing, I grabbed the metal and stabbed at the nearest piece of vulnerable flesh; the attacker's right leg. My left arm was raised to fend off the blow as I twisted down with as much energy as I could muster, and hoped to God I hit my target before he hit his.

I felt the metal rip through the fabric, dig into flesh and jolt against bone. I used the weight of my body to try and plunge through, but the metal gave way and twisted around my hand. I pulled my body into the foetal position, eyes closed tight, waiting for his strike. It didn't come.

A muffled cry of pain cleaved through the night air, definitely male, and I heard the club clatter to the floor, echoing in the dark. I looked again for a face, but the features were covered by a balaclava. Except for the eyes and mouth grimacing in pain. I was spent, and if he'd wanted to finish his work, he could have. But it was over as abruptly as it had begun.

I heard him grab the golf club and limp away toward the obscurity of a footpath leading down towards the canal, his uneven steps muffled by the night. Trying to look around, I only succeeded in throwing up on the road. The acid scoured the inside of my throat, leaving me spitting and panting for breath.

Having escaped serious injury, I crawled back onto the pavement, I didn't want to get run over. I laid my head against the cold, wet paving stone and slowly took in my surroundings from ground level.

The street was washed with pale light from the lamp post nearby, and I could smell the sour earth pressed between the concrete slabs by a million footsteps. A pool of blood trailed along my eye line and collected on the stone surface. I raised myself up and tried to clear my head.

The first blow had been the worst, unexpected, and my ears were still ringing. I felt for the source of the blood and cried out as my finger sunk into a deep cut behind my ear. I pressed my handkerchief hard against the wound to stem the flow.

I stood as best I could, my head still spinning so that I had to lean against the lamp post. The streets were deserted and the night had turned cold. I'd been attacked in a blind spot, tucked between the residential houses, an ideal position for someone to lie in wait.

The night was still, and the smell of stale cigarette smoke lingered. At the edge of the road, I noticed a couple of cigarette butts and reached down to pick one up; I almost fell over. My eyes filled with stars and a sharp pain jabbed through my head as I swayed and staggered. I reached for the cigarette a second time and touched the black, sooty ash. It was warm, and as I held it up to the lamplight, I could see it was un-tipped.

Whether it was linked to whoever attacked me, I had no idea, and I was in no fit state to think clearly. But I knew it wasn't a random attack. I hadn't been robbed, and crimes of this kind were rare in this part of Crossways. It felt like a warning or some sort of retribution. *But for what?*

I was starting to feel dizzy again, and the hotel was a couple of miles away. There hadn't been any passing traffic, so I began to make my way back to the only place I could think of.

I woke with a splitting headache, and it took me a while to work out where I was and how I'd got there. You don't see

BREAKING POINT

your ex-wife for almost five years and then twice in one night.

She'd wanted to take me to A&E, but I explained how impractical that was with Paul asleep upstairs. After cleaning my cuts and bruises, she let me sleep on the settee. I was grateful, the last thing I needed was lost time in a hospital bed.

I felt like I'd been run over by a truck as I pulled the blanket aside and raised myself to look at the clock. It was 5:30 in the morning. There was a brass band playing in my head, and every joint in my body was aching. *Slowly, slowly,* I said to myself. *Don't disgrace yourself and throw up on the carpet.*

I reached over to a table lamp and switched it on. The light stung the back of my eyes, and my head exploded in pain, causing me to cover my face with my hands until I could acclimatise. When I managed to sit upright, I looked around the living room and tried to take stock. So much had altered and yet everything felt so familiar. Convincing myself to stand, I realised I was still dressed in last night's clothes. Then everything came back to me.

It was still dark outside, and the sun wouldn't rise for at least another hour, but my eyes were becoming accustomed to the light. Wrapping the blanket around my shoulders, I wandered around the room in a daze; I needed a drink of water. On my way to the kitchen, my eyes were drawn to a photograph on the television. It was Paul in his school uniform. He was collecting a prize, and his mother was with him, surrounded by lots of other parents and children. I couldn't help smiling; he was such a lovely boy.

On the mantelpiece was another photograph, smaller and more discreet. I was surprised to see it was the four of us; Julie, myself, Paul and Alex. I picked it up to look more closely, trying to work out where and when it was taken.

'Who are you?' The strange voice jolted me.

I turned to see Paul, bleary-eyed and rumpled; his hair an untidy mop. He wiped his eyes with the back of his hand.

'Erm… hello, Paul,' I said, trying not to frighten him.

Wrapped in a blanket with crumpled clothing and bloodstains, I must have looked like an escaped convict.

'Your mother let me stay on the sofa last night.'

He pointed to my bandage. 'What happened to your head?'

I touched it, feeling embarrassed. 'Oh, it's nothing, I had an accident.'

'How do you know my name?' he asked.

I was close to panic and couldn't take my eyes from him. The room was filled with a dreadful silence.

'I'm your dad, Paul.'

The landing light switched on, and Julie appeared on the stairs, unkempt hair and wrapped in a lumpy dressing gown. It was apparent she'd rushed from her bed in a panic.

'You're up early, son.' Her voice was croaky from the wine, and she was looking at me as though I was an intruder. 'Why don't you go back upstairs, you've got school in the morning.'

He hadn't taken his eyes from me. 'Where have you been?' he said.

The innocence of the question filled me with despair, and I had to sit. I looked over to Julie, but she turned her head away.

'I'll make a cup of tea,' she said. 'I think we'll need it.'

I wrung my hands, ignoring the thumping in my head. 'It's a long story, Paul, I…'

He stopped me in my tracks. 'Did I do something wrong?'

I looked away from him and saw my reflection in the blank television screen. I couldn't help thinking of my father.

BREAKING POINT

'You did nothing wrong, son. After your brother's...' I tried to think of a suitable word. 'After your brother's accident, I wasn't a very nice person to be around.'

'I remember you cried a lot,' he said, sitting on the sofa opposite me. I thought my heart was about to burst.

Julie came in with a tray of tea and toast. She laid it on the coffee table and sat next to Paul as I continued.

'It was a difficult time for us all, Paul. It's just that you and your mother were... erm... stronger than me.' I looked over at Julie, she was close to tears, her hands coupled around a mug of tea. 'I didn't treat you both as well as I should have. That wasn't fair, and I'm sorry.'

'What happened to your head?' he asked again, biting into a slice of toast.

'I tripped over on my way to the hotel.'

'How did you end up here?'

'A lot of questions from a tired little boy,' said Julie, at last coming to my rescue. 'Now I think a couple more sips of tea then an early shower.'

'Are you going back to South Africa?' he asked.

I nodded, engulfed in shame and barely able to speak. 'I have to, son.'

His face remained impassive as he took another slice of toast and disappeared upstairs.

'What's going on over there?' Julie was looking at me through the steam rising from her teacup.

'I thought John would have kept you updated.' I replied and immediately wanted to take the words back. But it was too late.

'Don't you dare!' She snapped. 'John's been a good friend since you...' She bit off the last word as Paul reappeared in the hallway carrying a book.

'I've been keeping this to show you,' he said. 'Next time you came home.' He passed it over for me to look at.

It was a scrapbook. And as I flicked through the pages, I realised that every birthday and Christmas card I'd sent since I left, had been meticulously taped to the separate sheets. Above each card, in increasingly mature handwriting, he'd written, *From daddy*... along with the date it had been delivered. Even the envelopes, with my uneven writing and South African stamps, were preserved. I looked over at Julie, struggling to keep things together.

'He won't let anyone touch it,' she said.

His eyes moved from me to the book and back. I took his hand and drew him to me. He was soft and smelt of sleep and buttered toast.

'I promise I won't stay away so long next time,' I said as he wrapped his arms around me. I choked back my emotions, praying I could keep my pledge.

'Come on then, upstairs,' said his mother. 'Have a quick shower.'

He took the book and skipped up the stairs. Julie turned on me and whispered, menacingly. 'It's none of your business who I see, and don't you dare get sarcastic with me.'

'I didn't mean it that way,' I said.' John's a good bloke, and I wouldn't dare interfere. I just…' The words wouldn't come, and I couldn't summon up the energy to find them.

'I don't know what I'm saying any more. I just want to see a bit of Paul.'

She calmed a little.

'You're in trouble, aren't you?' she nodded at my hands as I picked at my fingernails. 'I can still read you, Danny Core.'

I stopped, embarrassed by my transparency. 'I'm investigating an accident that killed nine men.'

Her eyes widened. 'How does that involve Mathers?'

'It doesn't at the moment, I'm just gathering information.'

'There's more to it than that,' she said. 'You're not telling me everything.'

'I could be charged with manslaughter when I get back.' I hated burdening her with my problems.

'Manslaughter!' She said. 'Are you serious?'

BREAKING POINT

I was back working on my fingernails. 'It's a long story, but that's how the law works in South Africa.

She took a sip from her cup. 'Could you end up in jail?' I nodded, and her face dropped.

'In South Africa?'

I nodded again.

'So, this could be the last time Paul will see you?' Her tone sounded incredulous, but it was the finality of the statement that brought everything into stark focus. I realised that by convincing myself I could prove my innocence, I hadn't considered the consequences of failure.

'You're making all these promises to him, but you may not be able to back them up. Could you really end up in jail?'

I nodded. 'It's a possibility,' I answered. 'But I'm…'

'Don't go back,' she interrupted.

Three words. An instant solution in one sentence. For a nanosecond, this lightning bolt of logic was my way out. *Why hadn't I considered it?* And then I remembered.

Good Luck… Van Heerden's words rang in my ears, and I believed in them. I couldn't hide away in clear sight; I wasn't a criminal.

'I have to, Julie. It's a long story, but I'm determined to clear my name.'

'Looks like you've made some enemies over here,' she nodded toward my head. 'Why would someone attack you?'

'I don't know.' I needed time to think it through.

'Do you think it's linked to the accident?' she asked.

It would be a hell of a coincidence if it wasn't, I thought. 'I don't think so,' I lied. 'Last night, you saw what people think of me, it would be a long queue of suspects, wouldn't it?'

She rolled her eyes. 'You're still okay for Paul's football match?'

I touched the bandage at the back of my ear. 'I'll be fine, will he be alright?'

'You saw him just now; I don't think he'll mind.'

She smiled, and I gave her a thumbs up. It was going to be a good day.

'Is he too old for me to help him get dressed?' I asked.

'By quite a few years,' she replied. 'But be my guest, it'll make a nice change.'

As I made my way to the door, she touched my arm. 'Don't make him promises you can't keep, Danny.'

Chapter 31

Deep underground, Piet Reiss was circling the front end of the MK6 Stabiliser. It was the fourth time he'd reviewed the dismantled carcass.

'What do they do, Boss?' The voice came from Chaka. He and another mineworker, Daniel, had been chosen to help Piet and Embele dismantle the MK6. Short and wiry with tightly cropped hair, Chaka was staring at the array of steel bearings lying on the concrete floor.

'I wish I knew,' Reiss replied, scratching his chin. After removing the front of the Stabiliser from the central, *smokestack* section, they were reviewing the components for the first time.

Four-inch diameter; they must be doing something significant, he thought. 'Are you sure about the count?' He spat on the ground as the three exhausted faces looked up at him. They'd counted them a dozen times at least.

'Twenty-four, Boss,' replied Embele. 'None missing.'

Reiss looked across at the bearings, lined up in four rows of six. Next to them were the matching nuts and bolts, laid out in two rows of twelve. He went through it one final time for the everyone's benefit.

'Bearings, twenty-four. Nuts, twenty-four. Bolts, twenty-four.' They nodded in agreement.

'None missing?' Embele's response was more of a question.

'Agreed, none missing,' Reiss repeated and made a final note in his book.

The rubber flange seal lay spread across the ground. It looked, almost inconsequential, against the metal body. They'd checked along its circumference for splits or cuts; anything that would have allowed the high-pressure water to leak. There were none.

Another dead end on a day full of them, thought Reiss.

Embele stood up. 'You want to take pictures of the bearings, Boss?' Piet nodded with no great enthusiasm.

Embele rolled them over one by one, looking for signs of damage. He found four cracked, and another two sheared in half. He separated them from the others and laid them in an orderly line.

'Take some photographs of these, Boss,' he said. 'Close up, to show the detail.'

Piet clicked away with the camera.

Embele moved over to the bolts and told Chaka and Daniel to help him separate the ones that were damaged. Within half an hour, they found six. Three were fractured, and another three stretched so badly they'd had to be removed with a flame cutter. He looked over at Reiss.

'And photographs of these, Boss?' It was put as a question but was more of an instruction.

He knows what he's doing, thought Reiss, and gave a thumbs up. The camera flashed with small explosions of light until he finally shut it down and returned it to its leather case.

Their work was done, and they all sat down, shattered. Reiss passed the cigarettes around to Chaka and Daniel and lit them. He took three long draws, sucking each into his lungs, the tip glowing red. After two minutes of silence, the smoke was still exhaling from his nostrils. He wiped the sweat from his forehead and stared at Embele.

'You seem to know what you're looking for. Is there anything that stands out?'

Embele pointed to the gallery of damaged components. 'Only those, Boss.'

'Not good, huh?' said Piet. 'Have you ever seen damage like that?'

Embele shook his head.

Piet took another drag on the cigarette. 'Do you think it was caused by the fall?'

Embele just shrugged.

BREAKING POINT

'Our Chief Engineer seems to think the pipework tells a story,' said Piet. 'Did you see anything down on 120 to make you think it wasn't a pressure burst?'

'Some things don't add up, Boss.'

'Mmm.' Another two drags and Reiss threw the cigarette aside.

Chaka looked across. 'Are we finished, Boss?'

'Ja, I guess so,' said Reiss. 'I'll report what we've seen and get these photographs developed and fax copies to the UK.' He looked across at Embele again. 'Are you all finished down here?'

Embele stood and stretched his back, extending his arms toward the hanging-wall. His hands were clenched into fists making the biceps and triceps of his upper arms bulge like swollen blisters. As he relaxed, he turned and pointed towards the second MK6.

'I think we should start it up, Boss.'

Chaka and Daniel lifted their heads to look at where he was pointing.

'No chance,' said Reiss. 'We've got strict instructions not to start-up any of the Stabilisers while this investigation is ongoing.'

Embele sighed, his hands now on his hips.

'Mmm, we may not have a better chance to prove it's okay, Boss. The shaft is empty.'

'And what about us?' replied Chaka.

'He's got a point,' said Reiss.

'Thanks, Boss,' said Chaka.

'I meant Embele.' Reiss smiled and turned back to him. 'What would it prove?'

Embele sighed again, looking toward the MK6. 'That Stabiliser feeds the Water Cooling Plant down on 140 East. If I go down there and switch the plant on, I can check for vibration or any other effects to the pipe system.'

Chaka and Daniel were shaking their heads.

'And if everything was working alright, we could eliminate the MK6 as a cause for the collapse?' asked Reiss, noticing the doubts from the other two mineworkers

'Mmm, maybe.'

'Well, none of us here are convinced there's a problem with the Stabiliser.' Reiss looked at the others. 'So the risk is low.'

'Agreed, Boss,' said Embele. 'And we'll get an idea of how the pipes cope with the flow.'

'Okay, we'll do it,' said Reiss.

Embele wasn't finished. 'We'll need to shut the cooling plant down at some point.'

'Why?' asked Reiss.

'To see if the failsafe switches do their job and divert the high-pressure water.' Embele spat on the ground; the conversation was finished.

Reiss was impressed. 'That's a bloody good idea, we'll make an engineer out of you, yet.'

The big man looked uncomfortable with the compliment.

'Boss Core said that's what caused the fall.'

Reiss smiled. 'Sounds like he's got a convert.' He looked at his watch. 'Chaka, Daniel, you stay here and switch the Stabiliser on in one hour, that'll give us time to get to the Plant.'

Reiss saw the confusion on Embele's face. 'I'm coming with you,' he said, 'I want to see the effect for myself.'

Embele shrugged his shoulders and turned to the others.

'Run it for exactly forty-five minutes, during that time we'll switch on the cooling plant for fifteen minutes and see how everything's working. When we switch it off, you should see the water pressure start to drop…'

Piet interrupted. 'You should also hear the flow redirected through the exhaust system and into the auxiliary pipe network. If you don't, and the pressure gauges start to rise, switch the Stabiliser off immediately.'

'You got that?' said Embele.

BREAKING POINT

Chaka checked his watch. 'Okay. We switch on, one hour from now.'

'Report back to me on the surface,' Piet shouted over his shoulder as he and Embele made their way to the ventilation shaft.

And within the eerily silent chamber, Chaka and Daniel disappeared in the opposite direction toward the MK6.

Chapter 32

I arrived back at the hotel about 10:30am and was surprised to see Steyn sitting in the resident's bar having a coffee.

'What the hell happened to you?' he said, looking like he needed the caffeine.

'Cut myself shaving,' I replied.

'Cut the crap, that's not even funny. What happened?'

'Sorry,' I said. 'I was walking back to the hotel last night, and someone tried to crack my skull.' I winced as I rubbed the bandage.

'Did you see who it was?'

I sat at the table. 'No, it was dark, and he hit me from behind.'

'Christ, that's serious, man. Did you report it?'

'Not yet,' I looked at my watch. 'Why aren't you at Mathers?'

He pointed over my shoulder and raised his eyebrows. I turned around and saw John approaching. He was walked unsteadily and looked like he'd slept in his clothes.

I turned back to Steyn. 'Bloody hell, what did you two get up to last night?'

John sat between us. 'Sorry I'm late, can I have one of those?' he pointed to the coffee.

Steyn ignored him, so I poured a cup. He gulped it down noisily and asked for another, which went down as greedily.

'Ahh, that's better.' He wiped his sleeve across his mouth and looked up at me for the first time. 'What happened to you?'

'Someone attacked me last night.'

'Any idea who did it?'

'No, it was dark.'

'There's a bit of it going on at the moment,' he replied. 'Did he take anything?'

BREAKING POINT

'No, I think it was personal.'

'Where did it happen?' he asked.

I held my breath a little. 'The top of town, I'd decided to go for a walk.' He nodded his head.

'Where did you disappear to last night?' Steyn was tapping his fingers on the table, looking directly at John.

I looked across at both of them. 'I thought you were both together?'

John looked up, sheepishly. 'Yeah, sorry about last night, Steyn. I was out of order.'

Steyn shrugged and grunted.

'What's going on?' I asked.

John was going to say something, but Steyn got in first.

'It was nothing. Socket turned up at the club and managed to stir up an argument. John got a little wound up, and we ended up going home separately. Apart from that, it was a good night. Right, John?'

He nodded his head without enthusiasm.

'Can you hang around a while for me to change?' I needed to clean myself up.

He looked at his watch. 'Fine, but I can't stop for too long; they'll be wondering where we are.'

'I'll cover for you,' Steyn interrupted. 'While Danny freshens up, I'll get some more coffee. You look like you need it.'

'I'm okay thanks.'

'No, I insist,' said Steyn, and he made his way to the counter.

'I won't be long,' I said and turned to make my way back to the room.

'You saw Julie last night.'

John's comment wasn't a question and stopped me in my tracks. I turned back around.

'How do you know that?'

'She told me yesterday.' He was looking down at the table, his hands wrapped around the empty coffee cup. 'Why do you think I agreed to take Steyn out.'

He looked up at me, his face rigid as though it was an effort to stay calm.

'Any problem with that?' I asked.

He shook his head.

'Good.' I made my way back to the room.

Steyn returned to the table. 'Are you okay?'

'Yeah, fine,' John answered.

Steyn poured two cups. 'Black?'

John nodded, and they drank in silence. After they finished, John looked at his watch again. 'We need to be making tracks soon.'

Steyn leant back in his chair. 'I think we need to talk, don't you?'

'About what?'

Steyn saw the nervousness in John's fingers as they tapped haphazardly on the tablecloth. 'You didn't answer my question earlier, where did you disappear to last night?'

'Yeah, I didn't mean to leave you high and dry. Can't remember much about it, to be honest.' He smiled and made a drinking motion with his hand. 'We both had a few too many.'

'Did you go home?' asked Steyn.

'Yeah, like I say…'

'To Julie's.' Steyn's question drew the blood from John's face.

'Julie's? No, I went back to my house. Why would I…' There was a delayed reaction.

'Hang on. You don't think I had anything to do with what happened to Danny.'

Steyn tried to read his face. 'You seemed to think he was enough of a threat last night.'

'That was just the drink talking, I seem to remember you talking a load of crap as well.'

Steyn saw his neck flush with patches of red skin. He was getting angry… again. John stood.

BREAKING POINT

'I'll arrange for one of the other engineers to come and pick you up, I don't think my presence is helping.' He turned and walked toward the exit.

'Wait!' Steyn stood up and followed him.

John stopped and turned around. 'You really think I could be capable of doing that to Danny?' his breath stank of stale beer.

Steyn looked down at the floor. 'Sorry, it's just that…'

'Just what? I've just said that I knew he was meeting Julie last night, why would I implicate myself like that?'

Steyn looked up at him. 'You're right, I just thought…'

'Thought what? That I'd be so jealous, I'd attack him with a golf club?'

'You're right, I think my mind's muddled after all that beer. No hard feelings?' Steyn held out his hand.

John shook it with no enthusiasm, then smiled.

'I'm looking forward to seeing Socket's face when I give him the expense sheet.'

'You must admit, it's a peculiar situation with you and Danny's ex-wife?' Steyn knew the question was uncomfortable and, on cue, John's smile disappeared.

'Julie and I have talked about how to break the news to Danny, but it wasn't a priority when he was in South Africa. I never meant it to come out so suddenly, but I didn't want him finding out from someone else.'

'Like Socket, you mean?'

'There were already rumours,' John said.

'Are you serious about her?'

He looked at Steyn directly, his broken nose reddened over the scar tissue. 'What do you think?'

'And his son, how does he feel about things?'

John looked at Steyn, and for a moment seemed like he wasn't going to reply; that Steyn had crossed a line.

'He's a good kid, he's been brought up properly, and he talks about Danny a lot.'

'Asks lots of questions?' Steyn knew this was an uncomfortable conversation, but he wanted to probe as far as he could.

'What, like you, you mean?'

'I'm only asking for Danny's benefit,' said Steyn.

'Yeah, well I think Danny can ask for himself, don't you?'

'Hey!' I called out to both of them from the resident's bar. 'You two sharing secrets from last night?'

They joined me at a table, and we began talking about Mathers and the MK6 development. John seemed transparent, considering his involvement, and I wondered if the hangover had loosened his tongue.

'It was obvious the cost-saving targets were out of reach,' he said. 'I knew it, Jack Smelt knew it and Socket too; except he kept quiet.'

'Typical,' I said. 'Was that why you were taken off the team?'

John smiled back at me. 'I aired my doubts and Terry didn't like it; he said my presentations lacked enthusiasm. But there were other reasons behind the decision, I knew Stremsen was putting pressure on Jack to drop me.'

'But the MK6 project was a success?' I asked.

John looked up at the ceiling and shook his head.

'It's in Stremsen's interests to present anything that runs through the PMT as a phenomenal success; plus, he gets a very nice bonus out of it. Targets were being manipulated, and most of the team were demoralised, desperate to follow me out. Then at the eleventh hour, the project achieved its targets; no one working on the project could believe it.'

'Are they hiding something?' Steyn was on my wavelength.

'I can't say,' said John, his eyes moving between us. 'I wasn't close enough, and Jack had left.

'How *did* they achieve it?' I asked.

BREAKING POINT

He leaned forward on his elbows, looking keen to release his frustrations.

'The MK5 project was all about cheap supply from low-cost countries, and we smashed the targets with minimal redesign. I'm sure if Jack had his time again, he'd have reined it back.'

'What do you mean?' I asked.

'It made a hero of Stremsen and his PMT process, and raised expectations on all future projects.'

John leaned further forward as though someone might overhear. 'You know how critical the quality of the parts is?'

'Yes, of course.'

'Well some of the "*cheaper*"...', he did that annoying thing with his fingers, '...components on the MK5 didn't perform well. We had a lot of complaints from customers, and we ended up going back to a lot of our original suppliers.'

'I bet they loved that?' Steyn said.

John smiled. 'Yeah, they doubled the original price.'

'So the cost of the MK5 started to rise again, how did they take that?' asked Steyn.

'No one cared,' said John. 'The project was complete; all eyes were already on the MK6 Project. Stremsen put a smokescreen around the whole thing.'

Now I leaned forward, we were like a trio of spies.

'So what sort of *issues* did you have with the MK6?'

He looked at me warily. 'Sorry, Danny, I know where you want this to go, but the difficulties weren't serious; certainly not on the scale of those at Rinto Gold.'

I needed to question the points he was making.

'So how was the MK6 a success, if it was late at every stage?'

John smiled at my question. 'Because it achieved its cost reduction target.'

'But you said all the fat had been trimmed with the MK5?'

He seemed to stall a little before continuing.

'That's why Jack had to look at serious design changes to try and find the savings.'

'Does that explain the modified bolting pattern?' I asked.

John nodded and gulped his coffee.

'And the revised shape to facilitate the bearings,' he added.

'Ah, the steel bearings,' I said. 'I saw those in the racks when we were shown around the assembly department. I wondered what they were for.'

John began sketching on a paper napkin.

'It was really innovative. The bearings are in a circular pattern but concealed inside the flanges. The bolts manage the tensile forces, and the bearings take care of the shear forces. I'd like to say it was my idea, but it was all Jack's.'

'It's brilliant,' I said.

'And a major step forward in reducing the costs,' John continued. 'The bearings are a fraction of the price of the nuts and bolts.'

'How big are they?' asked Steyn.

'Ten centimetres in diameter,' John grinned. 'We say steel, but they're actually Super Duplex 198, a non-magnetic stainless steel. Great shear strength properties and corrosion resistance, though you wouldn't want to drop one on your toe.'

'Sounds expensive,' Steyn said.

John's voice seemed to lower. 'Well that's the thing, it's only used in the aerospace industry so you can imagine it's not cheap. We looked to India and China, but the special nature of the product still made the prices prohibitive.'

'So, what happened?' I said, still not sure where all this was going.

'Stremsen happened, that's what. He gets one of his machining suppliers in America to supply them.'

'You said a *machining supplier?*' Steyn again.

BREAKING POINT

'Yes, Machine Inc., based in Houston. They have some kind of relationship with a Mexican foundry, which supplied the raw material cheaper than anywhere else in the world.'

'And all the material certification?' I asked wide-eyed.

'Yes, full traceability. The overall outlay was reduced dramatically. The bearings were good quality and easier to install, so we made savings on the assembly time as well. And, *voila*, the cost-saving objectives were met.'

I looked at the sketch, trying to transform it into the Stabiliser. 'Did anyone question how it was achieved?'

John smiled. 'Jack had gone, and the rest of the team were demoralised. Why would they question it? It was the only part of the project they achieved their bonus.'

I looked at my watch, it was 11:30 and time was moving on. All this information was whetting my appetite, and I was keen to get back to work on the calculations. My stomach was telling me I hadn't eaten, but I could get some chocolate from the dispenser on my way back to the room.

I looked at John. 'Can you take Steyn in with you this morning? With all that went on last night, I need some time to check out the reports.'

I rubbed the bandage at the back of my ear, my head was throbbing like hell.

'If I can help, Danny, let me know,' John replied.

'I will. You okay with that, Steyn?'

'Sure, I'll have a sniff around and see what I can find out. I promised I'd get those files back to Billy Jones today, they'll be pissed if they find out he gave them to me.'

'I'll do my best to get them back to you today,' I said and walked them both out to the car park.

John had brought his own car from last night, the same old banger he had when I left five years ago.

'When are you going to replace this wreck?' I asked jokingly as Steyn got into the passenger seat.

'I only got it back on the road yesterday,' he said, stroking the bonnet.

'I hope you don't run my family around in an old jalopy like this.' I whispered in his ear.

He smiled back at me, looking embarrassed. 'Thanks, Danny.'

'They say it's the hardest thing to love someone else's child,' I said.

'I'm not so sure about that,' he replied and slipped behind the wheel.

BREAKING POINT

Chapter 33

I was in a building, surrounded by flames. Across the room, a woman was holding a baby. I shouted something to her, but she couldn't hear me over the screeching of a fire alarm.

She was wearing a white, silk dressing gown and clutching the child, shouting something at me. But as much as I tried, I couldn't move my legs, couldn't hear what she was saying.

'Reach over,' I cried out, but the words stuck in my throat. My arms hung limply. The alarm continued blaring, piercing my ears, then the floor gave way. I reached out for something to hold and woke with a start, biting my tongue. My heart was pounding.

The telephone rang next to me, but it took a couple of seconds to disengage from the dream. I grabbed for the phone in a cold sweat and winced as my shoulder reminded me of the damage done last night. My eyes felt like they'd been super-glued and I rubbed them with my spare hand, creating a galaxy of stars, flashing around in a pitch-black space.

'Hello…' I croaked, coughing to clear my throat. 'Hello?'

There was an unmistakeable hiss on the other end of the line as a delay kicked in. A shiver ran through me… *an overseas call.*

My eyes began to focus, and I looked around. The sun was glaring through the open curtains onto a room scattered with a mess of papers and notes. I couldn't get the girl with the baby out of my mind.

'Mr Core?' I froze. The voice seeped out of the receiver like audible syrup. I don't think my blood pressure had dropped from critical since my last meeting with Van Heerden, and here he was again, sounding like a blackmailer about to issue his terms.

Ian Holland

I sat on the edge of the settee, and a folder slipped from my lap, thumping to the floor. Looking at my watch, it was 4:30pm UK time, 5:30pm in Johannesburg. *Van Heerden was working late.*

'I hope you can hear me, Mr Core.'

He knew damn well I could hear him. More hissing.

'Mr Van,' I said. 'Good to hear from you.' *Even he wouldn't buy that one.*

'I've been waiting for an update on your progress,' he said. 'I hope the delay is a good sign.'

I held back, making sure he'd finished his sentence, otherwise we'd be tripping over each other with the phone delay. More importantly, it gave me time to think.

'It was a long day yesterday, Mr Van, and I believe there are issues that Mathers haven't addressed.'

The delay stretched out; he was thinking. 'What sort of issues?'

'They're only giving me access to what suits them.'

'That's not ethical. Do you have proof that Mathers is withholding information?'

I needed to be tactful until I knew more. 'Not yet, but I have found some anomalies in the new design that haven't been explained.'

A long silence followed, which I tried to fill.

'They've invited me over to America to discuss the issues with their CEO.'

Hissing and crackling bled through the phone like an alien intelligence about to make contact, but no response.

'Mr Van, can you hear me?'

'Perfectly, Mr Core.' His voice had chilled a few degrees. 'Tell me, what would be gained by wasting your time on a trip to America?' I was about to tell him but realised it was a rhetorical question. 'For whatever reason, it's a delaying tactic and will have no bearing on finding out the truth. Do you agree?'

'Yes,' I said, embarrassed that I'd even considered it. I could hear him breathing on the other end of the line and imagined him staring outside the office window, carefully constructing the next sentence.

'Did you sanction the dismantling of one of the Recycling Stabilisers near the site of the accident?'

How the hell did he know about that? I thought.

'Erm, yes, I did. I wanted to…'

He wasn't allowing me to finish. 'And has anything been revealed?'

'It should be completed soon,' I bluffed. 'And I hope to get the report by tomorrow. I know I should have made you aware…'

'If nothing is found, you will have jeopardised your position even further.' His voice was getting sharper. 'Are you still convinced that the Stabiliser is implicated in this accident?'

His tone seemed to give away doubts. 'Yes,' I said.

'And you have gathered enough evidence to prove that?'

I paused, thought about the question… and lied.

'Yes.'

'And, your Mine Captain agrees with you?'

I paused… and lied again.

'Yes.'

'Are you being truthful with me, Mr Core?'

I paused… and sold my soul to the devil. 'Yes.'

'Very well, then I see no reason to waste further time in the UK. I have already had the police authorities knocking on my door, asking for additional information, so time is of the essence. This deadline, in five days, is non-negotiable. You have my support up to that point, but, while you are still an employee of Rinto Gold, you will now follow my instructions. We have further work to do over here.'

I imagined him standing upright, perfectly dressed, his features hard as flint. I was about to agree with him, but he didn't give me time.

'You will return to South Africa immediately with your findings, and invite the main players from Mathers to join you. Rinto Gold will cover the costs, but no more than three people, and they must be decision-makers. I will invite the CEO of Heron, which should provide us with a quorum. The meeting will bring this process to a close.'

Now it was my turn to go quiet. Was this a sign that Van Heerden was supporting me, or that he wanted witnesses for the prosecution? I was about to say something to that effect, but this was a one-way conversation.

'We are six thousand feet above sea level, here in Johannesburg, and I believe we should maintain the high ground,' he continued. 'We will assemble everyone here in the Transvaal and make our introductions. I expect you to brief me beforehand when you come over. The following morning, the company jet will transfer us all to Concorde IV, where I will chair the main meeting. Our secretaries will ensure a room is made available. You will present your evidence, they will present theirs, and we will conclude this matter once and for all.'

It's strange, but, perversely, I felt relieved that someone else was making the decisions.

There was more static and a long delay.

'Are we clear about our responsibilities?'

'Yes,' I said, wondering how I was going to get proof with so little time left. Then he surprised me.

'I hope you've found your chicken, Mr Core?'

I thought I sensed a smile behind the comment, but the phone went dead.

I put the receiver down and tried to excuse the culpability of the lies I'd told him, but there wasn't enough time.

BREAKING POINT

Chapter 34

Almost immediately, the phone rang again. It was Steyn, and it wasn't good news.

'There's been another collapse on Concorde IV, Danny.'

I couldn't believe it.

'Where?' I said, wondering if the world was conspiring against me.

'140 East.'

'Was anyone injured?' I braced myself.

'Looks like Piet and Embele got caught up in it, but it wasn't a major fall. Apart from some cuts and bruises, they're both fine.'

'Thank God for that, did they explain how it happened? Was it an aftershock?'

There was an ominous silence on the other end of the line.

'Steyn?

'Erm, it seems they were carrying out their own investigation.'

'That's all I need, more men putting their lives at risk. What were they up to?'

More silence.

'Steyn?'

'They decided to start-up the second MK6.'

'What the hell... Against my orders!'

'Hang on, Danny, hear me out. They may have done us a favour.'

'What do you mean, a favour?'

I was scratching the raw patch of skin that had broken out on the top of my left hand.

'Well...' I heard him draw on his cigarette. 'They got two of the guys on the team to start-up, while they went down to 140 East and switched on the Water Cooling Plant.'

'What was the point of that, they could have brought down...'

'I'm coming to that, Danny. Once the Plant was up to speed, Embele performed an emergency shutdown to see how the Stabiliser would react. The two guys at the MK6 were told to verify that the failsafe switches had operated.'

I was beginning to realise Embele was behind this, he was testing out the scenario we'd spoken about. Although he'd shown no enthusiasm for my theory, he was testing it anyway. *Still waters ran deep, with Embele Ngozi.*

'And did they?' I asked.

'Did they what?' asked Steyn.

'Did the switches redirect the water?'

'No, that's how they knew something was wrong. The pressure gauges were going into the red, and the vibrations getting worse. Water was leaking from the seals, and the pipes were trying to rip themselves away from the brackets. They knew something was wrong and switched it off immediately.'

'How long was it between shutting down the plant and switching off the MK6?'

'They reckon, at least fifteen minutes.'

'Christ, the pressure could have pulled the whole system apart during that time. The whiplash effect on the pipes down on 140 would have made it a hundred times worse. It's a wonder no one was killed.'

'That's exactly what happened, Danny. Piet said the pipework started to shake violently, damaging the supports and making the hanging-wall unstable. If those supports hadn't held...' The unfinished sentence said it all.

'How did he sound?' I asked.

'A bit shaken up. They knew what was happening, but hadn't planned an escape route. Piet said they just ran like hell. The damage was kept to a minimum because of the other guys intervention.'

'How did Piet and Embele get away?' I couldn't believe they'd put themselves at risk like that.

BREAKING POINT

'Luckily for them, there was a pump station nearby,' said Steyn. 'They reached it before the collapse. It was nowhere near as dangerous as the fall on 120, but it could have been nasty.

'If they hadn't switched the Stabiliser off when he did,' I said. 'We could have had a major collapse like...' I couldn't believe it. 'Bloody hell, was it only nine days ago?'

Steyn nodded. 'Ja, seems like weeks ago.'

It didn't bear thinking about. I asked him to pass on my best wishes to both of the men and smiled.

'Tell them to expect a bollocking when I see them; gross misconduct.'

Then I remembered the reason for their trip. 'Ask Piet to fax over all the photographs they've taken so far, but tell him to use the hotel's fax number.'

I was becoming paranoid that anything sent to me via Mathers would be intercepted. More than ever, I was convinced that the Stabiliser was flawed, but I was running out of time to find the proof.

I put the phone down and surveyed the detritus from a night and day of snacking on chocolate bars, trying to get my head around the calculations for the MK6. I'd been asleep for over an hour, and my stomach felt like it was full of cement. I decided to have a shower to wake myself up.

I closed my eyes as the water splashed around me, doing my best to keep the bandage from getting wet. The water stung my knees, where they were scraped raw from the previous night, and there was a nasty bruise on my shoulder, which made any movement with my right arm stiff and painful. I think I got off lightly... maybe more lightly than my attacker, who would be nursing a seriously sore leg.

The sound of the water was soothing, and the heat relaxed the tension in my shoulders. I was alone with my thoughts and examined what I'd found out.

Ian Holland

The two folders Fred Stremsen had given me were worthless and contained the barest of information; mostly photocopies from published books. Considering the amount of secrecy involved, I'd expected the calculation sheets Steyn had given me, to reveal something. But I'd been disappointed and could find nothing suspicious.

The material certificates were in order. The metals were traceable back to the foundry that processed them, and the test results were as they should have been.

The Mexican foundry was called *Almeja Fundicion*. I'd never heard of them before, but I'd made a note for reference; it was unlikely I'd have the time to investigate further. I was quickly running out of options.

I squeezed the water from my eyes and looked at the shower pipe leading down from the ceiling, imagining the rate of flow from the main supply. The restriction through the heating elements and the final release through the showerhead... *I'd become obsessed with analysis.*

With so many calculations going round in my head, I needed to get out. I switched the shower off, and the water stopped with an audible *thump* transmitted through the piping.

Exactly how the Stabiliser should have reacted, I thought. Once the *dead man's handles* were released, the flow should have stopped immediately.

I restarted the shower, and cold water spat out, making me catch my breath. I switched it off, and again it stopped with a *thump*.

I switched it on once more, this time avoiding the cold spray, and put my finger on the supply pipe bracketed to the wall. I switched the shower off for a third time, and again there was a *thump*. This time I was able to feel the force pull at the pipe, as it reacted against the back-pressure created by the instant shut-off.

It was a microcosm of how the fail-safe switches should have worked. Without brackets, the pipe would flex and compromise the joints, just like the piping from the

BREAKING POINT

Stabiliser. Tensile forces pulling along the length and shear forces across the diameter.

Shear forces across the diameter... that's what I'd missed!

The forces on the MK6 would be at their most critical when the failsafe switches sensed the rise in back-pressure and redirected the high-pressure flow to the exhaust system. It would create the same *thump* I'd felt in the shower, only a thousand times more powerful.

I opened the shower door and grabbed a towel to dry myself. Stepping back into the bedroom, I tied it around my waist and clasped the test certificate folder that Steyn had given me.

Sifting through the specification sheets, I located those relating to the bearing material and scrambled through the calculation folder. My fingers were clumsy in their haste to find what I wanted; the calculation sheets relating to the bearings.

I laid both sets on the bed, side by side. My heart was racing. Were the tensile strength values, used to determine the strength of the bearings, the same as those on the material specification sheets?

It took me three checks before I could believe what I was looking at, but sure enough, they were the same figures.

And that's when I finally had proof that the MK6 Stabiliser calculations were flawed.

Chapter 35

'**What the hell's** going on over there, Luca?'

Rik Last was pacing his office floor, catching his reflected profile in Uncle Billy's photograph. Luca's mind was still concentrating on the fax from South Africa Last had given him.

'You mean in South Africa, Rik?'

Last flicked his head around angrily.

Listen up, Majori. Likky piped up.

'In Mathers, Luca. In Mathers, for God's sake!'

Majori looked up, surprised at the sharpness of his tone.

There was tension in the old man's face, and it wasn't often he showed himself under pressure.

'Sorry, Rik, I was distracted. This fax looks less like an invitation and more like an order. Does this guy, Van Heerden, realise who he's dealing with?'

Last sat back down and smoothed his hair.

'It's obvious he's being briefed by Core. And I assume, from the tone, he believes we have some questions to answer, concerning the MK6.'

Likky was starting to cuss.

'This is getting out of control.' Last's hands were resting on his lap, but his fingers were twitching. He put the fax down and pointed at Majori.

'Luca, you're overseeing this investigation. What do we do next?'

'Leave it with me,' said Majori.

Last frowned back at him.

'And the trip to South Africa?'

'I'd recommend you take him up on his offer,' said Luca. 'With such a serious accident, it would look suspicious if you didn't.'

Suspicious! Likky again. *Years of excellence, and now we're looking suspicious because of Fred, fucking, Stremsen.*

BREAKING POINT

'I know it's not palatable, Rik, but…'

'Have we found out why the failsafe switches didn't work?' asked Last, impatience getting the better of him.

'I've asked Fred, and he believes that the severity of the collapse stopped them functioning.'

'Do we know that for certain?'

'I asked the same question, and he assured me that it would be impossible to prove otherwise. A visit by the Heron CEO will be a good public relations exercise and help develop our profile in Africa.'

Last looked up. 'We cooperated too much, too early, Luca. You know that, don't you?'

He was staring him in the eye.

That was your fucking call, Majori. Likky wasn't happy.

'I still think it was the right thing to do,' said Luca, looking less than convinced.

'Mmm, we'll see.' Last's gaze moved to the photograph on the wall. 'As long as I'm not going there to get caught up… behind enemy lines, so to speak.'

Majori shook his head.

'You're *absolutely* sure that Stremsen has this thing under control, Luca?'

'From what he's telling me, Rinto Gold has nothing to link the accident to the Stabiliser.'

'So be it then.'

A calm seemed to come over Last.

'Maybe it's about time we met up with Thys van Heerden; see if he's as spunky in the flesh. I want you to put together a short report with all the information we have so far. Don't copy anyone else for the moment, you can brief me when we leave.'

Luca's jaw dropped.

'When *we* leave? But the invitation is for you, Rik.'

Likky laughed out loud.

'I'll decide who the invitation is for Luca. Now pack your bags and have that report ready for me to read on the plane.'

BREAKING POINT

Chapter 36

I got a taxi to Mathers and met Steyn in the office next to the reception. It was 5:30, and apart from the afternoon shift on the shop floor, everyone had gone home. He looked like he was getting ready to leave.

'You look a bit rough,' I said.

'I'm alright,' though his eyes told a different story.

I wondered whether he had more bad news.

'You did say, *no serious injuries*?'

'No, no, everyone's fine, how's your head?' he touched behind his ear. 'No bandage?'

'It was a nuisance,' I said. 'I've put a couple of plasters on to stop it bleeding. I don't want it to become a talking point.'

He looked at the damage. 'Nasty... what the hell did he hit you with?'

'A golf club,' I said, almost giggling at the stupidity.

'Mmm, that narrows it down,' he said. 'Someone jealous of your handicap?'

I laughed out loud and was reminded that my jaw was still sore.

'You were lucky,' he said, his face expressionless.

'Doesn't feel like it.' The aspirins were starting to wear off.

'Let's get a coffee, we need to talk.' He led me toward the machine.

When I worked at Mathers, I loved this time of day. Everyone from the offices had gone home, and the phones fell silent; no distractions. I was optimistic after my shower, and the warmth of my old company enveloped me like a familiar friend. My body shivered with subdued excitement.

Steyn struggled with the *bloody stupid,* coins before finally winkling out two cups of black coffee, no sugar.

'Did John behave himself last night?' I asked.

Steyn thought about it for a moment.

'I can see what you mean about his temper.'

'He looked like he drank too much.'

'Ja, his mouth could get him into a lot of trouble.'

'He's a good bloke Steyn, he hasn't had it easy.'

'What do you mean?'

I thought back to John's family and him as a young boy.

'His old man was a bastard. He was a miner in the local pit and used to drink most of his wages every Thursday. He had a temper as well, and everyone in the village knew John took the brunt of it.'

'Beat him?' asked Steyn.

I nodded.

'It was a small community and difficult for his mother to hide the bruises.'

'Only him?' asked Steyn.

'He never laid a hand on his wife or John's sister. It was as though he was jealous of him.'

'What happened?' Steyn sipped his coffee.

'A group of miners had a word with him and, not long after, he disappeared.'

'They killed him!' Steyn nearly choked on his coffee; his eyes wide with shock.

I burst out laughing. 'Of course not, it wasn't Dodge City. They confronted him in work and made it clear that the whole village knew what was going on. Told him to tidy his act up or else.'

'Then they killed him?' He beamed an ironic smile.

I ignored his teasing. 'Rumour has it he took offence at the advice and ended up in the hospital.'

'Vigilantes?' asked Steyn.

'Maybe, but that's the way things were done then. The police knew what had gone on and turned a blind eye. Within a week of being discharged, he left the house and never came back. No forwarding address or anything.'

'What about his family?' asked Steyn.

'John's mother and sister were okay, they still had their council house, and she had a part-time job.'

'And John?'

'He was always difficult to read. Those years with his father must have been hard, but I think he missed him more than anyone realised.'

'Doesn't excuse him, Danny.'

'No... maybe not.'

As we stood there sipping at our coffees, I felt his eyes on me.

'What?' I asked.

'Were you up to something last night, to make someone attack you?'

I smiled at him and winced as the muscles in my jaw stretched and burned. 'Nothing in the way your dirty mind is thinking. And anyway, he didn't get away scot-free.'

'What do you mean?'

'I managed to stab the bastard in the leg. That's what made him run, or should I say limp.'

'Any idea who it was?' He pulled at the bandage on his injured hand.

'Not really,' I said. 'I've got my suspicions, but no proof.'

'Want to share?'

'No, not without evidence.'

'Mmm...'

I sensed he was holding back on something. 'Is there something else on your mind?'

He fumbled with the bandage a little more, and I put my hand out to stop him.

'Steyn, if there's something you want to say?'

'How long have you known Dread?'

The question came out of the blue.

'Longer than I've known you, why?'

'Do you trust him?' He was looking uncomfortable.

'You're not suggesting he was behind last night,' I said.

'I'm not saying anything.' He'd gone back to his bandage. 'But he seemed pissed off about you returning to the UK.'

'That was just the drink talking. He's not capable...'

'What time did you get attacked?' he interrupted.

I thought back to last night.

'About 11.30.'

'He had plenty of time after he disappeared from...'

I held up my hands. 'Please Steyn, don't go there. We've got bigger issues at the moment.'

We said nothing for several minutes until I broke the impasse. 'I think I might have some good news.'

'Mmm, I thought you looked happier. What's happened?'

I slurped my coffee and told him we'd be leaving sooner than planned, now two of us were in higher spirits than yesterday.

'When?' he said, barely able to conceal his relief.

'Van Heerden has told us to return immediately. He wants me to invite some Mathers people to a meeting at Concorde IV.'

'Good luck with that. Who are you going to invite?'

'I'll get Stremsen and Socket to come along.'

'What makes you think they'll say yes?'

'I don't think they'll have a choice.' And I told him more about my conversation with Van Heerden.

When I'd finished, he looked puzzled.

'Christ, how does that make you feel happier, we have no evidence?'

'I've found a flaw in the calculations for the MK6,' I said, tingling with the hope generated by that simple sentence.

Steyn became more animated. 'Enough to get you off the hook?'

'I'm not sure, but it's enough for me to question the changes.'

'So, what do we do next?'

BREAKING POINT

I hadn't thought it through, but first I needed to confront Stremsen and Socket with the information.

'It'll mean exposing Billy Jones,' I said. 'They won't be pleased he gave us the folders.'

'Tough, 'Steyn replied, 'they told us... *all of our documentation is ready and waiting for you to look at*. And they lied.'

He was right, of course.

'Any news from Piet and Embele?' I asked.

'Nothing yet, have the photographs arrived?'

'Not when I left the hotel,' I said. 'It'll be interesting to see if any of the bearings are missing.'

He looked confused. 'Missing?'

I threw my empty cup into the bin. 'When we were taken around the site, did you notice the way they assembled the flanges?'

'Yes. So what?'

'Before MK6, the assembly process only used high tensile bolts, so it was evident if one was missing.'

'Sure,' he said. 'Bloody obvious.'

'But what if a steel bearing was missing, how would you know?'

Steyn thought. 'They'd have a bearing left over after assembly,' he answered.

'They would if they allocated the exact number of bearings,' I said. 'But they don't, they pull them out of racks, central locations, so they don't get counted out.'

'So they're relying on the skill of the assembler,' said Steyn.

'That's right,' I agreed, 'but mistakes happen.'

'Do you think that could be the problem with the MK6 on Concorde IV?'

'I don't want to get too far ahead of myself, let's see what Piet and Embele have found first. We can discuss it with Stremsen's team once we know the facts.'

Steyn was writing reminders on the back of his hand. Even though this was out of his comfort zone, he was learning fast. I suggested he made his way back to the hotel to see if the photographs had arrived.

'Maybe give Piet a ring, and I'll join you later.'

'I'll get on to it,' he said. But didn't move.

'Anything else?' I asked.

He was looking away in the distance, clumsily rubbing his bandage.

'I was talking to Dawn, and she was telling me about you and… erm… your family.'

I went cold. I'd been concentrating on so many things over the past few days…

'I should have told you,' I was embarrassed at my pathetic response.

'No, man, I understand.' He was trying to make light of it, but I saw the hurt on his face.

I pointed to two chairs and asked him to sit with me. It took a while to think through what I wanted to say, and with each second, I was aware of him watching.

'You don't have to…' he began, but I stopped him.

'Ever since I arrived in South Africa, you've been like a brother to me, Steyn. I should have told you… should have prepared you. I just couldn't…'

'You know you could have trusted me, Danny?' he looked upset.

'I'd trust you with my life, but that wasn't the reason I didn't say anything.'

'What do you mean?'

I looked at him and put my hand on his shoulder. 'I'm ashamed of the person I was back then.' The words barely escaped my mouth, and I was already struggling to hold things together… *two deep breaths.*

'My son didn't deserve to have his life cut short like that.' *More deep breaths.*

'I took away everything he had to look forward to… his whole future lay ahead and…'

Steyn grabbed my arm with his bandaged hand.

BREAKING POINT

'Shame doesn't come into it, man. It was an accident, a tragic accident. You can't blame yourself.'

I couldn't contain my emotions any longer. I'd barely managed to stifle the memory and close my eyes to the images, but now they spilt like blood from a mortal wound. Over the last five years, my mind had tried to purge the emptiness and self-loathing, but I wouldn't let it. Not unless it could bring my son back.

My body was shaking, and I was sobbing uncontrollably. I hated showing myself up like this and wondered what Steyn thought of it all… a grown man crying like a child.

I felt him pull me towards him; wrapping his arms around me as though absorbing my grief. His body was shaking, and I heard him sobbing against my shoulder.

'It's okay, Danny… it's alright,' he whispered.

And I held on to him, as though it was for life itself, knowing it never would be.

After Steyn left to make his way back to the hotel, I decided to visit the Centre of Excellence. I felt empty and needed quiet.

The entrance door was open, and the cleaning staff just finishing their chores before moving on to another part of the factory. As they left, I moved around the building, drawing in memories of my past. At the far end was a new set of double doors marked *No Entry*. I tested one of the handles and was surprised when it turned.

Pulling the door open, the room was shrouded in darkness, and a musty smell tickled my nostrils. A cold chill wrapped itself around my body. I flicked a switch inside the door, and the room was bathed in yellow light. This was the antipathy of the pristine laboratory behind me, but more recognisable. The paint on the walls was flaking and cracked, the green disfigured with layers of dust and grime.

Ian Holland

Backed against the left-hand wall were the remnants of some old equipment; test benches, pillar drills and an ancient centre lathe and milling machine. All familiar and looking like they were destined for the scrap yard. On the opposite wall were remnants of the *Ballbreaker,* the original test equipment; looking more like bomb damage.

In the far corner, a chair was lying on its side. I lifted it onto its legs and dusted it down. It was my old chair, and I couldn't resist sitting down. It creaked and groaned as I stroked the arms with my fingers. I saw myself reflected in a mirror on the opposite wall and smiled. *You're showing your age,* I thought and laughed at myself; quickly turning to look at the open door in case anyone was watching... *there was no one there.* Spinning the chair through three-sixty degrees, I looked back at the mirror, the smile had disappeared.

I scratched at the inflamed patches of skin showing through my hair and thought back to the Brig Uchel mountain.

In the most terrible of conditions, Alex and I had become one. The blood running through both our bodies, driven by a single heart. In the final moments of his life, he'd become more than my son; we'd become one person, understanding the other on an ethereal plane. The moment would never leave me, and I was eternally grateful.

With all the issues I had with my own father, how could I have deserted my family in the same cruel way.

BREAKING POINT

Chapter 37

A thin drizzle tapped against the window of the small room that housed the communal coffee and snack machines. The light was on and reflected against the window looking out onto the early morning darkness. It would be another hour before the sun rose.

The office heating wouldn't kick in for some time, so the room was cold and uninviting. Steam rose like smoke from two styrofoam cups of coffee sitting on one of the plastic tables strewn with yesterday's newspapers and waste packaging. The cleaning staff wouldn't start for another half an hour.

Stremsen was looking at his reflection in the window, but Socket sensed that his mind was elsewhere. A five o'clock phone call had summoned him to meet Stremsen at six. It was now 6:30, and for the first time in his working life, he felt outside his comfort zone.

'I'll be honest with you, Terry, you're starting to disappoint me.' Socket looked at him, waiting as Stremsen gulped at his coffee. 'I've got great plans for us, but all I see at the moment is Danny Core running rings around you. I'm not sure you can handle the WQD role.' Another gulp of coffee.

Socket stared at his cup, holding back his temper.

'He's making us look ridiculous, questioning our processes, our systems. Even questioning your competence.'

'Billy Jones was the Project Director, not me. I followed the instructions, so don't try and lay any blame on me. He's the one you brought in, and he's the one on the salary.' His face had begun to flush.

Stremsen turned to look at him directly. 'You were the Project Manager, a key position. You have to bear some responsibility.'

'Responsibility for what, Fred? You're making it sound like you agree with Core; that the MK6 is flawed.'

Stremsen's eyes moved back to his coffee cup. 'I'm not saying that!' A little bit of temper crept out. 'Core is the one making the accusations, and you're letting him get away with it.'

Socket's fist clenched under the table.

'None of his rhetoric is based on fact, he's bluffing.'

'And you know that for sure, do you?' Stremsen peered at him over the coffee cup.

'Of course, and you do too. All the data was assembled using the PMT process. Jack Smelt left no stone unturned, and although the project was late, we all agreed it was a sound development.' He heard his voice pitching higher, and consciously slowed down. 'You signed off each stage, Fred. Your name is all over this as well.'

'There you go again,' Stremsen remained impassive. 'Not taking responsibility. It's something I've started to pick up from you.' He pushed his cup to one side. 'Listen, I need you to show me what you're made of. This is your first real test of what it's like to be in charge, and I want you to show some leadership. Demonstrate you've got what it takes; that you can handle the pressure.'

'I can do that, but you need to back me up. I can't do it all on my own.'

'I'll be with you every step of the way.' Stremsen clenched his fist. 'But you need to get the upper hand with Core, he's treating you like a subordinate.'

Socket tensed. 'Okay Fred, I'll get to grips with him, you can count on it.'

'Good, let's start with a new resolve to discredit him and his insinuations, okay?'

Socket looked up with a new purpose. 'No more, Mr Nice Guy.'

'That's what I want to hear, Terry. Now let me fill you in with a phone call I had last night.' He looked over his shoulder and leaned in closer. 'You've been invited to a significant meeting along with me, Rik Last and Luca Majori.'

Bloody hell, Socket sat up as though the CEO had entered the room. He was part of the executive group, and a tingle ran up his spine.

'No problem, Fred, in the States?'

Stremsen gave him a humourless smile.

'No, in South Africa.'

Chapter 38

'**You've been busy,** Danny,' Socket said sarcastically.

We were in Billy Jones' office along with Steyn, Stremsen and Billy who was peering out of the window, looking like he wanted to be somewhere else.

'You must have been up all night working on this. Is that how you got injured?'

I instinctively touched the plasters at the back of my head.

'Tripped over in the dark?' he asked, smirking.

He was looking for a reaction but now wasn't the time. Steyn lit up a cigarette and stared at him.

'I wouldn't say all night, Terry,' I replied. 'But I believe there's a discrepancy in some of these calculation sheets.' I tapped the folder in front of me.

Socket looked towards Billy.

'These folders you issued to Mr Broed,' he pointed towards them. 'Did he sign for them?'

Billy squirmed in his chair as Socket continued.

'You know they shouldn't be released without a signature. It's not how the system works.'

Socket was trying to humiliate him, but Steyn was having none of it.

'Billy *did* ask me to sign for them,' he said and leaned back into his chair, drawing heavily on his cigarette. Billy couldn't disguise the surprise on his face as Steyn continued.

'I promised I'd sign the forms before I went home, but it must have slipped my mind. Jammer heer.' He gave Socket and Stremsen his best smile.

'And anyway, I thought we had full access.'

Stremsen's jaw was tightening.

'And so you have, it was simply...'

Steyn cut him off. 'Then there's no more to be said. We're returning all the files today, and I'll be happy to sign for them retrospectively to keep your *system* in order.' He turned to look at Billy, who nodded his head in appreciation.

Steyn was spoiling for a fight, but I couldn't let that happen, not with an opportunity to put them on the back foot. I passed the files back to Billy.

'Let's get onto the main reason for this meeting, Fred,'

I handed over copies of Mathers calculation sheets and straightened my own which was plastered with handwritten notes.

I cleared my throat and began. 'Can you confirm that the calculations you have in front of you, were the basis for determining the size and strength of the bolts and bearings for the MK6 Stabiliser?'

Socket looked at me with his arms crossed, defensively, over his chest.

'You know the answer to that,' he said. 'This is a revolutionary design Danny, a bit different from your day.' His words were soaked with contempt, and he smirked at Stremsen, who remained stony-faced.

'I'm just asking for confirmation,' I said.

'Yes, that's correct,' replied Billy, ignoring the posturing from Socket.

'Thanks,' I said. 'This *is* an innovative design and one which, in my opinion, deserves a lot of credit.'

'Oh, that's very big of you,' Socket again.

'Terry! Let Mr Core continue.' Stremsen was on edge. He'd raised his voice, and I was *Mr Core* again.

'Thanks, Fred,' I replied and continued. 'I've recognised the calculations used, and they form, what I believe, is a sound platform for determining the size and number of bolts around the flanges.'

Socket looked confused.

'But you said there was a discrepancy?'

'Yes, and a serious one,' I replied. 'You've overestimated the strength of both the bolts and the bearings.'

'Bullshit, you're just trying…'

'Terry!' Stremsen raised his voice for a second time, making even Steyn jump. 'Let Mr Core finish please.'

I continued. 'I've completed my preliminary calculations,' I handed out the second set of sheets with my own calculations. 'And concluded that using the *correct* material strength data, the overall safety factor of the MK6 is below the industry standard.'

I had everyone's attention now. Billy Jones and Socket pored over the sheets; Stremsen laid them on top of the first set and looked toward Socket.

After a few minutes of deliberation, Socket looked up.

'You know, as well as I do, there is no optimal safety factor, only a suggested range.'

For all the things I disliked about Socket, I could never underestimate his years of experience.

'That's right Terry, but that range, between 5 and 6, has been the bedrock of every Stabiliser designed since Franklyn Mather's time. He set the standard, and we've never allowed it to go below 6.'

Socket immersed himself in my calculation sheet again.

'Your scribbling's show the safety factor is down to 3.'

'As far as I could go with manual calculations, that's the figure I came up with,' I replied. 'You'll get a more accurate figure running them through the calculation database.'

Stremsen finally picked the sheets up and began to compare them. 'Our calculations show a safety factor of 5.8,' he said. 'That's quite a difference.'

He looked accusingly at Billy Jones before continuing.

'You say the strength of the bolts and bearings have been overestimated. Can you explain this *perceived* anomaly, this discrepancy which *you say* has reduced the safety factor?'

'Hang on, Fred,' Socket jumped in. 'You know which database we used for our calculations?' he waved the sheets at me, and I shrugged my shoulders.

BREAKING POINT

'The same one that you set up before you left,' he continued. I thought he was going to laugh out loud like a pantomime villain.

Stremsen was watching for my reaction.

Stay calm, I told myself. 'As I said at the beginning, Terry, but I'll repeat it for your benefit. The calculations are a sound platform for determining the size and number of *bolts* around the flanges. But you've substituted half of them with bearings.'

'Doesn't make any difference,' said Socket, in a petulant voice.

'I think it does,' I said, trying not to provoke another argument. 'And it explains why you have overestimated the strength of the fastenings.' *I hoped to God I was right.*

'The database is set up to calculate the forces on a Stabiliser secured *exclusively* with bolts,' I continued.

'Correct.' Socket reverted to his defensive stance.

'Where each bolt provides a clamping force to hold the flanges together.'

'Correct again, well done.' Socket was becoming more disruptive, and Stremsen waved an exasperated hand at him.

I ignored him. 'Your calculations only take into account the tensile force acting on the fastenings, which is fine when they're all bolts.'

'Explain,' said Stremsen and I took a deep breath.

'The clamping force is strong enough to eliminate any shear forces on the bolts, that's why they're ignored in the database.'

Socket wanted to interrupt again, but Stremsen gave him a look.

'But by reducing the number of bolts, you've reduced the clamping force. This means you've exposed the remaining bolts and the new bearings to shear forces. None of which is accounted for in the calculations.'

Socket had something to say and looked over at Stremsen who gave him a nod.

'But we haven't reduced the quantity,' he said. 'The original Stabilisers had forty-eight fastenings on each flange, and the MK6 has the same forty-eight fastenings. Twenty-four bolts and twenty-four bearings; the same combined number, the same calculation.'

'Not quite, Terry,' I said and noticed Stremsen lean forward.

'As I said before, your calculations consider the *tensile strength* of the fastenings, but with the changes you've made, you have to consider the *shear strength* as well.'

I saw the confusion in Stremsen's furrowed brow and tried to simplify. 'In basic terms, Fred, the tensile force is trying to stretch the bolts, and the shear force is trying to cut them and the bearings in half, like a guillotine.'

'I know that,' he said.

Lying bastard, I thought.

'They're the same values, Fred, this is all bullshit!' There was a maniacal smile across Socket's face.

I turned away from him and handed out a single sheet of paper, doing my best to stop my hand shaking. As I passed a copy to Steyn, he gave me a reassuring smile; it was just what I needed to steady my hands.

The room went still. Stremsen ignored his copy and watched Socket and Billy Jones poring over theirs.

Clearly, from the body language, they were troubled. Socket appeared to have swallowed his tongue and Billy had turned grey. I pushed home my advantage.

'The sheet in front of you is a copy of the *Distortion Energy Theory* or *von Mises* as it's sometimes known.'

'What the hell is that, Terry?' Stremsen looked worried. I think Socket had gone numb and hadn't heard the question, so I answered for him.

'It shows that tensile strength and shear strength should have been treated differently in your calculations. The shear strength could be fifty per cent less than the figure you've used in your calculations. And to paraphrase Terry, none of this is *bullshit!*'

BREAKING POINT

I couldn't resist the final flourish which gave Steyn something more to smile about.

'How does that change things, Terry?' Stremsen was clearly agitated. He didn't have a clue what I was talking about and was finding it impossible to hide the fact.

Socket was still looking at the last sheet when he answered.

'It means,' he quickly corrected himself. 'It *could* mean the fastenings are not as strong as we thought.'

'Only half as strong,' said Stremsen. 'Does that mean the safety factor is halved?'

Socket was nodding, absorbed with my final sheet, and took a full minute to answer. 'We'll have to run it through the database. It *may* lower the safety factor, but we'll have to see.'

Steyn was still looking for an argument. 'What are you saying, it *could* mean, and, it *may* lower, Terry? I've never met this, von Mises, but I sure as hell know that if the fastenings are only half as strong as you thought they were, then the safety factor's only going one way.' He pointed his thumb down like a Roman emperor.

Billy Jones had remained quiet for most of the meeting, chewing on his pipe, but now he gave me the opening I was waiting for.

'Even if the fastenings failed, and I'm not saying they did, how could that have caused the accident?'

I heard Terry groan.

'May I?' I said, taking a marker pen from Billy's desk. *A picture's worth a thousand words,* I thought.

They all twisted in their seats as I began to sketch the rough shape of a Stabiliser on Billy's whiteboard. Below the Stabiliser, I drew a tunnel and marked it, *Level 120, Accident Site*, to identify its relationship to the MK6, then turned to face them.

'If one bolt or bearing failed, it would set off a devastating chain reaction. The force of water running through the Stabiliser would increase the stress, exponentially, on each of the remaining bolts and bearings. They, in turn, would start to fail and cause the flanges to split and the seals to leak.'

I drew arrows to indicate water, spewing out from the flange joint.

'Failure of these seals would cause a pressure-drop inside the Stabiliser, which would prevent the failsafe switches from operating.' I prodded the four crosses on the diagram.

'Why?' Jones again, acting as my prompt.

Socket looked out of the window as though he was unconcerned, but I could see that he knew where this was going. Stremsen was focused, but this was way over his head. I pressed on.

'The switches need to detect back-pressure to work. Once triggered, they open a set of valves which redirect the flow from the Stabiliser.'

I was absorbed by the detail and elaborated the features on the board.

'This prevents the pressure from rising to dangerous levels inside the main body.' I tapped my pen at the arrows coming from the flanges.

'And any back-pressure would be lost through those leaky seals,' said Billy following the logic.

'Exactly,' I replied. 'And a chain reaction would be set in motion. High-pressure water would continue pumping through the system with nowhere to go, the resultant rise in pressure would put the whole system under enormous stress. The water hammer alone would be like a minor earthquake, forcing the piping or the Stabiliser to rip itself apart.'

Stremsen and Socket were now listening intently.

'What's *water hammer*?' asked Stremsen.

Socket answered for me. 'It's *hydraulic shock*, Fred. A pressure wave or surge.'

BREAKING POINT

I jumped in. 'About ten years ago, we tried to replicate the effect of *hydraulic shock* using the old *Ballbreaker*. Do you remember, Terry?'

He nodded unwillingly.

'We had to abort the experiment within minutes The vibration of the Stabiliser nearly brought the lab building down.' I pushed home my advantage. 'Under these conditions, a Stabiliser would be trying to twist and shake itself away from anything holding it down.'

'Which is what we believe happened on Concorde IV,' said Steyn.

Socket was bright red and flustered, but managed to stay belligerent. 'Prove it!'

I ignored him. Stremsen was looking at me directly, copies of the calculations lying limp in front of him.

I saw it all clearly in my mind's eye.

'The knock-on effect wouldn't have stopped there. The destructive energy would have been magnified throughout the external piping. The further down it went, the greater the effect,' I pointed to Level 120 on the whiteboard.

'Until all that energy would tear down the walls that are trying to hold the pipes... here on 120.' I gave my sketch a last look, nodded, and went back to my seat.

There was an eerie silence, broken only by Billy Jones sucking on his empty pipe.

Stremsen stood. 'Very dramatic, Mr Core. I'd like to adjourn while we discuss this in private.'

As the three of them disappeared outside, I noticed Socket was limping.

Steyn leant across. 'Does this, von Mises, make that much of a difference, Danny?'

'To be honest, I don't know,' I said. 'It would take me a day to work out the calculations manually, but they can run it through the database in less than an hour. It *will* lower the safety factor, as you said, but Socket's right. Unless the factor is less than 1, it's going to be difficult to prove culpability. But it's the only thing I've got left.' I grabbed his arm. 'I'm not sure how this is going to go, Steyn, but I need copies of those photographs from Piet and Embele. I need to know if any of the bearings were missing.'

He tapped me on the shoulder. 'Dread owes me a favour. I'll get him to give me a lift back to the hotel.'

'If you can speak with Piet…'

'Leave it with me.' And he was gone.

The three Mathers men returned after half an hour. This time I watched Socket make his way back to his seat. He was definitely dragging his leg.

'Sorry to keep you waiting, Danny,' Stremsen was back in charge and didn't even acknowledge that Steyn had left.

'We've passed this new information to our engineers, and it seems that there is merit in what you're saying. We don't agree with your doomsday scenario. Still, we'll run the revised calculations through our database and find out the precise safety factor. I'm informed it should take no longer than an hour, so I suggest we reconvene in…'

'There are some other things I'd like to discuss while we're here, Fred.'

The three of them looked up at me, and I heard Terry groan again.

BREAKING POINT

Chapter 39

'**How's the meeting** going?' John asked.

Steyn was lost in his thoughts as they made their way to the hotel.

'Oh, pretty good,' he answered. Then a long silence.

'Are we okay, Steyn?'

The words jolted him. 'Ja, sure. It's just that I don't want to say too much... you know.'

'What do you mean?' said John. 'Don't you trust me?'

Steyn looked across at him for the first time since they'd left the factory.

'The thing is, whatever you and Danny had in the past, you're on opposite sides now.'

'What do you mean?'

'Well, whatever's good news from Danny's point of view is going to be bad news for you.'

'Is that why you're having photographs sent via the hotel, you don't trust us?' John pulled his car into the car park and switched off the engine.

Steyn was staring out of the windscreen, at nothing in particular.

'I'll let you into a little secret, John. Danny isn't here on company business, and he wasn't *asked* to investigate this accident. He's funding this trip himself.'

John removed his safety belt and twisted around to face him. 'What do you mean, *he's funding it*? You're both here on work-related business, aren't you?''

Steyn's eyes were focused on the hotel entrance. 'He won't like me for saying this, but time is running out for him.'

He took a deep breath and explained the situation back in South Africa. When he'd finished, John sat there, his hands on the steering wheel.

'Manslaughter! How can he be held responsible for an act of nature? How can they...'

Steyn broke in. 'They need someone to blame, and at the moment, Danny's Safety Initiative is being questioned.'

'But that's ridiculous, you said the system has been running successfully for over two years. How can they point the finger now?'

'South Africa's changing,' said Steyn. 'And so is gold mining. Safety's a big issue, and Rinto Gold has been setting standards. They can't pass over an accident like this. Not one that's taken so many lives and been highlighted in the media. Someone's got to be made responsible.'

He turned to look at John, gauging his reaction.

'Danny believes the problem started with the MK6. If he finds the proof to clear his name, then the responsibility will shift to you, Mathers. And that's why, until this is resolved, you're on opposite sides.'

'How long has he got?' asked John.

'He's been given ten days to come up with proof. We thought we had four days left, but they're getting impatient, a phone call today told us to return to South Africa, immediately.'

Steyn stared into John's eyes. 'You want to tell me anything more about last night?' The atmosphere was uncomfortable, but he wasn't going to let go.

Finally, John answered him. 'You're not going to start all that again, are you.'

'Sounded like you were pretty angry before you disappeared.'

'I had a few too many beers. I didn't know what I was saying.'

Steyn shook his head. 'Danny needs all the help he can get at the moment. I don't know what your relationship was like before, but I'm pretty sure it's changed since he found out you were going out with…'

'I told him about that, he didn't *just* find out,' John banged his hand on the steering wheel.

'Okay,' said Steyn. 'I just needed to hear it from you, one last time. No hard feelings?'

BREAKING POINT

John nodded reluctantly. 'We've just put the revised figures through the calculation database, the results should be ready by the time we get back.'

'Mmm, any thoughts?' asked Steyn.

John shrugged. 'I don't know, but they've asked me to present the figures.'

'What result are you hoping for?' Steyn peered into his eyes then gave him a cold smile. 'See what I mean about being on opposite sides?'

'I think you need to get those photographs,' John turned his head away.

'Wait here,' said Steyn. 'I need to make a phone call first.'

Twenty minutes later, the passenger door opened and Steyn sat heavily, pulling at the seal of an envelope. He counted out twenty-four colour prints and a written report. Twenty-six sheets in all.

'Can I have a look?' asked John.

'Not yet, I want Danny to look at them first. A lot is riding on these.'

John nodded. 'Still can't trust me.'

Steyn pushed them back in the envelope. 'After last night, I'm not even sure I like you.'

He looked for a reaction, but there wasn't one.

'Okay, I understand why you would think that,' said John. 'But let's get one thing straight.' He watched the big man put on his seat belt. 'After what you've just told me, I'll do everything I can to help Danny clear his name.'

'Good,' said Steyn. 'So, we all know where we stand. Now let's get back.'

Chapter 40

I pulled out some of the notes I'd taken. They weren't essential, but I was delaying as much as I could until Steyn returned.

'It was interesting visiting the assembly department, but I was concerned about the lack of control in the selection of the bearings.' I thought I'd confront them head-on.

Both Stremsen and Socket looked suspicious.

'It's *fully* controlled,' said Stremsen.

'I disagree,' I said, referring to my notes. 'How do you know whether you've put the correct number of bearings between the flanges?'

Socket smirked at me. 'Are you taking the piss?'

'It's a reasonable question.'

'I told you before, but I'll repeat myself.' He looked across at Stremsen with that annoying self-confidence. 'The MK6 has forty-eight fastenings on each set of flanges. Twenty-four bolts and twenty-four bearings.'

'Yes, I know that Terry, but they don't allocate the exact number of bearings. The assemblers randomly pick them from a central location, just like the bolts.'

'It's worked for the last seventy years; I don't think we're about to change things now.' He was full of confidence and enjoying the attention Stremsen was giving him.

'It's fine with bolts,' I replied. 'You can visually check if one is missing after assembly. But how would you know if a bearing was missing?'

My question caused him to delay a fraction. 'Erm, it's given a final inspection certificate.'

'But how do they inspect and count what they can't see?'

I expected more of a reaction to my question, but Stremsen interrupted.

BREAKING POINT

'Have you heard of Process Capability, Danny?' Before I could answer, he got up and rubbed out my sketches on the whiteboard and began drawing a grid.

My stomach turned over as he faced me. I felt another lecture coming on.

'We've implemented a new process whereby the assemblers tick off a sheet as they locate each of the bearings. Terry, show Danny our SAP.'

Socket passed me a foolscap folder. 'It stands for, Stabiliser Assembly Pack,' he said.

'Oh, right,' I replied, none the wiser.

'If you look through the pages...' Stremsen was in full schoolteacher mode now and began replicating the tasks on the sheet to the whiteboard. 'You can see how each task, carried out during the assembly process, has to be verified by the operator's signature. This includes the time and date of completion. This is checked by an independent inspector before the next stage of the assembly process can begin.'

He was drawing extravagant arrows on the board, veering from one matchstick man to another.

'It's all handwritten,' I said.

'That's right...' he stalled, but his tag teamer filled in.

'If a customer has a problem,' said Terry. 'With any one of our Stabilisers, we can match up the serial number with the appropriate SAP, and check whether there were any underlying issues with the assembly or the final testing procedures.

Stremsen had regrouped. 'When I set up the PMT process, I demanded that all statistical data needed to be collated at every stage of the production process. Are you familiar with the principle of Process Capability, Danny?'

I looked up at him; this time he allowed me to answer. 'A little.'

'Then you'll know it provides tangible proof that a process is working within specified limits.'

I nodded as I ran through a number of the pages in the folder. 'I take it this is the SAP for the MK6 at Concorde IV?'

Stremsen was glowing with pride. 'The sales department matched it up with the serial number you gave us and that's your copy.'

'And everything's in order?' I asked, already knowing the answer.

'Of course,' he said, back in control. 'There was nothing during the process of building your MK6 Stabiliser to suggest anything other than a first-class product.'

I needed a cigarette. My pulse thumped inside my head, and I squeezed my eyes shut to ease the pain.

'Can I get you a glass of water?' Billy Jones joined the conversation.

'No, no, I'm fine thanks.' I found the page I was looking for and felt their eyes all over me.

'I see you've found the sheets referring to the assembly of the bolts and bearings,' said Stremsen. He referred to his copy. 'As you can see, each bearing was fitted and signed off by the assembler, then independently verified at final inspection.'

'They're all handwritten,' I repeated.

Socket gasped in frustration. 'So what!'

I was getting aggravated by the stupidity of their argument.

'This document tells me that someone signed to say they fitted the bearings, but that's not conclusive proof that they actually did. It doesn't remove the risk of an error.'

Socket laughed. 'And that's why we have a final inspection process.' He raised his sheet toward me and pointed. 'There's the signature, totally independent.'

He crossed his arms and shook his head as if I was a moron. It was enough for me to doubt my logic.

'Final inspection *is* still carried out after assembly?' I asked, hoping to God I was right.

BREAKING POINT

By the look on Stremsen's face, I think he knew where this argument was going and tried to shut Socket up; but it was too late.

'Of course, it always has been. That's why it's called final inspection... *Duh!*' He made a silly face to humiliate me and looked to Stremsen for approval, but there was no reaction.

I breathed a sigh of relief; I *was* right and continued. 'So after assembly, how did the final inspector...' I looked at the signature. 'Ralph Potts, check that the correct number of bearings were in place before he signed this sheet?' I waved it at Socket.

The air seemed to be sucked from the room. Socket looked toward Stremsen, but all he could do was shake his head.

Strangely, Billy Jones seemed to be enjoying the experience, and I pressed my advantage home. 'The only statistical analysis you're making is based on the reliability of the operator to sign a piece of paper. That's not how Process Capability works.' I looked at each of them expecting a counter-argument, but they were speechless, so I hammered my advantage home. 'You have a critical part of the process that's not in control. It's manual and subject to human error, no matter which way you try to spin it with your SAP.'

Billy coughed awkwardly as though he wanted to say something, but stayed silent. I addressed both Socket and Stremsen.

'You haven't changed your processes to cope with the new bearings. Within the next fifteen minutes, I expect to learn how many bearings were in the MK6 Stabiliser. If you have faith in your Process Capability, will you guarantee there will be none missing?'

I'd crossed the Rubicon. Without proof, it was a huge gamble to taunt them, but it was done now. *Alea iacta est,* the die is cast, I thought.

Stremsen sat back down and dropped his coloured markers on the desk. He and Socket got into a whispered conversation while Billy and I looked at each other and shrugged; he'd clearly been sidelined.

They broke away from each other and Stremsen gave me a long stare.

'You've dismantled the Stabiliser?'

'Yes,' I replied.

'Tampered with the evidence?'

'A bit formal, but if you want to put it that way, yes.'

'We seem to be at odds once more, Mr Core. I think we've given you all we can in terms of…'

The door opened abruptly, and Steyn peered through waving an envelope. I asked to be excused and left Stremsen's unfinished sentence hanging in the air. My legs felt weak, and I was sure they could hear my heart pounding against my chest as I walked past.

Steyn stood in the corridor outside Billy's office. He didn't need to say anything, his body language told me everything.

'I'm sorry, Danny.'

'Shit!' I spat the words out as I opened the envelope to look at the photographs. Each page I turned was an effort, I didn't need to count the bearings. 'Did you manage to get hold of anyone?'

'Yes, I spoke with Piet, he said they took it in turns to count the bearings and came up with the same answer. All the bearings were in place.'

'Fuck! That's made things a lot harder, Steyn… a *lot* harder.' I couldn't come up with a more articulate reply.

A young girl passed us and turned to look at me.

'Sorry about his language, love.' I heard Steyn's words through a fog of disappointment. I was numb and slumped into a chair, my head heavy on my shoulders. I dragged my eyes through the pages.

'Some of these bolts and bearings show signs of severe damage,' I said. 'That ties up with my hypothesis about the

BREAKING POINT

distortion energy theory. It's exactly the scenario I talked about. Look here?' I passed over three of the prints showing the groups of damaged parts lying next to one another.

'I mean, what else would have caused that?'

Steyn looked at the pictures as I continued. 'These bolts have stretched, and two of the bearings have sheared.'

I got up to point them out to him, realising that my words lacked credibility. He was looking at me in a way that unnerved me.

'What? Spit it out, Steyn.'

'I asked Piet what he thought,' he said quietly.

I nodded, I had no energy left.

'He still thinks the accident is linked to a pressure burst on 120.'

I went cold. 'And Embele?' I asked.

He paused. 'The same.'

'And you, Steyn, what do you think?'

He pulled out his cigarettes and gave me one. I took a light from him, and we both filled the corridor with smoke. I heard the telephone ringing in Billy's office and sucked another lung full, knowing it wasn't healthy, but past caring. Steyn was halfway through his before he finally gave me an answer.

'Ek dink hierdie bastards is wegkruip iets,' *I think the bastards are hiding something.* And he winked at me.

I wasn't expecting that response, which made it feel all the more remarkable. Nor was I expecting the slap on the back, which nearly knocked me back into the chair. It brought a smile to both our faces. Dousing our cigarettes, we walked back into the office, armed with the prints.

'Ah, gentlemen, welcome back,' Stremsen's mood had improved. 'I've just had a phone call from the engineering department. They've had the results using the reduced values, in line with the distortion energy theory...'

Half an hour ago, he hadn't heard of it, and now you'd think he'd created the principle.

'They're bringing the printouts as we speak.' The smug look on his face was dashing the last hopes I had.

He saw the images in my hand. 'I see you've got some pictures,' he looked wary. 'It hardly matters now that you've tampered with the Stabiliser, but I'll ask the question anyway. Are there any bearings missing?'

I sat and passed the prints to Socket. He snatched them off me, and both he and Billy scanned the pages.

'I'm surprised you need to look,' I said. 'If you have so much faith in your Process Capability.'

No one replied, they didn't have to.

Socket looked up, smiling.

'All present and correct, Fred.' He was cocky again.

Stremsen's wariness evaporated. 'As I said, it never was in doubt.'

The door opened, and John walked in, followed by Richie Tick.

'Are we okay to…?'

'Come in both,' said Billy.

'You asked for the revised calculations,' said John, looking across at me. His body language dissolved the last hopes I had.

'I don't want to take up too much of your time,' said Stremsen. 'So let's get down to facts. What was the final safety factor of the MK6 Stabiliser with the modified figures?'

He was showboating and clearly knew the answer.

John looked at me again. 'I've already told you over the phone, Fred.' The distaste between them was plain, and the comment took some of the wind from Stremsen's sails.

I smiled. 'Just for the record, John, what are they?'

'We've run it through the database, Danny, and it works out at 3.6.' He passed me the printout.

'Are you okay with this, John?' I asked.

He knew what it meant as much as I did. 'It's accurate, Danny. But you were right, we made an error with the original calculations.'

BREAKING POINT

'Thank you, John, that'll be all,' Stremsen tried to cut him short, but he didn't move.

I had nothing to lose now… *big breath*.

'So it's well below the accepted value, John.'

'We'll take it from here, John,' Stremsen was desperate to get him out.

'Yes it is, Danny,' John replied with no enthusiasm.

'So the MK6 wasn't fucking safe and was a major factor in the accident?' Steyn's question was angry and aggressive.

I turned to look at him, his jaw was set for an argument.

'Well!' He was shouting now.

Billy tried to calm things. 'We've said before, Steyn, the safety factor is only…'

'Voetsek! Billy. I'm asking Dread.'

I'd rarely seen Steyn like this. And when I did, it usually ended unpleasantly. John was unnerved; something else I'd seldom seen. *What the hell was going on between them?*

John looked at me and shrugged his shoulders. I nodded for him to continue.

'Erm, in all honesty, I'd… I'd have to say… it's a possibility. But, erm… not a probability.'

'Christ, man, get off the fucking fence!'

'Steyn!' I grabbed his arm. 'That's enough!'

The room went quiet, except for the sound of him panting in frustration. He was seething, and I tried squeezing his arm as a warning.

'I'd have come up with the same conclusion myself, John.' I said. He looked relieved.

'Okay, gentlemen,' Stremsen stood looking nervously at Steyn. 'I think that concludes our work here.'

Steyn pulled his arm from my grip, grabbed the envelope from Socket and stormed out, catching everyone unawares. An embarrassed calm descended on the room before Billy broke the spell.

'Danny, I hope you're able to solve the mystery of the collapse, at least to give...'

Stremsen butted in again. 'I believe we've cooperated as much as we can, Mr Core. I hope you put as much effort in your underground investigations as you've done here. I will, of course, be taking up the invitation from your chairman to a summary meeting in South Africa, and assume you will be making plans to fly back home.'

'Tomorrow,' I mumbled barely able to move my mouth.

They all came to shake my hand, but I felt nothing. I heard John say *sorry*, but the rest was a blur.

BREAKING POINT

Chapter 41

Billy Jones came up to me after everyone had left.

'Looks like we just got away with it, Danny.'

It wasn't triumphalism, and he was probably right.

'Your point about the assembly was valid,' he continued. 'And we'll be making some changes.'

He pushed a set of keys into my hand.

'As it's going to be your last day, I thought you might like to borrow my car.' He saw my surprise and smiled. 'Red Cortina, parked outside reception, I'll use one of the pool cars. You can drop mine back tomorrow morning.'

'Thanks,' I said. 'That'll make a big difference; it's been a difficult couple of days.'

He looked uncomfortable and glanced toward the door to make sure no one was around.

'You seem convinced about a fault with the MK6.'

'I'm not sure I know, anymore,' I replied. I felt I'd reached the end of the line.

'I'm not proud of the way we've dealt with your investigation.' He looked genuinely concerned. 'But, for what it's worth, I believe the MK6 development *was* carried out professionally.'

'Were you one of those surprised it achieved its cost savings targets?' I asked, dropping the keys into my pocket.

He wasn't great at hiding his emotions. 'Who told you about that?'

'I think I read something in the reports,' I bluffed.

He seemed to be weighing whether to answer me before shrugging. 'Mmm, it was a *very* ambitious target.'

'But you all had a decent bonus from the success?'

It was a question too far, and he closed up. 'You know I can't discuss internal policy, Danny.'

'You're right,' I said. 'And I shouldn't put you on the spot.'

We shook, and he wished me a safe journey home. *Billy Jones was one of the good guys.*

I wandered around the factory looking for Steyn, it felt like I'd been anaesthetised. Every sound was muffled, and the pace of everything and everyone had slowed. My journey was over.

Up until this moment, I had been overwhelmed by the perverse excitement. Now it was just a massive anticlimax. I'd failed my greatest challenge, and everything before it seemed diminished.

The process had forced me to look inward and evaluate my abilities, and I'd been found wanting. The long-suppressed fear of what lay ahead revealed itself. *Would I ever get to see Paul again?*

I was lost in my thoughts when I turned the corner and bumped into Socket, making his way to the coffee machine. It was the last thing I needed, but I thought, *what the heck.*

I don't know why, but I grabbed his arm as he tried to ignore me. 'Fancy a coffee?'

He looked more surprised than I did. 'I'll get my own.' He spat the words out and moved on.

I paused a moment then decided to follow him. He was dispensing a cup when I arrived.

'Mind if I join you?'

He shrugged and pulled a steaming brew from the machine.

'Looks like we're all meeting up in South Africa,' he said, turning to face me.

'Yes, I know,' I replied. 'Who do you think made the suggestion?' My response caught him unawares.

'Why would you want me there?'

I ignored his question. 'Ever been underground, Terry?'

He looked at me suspiciously while he slurped his coffee. 'Who said anything about going underground.'

I had his full attention now and turned to put some coins in the machine.

BREAKING POINT

'Any recommendations?' I asked, my finger hovering over the buttons.

'Fuck off, Core,' he said and started walking away.

'Who do you think is setting the agenda for this meeting?' The comment stopped him in his tracks. 'I've arranged for us to visit the accident site and show you the suspect Stabiliser.'

He was angry when he turned back around.

'What for? We've proved the MK6 had nothing to do with it, and anyway, you've stripped it down. What the hell is there to look at?' His arrogance was melting away.

'We've got another MK6,' I replied. 'Identical to the one involved in the accident and installed at the same time.'

He moved closer to me. '*Involved*,' I could smell his coffee breath prickling the inside of my nose. 'Haven't you been listening to anything these past few days? We've put up with you and that captain of yours wandering around like you own the place. And what have you got?'

I snapped at the band on my wrist.

'Fuck all, that's what.'

I watched his spittle foam at the corners of his mouth.

'Nothing on the MK6, and nothing on us. I've waited a long time for this, Core, and I'm going to enjoy watching you get sacked.'

Now I was angry. 'How's your leg?' I asked and watched for his response.

Confusion, then anger. Not what I was expecting. The anger boiled over into rage and he grabbed me by the collar.

'I know it was you, Core...' he screamed.

I tried counting to ten and only got to three before the red mist fell. I pushed Socket into the dispenser with my left hand and grabbed deep into his groin with my right, squeezing the blood out of whatever was in my grasp.

The coffee cup flew out of his free hand, and he let out a strangled moan; instantly letting me go. I did the same, but the damage was done. His knees buckled, and his lungs emptied.

I pulled him up and tried to sit him on one of the chairs, but he pushed me away, grunting an expletive.

'What's all the commotion?' It was Dawn shouting from the doorway.

Socket groaned, his hands clasped between his legs.

'Call security, he attacked me.'

She looked across at me and shook her head.

'I've been watching you both, you should be ashamed of yourselves. You're as bad as one another.'

I would have smiled if I hadn't been feeling so guilty.

'Any more, and I *will* call security to get you *both* escorted from the site.' And with that, she shut the door on us.

Socket had begun to recover and lifted himself onto a seat. 'You'll pay for this, Core.'

'Me?' I said, my head thumping from the rush of blood. 'You're lucky *I* don't press charges.'

He looked baffled. 'What are you talking about?'

I felt uncertainty creeping into my voice. 'Two nights ago…' I pointed to the back of my head. 'When you attacked me.'

More confusion on his part.

My mouth was drying up. 'I saw you limping… after you got injured two nights ago…'

Without prompting, he pulled his trouser leg up and exposed two jagged scars running vertically and horizontally across his knee, the joint was swollen and inflamed.

'Remember what you did twenty years ago?' There was so much anger, his eyes were watering.

It was my turn to feel sick… *surely he was bluffing*.

'Let me see the other leg?' I said.

He pulled his other trouser leg up, there wasn't a scratch. I collapsed in the chair next to him, my head in my hands… *I was so sure.*

BREAKING POINT

He straightened his trousers and swayed as he stood, at that moment, I almost felt sorry for him.

'I know I'll never convince you,' I said, looking up at him. 'But it wasn't me who did that.'

He sneered down at me. 'If it had been me who attacked you, Core, you wouldn't be fit enough to walk around.' And he limped from the room.

I straightened my jacket; the experience had shaken me pretty badly. I took some deep breaths and felt Billy's keys rattle in my pocket. Paul… *I'd almost forgotten.*

I looked at my watch, it was 2 o'clock. I had time to drive to town and get a present, plus a bunch of flowers for Julie, and still be back to pick them up for football. My head was thumping.

Chapter 42

Steyn was still annoyed with the outcome of the meeting, and it had taken three cigarettes and two circuits of the factory to work out a new strategy. Key to that was enlisting John Dread, which meant building bridges.

He'd found John in the engineering office, staring at the computer monitor.

'Found anything different?' he asked, catching him unawares.

'Oh… Hi!' John stared up at him. 'I was just double-checking the calculations.'

'And?'

John looked back at the screen. 'They've been estimated correctly,' he replied. 'I've even done a rough manual check.'

'Still standing by your summary then?'

John looked up again. 'Whatever you think of me, Steyn, I'm not getting a kick out of this. Yes, the reduction in the safety factor isn't very professional, but it's still not enough to ring any alarm bells.'

Steyn looked around, one or two of the engineers were taking an interest.

'Can we find somewhere private to talk?'

John led him away from the laboratory and into a part of the factory Steyn hadn't seen before. Guiding him into an unlit corridor, John opened a green, wooden door marked, *Wages,* and switched on the lights. The room was cold and smelt of neglect.

'This place has been empty for over a year,' John said, looking around at the cobwebs on the ceiling.

'No one gets paid any more?' Steyn replied with a weak smile.

'Everything's automated these days. We had ten people running the wages a couple of years ago, now its two in the main office block. At least it means we won't be disturbed.'

John wiped dust and cobwebs off one of the tables. 'I assume you're ready to show me those pictures.'

Steyn passed some over. 'They're all from the MK6 we dismantled, see what you think.'

John went through them. 'What am I looking for?'

'You're supposed to be the engineer?'

John shook his head and blew out his cheeks. 'You may not like the conclusion, but the safety factor we came up with is legitimate. Even Danny agreed.' He started to lay the sheets on the table. 'Danny's seen them all?'

'Yes,' said Steyn.

'And he couldn't find anything incriminating?' John didn't wait for an answer. 'Help me move the table to the window, I can see better in the natural light.'

They dragged the table under the window, and John pulled the pictures up one by one. 'They're not the best copies, are they?'

'Jones and Socket didn't seem concerned,' Steyn replied, handing over the rest.

'They were only interested in counting them,' John replied.

'Christ! there's a bit of damage on some of these.' He pointed to the image of a sheared bolt, then another showing a fractured bearing. 'I can't begin to picture what happened below ground to cause that much damage.'

'Imagine being in the middle of it,' Steyn said, pulling out his cigarettes.

'I wouldn't if I was you,' John pointed to the ceiling. 'I think the smoke alarms and sprinklers are still active.'

Steyn grunted and returned the packet to his pocket. As he did, the sheet he was holding slipped from his grasp and fell between the table and the window. 'Damn!' He knelt awkwardly to pick it up. 'Mind your leg,' he said, tapping John's shin. He reared back as John gasped and clumsily moved his leg out of the way.

Steyn's fingers tingled. Beneath the fabric of the trousers, the leg was bandaged... *I managed to stab the bastard in the leg...*

He took his time reaching for the sheet, all the while gritting his teeth. Now wasn't the time, he needed him onboard.

He stood back up. 'I'm going outside for a smoke.'

'You should give those up.' John had recovered his composure and remained engrossed in the images.

Steyn smiled as best he could. 'Mmm, I won't be long.'

It took two cigarettes for him to calm down. He was still trying to weigh up a response that didn't include violence, when he heard the door open in the corridor and Dread's voice.

'I think I've found something.'

He doused the cigarette underfoot and almost fell through the door. On the table were four distinct images, each with red arrows pencilled in at strategic points. John had both hands leaning on the table, his eyes scanning over each of the sheets.

'Are there any more pictures to look at?' he asked.

Steyn shook his head. 'This is everything we've had so far.'

'So, there may be more?'

Steyn nodded. 'I could find out. Why, what have you found?'

John pulled two of the images together, showing fractured bolts. 'See these. They're made from ASTM A35 stainless steel. Excellent tensile strength and high corrosion resistance.'

He lifted the pictures to the window, so the natural light showed up the colours. 'Notice anything?'

Steyn looked closely. 'Like what?'

John didn't answer. Instead, he took the other two images, close-ups of two fractured bearings, and lifted them to the light. 'These are made from a similar material

BREAKING POINT

called Super Duplex 198. Excellent shear strength and high corrosion resistance. Notice anything?'

Steyn looked again, and this time his eyes were drawn to the arrows John had pencilled in. 'That discolouration inside the fracture?'

John nodded and pulled up the two images of the bolts again. 'Have another look at these bolts, and this time tell me what you *can't* see.'

Steyn put them up to the light, it was apparent.

'They're not discoloured,' he answered.

'Doesn't that strike you as strange?' John held all four images together. 'Both components exposed to the same environment, yet looking so different.'

He laid them back on the table.

'What do you think it is?' asked Steyn

'It looks like corrosion,' replied John. 'But that would be impossible.'

He lifted them up to the light once more, as though confirming his opinion.

'The photographs aren't great, so it's not inconceivable that it *is* contamination from the surrounding area.'

'What do we do next?' asked Steyn.

John looked at him. 'We? The question is, what do *you* do next?

'Ahh... so you're finally taking sides.' Steyn couldn't help himself. 'What happened to... *I'll help Danny all I can?*'

John looked him in the face. 'Look, I'm in dangerous territory here. If I'm seen to be helping you, I'm going to be in a lot of trouble.'

'What makes you think you're not already?'

John's eyes narrowed. 'You haven't told anyone about me helping you, have you?'

Steyn ignored the question. 'How did you know Danny was attacked with a golf club?'

The colour drained from John's face, and the reply came a fraction of a second too late.

'You're not on about that, again, I told you…'

'Danny told you he'd been attacked; he didn't say what with.'

This time the delay was longer, the nervousness more pronounced. 'He… he must have… I…'

'Only one way you'd know, and that's if…'

'This is crazy.'

'One way to prove me wrong,' said Steyn.

'I told you…'

'Show me your leg.'

Steyn took a quiet step back and adjusted his body weight evenly on both feet, clenching his fists. His eyes never left John's, and all he could see was frustration and anger. He'd seen enough of him to know he was unpredictable.

John's shoulders slumped, and he turned to look out the window. A train passed, filling the silence with a metallic rumbling of wheels, the sound vibrating through the floor.

'Are you going to tell Julie?' John's voice was muffled as though he had no energy to form the words.

'You're not worried about Danny knowing?' Steyn asked.

'I'm not proud of what I did, but he'd probably understand.'

'Understand?' said Steyn still on alert.

'Yeah, maybe Danny and I are too much alike, both running away from things. But I can't lose what I've got with Julie… and Paul.'

'You could have killed him.' Steyn tried to keep his voice neutral.

John turned around to face him, his eyes wet. 'I just wanted to scare him off.'

'He's here trying to clear his name, man. I wasn't joking when I said he could go to jail.'

'But I thought he'd come back to…'

'What! Take his ex-wife back?' Steyn finished the sentence for him.

BREAKING POINT

'Okay, I was wrong, I see that... now.'

'So you'll help?' Steyn saw him look toward the images.

'I never said I wouldn't, I just have to be careful. And you still haven't answered my question?'

'I won't say anything,' said Steyn. His hands relaxed.

'And Danny?'

'He won't get to know from me.'

'How do I know I can trust you?'

'I could ask you the same thing,' Steyn spat the words back at him. 'And the answer would be the same.'

'What's that?'

'Because you have no choice.'

John turned to look out the window once more.

'I've worked here all my life. If I lose this...'

Steyn was convinced that, whatever slim hopes they still had, relied on Dread's help.

John turned around. 'Let's get Danny here.'

It was 3 o'clock when I arrived back at Mathers.

'I've been looking for you everywhere.' Dawn looked in a panic as I entered the reception area.

'What's happened?' I said, expecting another crisis.

'John and Steyn have been trying to get hold of you, they're in the old wages office. It sounds important.'

By the time I got there, they were sitting around a table, copies of the photographs laid out in orderly lines.

'What's going on?'

Steyn nodded for John to answer.

'I think we may have found something,' he said, then took me through the images one by one.

The idea that some of the bearings had corroded seemed too subjective to me. They were poor quality photos, and there was a lot of contamination in the surrounding area.

'Can we get any more sent over?' Steyn asked, sounding more optimistic than I was.

'We're leaving tomorrow,' I said. 'I don't think there's enough time.'

'Maybe he's got some more he hasn't already sent us,' John said. 'They could be more relevant now.'

'Are you sure you should be this close to us,' I asked. 'If I was your boss…'

'I'm doing this as a friend, Danny. Steyn asked me to review the photographs, and I agreed. I'm not expecting it to lead to anything, it just looks odd.'

'You need to inform Socket,' I said. 'It's one thing helping us, but withholding information is a step too far. And they *will* find out.'

'How would I explain what I know?' asked John.

'Tell them I found the signs of corrosion and asked you to pass on the information. The next time I see them will be in South Africa.'

'Okay,' he said. 'He'll probably ignore me anyway.'

'Good.' I looked at my watch. 'Steyn, can you get hold of Piet. If he's got anything else to send over, give him Dawn's direct fax number.'

He nodded. 'I'll tell her to keep them safe from prying eyes.'

'Thanks,' I said. 'And tell him to bring the damaged bolts and bearings above ground. We can look at them in detail when we get back.'

'Okay, I'll get on with it,' he said and left us to it.

'Can you get me drawings of the MK6 flanges, John?'

'Why do you want those?'

'All our focus seems to be on the fastenings at the moment. I'd like to familiarise myself with more of the details.'

'No problem,' he said. 'I'll leave copies with Dawn.'

'Thanks,' I replied. 'You'd better leave this with us and keep your distance.'

He nodded his agreement. 'When you get back, let me know what you find,' he said. 'In the meantime, I'll do some digging this end and see what I can find.'

BREAKING POINT

'Thanks, John. I appreciate that.'

We shook, but there wasn't the same warmth behind it.

'Have a safe journey,' he said and seemed about to say something else, but changed his mind and left.

Back in our temporary office, Steyn was just finishing a conversation on the phone. 'Okay, thanks, Piet.'

I looked at my watch, it was 3:45. 'Any news?'

Steyn looked at his notes. 'Piet has got some more photographs that he's going to send over right away.'

'Did he notice any corrosion?' I asked.

'No, not really, he said they were more concerned about the fractures.'

'Okay, let's wait and see what he sends, and make sure John gets copies. Is Piet going to bring the damaged bearings back to the surface?'

Steyn nodded. 'Yes, but the main shaft is still on lockdown, and the ventilation shaft isn't accessible until tomorrow morning. He'll take Embele down with him.'

'Why, Embele?' I asked.

Steyn smiled. 'Seems he's made an impression on Piet. Reckons he's wasted as a Boss Boy.'

'I wouldn't argue with that,' I said.

Steyn reached into his shirt pocket. 'Fancy a cigarette?'

I shook my head. 'No thanks, I've got to make an important phone call.'

'Okay, I'll go and tell Dawn to keep an eye out for those faxes.' And he disappeared into the corridor.

I dialled Julie's number, she picked up on the third ring.

'Hi, Julie.'

'You're not coming, are you?'

'Something's come up, and I can't…' I was crushing the phone in my hand.

'I'd made arrangements to take Paul anyway, I knew you'd…'

'This is important, Julie…' I broke in before she started.

'More important than your son?' she asked, angrily.

I couldn't answer that. 'Can you tell him…'

'Tell him yourself, Danny, if you can find the time!' The phone went dead.

It took another hour for the faxes to come through. Dawn made sure that no one was around when she brought them in.

'I hope they help, Danny,' she said; I knew she meant it.

I thanked her and laid them out on the desk. Steyn and I pored over every aspect of the six new images but couldn't come to any conclusions.

'It's like everything we've found so far,' I said. 'Plenty of theories but no evidence.'

I looked at my watch, it was 6.30, then looked at Steyn. 'I'd better get you back to the hotel, you need to pack.'

'Are we walking?' he asked.

I forced a smile. 'No, Billy Jones lent us his car. He said we can drop it back here tomorrow on our way to the airport.'

'Mmm, that was good of him.'

BREAKING POINT

Chapter 43

It had been a long day. I drove into the familiar cul-de-sac and stopped outside the semi-detached house. Number sixteen displayed in plastic numerals on the red brick wall.

The curtains were open, and the living room lights were on. I could see Julie watching the television. It was 7.30 and a school night. Paul would probably be in bed.

I grabbed his present and one of the two bunches of flowers from the back seat and got out of the car. The rain had stopped, but there was still a dampness in the air. Knocking on the door, I braced myself. Warm air wafted in my face as it opened and I was enveloped in a familiar scent.

I was expecting an argument, but what I got was worse... indifference.

'You'd better come in.'

Julie didn't wait for me to enter and returned to the lounge, switching off the television as I walked into the room. We both sat down at opposite ends, me feeling awkward with the presents in my hand.

'Whatever you were up to earlier, was it worth missing your son's football game?' she said, brushing the legs of her jeans.

It was difficult to look her in the face. 'No,' I replied. It was all I could come up with.

'I was hoping to give him this before I leave.' I held up the present.

'You're leaving?' She seemed surprised.

'I've been told to return, so we managed to book a flight for tomorrow evening.'

'And the flowers?' She pointed to them on my lap.

'They're for you.' I held them out.

'Guilt.' She spat the word and took them to the kitchen.

'Probably,' I said quietly to her back.

Ian Holland

From the kitchen, I heard her busily drawing water into a container. I took a last look around the living room, the spaces once filled by Alex. I superimposed his image onto the carpet holding his favourite teddy. And I could say we were all here, as a family, for one last time… it was more than I deserved.

The warmth of the moment was soothing, and my eyes began to close.

'You're not falling asleep, are you?' Julie returned with the vase of flowers and set them on the mantelpiece

I woke with a start. 'No,' I lied.

'You were snoring,' she replied, fussing over the flowers.

'Sorry, erm, I was wondering if I could see Paul before I go.'

'It's late, and he's got school tomorrow. Couldn't you come round in the morning, before he leaves?'

'Dad?' his voice called from upstairs.

I looked at Julie before she waved me on with a sigh. I crept up the stairs as quietly as I could, the bedroom was cloaked in darkness. As I switched on the light, Paul sat upright, shielding his eyes.

'I thought you were coming to football today?' his voice was husky with sleep. There wasn't an ounce of anger, and that made it harder to answer.

'I had work to do, son, I'm sorry.' I handed him the package. 'I got you this.'

'Thanks,' he barely looked at it. 'What about next week?'

I sat on the bed next to him, he smelt of soap, and his hair was still damp.

'I have to go back to South Africa tomorrow, Paul, there are things I have to sort out.'

Julie appeared in the doorway and leant against the frame, arms folded.

'Will you come back soon?' he was fidgeting with the present, not looking at me.

BREAKING POINT

My eyes filled up, and I found myself unable to speak. I put my arm around him and kissed the top of his head, my tears soaking into his hair. Julie was watching me... *Don't make him promises you can't keep.*

'I'm not sure,' I said. 'I need to go back and find out... erm, find out if... erm,' I couldn't think of an answer.

'Your dad *will* be back,' Julie's tone was unwavering. 'He made me a promise.'

I looked toward her. It didn't make sense, but I felt strengthened... *I had to find a way.* She smiled and left me alone to try and cram in five lost years. And the more I listened to his stories, the more profound was my regret.

'Not going to take my advice and stay put?' Julie asked as I opened the door to leave.

I turned to face her. 'And be a fugitive for the rest of my life?'

'Will you clear your name over there?

'Yes... yes,' I answered. 'I've got a lot of information that will support my case.'

'Has John helped?' His name came out so casually, I felt as though he'd walked into the space between us. She was watching me.

'Yes... yes, he's been great,' I said.

'Then you won't be charged with manslaughter?'

'No... no, that's unlikely now.'

'Yes, yes... no, no, you still repeat,' she said.

'Old habits,' I smiled.

'It used to be a sign of you lying, Danny.'

'Maybe I've changed,' I said, shivering as I stepped out into the cold evening.

Julie moved into the opening, holding the door ajar.

'What time are you leaving tomorrow?'

'About ten,' I said. 'I've borrowed a car, so I'm going to the cemetery first, take some flowers for Alex.'

'Say hello from me,' she replied.

'I will.'

Ian Holland

A familiar barrier had fallen between us, and there was nothing else to say. I walked to the gate and turned to wave goodbye, but the door had closed.

Without light from the house, the night closed in around me. The air was cold and miserable, condensation glued itself to my jacket. I got in the car and looked up at Paul's bedroom window. The curtains cracked open, and his head appeared. He was waving.

I got out and waved back, thankful my emotions were hidden in the darkness.

BREAKING POINT

Chapter 44

It was 10pm and a misty rain swept across the dim orange light leaking out from the windows of the engineering office. Inside, John Dread was sitting at his desk, sifting through a folder marked, *Quality Control, Material Certificates,* a cold cup of coffee sat close by. Beyond the office, the laboratory was in darkness.

A noise from behind made him turn around nervously. He peered, through his reflection on the glass panel and into the gloom beyond... *no one there*. He looked at his watch, the nightshift had just started, and the light from the office could attract unwanted attention. He returned to the paperwork with added urgency.

He'd borrowed the master keys from gatehouse security on the pretext that he needed to access the engineering office.

'I need to send some urgent information to a supplier,' he'd told them. The keys would also open Billy Jones' office. Once inside, he was able to access the MK6 material certificates folder without having to sign for them.

You've crossed the line, he thought, as he sifted through the certificates. This was a serious breach of the regulations and would lead to instant dismissal.

He eventually found the document relating to the MK6 bearings and took a photocopy. According to the records, there had only been one shipment from Houston. Reading down the information, he checked off the values with his own technical details.

Material Grade... tick. Tensile Strength... tick. Shear Strength... tick. Everything was in order.

The list detailing the chemical composition was beyond John's expertise. It might as well have been written in Latin. *Must be okay...* he thought.

He looked at the supplier's name again... *Machine Inc.* It had details of their Houston address, which he'd checked out and was legitimate. Below that, under the title of, *Subsidiary Supplier*, was the name of the foundry, *Almeja Fundicion;* which struck him as unusual.

This was a material certificate, and he would have expected the foundry to be classified as the supplier. He looked at other documents in the folder, and none included a *Subsidiary Supplier* reference, so he grabbed a dictionary to confirm the meaning.

Subsidiary company: A company owned or controlled by a holding company.

As he passed his green highlighter over the name, he heard the door of the laboratory creak open. Switches clicked, and the fluorescent lighting flashed and popped before illuminating the whole area. He spun around, pushing the documents into his drawer.

'Haven't you got a home to go to?' A security officer was shouting from the doorway.

John's heart was thumping. He shot up, opened the office door and poked his head out. 'Yeah, I'm just packing up,' he shouted across the laboratory.

'Finished with the keys?' the officer asked. 'Only I need to do my rounds.'

'No problem,' said John. 'I just need to send one more fax. Can you give me five more minutes?'

'Okay, I'll meet you at the gatehouse, just make sure you lock up.' The lights clicked off, and he disappeared.

John put the certificate back in the folder and slipped his own photocopy in his back pocket. He switched everything off and locked up the laboratory.

Moving outside, he made his way back to Billy's office and managed to replace the folder without bumping into anyone. It was bitterly cold and yet he was sweating. Making his way outside the building, he took the circuitous route back to the gatehouse; less likely to be seen.

'I hope the bastards are paying you for this?' the officer said as he looked at his watch and recorded John's exit time in the logbook.

BREAKING POINT

'Can't do enough for a good company,' John replied, trying to be casual while his stomach was churning.

'Is this to do with the accident?' the officer asked, turning the book around for John to sign.

'No, nothing like that,' John lied. His hand was shaking as he scribbled his name. 'See you tomorrow.' He made his way out as quickly as he could.

Hunching against the cold, he made his way through the car park. Everyone was talking about the accident, and all sorts of exaggerated rumours were passing through the Mathers grapevine. It was getting serious, and here he was breaking into a director's office. And, if anyone did do any digging, his presence was on record in the logbook.

It had been high risk, for very little return.

The certificate seemed to be in order, he patted his back pocket to make sure the copy was secure. *If,* and it was a big *if*, there was corrosion in the bearings, how was that even possible? Super Duplex 198 was a high quality, corrosive resistant material. He would have to wait for confirmation from Danny, but that would take time.

Meanwhile, he could find out more about the company's involved with the supply of the bearings. Machine Inc. in Houston and the subsidiary supplier, Almeja Fundicion in Mexico.

He jumped in his car and turned the ignition, the engine spluttered into life. He thought about going round to see Julie but put it out of his mind. He wasn't proud of what he did to Danny and felt sure he'd give himself away to her.

He put the car into gear and headed home.

Chapter 45

Stepping down from the hotel entrance, I breathed the morning air deep into my lungs. This was my home, and I craved to feel a part of it once more. The clouds were clearing, and the sun bled through the steel-grey sky. I'd explained to Steyn where I was going and that I'd pick him up later.

Driving north for half a mile, I passed through the new town and into Old Crossways. The roads narrowed considerably, built when life existed at a slower pace. A sign pointed the way to St. David's church, but I knew the turning well.

I pulled left onto the single-track lane, trying to avoid the dips and potholes muddying Billy's car, and within a minute I'd reached the tiny car park. It was 7.30 in the morning and, unsurprisingly, the place was empty.

Removing the bunch of flowers from the passenger seat, I got out of the car. It wasn't cold, but a shiver went through my body. It was so quiet and calm, almost eerie… *but there was nothing here to harm me.*

The gate had a rusty plaque, *Gods Acre,* and it squealed as I entered the lichen-covered graveyard, frightening two pigeons from a large oak tree. Their feathers whistled in flight and broke the silence before it finally settled once more. I carried on past the Norman church and the ageing headstones before coming to a modern stone cross.

I stood and looked at its inscription, trying to remember the good times and disregarding the bad, but shadows were already forming. The love and happiness I cherished became overwhelmed with dark thoughts. My body shivered, and the reek of damp earth turned my stomach.

My fingers tingled, and my hands unconsciously tightened, crushing the stems of the flowers. I tried to focus on the words etched into the marble, but my eyes were blinded with tears. Only when I closed them could I see him. Alex... my little boy.

I knew he was somewhere else, prayed he was somewhere else; yet all I could see was the cold, wet earth, hiding him from me. I wanted to explain, but this was far worse than I imagined... I couldn't leave him again.

I knelt, oblivious of the wet grass soaking through my trousers, and put the flowers into the ceramic vase next to his name.

'He'll like those...'

I turned, wiping the moisture from my nose and eyes with the arm of my jacket. Julie was smiling down at me, holding out a handkerchief.

'Pink was his favourite colour,' she said.

I got stiffly to my feet and took the hankie. 'Thanks,' I replied. 'How long have you been there?' My body was still trembling.

'Long enough.'

'Sorry...'

'What for? Missing your son... our son.'

'I wasn't expecting you,' I replied. 'But thanks anyway.'

She bent and finished arranging the flowers.

'There, that looks better.'

Then she stood beside me, staring at the display.

'Alex would have been eight years old,' she said.

'He'll always be three to me,' I replied and realised it was a stupid thing to say. Julie was grieving as well.

'How's Paul?' I asked.

'He's fine, he asked about you when he woke up. He's going to miss you.'

'I'll miss him,' I turned to look at her. 'You've done a great job.'

'Mmm, maybe.' She looked up at the sky. 'There's still time to miss your plane.'

'Would anything change if I did?' I asked.

We were facing one another, and I could see the question had made her feel awkward.

'Yes, for Paul,' she eventually answered. 'He needs his dad.'

I braced myself. 'And you?'

She looked at me, confused, and I felt foolish.

'Sorry... I... I didn't mean to...'

She touched my arm and smiled. 'We had our time, Danny.'

I nodded lamely.

'It was good for Paul to see you again, and for a moment...' She let go of my arm. 'For a moment I wondered...' Her voice began breaking. 'But things have moved on,' she said quietly, regaining her composure.

With John? I wanted to ask but was afraid of the answer.

'Paul and Alex will always be our sons,' she continued. 'And that's all that really matters.'

She turned back to the flowers. 'What time does your plane leave?'

'12.30.' I replied, afraid to give myself away.

She turned to look at me. 'I really hope everything works out when you get back home.'

It's not my home! I wanted to shout out, but no one was listening.

'I've made a promise to Paul,' I said. 'And I can't let him down again.'

I tried to discreetly wipe the tears from my eyes, and as the moment threatened to overwhelm me again, Julie took my hand.

Steyn and I didn't speak much on the journey back to the airport. We'd been driven by one of the young engineers who may have been briefed to report back on anything we said... *or maybe I was getting paranoid.*

In reality, there wasn't anything more to say. The trip had been inconclusive, and I was returning to an uncertain future; one that could exclude me from seeing my son again.

I'd given Van Heerden the impression I had evidence to prove the MK6 Stabiliser was at fault, but it was all circumstantial. The meeting in the Free State would be one-sided.

We arrived at Heathrow in good time. After despatching our luggage and picking up our tickets, we made our way to the departure lounge.

'I'll get coffee for the two of us,' I said.

Steyn nodded and made his way to one of the tables.

The concourse was busy, and as I looked around, I thought how easy it would be to disappear out of the main door and catch the first bus back to South Wales... but who was I trying to *kid.* I ordered two coffees and took them back to the table.

'Want to help me finish these?' Steyn said, pulling out his last pack of cigarettes. 'I'll be glad to get home and smoke something decent.'

'No thanks,' I said. 'I'm giving them up. You should too.'

'Again? No bloody way, man. These things keep me sane.' He lit up and disappeared behind a fog of smoke.

'Thanks for all your help,' I said. 'I know it hasn't been easy, but I don't think I'd have got through it without you.'

'We're not finished yet.' There was menace behind his statement. I looked at his grizzled features and smiled.

'There's nothing left in the tank, mate.'

'Don't start talking like that.' He pointed his cigarette at me.

I looked down at the band on my wrist. 'Which came first, Steyn, the chicken or the egg?'

'What you talking about?'

'It's an impossible question, isn't it? And this has all been about trying to find the answer to a similar one.'

'You've been overdoing it.' He was smiling at me, but I didn't have the energy to return it.

'I've been convinced the MK6 failed and caused the collapse on 120, yet I haven't found proof. A good engineer would investigate the counter-argument. Did the collapse on 120 cause the MK6 to fail?'

I took the elastic band off.

'But I've ignored that fact, and Stremsen is right about one thing. I haven't considered the possibility, even though everyone at Concorde IV thinks the same.'

Steyn was watching me, drawing in the smoke and exhaling it through his nostrils. He finished his coffee in two big gulps and squashed the cigarette into the ashtray as though he was trying to push it through the tabletop.

'So that's it, you're giving up?'

'No, I won't give up, I've got a son who's relying on me. I've just got to fight a new battle.'

'What new battle?' I could see he was getting angry.

'We have to find out *why* the 3S Initiative failed.'

It was the first time I'd said it out loud, and it hurt.

He was giving me the evil eye.

'What's wrong?' I said.

'Why the seismic sensors failed... listen to yourself, Danny, you're starting to sound like them.' He pointed into the distance. 'You've been around that lot for too long, and you know what they say?'

I wasn't really listening.

'He who walks with the lame learns how to limp.'

'Very profound,' I said. 'Did you hear that in the Broederbond?'

He banged his fist on the table, and I jumped up, along with half a dozen others around us.

'I'm sorry,' I said. 'That was uncalled for.'

'I'll put it down to your state of mind,' he replied through gritted teeth. Then leaned in close.

'The 3S Initiative was never meant to be infallible, and every man who went underground knew that, but look at the record. Over the last twelve months, Concorde IV has logged ten Amber warnings and two Red. The engineering

BREAKING POINT

team found seven of the Amber's warranted additional maintenance work, and one of the Red's justified sealing off and rerouting.'

I was about to interrupt, but he held up his hand.

'The remaining three Amber's and the Red, that didn't require work, tell a lot about the system.'

'What's that?' I asked, impressed by his recall.

'That it doesn't take chances, it's a *low-risk* system. Christ, we were close to one million Fatality Free Shifts.

'So, what's your point?' I said.

He dabbed his finger on the table. 'Isn't it a bit of a coincidence that within months of installing two MK6 Stabilisers, we get a collapse on 120, directly linked to one of them.'

He let the statement hang then let me have it.

'So don't give me this bullshit about failing, that bastard Stremsen is covering up something. Ever since we arrived, he's been putting obstacles in our way.'

'I agree, Steyn, but we've got nothing to show.' I couldn't get excited any more.

'We've still got things going on,' he said. 'Piet Reiss is bringing the damaged bearings up for us to look at when we get back, and *your mate* said he's going to do some digging around.'

Your mate... it wasn't difficult to hear the sarcasm in the tone.

'You don't like him, do you?' I already knew the answer.

'You're too loyal, Danny,' he pointed his finger at me. 'There's a lot about him you don't know.'

'Like why he attacked me,' I said.

He looked up, shocked. 'You knew!'

His voice carried across the coffee bar and made more people turn their heads.

'Not straight away.' I was uncomfortable talking about it but owed him an explanation.

'I believed there were only two people who had a motive. Socket because he hates my guts and John because...' I struggled to say it. 'Well... because of our connection with Julie.'

'So how did you find out?' he asked.

I was fiddling with the band and looked up at the flight-board. Unfortunately, ours wasn't being called, so I was on the spot.

'Yesterday I got proof it wasn't Socket, and that only left John.'

I put the band back on my wrist, pulling gently and releasing. The sensation ran up my arm and through my body.

'Has the bastard come clean?' asked Steyn.

I looked at him and smiled. 'What do you think?'

'Well he admitted it to me,' he replied. 'After a bit of persuasion.'

'Mmm, he must have been pretty angry, me coming back, meeting up with Julie. I know what he's like in drink, and that probably tipped him over the edge.'

'Don't justify it, Danny, are you going to say anything to Julie?'

'What for?' I said. 'There's nothing to gain from it. She told me she needs someone to rely on, and John seems to fill that space. I can't even promise I'll be a free man.'

He grabbed my arm. 'You can cut that crap out! I told you before, they're hiding something... we've just got to find out what.'

BREAKING POINT

Chapter 46

Now that Socket was on his way to South Africa, Billy Jones had asked John to take over the running of the laboratory. With no one looking over his shoulder, he'd found the contact number for Machine Inc., in Houston. He was waiting for an opportunity to ring them and for the first time, the office was empty.

He looked at his watch, it was 3:30pm, that meant 9:30am in Houston. He stood and checked the lab... *no one*, everyone was enjoying the freedom of Socket's absence.

He knew there was no going back once he rang the number. Stremsen would find out, and that would be the end of his career. He looked at the contact number, and his fingers punched them in. As it rang, he got cold feet and put the phone back down... *was there another way?*

Deep down, he knew there wasn't, took a deep breath and repeated the numbers. After a few seconds, a woman answered.

'Good morning, Machine Inc. How can I help?'... *there was still time to bail out.*

'Hello, Machine Inc. How can I help?' she repeated.

'Erm... hi... I wonder if I can talk to the CEO, please.'

There was a pause.

'Can I ask what this relates to, sir?'

He was already regretting his decision. 'Erm... I've got a query on one of your material certificates.'

Another pause.

'And the name of your company?' her voice seemed less friendly.

'Mathers in the UK,' he said... *he'd started to dig a hole.*

'Let me transfer you to the Quality Manager, I'm sure he can deal with your inquiry. Who should I say is calling?'

'Erm... John Dread,' he replied... *no turning back now.*

'One minute, please.'

The phone began ringing once more.

'Hi, John, Dwight Kerbow here, Quality Manager. How can I help?' The voice was bright and breezy.

'Hi, Dwight, I'm the design engineer from a company called Mathers, in the UK. You supplied us with a batch of Super Duplex 198 bearings, and I've got a question I'd like to ask about the material certificates.'

'Okay, fire away, and I'll do my best.' He didn't sound threatened or evasive... *a dead end?*

John pulled out the photocopy he'd taken the previous night and focussed on the highlighted text.

'I've noticed the suppliers name is shown as Machine Inc.,' he said.

'That's right, we're the suppliers of the product, are you having any problems?'

'I'm not sure,' said John. 'I understand that you supply us with the final machined product, but this is a material certificate. The supplier's name would normally be that of the company that produces the raw material.'

'Okay, just hold on a moment, I'll get our copy.'

The phone line clicked, and *mood music* took over. After a couple of minutes, another click.

'Hello, yes, I've got the original in front of me, and it does show the name of the foundry.'

'Yes,' John agreed. 'But it's under the title of *subsidiary supplier*. Does that mean that Almeja Fundicion isn't an independent foundry and is part of Machine Inc.?'

There was a long pause, and John had one of those sixth sense moments... *Dwight Kerbow was weighing up a response.*

'I can only answer for the certification, John. The foundry *is* part of Machine Inc., and that's why we have it clearly marked on the paperwork.'

His tone had become business-like, all the warmth evaporated into suspicion. The back of John's neck began to prickle as the conversation became uncomfortable.

BREAKING POINT

'Do you have a telephone number for them?' he asked.

Now there was a longer pause.

'I can deal with any questions you have, John.' He sounded irritated.

'I'd rather speak to the foundry directly if that's okay,' said John.

'You are speaking directly,' Kerbow answered. 'I'm Almeja's quality representative. Anything I can't answer, I will pass on to the appropriate person and get back to you by the next working day.'

'But why can't I ring directly and save all that delay?'

'That's not how the business is structured, Mr Dread, now can I have your question?'

Mr Dread, thought John… *time to bail out.*

'No, that's fine thanks, Dwight. I was just querying which name I should use to file the certificate. I'll put it under M, for Machine Inc. It's just that my boss is a bit of a stickler when it comes to paperwork. I appreciate your help.'

'No problem, John…' *He was bright and breezy again.* 'Y'all have a nice day.'

The phone went dead.

John couldn't take his eyes off the highlighted text; *Subsidiary Company*. He needed to ring the foundry direct, but he needed a plan. He was in so deep now; he couldn't see over the top.

The last engineer made his way from the office. 'See you, John.'

John looked up. 'Cheers, Richie.'

He'd been waiting for him to leave for the last half an hour and looked at his watch. It was 5:30pm, which made it 11:30am in Mexico.

He pulled his handwritten notes from the drawer and went over them once more. They were covered in doodles; distractions while he tried and failed to form a written strategy, there simply wasn't one for this kind of conversation. He went over everything in his head once more.

He'd found out about the relationship between Machine Inc. and Almeja Fundicion. It had been a surprise, and he doubted anyone else in Mathers was aware of it, but that didn't mean there was a conflict of interest. The question had provoked a frosty response from Kerbow, but he had confirmed the connection without prompting; no awkwardness or outrageous lies.

Not being able to contact Almeja directly was unusual but not enough to be suspicious. *Then why am I risking everything?* He wondered.

He scanned the words once more, *Subsidiary Supplier*, it just didn't look right. He pulled back his notes.

He'd tried to get the number of Almeja from Mathers purchasing department, but they'd started asking awkward questions and he didn't want to push it. Only one other person could help him out, but it would have to wait until tomorrow morning.

BREAKING POINT

Chapter 47

'**It's not much,** Mr Core.' I could hear the disappointment in Van Heerden's voice.

Steyn and I had managed to get some sleep on the plane ready for the de-brief, but we were still exhausted.

We stood across from his desk, arms behind our backs. All we needed was a blindfold, and the picture would be complete. I gripped the report of our findings in the UK, having just finished presenting its contents.

After the low temperatures of Crossways, the late afternoon heat of Johannesburg was stifling, though it didn't help that we were both overdressed. I'd explained my concerns about the safety factors and the lack of control during assembly. Still, it was a poor return for seven days of work.

'But they've answered those concerns, haven't they?' Van Heerden's point hit home, and it was an effort to nod in agreement. I showed him the images of the damaged bearings and saw the shock on his face.

'Is this amount of damage possible if the safety factors were adequate?' he asked.

'They're saying the collapse caused them to shear, and ditto why the failsafe switches failed.' I pointed to the discoloured areas on the photographs.

'We believe these could be signs of corrosion.' He glared down at the images. 'Once it's confirmed, we have a contact in Mathers who'll work on our behalf.'

His eyes turned back on me. 'Don't you mean, *if* it's confirmed? And this contact, what responsibility does he have?'

'He's a senior engineer,' I answered. 'And we trust him.'

'Mmm, I'm assuming none of the people we're meeting tomorrow have any knowledge of this?'

Steyn and I both shook our heads.

He looked at Steyn.

'Do you trust this contact, Mr Broed?'

I was about to say something, but Van Heerden put his hand up. 'I asked your Mine Captain.'

Steyn took an age to answer.

'No I don't...' he finally said, and Van Heerden's tanned features glowed beneath his grey hair. 'But my head's not on the block. I only met him a week ago, but Danny's known him for years, and that's good enough for me.'

Van Heerden turned to look out of the window over the metropolis. I looked at Steyn and mouthed, *thank you.* He winked back. The seconds ticked by and Van Heerden didn't move. A thin, dark profile against the vast panorama; dead centre and hands clasped behind his back.

The morning sun reflected off the pristine stinkwood desk, casting an elongated shadow from the expensive pen, equispaced and adjacent to the front edge. I'd travelled thirteen thousand miles, yet everything here seemed to have stood still.

'I commend you for such an honest answer, Mr Broed.'

Steyn raised his eyebrows to me, and I couldn't help smiling.

Van Heerden turned back around, his face giving nothing away. The immaculate suit, white shirt and cufflinks with the Rinto Gold logo protruding below the dark sleeves.

'This *contact* is highly irregular, and if your visitors were to find out, I would deny knowledge of this conversation.' His hands tugged his cuffs, teasing them out to expose equal proportions.

'You are taking a huge risk, but that's the path you've chosen. I will make judgements on facts alone, you understand?'

We nodded.

BREAKING POINT

He pulled a sheet of paper from his drawer. 'I've had notification from the other attendees.' He looked down the page.

'The CEO, Rik Last and someone called Luca Majori are flying in from Houston. Fred Stremsen and Terry Socket are flying in from the UK. They've declined my offer of seats on the company jet, preferring to make their own travel arrangements to Concorde IV.'

'Did they give a reason?' I asked.

'No, but I would have done the same in the circumstances. They're keeping their distance from us.'

I couldn't help feeling I'd contaminated everyone associated with the accident.

His attention turned back to the sheet of paper.

'Mr Last is at pains to point out they have already proved, beyond doubt, that the MK6 Recycling Stabiliser is not implicated in the accident at Concorde IV. And they are only attending the meeting as a mark of respect.' He looked up and raised his eyebrows.

'I challenged them about your complaint about Mathers withholding information. His denial was expected, but it keeps them on the back foot. However, none of this will be enough without absolute proof.'

He looked at the two of us.

'Do you still believe the MK6 is implicated in the accident?'

I nodded.

'The bastards are hiding something,' said Steyn. His outburst brought a rare smile to Van Heerden's face.

'Then let's hope we can get this resolved without further injuries.'

He pointed to the plasters at the back of my ear and the strapping on Steyn's hand. It broke the ice, and we both smiled in embarrassment.

'The meeting is arranged for 9 o'clock tomorrow morning,' he continued. 'I suggest we have an early night and reconvene here at 7 am. I've arranged for transport to the airport where the company jet will be ready to take us to the Free State.'

As Steyn and I walked away, my stomach turning at the thought of another journey in the small plane.

'Could you give us five minutes alone, Mr Broed?' Steyn grunted his assent and closed the door behind him.

What now, I thought.

Van Heerden stooped to press the intercom button and seemed to brace himself.

'Mr Van?' The voice of his secretary screeched through the speaker.

'Can you bring in the letter, Jean?' he said and looked up at me.

Almost immediately, she walked in with a manila envelope and touched my shoulder as she passed it to Van Heerden. I remembered her consideration the last time I was here and smiled as she left.

'Please sit down, Mr Core.'

I took a seat, and he did the same, placing the envelope carefully on his desk.

'I've received a letter from the police authorities.' He tapped the envelope with his finger, and I went cold.

'It contains a form which I have to return to them by midnight tomorrow.'

'To do with the accident?' I asked, knowing the answer.

He nodded. 'I'm obliged by law to comply.' The intonation made it sound like an apology.

'Have you done this before?' I asked.

My tongue was dry, and I clasped my hands together to stop them shaking.

'No, these are recent changes to the law.'

He was speaking so quietly, I had to strain to hear him.

'Mining is in a state of flux,' he continued. 'What was tolerated under your predecessor is now history. It was one of the reasons we promoted you.'

'A scapegoat,' I said. I couldn't help myself.

BREAKING POINT

He ignored my comment. 'I've been advised to ask you for your passport.'

Despair turned to anger, and I shook my head in disbelief.

'If you thought I was to blame, don't you think I would have stayed in the UK?'

He smiled at me. 'If I thought you were to blame, Mr Core, do you think I would have let you go to the UK?'

'Mmm, I suppose not,' I said, embarrassed at my outburst.

His smile evaporated.

'In the event of the worst scenario, I've arranged for you to be represented by the Rinto Gold legal team. I can't guarantee what the outcome will be, suffice to say the company will fund all your costs.'

I was stunned. 'That's very generous.'

'It's a calculated risk, nothing more. You have just over twenty-four hours to find proof that Mathers is responsible and I will do all I can to help, but ultimately the onus is on you.'

He stood and led me to the door.

'Do you want me to leave my passport?' I asked.

He shook his head. 'We have work to do.'

Chapter 48

'**Are we going** to get ambushed, Fred?' Rik Last was still weary with jet lag.

He'd arrived with Luca Majori four hours ago from Houston, and had only managed a little sleep. It was now 6.30 in the evening, and the sun wasn't budging in the clear blue sky of Johannesburg. The streets were noisy and breathless with heat. The humidity was playing havoc with his hair.

'In what way?' Stremsen looked pained.

Don't, fucking, start, said Likky.

Last rolled his eyes. 'If you think I've come all this way to be embarrassed.'

Stremsen gave him a smile. 'We've been with Core for over six days, Rik…' He looked across at Socket who nodded and took another drink of beer. 'He's had full access to the data and hasn't found a shred of evidence to back up what he's saying.'

Stremsen and Socket had flown in a couple of hours earlier from Heathrow and been summoned to an early dinner before either had time to unpack. None of them had much of an appetite.

'And the failsafe switches?' Majori added his concerns. 'Have they accepted they didn't function *because* of the collapse?'

Socket nodded and Last saw the gesture. 'Is that a yes, Terry?'

The nodding stopped. 'Erm… well, not exactly.'

Then why are you fucking nodding! Likky hated empty gestures.

Stremsen jumped in. 'They haven't signed anything, if that's what you mean, Rik?'

'I'm not asking for a signed document, Fred, just an opinion… your opinion.'

BREAKING POINT

He pushed his plate away. He had no desire for *any* of this and looked toward the window to the street beyond, just managing to catch his reflection.

'Core will never openly admit it,' said Stremsen, leaning forward on his elbows. 'But he hasn't been able to produce evidence that implicates the MK6, and we have the PMT process to thank. Every question they've put to us, we've been able to substantiate with documented proof.'

'The chairman of Rinto Gold suggested you've withheld information, is that true?' Last despised deception from others.

'No,' Stremsen replied. 'There was a mix-up with some of the files, but that was sorted out by our Engineering Director.'

'I'm glad you brought the subject up.' Luca looked first at Socket, then at Stremsen. 'Why isn't Billy Jones here? Surely as the Engineering…'

'I'm restructuring at Mathers.' Stremsen cut him off. 'A new position of Worldwide Quality Director is being made to oversee quality measures and new developments in the future.'

What the fuck! Likky didn't like surprises.

'Were you planning on sharing this information, Fred?' Last fidgeted with his glass of iced tea.

'Of course, Rik, I wasn't going to make a formal announcement until I'd cleared it with you. But with all this going on…'

'So what's the relevance of giving Billy Jones a different title?' asked Last.

Majori looked confused as well. 'And how does that explain Billy Jones' absence.'

Socket squirmed in his seat as Stremsen loosened his collar button.

'Because Terry Socket will be taking up the new role,' he replied.

An embarrassing silence hung around the table.

Is this a fucking joke? It was a step too far for Likky.

Last reached for his comb again. 'And where is Billy Jones in all this?'

'Billy's role will be redundant.' Stremsen's voice tapered off, but it didn't lessen the impact.

Last gave his hair a few strokes, musing over what he'd just been told. He looked over toward Socket then back to Stremsen.

Fucking morons, said Likky.

'Put that decision on hold until we deal with this issue.' The bluntness of the statement created an embarrassing silence.

'Of course, Rik,' Stremsen tried filling the gap. 'But Terry has led this investigation and countered all of Core's ridiculous accusations. He's proved himself as a real leader.'

Socket decided to add his weight to the argument.

'Danny Core is trying to deflect the blame from his safety Initiative, I wouldn't believe a word he says. I've known him for a long time, and he'll find any way to twist the truth.'

Luca turned to face him. 'I met Core five years ago, and he didn't give me that impression.'

'You don't know him,' Socket replied, gulping down his third bottle of Castle lager. Johannesburg's altitude on the Highveld plateau was exaggerating its effect.

Stremsen tried to cut in. 'Thanks, Terry, but let's keep personalities out of this.' It was to no avail.

'Take this business with the bearings,' Socket continued. 'It's just another desperate attempt to undermine the design.'

Bearings! What fucking bearings? Another surprise for Likky.

Luca's face went rigid as Rik spun round to face Stremsen. 'It seems two people have knowledge that hasn't been shared,' he said.

BREAKING POINT

Stremsen put his face in his hands. Only twenty-four hours ago he'd told Socket to... *keep this information between us, it'll only complicate matters.* And now...

'What's the *problem* with the bearings?' Luca's question was directed at Stremsen.

'Nothing, it's all under control now.'

Business with the bearings... since fucking when? Likky was doing somersaults.

Rik's stare seemed to threaten the lenses in his glasses. 'Why haven't we been told, Fred?'

'Because it's been dealt with, Rik.' Stremsen was glaring at Socket.

'What's the issue?' asked Luca more pointedly.

Stremsen looked from one questioner to the other.

'They took photographs of some of the damaged bearings and *claim* they show signs of corrosion, but it's bullshit. The whole area is contaminated with mud and crap from the site. The photographs are way too grainy to show any detail.'

'Do we have copies of these photographs?' asked Rik.

'No,' said Stremsen.

'Why not, surely they're evidence?' Luca was back in the conversation.

'Because at the time, they were accusing us of having bearings missing and, once again, we proved them wrong by explaining the process, and showing them the PMT documents.'

Luca turned to Socket who had gone very quiet. 'Anything to say about that, Terry?'

'Well, they did...'

'They did nothing, Terry...' Stremsen was angry. 'Except try and undermine the integrity of the process.'

Socket shut up as the rant continued.

'The photographs proved that the Stabiliser had the correct number of bearings, and once again, they had to agree. So there was no need to keep copies.'

'What would be the significance of corrosion, Terry?' Last's question caught Socket off-guard, and he glanced at Stremsen.

Last saw the look and pointed his finger.

'I asked *you* the question, and I want the truth.' He felt the back of his neck bristle. 'Or so help me God, you will not see your next pay-cheque.' His raised voice had attracted the attention of the diners nearby.

Answer the fucking question? Likky didn't care.

'It can't happen,' Terry said with a little more humility, though his face was crimson. 'The bearings are corrosion resistant, what they see as corrosion is surface contamination.'

'And you've explained that to them?' Last was still pointing.

Stremsen and Socket nodded in unison.

'Hypothetically, what if the bearings were corroded?' This time Majori asked the question. 'Would that cause a failure?'

Stremsen answered. 'Not in such a short time frame.'

'Your opinion, Terry?' Last wouldn't let him go.

'They've only been installed for six months, Rik, it's not possible.' He was squirming again.

Last looked across at Majori, then again to Stremsen and Socket. 'Fred, I asked you to keep me informed of everything. Now, twelve hours away from a meeting to discuss why nine men died, you drop this bombshell.'

Stremsen held out his hands. 'It's covered Rik, we have certificates.'

Shut the fuck up! Likky had had enough.

'Quiet, and listen to me,' Last's voice was calm and controlled. 'I'm still convinced we've been too cooperative, and if I had my way, we would not be here.' He gave Majori a fierce stare.

Fucking moron, Likky wasn't happy.

'We've underestimated Core, he's got spunk, and we should have been more cautious.'

BREAKING POINT

Once again, he pulled the comb out and ran it through his hair. Left side, right side, three times through the centre and smooth down. He glanced toward his reflection in the window and replaced the comb. All eyes were on him as he turned to Stremsen.

'Are we walking into an ambush, Fred?' he asked once again.

Stremsen didn't falter. 'No,' he said. 'One hundred and ten per cent, no!'

'Mmm, okay. I've declined an invitation to join the Rinto Gold team on their private plane and instead arranged for an air-conditioned bus to pick us up from the hotel at 5 am. The three-hour journey will be in the cooler part of the day, which should make us the first to arrive...' he pointed at Stremsen. 'Fully briefed. Fred, you and Terry will be visiting the accident site, as agreed, but you will say as little as possible.'

'Yeah, about that...' said Stremsen.

Luca was shaking his head in warning.

Likky was going ballistic!

'Don't go there.' Rik waved the comment away. 'I hope we'll have this business concluded in time for an early evening journey back to Johannesburg. Only *if* we get a satisfactory conclusion to this, will we discuss the reorganisation.' He peered at Socket under his dark, bristly eyebrows.

'Until then, everything is off the table.'

Chapter 49

It was strange returning to Concorde IV. When was the last time I'd been here; seven… eight days ago? I'd lost count. There were moments in Crossways when it seemed like years, but right now it felt like yesterday.

The flight from Johannesburg had been smooth and given me a rare opportunity to admire the beauty of the Orange Free State from the air. I hadn't realised how diverse the scenery would be. The land was washed in so many shades of blues, browns and greens, I wished I had a camera. One moment verdant fields were bursting with crops, the next, grasslands interspersed with acacia trees and rocky outcrops reached hundreds of feet toward a vast blue sky.

When we crossed into the industrial goldfields, the setting became utilitarian. Headgears and mine dumps dominated the landscape, and townships became more prominent. Modern roads linked them with more substantial towns, but politics provided unseen barricades to keep them apart.

Our taxi pulled into the Concorde IV car park, which was virtually empty. Only the maintenance teams and other vital workers, linked to the repairs, were necessary while the mine was on shutdown.

As we walked toward the gatehouse, Van Heerden pointed to the motionless headgear in the distance.

'That inactivity is costing us one-hundred thousand rand a day, Mr Core.'

It seemed like every time he raised me up, he needed to drop me back down; I could never understand his motive.

'Good morning, Boss.' Marshall, the gateman, immaculate in his uniform and cap, greeted us from the entrance with his unmistakable voice.

'How's the hand?' asked Steyn while Van Heerden looked on quizzically.

BREAKING POINT

Marshall surprised us all and pulled it out of his jacket. The gaps in the white bandage where his fingers should have been made me wince.

'I believe they are starting to grow back,' he said, and laughed out loud.

It put my issues into perspective. Steyn and I laughed along with him, and I felt better. The look on Van Heerden's face was a picture, and I'm sure he wanted to smile.

'Your visitors have arrived,' Marshall said, waving us through.

We walked across the compound following the winding concrete path. On the far side, the conveyors were silent, hidden within the confines of the reduction plant. The covered walkway, generally filled with workers, was empty and cast a long shadow in the morning sun. The bushes and protea plants lined up along the pathway were starting to wilt from the lack of attention, and the lawn had the consistency of hay.

I saw Van Heerden look up at the dormant winding house emblazoned with *Rinto Gold* in black and *Concorde IV* in red.

'Very impressive,' he said. *I wondered if he was complimenting the signage, or being derisive about the lack of production.*

'What happened to his hand?' He nodded back toward the gatehouse.

'He lost three fingers and part of his thumb,' I replied.

'Mmm, about six months ago, at the stopes?' he enquired.

Steyn and I looked at one another.

'Yes,' I replied. 'I'm surprised…'

'That I'd know?' he interrupted.

'Well… yes.'

'Every accident report passes across my desk,' he replied. 'And I make it my business to read them all.' He brushed down his suit and straightened his tie pin. 'Rinto Gold has to be efficient, Mr Core, but it's not heartless.'

I felt he wanted to say more, but walked on.

We entered the Engineering Office and were met by Laura, my secretary. It was good to see a friendly face.

'Mr Core, so nice to have you back.' She gave me a hug and turned to point at Steyn. 'I hope you've been looking after him?'

I was cringing, but Steyn loved every minute of it.

'I tucked him in every night, Laura,' he replied.

'Don't believe him,' I said.

'You know Mr Van Heerden?'

'Only through Jean, your secretary,' she replied, offering her hand. 'Nice to meet you.'

'And you. Our guests are waiting?'

'Yes, they've been here for about half an hour.'

I looked at my watch, it was 8:30.

'Is Piet Reiss here?' Steyn asked.

'Yes, since 6 o'clock. He's waiting for you in your office.'

'Right, shall we get on?' Van Heerden sounded impatient.

'Steyn, why don't you catch up with Piet,' I said. 'See if he's brought those samples for us to look at. Maybe check if everything's okay for us to get down to 120.' I didn't want more surprises.

'No problem.' He gave me a knowing wink as he made his way out.

Laura led us toward my office. 'I'll bring in some fresh coffee.'

Van Heerden nodded.

'You've been here since 6 o'clock?' I whispered to her as we entered the room.

She waved me away with a smile. 'Someone had to reorganise your office.'

'Thanks,' I said and turned to follow Van Heerden in.

BREAKING POINT

He stopped and turned around to face me, so close I could feel his breath on my face.

'We will not take a backward step,' he said in a menacing whisper. It was like an electric charge through my body.

'Thanks,' I said and followed him in.

I barely recognised the place, there was so much space. My desk and drawing board had been pushed against the walls, and my camp bed had disappeared. In the right-hand corner, the computer lay untouched, and the space in the middle was now occupied by a large, circular table.

Four faces looked around as we entered. I recognised Stremsen and Socket, the other two I hadn't seen for a long time.

Chapter 50

John picked the phone up on the first ring. The office was full, and he was aware that he could be overheard.

'John, it's Dawn. I've tried every way I can to find this number for Almeja Fundicion, but everything directs me back to Machine Inc. in Houston.'

'I had the same problem,' he replied.

'Are you going to tell me what all this is about?' She sounded suspicious.

'I can't say at the moment, you've got to trust us.' He looked around, making sure no one could hear.

'Us, as in you and Danny?' she replied.

'It's complicated.'

'Is he in trouble?'

'Yes, and I'm trying to help.'

'Okay, I'm assuming you'll tell me when the time's right. Let me know if I can do anything,' she said.

'Thanks. You won't be implicated in anything.'

'I don't care. Just let me know.' The phone went dead.

It had been a long shot... *and probably another dead-end*, he thought. But what next?

He pulled out the certificate once more, the green highlights seemed to be taunting him. His phone rang again.

'John, it's Billy Jones here. Can you pop over for a minute?'

Putting the certificate back in his drawer, he pulled out yesterday's laboratory test results, Billy probably wanted them for his monthly report.

He took the same circuitous route as the previous night; it would give him time to think through the next step.

When he arrived, he tapped the door and walked in. Billy was standing next to the window, filling his pipe.

'These are copies of the latest test results,' John said and laid them on the desk.

BREAKING POINT

Billy looked up. 'Close the door and take a seat, John.'
All very formal, thought John.
'Everything okay, Billy?'
No answer. Billy sat opposite and lit his pipe. Three puffs of increasingly dense smoke were followed by a deep intake of breath, the smoke would take an age to exhaust from his mouth and nose. The pleasant aroma from the tobacco had a calming effect and the sun, shining through the window, exaggerated the smoky plumes as they floated toward the ceiling.

'Working late last night?' Billy's question set off alarm bells with John.

'Erm, yeah, I had to fax some documents.' He could feel his face redden.

'Taken from my office?'

Billy's voice was calm and reasonable, smoke sputtering out with each syllable, but he wasn't smiling.

'What do you mean, your office?'

John tried crossing his legs, then folding his arms, trying to make himself smaller. Less of a target.

'Security reported that during their second security check, at midnight, they found my door unlocked.'

'So?' said John. 'What's that got to do with me?'

'They confirmed the office was locked when they did their first check at 7pm,' Billy was still breathing out smoke.

'Do I need my union rep?' John was trying to stay calm, but his heart was pounding. *How could he forget to lock the bloody door?*

'Fine by me,' said Billy. 'But then you'll have to explain to both of us why you borrowed the master key in between those security checks.'

Bollocks! No point in denial, he thought. 'I needed to get some documents, at short notice.'

'What documents, and who needed them so urgently?' said Billy. The last of the smoke seeped from his nostrils.

'I can't remember, I had a lot on.'

'Was it the MK6 material certificates?' Billy relit his pipe and went through the same process; three deep puffs and inhale.

He knew which documents… John was desperately trying to excuse his lies when Billy put him out of his misery.

'You *must* have had a lot on because you returned them to the wrong drawer.'

John felt his legs shake uncontrollably as Billy continued.

'I've been trying to get my head around why an intelligent person like you would risk your career doing what you did.' Billy was shaking his head. 'You could have waited until the morning and had full access. And then it came to me.'

He put his pipe in the ashtray.

'You didn't want to sign for them, did you?'

Billy stood and removed a folder from the drawer marked Quality Control and dropped it on the desk in front of John… *MK6 Material Certificates.*

'What were you looking for in there, that you didn't want anyone to know about?'

John was floundering, all reason hanging by a thread. He couldn't speak, let alone come up with a plausible excuse.

Billy sat back down and opened his hands toward John. 'Tell me the truth, no bullshit, and maybe we can find a way past this.'

'How do I know I can trust you?'

John wasn't going to expose Danny, not after all that had happened.

Billy gave a lop-sided smile. 'You've seen my relationship with Socket and Stremsen, do you really think it's in my best interests to tell tales. I'm just curious to know why?'

'What about Security?' John asked.

BREAKING POINT

'They're waiting for my response,' said Billy. 'That's why I'm giving you this chance. I can explain that I gave you permission and forgot to inform them, but only if you tell me the truth.'

John thought it through and realised there was *nothing to lose now*.

He told Billy about the photographs and the signs of corrosion on the bearings.

'Have you informed Stremsen?' asked Billy.

John frowned. 'I told Socket about *possible* corrosion and assumed he'd pass the information on to you.'

'First I've heard of it,' said Billy. 'But, like I said, that doesn't surprise me. Can I have a look?'

John collected them from the lab, and when he returned, Billy asked him to lock the door.

'It has to be some form of contamination,' Billy said, squinting at the images under his desk lamp. 'Super Duplex 198 wouldn't corrode like this.'

'Agreed,' said John, 'But Danny's got other ideas. He's having the bearings brought up for a proper examination. They might even be looking at them as we speak.'

'So why the cloak and dagger stuff based on some *dodgy* photographs?'

'Look at the certificate.' John pointed to the folder.

Billy removed the sheet from the manila cover.

'What am I looking at?'

'The Subsidiary Supplier reference. Doesn't it strike you as odd that they've got the foundry down as a subsidiary supplier, and the machining company as the material supplier?'

Billy scanned the document. 'I've never seen that before,' he said. 'But it's hardly a reason to risk your job.'

John was looking at his hands. 'There's something else.'

'Come on then, full disclosure.'

'I tried phoning the CEO of Machine Inc.' Saying it out loud made it sound like a misdemeanour, and Billy's reaction didn't help.

'You did what!'

'Why not?' said John, lifting his hands up.

'You're investigating them,' said Billy. 'If they put two and two together... Just give me the whole story.'

John spent half an hour trying to explain what he'd unearthed. When he'd finished, Billy lit up his pipe.

'You're in deep shit, John. If it gets out that you've been making enquiries on behalf of Danny Core and Rinto Gold, even I wouldn't be able to defend you.'

'But doesn't it strike you as odd that the Quality Manager for Machine Inc. is the spokesman for the material supplier, Almeja Fundicion?'

Billy pointed at the document. 'From where I'm sitting, you're trying to find evidence to implicate Mathers, and that's something I can't ignore.'

'So you're going to report me?'

'This is a different level from breaking into my office, John. I've been open-minded throughout this process, even when it could have cost me my job. But Danny Core has consistently failed to find evidence that the Stabiliser is implicated in the accident. You realise who pays our wages?'

'I'm trying to clear up a loose end,' John replied. 'You've got to admit it's odd. And, as the Technical Director, if our auditors found out about this anomaly, you'd have some explaining to do.'

'And you're going to tell them?'

'I'm like you, Billy, maybe it's something I can't ignore.'

'Mmm,' Billy looked once more at the document. 'I've still got a few contacts working in metallurgy labs, I'll see if I can get more information on Almeja Fundicion. In the meantime, shred your copy of the certificate. I'll make a few phone calls, then we can talk again.'

'And this is between us, Billy?'

John saw the irritation in his eyes. 'You've given me no choice.'

Chapter 51

Van Heerden walked into the room with a purpose. 'Good morning, gentlemen and welcome to South Africa.'

He made a beeline toward the tall man with the glasses and the Heron badge. 'Mr Last, good to meet you, even though it is under difficult circumstances.'

Last shook his hand warmly. 'And you, Mr Van Heerden, please call me Rik.' He extended his arm toward the other men.

'This is Fred Stremsen, Terry Socket and Luca Majori.' They shook hands.

Van Heerden introduced me, and there was another round of handshakes. At least it went better than the last time we introduced ourselves.

'We've met before, Luca,' I said as I shook his hand.

'Yes, we have. Good to see you again, Danny.' His handshake was the only one that felt genuine.

Stremsen didn't look best pleased when Rik Last gave a complementary anecdote about a meeting we had over five years ago. I was surprised he remembered.

The large table had name tags allocated, so everyone knew their place. Rik Last was next to Van Heerden, and I was between Majori and Stremsen, facing Socket. It looked like Dawn had done her best to avoid conflict.

She came in with fresh coffee and biscuits, and after some small-talk, Van Heerden called the meeting to order.

'Gentlemen, we are not here to apportion blame, our role is to try and resolve the circumstances that led to the tragic events of ten days ago. It's hoped that your support, and willingness to cooperate, will allow the families of the victims to move on.'

Rik Last interrupted. 'Thank you, Thys.' He spread his arms wide. 'But as I said, when accepting your invitation, we have already cooperated with Danny at our Mathers

BREAKING POINT

facility. And the MK6 Recycling Stabiliser, at the centre of his investigation, has been cleared of any involvement.'

'That's quite right,' Stremsen added his approval and Socket nodded.

Van Heerden looked around the table, his expression didn't change. He crossed his legs and adjusted his shirt cuffs so that the *RG* logo of his cufflinks faced the same way.

'Are you all aware of corrosion on the damaged bearings?' he asked.

The silence deepened, and I saw Rik Last turn to look at Stremsen.

'Have you seen the photographs?' Van Heerden directed the question to Last, but Stremsen jumped in.

'Yes, we saw them at Mathers, Thys, and we were all agreed that it was contamination from the collapsed area.'

Van Heerden looked at me. 'Did you agree, Mr Core?'

I shook my head. 'No, the photographs weren't conclusive. That's why we've arranged for the bearings to be made available for everyone to look at today.'

What the fuck! Likky joined the meeting.

Last stroked his hair and tapped his inside pocket.

'Have you looked at the bearings, Danny?' Luca looked calm, but his voice sounded strained.

'No, the process of stripping down the Stabiliser began while we were in the UK, I've only seen the photographs.' I tried to sound positive.

'And that's another thing, Thys,' Stremsen's voice had gone up a couple of decibels. 'Your people dismantled the Stabiliser before we had a chance to send in our own engineers. That's tampering with the evidence.' His face was reddening.

'We came here as a goodwill gesture. We gave Core full access to the Mathers facilities, and you've responded by ambushing us with a trumped-up issue about corroded bearings. What sort of thanks is that?'

I looked around the table, the outburst had caught everyone by surprise. All eyes were on Stremsen except Van Heerden who was looking directly at me with a wicked smile.

'Yes!' It was the first word Socket had spoken.

Van Heerden's smile disappeared, and he turned to look at him. 'Pardon,' he said.

Socket sunk into his chair as he tried to finish what he'd started. 'The bearings, they've been dealt with. We checked the photographs and the correct numbers were assembled.'

Van Heerden ignored him and turned to Stremsen. 'We're not talking about quantity, as you well know, the question mark surrounds the quality of the bearings. Please explain, Mr Core.'

All eyes turned on me, I gave the band on my wrist a couple of pulls. I was so uptight, I couldn't feel a thing and looked across at Last... we *will not take a backward step*. Right, here we go...

'We discovered signs of possible corrosion on some of the photographs...' I began.

'And we've already agreed that that's impossible.' Stremsen was getting animated again.

Shut the fuck up, Likky was fretting.

'Let Mr Core finish, Fred.' Last pulled his comb out of the inside pocket of his jacket and ran it through his hair. Left side, right side and three times through the centre. I noticed his hand shaking a little as he looked toward the window of the office.

I tried once again. 'I emphasise, *possible corrosion* because the photographs weren't the best quality and that's why we've arranged to carry out a visual inspection, with you in attendance. This way, we can come to a joint agreement.'

It was the most significant gamble of my working life, and I had no control over events. My future was about to be decided with a subjective examination by two partisan groups, and I was in the minority.

BREAKING POINT

I might have laughed if I hadn't felt like throwing up.

Van Heerden pointed at Stremsen. 'You are under no obligation to look at the bearings, we just thought it proper to share the physical evidence. I'm disappointed you believe it to be some sort of trap.'

Stremsen, you're making things fucking worse! Likky sensed problems.

Rik Last raised his finger. 'Fred, I think you've misinterpreted Thys' offer. Of course we'd all like to see these bearings, then we can put this issue to bed, once and for all.'

Van Heerden gave me a nod, and I left the room to find Piet and Steyn.

Chapter 52

Within an hour of leaving Billy's office, John had a phone call summoning him back. When he arrived, Billy was staring out of the window and barely acknowledged him as he walked in.

'Lock the door behind you,' he said.

John turned the key and took a seat. He noticed the material certificate for the bearings laid out next to a thick reference book. On top was a sheet of paper with handwritten notes. He craned his neck, trying to read the remarks.

Billy turned around and sat opposite, blowing out his cheeks. John didn't know whether this was a good sign, or not, everything was turned on its head.

'Well?' John snapped the question at him. They were both implicated by their enquiries, and status meant nothing at this moment in time. 'Did you get a contact for the foundry?'

Billy nodded. 'Mmm.'

'Is that a yes?' John was getting impatient.

'I'm not sure we should be doing this,' said Billy. He looked upset.

'We've been through this,' said John. 'We agreed…'

'This has got implications, John, way beyond our pay scales.' He pulled out a pouch of tobacco and filled his pipe, but his hands were shaking and some spilt onto the desk. John watched him brush it off and try again; the result was no better.

As Billy reached for the matches, John grabbed them and pulled them away.

'You've rung the foundry, haven't you?'

Billy nodded and put the pipe down. 'I got the number off a friend of mine.'

'And…' John leaned in closer. 'Are they're crooked?'

Billy shook his head.

BREAKING POINT

'No, just the opposite. His company uses them *and* Machine Inc. Both companies have good track records.'

That caught John unawares. 'Then why do you look like you've been caught with your hand in the till?'

Billy lifted the blue reference book and passed over a sheet of paper hidden underneath.

'This is what Almeja have sent me.'

It was a material certificate, grainier than the original because it had been faxed. John read through it, trying to understand what he was looking at.

'It's Almeja's material certificate for the MK6 bearings,' Billy explained, his eyes darting between John and the locked door.

'I don't understand,' John couldn't make sense of it. 'It's the same certificate… but different.'

He scanned across it again. 'There…' he said, turning it around to show Billy. 'It says, *Material Supplier, Almeja Fundicion*, there's no mention of a subsidiary supplier.

Billy didn't respond and looked at him with glazed eyes.

'What's the matter?' John could feel himself getting angry.

'Look at the material grade?' said Billy, his head disappearing into his hands.

John scanned the top of the sheet… and then again. He squeezed his eyes tight and tried for the third time… *he must have misread it*. But the letters and numbers refused to match.

He looked up at Billy.

'Jesus Christ! What the fuck's going on?'

Chapter 53

The sliding door of the workshop gave a metallic screech as I pulled it open; it echoed across the dormant machinery cluttering the work-space.

As I made toward the chatter of distant voices, shafts of sunlight pierced through the dirty windows, spotlighting the tangle of metal components waiting to be repaired. It conflicted with the sterile environment of Mathers' Centre of Excellence, but I knew that looks could be deceiving.

Halfway along, I saw three people surrounding a metal bench, and a familiar voice boomed out.

'Have a look at these, Danny.' Steyn beckoned.

I acknowledged Piet and Embele.

'How are you, Piet?' I said.

He shook my hand, 'Good, Danny.'

There was a flesh-coloured plaster on his forehead. 'How's your head, I heard you were doing a bit of detective work?'

He smiled and pointed to the plaster behind my ear. 'That makes two of us, eh?'

'Touché,' I replied and walked around the bench.

'Good to see you, Embele.' I shook his hand and patted his shoulder. 'You're well?'

He smiled, 'Good, Boss.' It had seemed a long time since we spoke. 'And how are you after the accident?'

'A few scratches, Boss.'

Still economical with his words, but it was good to see him.

'This is what we've got,' said Piet. 'We've hosed them down as best we can.'

It was a sobering image. On the bench were six bolts and bearings, destroyed.

'The photographs were bad, Danny, but a hundred times worse in the flesh.' Steyn summed it up.

BREAKING POINT

I shook my head. 'This can't be right, not this much damage.'

Working my way around the bench, I segregated three fractured bolts and peered into the fissures.

'Here, use this.' Piet handed me a torch and magnifying glass. Everything was so much clearer, no room for doubt. There was contamination in the constricted area of the fracture, but overall, just as expected, no signs of corrosion.

'What do you think?' Steyn asked, leaning on the bench. I sensed he was on edge.

'They look okay to me,' I said. *Now for the bearings*.

I segregated the two with the worst damage, they'd tell me more of a story. Both had split unevenly into four separate sections and were heavy and awkward as I pulled them toward me for a closer look.

'Watch you don't cut yourself, Boss,' Embele warned and passed me a rag. Now they were closer, I noticed the line of fracture was jagged and sharp.

I rolled them onto their rounded faces, with the damaged area facing upwards, and followed the light from the torch with my magnifying glass. I scanned the exposed inner structures, once, twice, three times, just to make sure. But it didn't need a magnifying glass.

'These have corroded,' I said. Relieved when they nodded.

I turned one of the bearings over and ran my hand along the outer face. Instead of a smooth and shiny surface, it was grainy and pitted. There was an uneven groove about ten millimetres deep on the edge of the fracture point. When I ran my finger along, it was surprisingly smooth.

'The outside is pitted. But this groove looks like abrasion of some kind.'

They nodded again.

I checked the other three sections, and they all had the same features by varying degrees.

'Can we match up each of the two halves?' I asked. It was awkward because of their weight and shape, but eventually, we got them to join into two spheres.

Steyn was the first to spot something. 'The groove is right along the fracture line on both of them,' he said. 'That must mean something.'

It was smooth, misshapen and stained brown against the stainless steel.

'It's split along the weakest point,' I agreed. *I had an idea, but I'd need to check the drawings John had given me.*

'Your mate, Dread did us a favour spotting this,' said Steyn. It should have been a compliment, but the tone gave away his distaste for John.

'It's certainly odd,' I replied and turned to Piet. 'What do you think?'

He looked over at the others. 'We've already agreed its corrosion.'

I felt elated, this was a real breakthrough.

'Is everything ready on 110, for us to go down and take a look?' I asked.

'Ja,' said Piet. 'The ventilation shaft is manned, but it'll be a bit uncomfortable for them in the kibble.'

'That's something they'll have to put up with, Piet. I think it's best if I take Stremsen and Socket down, I want to see their reaction when we switch on the MK6.' I looked at Embele, 'Will you come down and help me start it up?'

He nodded. 'No problem, Boss.'

I took him to one side, while Steyn and Piet shared a cigarette. 'This could be dangerous,. The switches failed once, and there's no reason they won't again.'

'Then why are you going down?'

The simplicity of the question made me realise I didn't have an answer.

'I… I thought it was because I wanted to find the truth,' I answered. 'But I'm not sure what that is any more.'

He frowned. 'We can't let it happen again, Boss.'

BREAKING POINT

I smiled at him. 'You don't say much, Embele, but you have a way of getting to the point.'

He smiled back. I think he was beginning to like me.

'I'll run the MK6 on half-pressure, just to be safe, Boss. There's a pump-room close by if anything happens.'

'Do you think we'll need it?' I asked.

He shrugged. 'I've seen enough to know that something's wrong.'

We rejoined the other two.

'Steyn, I need you and Piet close to the meeting when we're taking them down. Make sure Laura keeps you informed of any breaking news.'

'Okay with me,' said Steyn, Piet nodded.

'And the second MK6 is powered up?' I looked at Piet.

'Ja, it's been checked out and seems to be okay.' He made a bit of a face. 'You need to be careful down there, Danny.'

'Still not sure about it?'

'Readings are all fine, but it sounds like shit.'

'We need them to hear that. The shittier, the better.'

He smiled. 'We've got lamps, boots and overalls ready in the changing rooms for your guests.'

'Good work.' I pointed to the components on the bench.

'Can you take one of the bolts and these two fractured bearings back to my office for the group to review.'

I looked at Steyn.

'I'll get a message back to John, confirming the bearings *have* corroded. Hopefully, he can find some clues.'

Chapter 54

Someone was knocking on Billy's office door.

'Leave it,' he said impatiently and stared at John. 'I don't know what we're getting ourselves into.'

'Yeah, you said that Billy. Pull yourself together.'

John looked at the top of the faxed sheet and read it out loud. 'Super Duplex 193 stainless steel. What material is that?'

Billy pulled out the original material certificate. 'It's not what it's supposed to be,' he replied.

'I realise that, but is there such a material?'

'Oh yes, and all the chemical and material properties comply with 193. But it's still *not* 198.'

He passed the original sheet over. 'Compare them?'

John laid the two sheets side by side and ran his finger down each.

'They're identical except for the grade description, I don't understand.' He looked up, confused.

'It's been doctored.' Billy's words sent a chill through John's body.

Billy continued. 'Look at the way the material grade is described on the two sheets?'

John looked again, focussing on the text.

'The type is different,' he said. '*Subsidiary Supplier* has been added and so has *Material Supplier: Machine Inc*. Very similar, but slightly different from the original.' He couldn't believe what he was seeing.

'Look closely at the number *198* with this.' Billy passed over a magnifying glass.

John focussed on the sheet and saw it straight away.

'The *3* in *193* has been typed over with an *8*.' It took a full minute for it to sink in.

'What does this mean, Billy?'

'They're different materials,' he replied.

'I realise that, but how different?'

BREAKING POINT

Billy pointed to the reference book.

'*193* is classed as a ferritic stainless steel whereas *198* is an austenitic stainless steel.'

'Plain English, Billy?'

Billy rolled his eyes. 'Put simply, *193* is an average strength stainless, whereas *198* is a high strength stainless. However…'

'Hang on, Billy…' John looked at both sheets with a new purpose. 'Both these certificates have identical strength values. Only the material description has been doctored.'

Billy was looking at him. 'So what?'

John was studying the numbers, making sure his logic was right before revealing his thoughts.'

'John, what are you trying to say?'

He looked at Billy and smiled.

'When Danny asked me to rerun the calculations in the database using the revised shear strength values, Von Mises and all that, I used the same figures that are on both these sheets.' He waved them at Billy.

'So what?' Billy looked confused.

John looked up with a triumphant smile. 'So the revised calculations were based on the weaker values. Yes, the safety factor dropped from 5.8, but the revised figure of 3.6, is one-hundred per cent accurate. Even though it's not, *technically* the correct material, it's still fit for purpose.'

Billy's face lightened up.

'So we're in the clear?'

'More by luck than judgement,' said John. 'But yes, the Stabiliser is essentially safe.'

John's smile left him. 'But it still doesn't explain why the material has been switched.'

'It's obvious,' said Billy, '193 is a lot cheaper than 198.'

And the penny dropped. 'That bastard, Stremsen,' John shouted. 'He's the one who recommended Machine Inc., and it explains how he achieved the cost savings.'

'That's a big leap,' said Billy. 'We'd have to find proof and...'

He was about to say something else when there was more knocking. 'Whoever it is, get rid of them, John.'

John unlocked the door, it was Dawn.

'I've been looking everywhere for you,' she said. 'We need to speak in private.'

'I'm a bit busy at the...'

She grabbed his arm and pulled him outside.

'Danny left a message for you,' she whispered. 'He said the bearings *have* corroded and he's only got twelve hours to find out why.'

'When did it come in?'

'About half an hour ago, but no one knew where you were. Is everything okay?'

John shook his head.

'Is this bad news?'

'It's not great, Dawn, so keep it to yourself for now.'

She passed him a piece of paper.

'This is the direct number to Danny's office.' John thanked her and returned to the office, relocking the door.

Billy was hidden behind a cloud of pipe smoke. 'What was that about?' he said, waving away the smog.

'Dawn,' answered John. 'Danny's confirmed the bearings *have* corroded.'

'Not surprising,' said Billy. 'That's what I was about to tell you.' His voice had gone up an octave.

'193 stainless is ferritic, meaning it has poor resistance to corrosion.'

'And 198 stainless?' John was dreading the answer.

'It's austenitic; corrosion-resistant.'

'Bollocks!' said John. 'Well, that explains what we saw in the photographs.' His chin was resting on his hands, his head nodding up and down to the rhythm of his knees.

'How long ago did the MK6 Stabilisers get installed?' he asked Billy.

'About six months, why?'

BREAKING POINT

'Danny is suggesting the corroded bearings played a part in the failure of the Stabiliser. But even with high-pressure water rattling through 24/7, they wouldn't deteriorate to that extent, would they?

'No, of course not,' Billy replied.

'Not in a dry environment.'

John looked up at him.

'What do you mean, a *dry environment*?'

Billy looked confused. 'The bearings are sealed off from the water supply.'

Now it was John's turn to look confused.

'What makes you think that, Billy? They're on the wet-side of the seal... hit by every one of the thousands of gallons of water running through the Stabiliser.

'I didn't know that!' Billy's face was ashen as he pulled the reference book toward him.

'What's wrong?' asked John.

'I think our luck just ran out,' Billy said, frantically flicking through the pages.

Chapter 55

Our entrance couldn't have been more disruptive.

Steyn told Stremsen and Socket to vacate their chairs, almost pushing them out of the way, while he and I laid a sheet across the top of the conference table. Piet and Embele followed us in and put the damaged bolts and bearings on top.

'We'll wait for you in the changing rooms, Danny,' Steyn said, and led the others outside.

Stremsen and Socket returned to their seats.

Fucking hell! Likky was shocked.

'That's an extraordinary amount of damage.' Rik Last looked stunned.

Stremsen remained seated while Socket got up and began handling the samples. I passed him the rag, torch and magnifier. Majori and Last were craning their necks to get a better view of the damage, and I noticed them wince at one another.

'You've looked at these already?' Socket asked me over his shoulder.

'Fifteen minutes ago,' I replied.

'And?'

'*And*... I'll wait for your opinion.' He wasn't going to get any prompts from me.

He looked at them for no more than a minute. A few cursory pokes with his finger and then switched off the torch. He took his seat and looked at Stremsen.

'It's surface contamination, Fred, no doubt about it. To be fair, I can see why everyone's been fooled,' he looked across at me. 'But Super Duplex 198 doesn't corrode.'

I stood and showed him the abrasion and pitting on the surface of the bearings.

'And what about these?' I asked.

BREAKING POINT

He got back up with a sigh and impatiently rubbed his hands across them. After another quick glance through the magnifier, he sat back down.

'Damage caused by the collapse,' he answered.

'And these?' I pointed to the grooves on both bearings.

He crossed his legs and leaned back.

'We don't know what your people got up to when they stripped it down.'

I felt like taking him by the throat. 'I've looked at the drawings, Terry. Do you really believe it's a coincidence that the damage seems to be where the two flanges come together?'

Stremsen stood and peered at them from a distance as though they were going to bite.

'The truth is we don't know what you've been doing with them. You've forfeited any credibility by having the Stabiliser dismantled without independent witnesses.'

'It's some sort of chemical reaction,' Socket re-emphasised for good measure. 'Pure and simple.'

I had no answer because anything suspicious would be attributed to the strip down. At the time, it seemed like a risk worth taking, but now, with no tangible evidence, I realised the magnitude of my mistake.

Rik and Luca sat impassively, while Stremsen and Socket were having a smug-fest.

Van Heerden was fiddling with his cuff, deep in thought. He caught me watching and stopped.

'This would seem to contradict your own opinion, Mr Core,' he said, out of the blue. 'May I take a look?'

I handed him the torch and magnifier, and all eyes bore down on him as he moved around the table. He never touched the bearings, preferring to direct me to move them into various positions.

The room was quiet except for his instructions and the occasional *thump,* as I manoeuvred the sections around the table. I caught Luca and Last glancing at one another; they weren't looking comfortable in this environment.

After about fifteen minutes, Van Heerden gave me back the equipment and returned to his seat. He took out a handkerchief, unfolded it and slowly wiped his hands; his eyes never left Socket.

'How long have you been an engineer, Terry?' he asked.

'Eh, what's that got to do with anything?' Socket was taken aback.

Van Heerden folded the handkerchief precisely along its creases and placed it back in his pocket. Socket coughed nervously.

'This is a serious matter…' Van Heerden's eyes were pinched, as though looking for something specific on Sockets face. 'And should be treated accordingly. Would you agree?'

Socket nodded, and I tensed as Last continued.

'If what I've witnessed is a measure of the effort you put into developing the MK6 Stabiliser. Then Mr Core is right to be concerned about your competence.'

Socket went from cocky to seething in a nanosecond, and the room seemed to shudder.

Out of fucking order! Shouted Likky.

'Thys!' Last raised his voice. 'I don't want to be rude, but you can't make statements like that about one of my senior engineers. I made it clear that we're not here to…'

'Point taken, Rik.' Van Heerden held up his hands.

'You're right, maybe I expected too much.'

The wily bastard's made his point, I thought.

Van Heerden pulled his sleeve up to look at his watch, and I noticed an elastic band around his wrist.

'Time is moving on,' he said, 'and I don't want to keep you here all day. I suggest that while the others proceed with the underground inspection, we…' he nodded towards Majori and Last. 'Continue with the meeting until they return. Afterwards, a bite to eat, and then you can be on your way.'

'Is it necessary to go down?' Stremsen looked like he'd sucked on a lemon.

I didn't want him wriggling out of this and jumped in.

'I want you to hear the MK6 in operation and tell me if you're happy with it,' I said.

'What's the point of that?' Socket was still smarting from Van Heerden's put down. 'We've answered all your questions.'

'I want you to hear and feel the experience,' I said. 'Then you can tell me to my face it's operating efficiently.'

He made a big show of annoyance before Last and Majori waved them both out.

Chapter 56

'**Galvanic corrosion!**' John's expression was one of disbelief.

'I'd assumed the bearings were sealed off,' said Billy, searching through pages of the book and scribbling various numbers on a sheet of paper.

'How am I supposed to know every detail of the design?'

He crossed some digits out, rechecked the book, and applied new ones. Sighs of frustration and expletives followed, and the room crackled with nervous energy.

John watched in silence on the edge of his seat, his hands clenched. He was hoping for Billy to give a relieved smile or cheeky wink… *panic over, everything's okay*. But it never came.

Billy hurled the pencil at the door and slammed his fist onto the blue reference book.

'Someone's going to jail for this!' His eyes were brimming with tears.

John said nothing… not yet.

For almost ten minutes, he watched Billy come to terms with his frustration, drying his eyes and refilling his pipe.

Three long puffs and inhale. Smoke billowed, and Billy's body relaxed.

Now was the time.

John got up, retrieved the pencil and placed it in front of Billy.

'Are you okay now?' he asked.

Billy looked up at him, squinting his eyes.

'Sorry, it all got a bit too much.'

'None of this is your problem, Billy. Take me through it.'

Billy put his pipe down and took a deep breath.

BREAKING POINT

'The high-pressure water is treated with chemicals to inhibit corrosion. Unfortunately, it acts as an electrolyte between the bearings and the Stabiliser flange.'

'That doesn't sound good,' said John.

'It's okay if the two metals are compatible.'

Billy turned to a page in the reference book and showed John a list.

'Every metal has an *Anodic Index*,' he pointed to a list of numbers on the page.

'This is the index number for Monel T20, the flange material. And this...' he moved his finger further down the list. 'Is the index number for Super Duplex 193, the *actual* bearing material.'

He put the book down and showed John his scribbled notes.

'As the difference between the two numbers increases, the corrosion factor accelerates. To be compatible, the difference should be less than 0.15.' He went quiet as John looked at the calculation.

'Is that 0.4?' asked John.

'Unfortunately, yes,' Billy replied.

'That isn't good?'

Billy grabbed his pipe, sucked at the burnt ash, and put it back down. 'In the hostile environment of the mine, the high-pressure water creates an electrical conduction path between the bearing and flange. This creates an accelerated attack on the anode metal, dissolving it into the electrolyte.'

'Plain English, Billy.'

'The bearings are being eaten away by the high-pressure water,' he replied.

'Shit!' It was John's turn to take a deep breath.

'And this wouldn't happen if the bearings were made from Super Duplex 198?'

'No,' said Billy. 'Jack Smelt knew what he was doing.'

'Well whoever's involved in this obviously doesn't.'

John stood and paced, the room seemed much smaller. He passed Billy the note Dawn had given him.

'This is Danny's direct number. We need to ring him straightaway, tell him about this mess. Christ, when this comes out, we'll all be out of jobs. We're the ones who'll be charged with…'

'Stop!'

John froze. *Billy never shouts,* he thought.

'Sit down!'

He complied as Billy filled his pipe and lit up and became fascinated by the languid clouds billowing toward him. Three long puffs and inhale. As the smoke reached his own nostrils, he realised his leg had stopped twitching.

'Sorry about that.' Billy's voice was quiet and composed.

John looked away from the smoke and saw Billy grinning.

'I'm still in charge, no matter what Stremsen thinks.' There was self-belief in his tone.

He stood up and looked out of the window, it was early afternoon, and the sun was shining. A vapour trail ran across the clear blue sky, and a glint of sunlight reflected from an aeroplane thousands of feet up.

'Do you think Stremsen's involved?' Billy asked.

'Yes!' John's answer left no room for doubt.

'Machine Inc. could be acting independently,' said Billy. 'Getting greedy.'

'I can't see it,' said John. 'Look at the evidence.' He raised a finger.

'One, Stremsen recommended them. Two, he got a huge bonus for meeting the MK6 cost savings. And three, he's been holding back information ever since Danny arrived.'

'All circumstantial,' said Billy. 'And what about Socket, do you think he's involved?'

John shook his head in his hands. 'I don't think so, he's too much of a coward. He'd have given himself away by now.'

'Maybe we should tackle him when he gets back,' said Billy.

BREAKING POINT

'It'll be too late by then,' John replied. 'We need to resolve this in the next twelve hours.'

He explained Dawn's message, and the pending manslaughter charge facing Danny.

'That makes our planning *more* critical,' said Billy. He pulled out a sheet of paper before continuing.

'We're not implicated, but as whistleblowers, they'll come after us. They could argue it's an administrative error, so we need to consolidate our proof and report it to the top man.'

'Rik Last?' said John.

'Yes, particularly while he's over there with Stremsen.'

'What if *he's* in on it?'

'We'll soon find out, but we've got no choice.'

'We have to tell Danny,' said John.

Billy shook his head. 'We don't work for Danny, and he'll find out soon enough. But we must keep Stremsen and Socket out of the loop, they'll only muddy the waters.'

He began writing on the sheet. 'I'll give you the revised shear strength and tensile strength figures; based on the corroded bearing material. I need you to run them through the database and come back with the new safety factor calculation.'

'It's not going to be pretty.' John grimaced.

'No, but it's evidence. They'll interrogate everything we say, so our proof has to be watertight. While you're doing that, I'll ring Machine Inc. and confront them with the evidence from Almeja. If I don't get any answers, I'll threaten them with exposure.'

'Will they respond to intimidation?'

Billy looked up from his notes. 'I've been defending a pack of lies for the last week, and I've watched an innocent man incriminated with false evidence. It's time to put things right.'

'Is there a way we can get confirmation that the bearings *are* made from Super Duplex 193?' John asked.

'Otherwise, this could be excused as an administrative error by Machine Inc.'

Billy thought for a moment. 'A metallurgy test would take too long to get organised, so we'll have to rely on the background evidence we've got.'

After going through the reference book, he scribbled some numbers. 'Put these into the database and run the figures. Come back as soon as you've got them.'

John unlocked the door and left.

Billy looked at his watch, it would be, 7.30am in Houston. He'd wait for another half-hour; it would give him a better chance of catching someone there.

Something John said was niggling at the back of his mind… *could be excused as an administrative error.* He returned to the reference book, found the page he was looking for and read it out loud.

'Super Duplex 193… medium strength… poor corrosion resistance… ferritic properties.

'Ferritic properties!' he said out loud and picked up the phone.

'Hi, Dawn, can you put me through to Danny Core, I need to speak to him urgently.'

BREAKING POINT

Chapter 57

Socket and Stremsen looked like condemned men as I led them into the Mine Captains office. Piet, Embele and Steyn all looked up as we entered. Socket's neck was bright red, he was still seething from Van Heerden's put down.

Steyn reluctantly got up and shook hands with them.

'Welcome to Concorde IV,' he said. 'This is Piet Reiss and Embele Ngozi.'

I noticed they only shook hands with Piet.

'Embele will be joining you underground, so let's get you over to the changing rooms and into some overalls.' He gave Socket one of his stares.

'I've got a special hard hat for you, Terry, one with an anchor on it.'

Socket was about to say something, but the phone rang. Steyn picked it up.

'Hello,' he said, then nodded and passed it over to me.

'It's Laura. While you're busy, we'll make our way over and wait for you.'

I gave him a thumbs up. 'Hi, Laura.'

'Mr Van wants a word,' she replied. There was a shuffling noise in the background, then his voice.

'I'm not an engineer, Mr Core, but I recognise corrosion when I see it. Tell your contact in Mathers to pull his finger out. I need something tangible to convince me not to send that form back to the police authorities.' Then the phone went dead.

I was stunned. It still felt like a lost cause, but... *We will not take a backward step. We* sounded good. Six of us were in agreement about the corrosion, and that felt like a majority to me.

I looked out of the window and saw Steyn leading the way to the changing rooms. Pulling out a packet of cigarettes from my shirt pocket, I remembered I was giving them up and placed them in Steyn's drawer; they wouldn't go to waste.

My lips were dry, and my mouth tasted of stale coffee. It was so quiet I could almost hear the beating of my heart. I'd given my all, but it hadn't been enough and cursed myself for allowing the MK6 to be stripped down. It had corrupted any evidence I'd found and left me exposed.

I leaned across the desk and picked up a sheet of paper. It was the shift rota Steyn and I had looked at on the morning of the accident. Maybe Julie was right, and I should have put my son first and stayed in the UK.

I wasn't much of a role model, but to add that to my parenting CV would have been a step too far. My journey was coming to a close, and I was exhausted. My eyes began to close, and I felt oddly at peace.

Steyn's telephone woke me just as I'd begun to snore and I sat up in a rush, lunging for the receiver.

'Hello,' I said wiping the dribble from my mouth.

'I'm glad I caught you, Mr Core.' It was Laura again. 'I've got Billy Jones on the line…'

BREAKING POINT

Chapter 58

Piet drove us out to the ventilation shaft in his bakkie. Embele and I got shaken about in the back of the open truck, while Stremsen and Socket sat in the cab stony-faced. It was only a fifteen-minute walk, but there was no point in wasting energy, and outside it was twenty-five degrees and rising.

As we exited, I could see the horror on Stremsen and Socket's face. The new ventilation shaft was being excavated to help cope with the demand for clean air in the far reaches of the main shaft, but all work had stopped since the accident. It wasn't what they were expecting.

The steel kibble hung from three chains, linked to a steel cable that threaded up and around a spindly headgear, spread-eagled across the shaft. The cable continued along, down and around a winding gear housed in a temporary winding house.

It was a far cry from the sophistication of the primary headgear of Concorde IV but surprisingly versatile. It would remain the only way in and out for men, equipment and excavated rock until the shaft was completed.

Beneath the kibble were two rubber flaps. These opened to allow it to descend and then closed again so that no debris could fall through. Accelerating at 32 feet per second per second, gravity could turn an innocuous piece of rock into a deadly missile during an eleven thousand foot drop.

'You're not expecting us to go down in that?' Socket seemed appalled at the notion.

He and Stremsen looked unkempt in their white overalls, the belts holding their batteries hanging clumsily around their waists. The kibble didn't look big enough to manage four men at once, and it would be a tight fit.

'Don't worry Terry, it's perfectly safe,' I said, looking over at Stremsen who didn't look well.

We climbed a step ladder and scrambled inside where there was about three inches of muddy water slopping around in the bottom. Stremsen wasn't supple, and Embele ended up dragging him over. When he landed, he managed to splash us all in brown mud.

Inside, our heads and shoulders protruded above the top. I told them to crouch and press their backs against the inside chamber. 'Fold your arms and keep everything inside the bucket, don't get tempted to look out.'

I leaned over and switched Stremsen's lamp on. Embele tried to do the same with Socket but had his hand pushed away.

'Let him help you,' I said. 'It's going to get dark.'

He ignored the two of us and continued to struggle with the switch.

I shouted for Piet to start the descent and he signalled to the operator in the winding house. The rubber flaps opened and we dropped through. As they closed behind us, all the natural light disappeared, and the kibble gathered momentum. The only sound we heard was the air being displaced, and the only light was from three of our lamps.

Stremsen looked terrified. We'd had our differences, but I took no pleasure in his discomfort, and I squeezed his arm.

'Don't worry,' I shouted, 'you're going to be okay.'

I turned my light toward Socket, who was still struggling with his lamp. But as I stretched over to help, Embele grabbed my arm and angrily shook his head... *I was going to have to watch him.*

The kibble accelerated, occasionally buffeting us as it grazed the sides of the shaft. The sounds were magnified in the open-top container, but I found myself surprisingly calm. Stremsen and Socket had their eyes shut tight.

Eventually, I felt my feet pressing harder onto the floor as we decelerated. When we came to a stop, I held on to Stremsen's arm until the steel cable stretched and relaxed,

BREAKING POINT

before finally settling. We'd reached the cross-cut on Level 110, our access to the MK6 Stabilisers.

We climbed out onto a temporary wooden floor, then a couple of steps into a small haulage-way. I pushed a security button, and after a five-minute safety delay, the kibble returned to the surface. Embele was the only one who knew the way to the Stabilisers from here, and we fell into step behind him.

There was an eerie silence about our journey. Apart from the occasional maintenance worker, we were alone. Everything was well lit, and it didn't take long to get to the Stabilisers. I noticed that Socket had started limping, which wouldn't help his mood.

Embele stopped us in front of the first Stabiliser, the old model. I pointed out the traditional bolt pattern on the flanges to Socket, but he wasn't interested, and we moved quickly on to the dismantled MK6. The front was separated from the central *smokestack*, and the bolts and bearings lay in the same formation as displayed on the photographs, less the samples Piet had brought to the surface.

'This was the MK6 that fed the drills at the accident site,' I said.

Stremsen watched as I picked up the dismantled rubber seal and ran it through my hands, feeling for damage.

He shook his head.

'This should not have been done without our input. How are we supposed to believe that anything you find, wasn't as a direct result of the collapse?'

I ignored him and moved on to the bolts.

'Some of these have fractured,' I pointed them out. 'That shouldn't have happened, even in the event of a collapse.'

'How do you know?' Socket joined the fray. 'The Stabiliser's never experienced this kind of failure before.'

Unfortunately, he was right. In my time with Mathers, I'd never had to deal with the after-effects of a full-scale collapse on a Stabiliser.

'How do we know the damage wasn't caused during dismantling,' he continued, pointing up to the lifting equipment.

That was ridiculous.

'Embele's team stripped this down,' I said. 'And they…'

'I thought the blacks needed supervision.'

Socket's comment stopped me in my tracks, and I saw Embele tense up next to me.

'What?' Socket held his hands up, feigning surprise. 'You've already invalidated the warranty by dismantling it on your own. And now you're admitting it was done by unskilled labourers.'

Embele looked at me, and I shook my head. He held his ground.

'Terry does have a point there.' Stremsen was grinning.

'No, he doesn't,' I replied. 'Embele is the Boss Boy, which means he's the foreman in charge of a team of mineworkers. They had support from Piet Reiss, the maintenance supervisor, but Embele knows more about this equipment than anyone else on the mine.'

'Surely, not more than you?' Stremsen was trying to goad me, and it was beginning to work.

I moved towards them, and they instinctively stepped back.

'You say what you like about me.' I was pointing my finger at both of them. 'But Embele's already lost his brother in this accident. You disrespect him, you disrespect me.' My hand was shaking.

There was an awkward silence as I stood there eyeballing them, grinding my teeth.

'Boss,' Embele tapped me on the shoulder and prompted me to show them the bearings.

I took a few deep breaths. 'These are the rest of the bearings.' I rolled one of them along the floor. 'You can see signs of abrasion on the outside, similar to those in my office. Smaller maybe, but the same shape.'

BREAKING POINT

'Accident damage.' Socket's reply was expected, and he wandered aimlessly toward the other components.

I turned over other bearings and, in varying degrees, they all had the same discoloured groove. Feeling along each of them, they were all smooth... *this wasn't impact damage.*

'Embele, can you try this on each of the bearings?' I passed him the small magnet I'd been asked to take down.

'What's that for?' Socket and Stremsen were suddenly interested.

'Just a check I was asked to carry out,' I said.

Embele touched the first bearing, and there was a *click* as it attached itself to the metal. He moved on to the others.

'A magnet, what's that supposed to prove?' Stremsen wiped his mouth with his sleeve, his lips looked dry.

There was another metallic *click*, then another, then another...

'Just a routine check,' I replied.

Billy's request had confused me, and when I asked him why he wanted to know if the bearings were magnetic, he wasn't forthcoming.

It's essential for both of us... he'd replied, and I hadn't had the time to probe further.

Embele handed the magnet back to me.

'They're all magnetic, Boss.'

'Thanks,' I said. 'Would you like to confirm that, Fred?' I offered him the magnet, but he looked away.

'I'll take that as a no then,' I said.

He looked put out about something.

'Let's move on to the other MK6,' I continued. 'See if we can get it fired up for you.'

Chapter 59

It had taken an hour for John to run the new figures through the database. As soon as the results printed out, he rushed them back to Billy's office feeling as though he'd run a half marathon.

Barging through the door, he held up the sheets. Before he could say anything, Billy was on his feet.

'Coffee, black, no sugar?'

'Erm, yes, but don't you want to know…' John was panting and Billy was out the door before he could finish.

A couple of minutes later, Billy returned, nudging the door open with his feet, a cup in each hand.

'Lock the door,' he said. It was an order.

John had calmed down, though he was still waving the sheets.

He got up, turned the key, then tried again.

'I've got the results of the…'

'Relax, drink your coffee.' Billy passed the cup over. 'Before we do anything else, I want to share a phone call I've just had with Machine Inc.'

He pulled out a tape recorder from his drawer and plugged it in.

John gave a nervous laugh. 'You taped the call?'

Billy winked at him and pulled a cassette tape from his pocket. He slipped it into the recorder and closed the lid.

'Is this necessary?' There was apprehension in John's voice.

'It's not a great recording,' said Billy. 'But good enough. Necessary? I'll leave you to judge.'

He switched it on and began making notes.

After twenty minutes, he switched the tape off. John's coffee was untouched and stone-cold, his brain struggling to interpret the muffled conversation he'd just heard.

BREAKING POINT

'Now, do you think it was worth recording?' Billy asked, pulling out the cassette and placing it back in his pocket.

His fax machine started buzzing and screeching in the corner, interspersed with the sound of paper sliding out.

John counted them out in his head. *One, two, three...* then silence.

His mind returned to the voices on the tape, loud and soft... calm and angry... whispers and shouts... then silences, lots of silences. Still, he couldn't think of anything to add.

Billy removed the fax sheets and laid them on his desk. He read through each one, underlining words and sentences and scribbling notes in the margin. John watched, impressed with the calm determination. *A different Billy Jones was emerging.*

Billy dropped his pen and shuffled the sheets of paper.

'You've got the new safety figures?' he asked.

John had almost forgotten about them and pulled the sheets of paper from his pocket. He was still in shock and had to look at them again.

'Minus 2.8, Billy... *minus* 2.8.' It was so bad, it needed repeating.

Billy didn't falter.

'You said it was going to be ugly.'

He took the sheets and added them to the others.

'These are further evidence that the MK6 Stabiliser is unsafe?'

John nodded. 'Can I have a look at those?' He pointed to the faxes.

'Of course,' Billy passed them over. 'Are you ready for this?'

John didn't understand the question until Billy began dialling Danny's number from the note he'd given him.

'I'll put it on speaker-phone,' Billy said, pressing a red button on the microphone.

Long seconds passed before it connected, and the ring tone echoed through the speaker. Then a click and a strong South African accent.

'Goeiemore, Danny Core se kantoor, Laura praat.'

'Hello, Laura, it's Billy Jones again. Can you put me through to Rik Last, please.'

John looked at him. '*Again!* Then *you*'ve already rung her?'

Billy put his finger to his mouth just as the speaker burst into sound.

'Rik Last speaking…'

BREAKING POINT

Chapter 60

'**Mr Last, it's** Billy Jones here from Mathers, I've got some confidential information I'd like to pass on.'

Last looked across at Van Heerden and covered the mouthpiece.

'Thys, I wonder if we could take this in private.'

Van Heerden's chair scraped the floor as he got up and left the office without a word.

Last waited for the door to close then pressed the speaker-phone button. 'It's just myself and Luca Majori, Billy, you can speak openly.'

As Billy reported his findings, Luca turned the volume down, and both men leaned in closer. The voice delay wasn't an issue as the conversation was all one way. Luca scribbled notes as more and more details came forth.

Billy was reading from a script, and every sentence had been carefully prepared. He reported the facts. No editorials and nothing that could be used against him.

After fifteen minutes, the speaker let out a quiet hiss. Billy had finished. There was a lull while Luca finished his notes and Last fell back in his chair.

What the fuck! Likky couldn't believe it.

'You realise what you're implying, Billy?' Last said, looking exhausted.

'I'm implying nothing, Rik. I'm merely passing on information that's come to my attention.'

Get off the fucking fence! Likky wanted answers.

'The evidence looks damning,' Billy continued. 'But we don't have definitive proof that the bearings are made from the incorrect material.'

'When will we have that?' Luca asked, making notes.

'Is Danny Core still with you?' Billy's question surprised them both.

'No, he's gone underground with Fred and Terry,' said Luca, looking askance at Rik.

'Why, does he know anything about this?'

'Of course not,' said Billy. 'But I asked him to carry out an experiment on the bearings which should provide absolute proof.'

'We've got some of them in front of us,' said Rik. 'What did you ask him to do?' He reached out to touch one of the fractured bearings.

'Have you got a magnet?' asked Billy.

'Of course, we haven't got a...' Luca's petulance was cut short.

'Hang on,' said Last. He pulled out the hook holding his Heron badge to the lapel of his jacket and held it up to Majori.

'Okay, we've got one, Billy,' said Luca. 'What do you want us to do with it?'

'Check whether the bearings are magnetic,' Billy replied.

Last held it to the fractured bearing, and it attached itself to the metal with a *click*. Then he stood up and did the same thing with the three other sections.

Click... click... click... He nodded to Luca.

'All the bearings are magnetic,' Luca whispered into the microphone.

Last took his seat.

'Is that good news?' he asked.

The delay seemed to last forever.

'No, it's not,' Billy's voice was almost apologetic. 'Super Duplex 198 is non-magnetic. I believe the test you've just carried out confirms the bearings are made from low-grade, Super Duplex 193.'

The room was stuffy and the fan, whirring away on the desk, was only pushing around the warm air. Both men had beads of sweat, forming on their brows.

Billy's voice broke through again.

'Thank God we've only commissioned two MK6, and one has already been dismantled. I'll put production on hold this end until you hear Stremsen's version of events.'

BREAKING POINT

That bastard Socket's mixed up in this! Likky

Last was sliding his fingers continuously through his hair. A tuft stood up against the back of his ear, damp with perspiration.

'What about Socket, is he involved?'

'I don't know,' said Billy. 'His name wasn't mentioned by either Machine Inc. or Almeja. To be blunt, I could ask you the same question.'

What the fuck are you implying? Likky.

Last turned to Luca and raised his eyebrows... *this guy's got spunk,* he thought.

'I could take offence at that, Billy,' Last replied. 'But I appreciate your candour. I can assure you that this is the first I've heard of the problem. The details appear to have been confined to Mathers.'

'Okay,' said Billy. 'Then you need to tell Danny to quarantine the second MK6, immediately. It's unpredictable and dangerous.'

'But he's gone down to do a trial run with Stremsen and Socket,' said Luca.

'Then you've got to stop them!' Billy was shouting now.

'Under no circumstances must they operate that MK6. Someone could be killed!'

Luca got up and lunged for the door. Laura was at her desk, Van Heerden was staring out of the window. They both turned to face him.

'You've got to get someone down there,' Luca was almost gasping. 'The MK6 might be dangerous. It must not be switched on!'

Van Heerden turned to Laura. 'Get Broed on the phone.'

She rang the number, and Steyn answered on the first ring. 'What's the news, Laura?'

'Hold on.' She passed the phone to Van Heerden.

His voice was clear and steady.

'Core's group are in danger; you need to get to them and prevent them from switching on the MK6.'

'I don't understand, what's wrong?' Steyn sounded shocked.

'No time to explain, just get to them as soon as you can and don't go alone.'

'I'll take Piet with me.'

'There are risks,' Van Heerden warned. 'The MK6 may be dangerous.'

He waited for a reply, but the line had gone dead. He wasn't aware that Steyn and Piet were already running toward the bakkie.

He put the phone down and looked at Majori, who was still breathing hard.

'They're on their way.'

He walked past him into Danny's office where Rik Last was running his fingers frantically through his hair.

'I think you have a bit of explaining to do, Mr Last.'

In the background, Laura's fax machine started buzzing and screeching, interspersed with the sound of paper sliding out.

Rik Last counted them in his head. *One, two, three...* then silence.

'Bring those faxes in, Luca,' he shouted through the open door and wondered what Uncle Billy would do in the circumstances.

BREAKING POINT

Chapter 61

We stood in front of the MK6, and I remembered taking notes just after the accident. This was *Stabiliser 2*, imprinted on my brain.

The last time Embele and I were here, the noise was hitting us in the face. Now everything was quiet… for the moment.

With a week of inaction, the floors had dried to a hard crust. I assumed the wet patches below the pipes were a residue of the leakage experienced during Piet and Embele's unauthorised trial.

The gate was unlocked, and I led Stremsen and Socket through the safety fence and up the ladder onto the mezzanine. Embele was busying himself around the various gauges and switches in preparation for the start-up.

I tried explaining how severe the vibrations had been and the temperature inside the body of the Stabiliser. Still, there was no interest from either of them. I had to admit, it looked pretty bland now that it was at rest.

They were convinced the collapse was the root cause of any Stabiliser failures, and I was starting to believe that myself. But I was determined that they should experience the turmoil I'd witnessed when the Stabiliser was powered up. Without an ounce of enthusiasm, they made their way back down the steps.

'I've switched the power on, Boss,' Embele called from the outlet side of the Stabiliser. 'Do you want me to begin the start-up?'

'Hold on,' I said. 'I want to show them the pipework further down, while they can hear me speak.'

'I'll get the ear protectors ready,' he replied and made his way to the pump-room.

Showing Stremsen and Socket around the site was like dragging two dead weights. They were acting like spoilt children, sighing at every comment I made. I led them along the outlet pipes, explaining how the flanges showed signs of leaking and how the resultant pressure drop would create problems with the failsafe switches.

All they wanted to do was return to the surface, but I was determined to have my say. It was all I had left.

I moved them further down the pipework to the first change of direction, a thirty-degree horizontal bend. I pointed to the freshly repaired cracks in the plinth and pulled up a shard of concrete lying nearby.

'The vibrations inside the Stabiliser were transferred along the pipework; the further down they went, the worse the effect.'

I lifted the fragment. It was about two feet long and weighed around ten kilos.

'The pipes at these stress points were putting the plinths and brackets under intense pressure and starting to break the concrete into splinters like this.'

Stremsen rubbed his hand along the concrete. 'Did you photograph this area, after the accident?'

'Yes, they're all in my office.'

'You've argued that the whiplash effect started from the Stabiliser and ran down the pipework.' He was stroking the concrete.

'What's to say it didn't start from the collapse and ran *up* the pipework to the Stabiliser?'

I looked at Socket, but he turned away.

'I'd say you don't know what you're talking about, Fred.' *It was a ludicrous suggestion*.

'The collapse was a violent burst of energy and created massive destruction, but it dissipated immediately. There was no energy left to cause sustained whiplash in the piping.'

'That's just your opinion,' Stremsen said.

This is going nowhere, I thought. And led the way back.

'Let's get this Stabiliser running, and maybe you'll see what I mean.'

BREAKING POINT

When we got back to Embele, he gave us each a set of ear protectors.

'We'll go back onto the mezzanine,' I said. 'I want you to feel the full effect of the problem at the start-up.'

I dragged them back up the ladder and told them to hold onto the handrail.

'I'll have to use hand signals once it starts up.'

I gave Embele the thumbs up and shouted for him to begin.

He raised his hand and disappeared behind the control panel.

There was a gushing from inside the body as the valves opened and water flowed down from the *smokestack*.

I pointed towards it. 'The water from that pipe would normally feed the water-cooling plant on Level 140, but because we've shut the plant down, the back-pressure will build and trigger the failsafe switches. Once it's up to full pressure, I want you to feel the movement and tell me if you think it's normal.'

By the time I'd finished the sentence, I was shouting at the top of my voice. The noise continued to build, and the vibrations ran through my whole body. I'd forgotten how painful the sound could be, and I could see the others pressing their ear protectors tight against the sides of their heads.

I put my hand on the alloy body of the Stabiliser and felt it getting warm. Socket was starting to look concerned and pointed up at the *smokestack*. It was already beginning to vibrate. The noise was worse than I remembered and concerned me. I indicated to Stremsen and Socket to follow me back down the ladder; it would be safer watching from a distance.

I stepped onto the ladder, just as an explosive *thump resonated* from inside the body. It shuddered along the length of the Stabiliser and left the other two frozen; their eyes wild with fear.

I needed to get us down to ground level quickly, and started my descent. A second blast exploded to my right, twisting the Stabiliser body and throwing me from the ladder. I fell about ten feet and hit the floor on my back. My head ricocheted off the concrete, and all I could see were flashing lights. I couldn't breathe and grunted for air, desperate to fill my empty lungs. *It felt like I was suffocating*.

I thought I'd broken ribs as each breath I took stabbed at my insides... *had I punctured a lung?* I closed my eyes and breathed slowly... deeply, and my panic finally subsided along with the pain. I was soaking wet and raised myself on all fours. Lifting my head to take in the surroundings, the noise was agonising, and the floor awash with water.

To my left, a stream of high-pressure water was hitting the far wall, powerful enough to cause severe damage if anyone got in the way. My eyes traced the source back to the front flange of the Stabiliser. The seals had been breached, and the failsafe switches had failed... again.

Looking up toward the mezzanine, I saw the heads of Socket and Stremsen's appear over the top and waved them down. But they seemed too frightened to move. They were shouting, but it was hopeless with the mayhem around us.

I tried to raise myself further, but my head span and forced me down on one knee as I tried to avoid passing out... *Embele, where was he?*

I crawled forward, my legs and arms seemed okay. My ear defenders had fallen off, and it felt as though my head was going to explode. Creeping toward the control panel, I saw Embele prostrate on the floor, his face immersed in the surface water.

'Embele!' My words were useless in the chaos, but they were all I had left.

A pair of hands lifted me from behind and dragged me away. The heels of my boots created a wake as I was pulled through the water and dumped onto drier ground.

BREAKING POINT

In the foreground, Piet Reiss dodged the water spray and disappeared behind the control panel as Steyn stepped around me and ran toward the ladder. He climbed half-way up and coaxed Socket and Stremsen down. Eventually, the noise abated, and I sat there in a couple of inches of water, wondering what the hell had happened.

Piet came round from the control panel with Embele hanging on his shoulder. He was coughing and spluttering, but he was walking, and my relief was beyond words. The noise was reduced dramatically, and I could hear Piet shouting at Steyn.

'Get everyone into the pump-room.'

Steyn helped me up, and we followed the others. Once the door closed, the respite was immense.

'Are you okay?' Steyn was shouting at me, but I had a sharp whistling in my ears and couldn't hear a word. I held my nose and blew hard, my ears popped, and the whistling abated.

'Are you okay?' he shouted again.

'Stop bloody shouting,' I said and smiled as he started laughing.

Stremsen and Socket were in a daze, both staring blindly at the closed door in front of them. Steyn and I watched in silence as Piet took down the first aid kit and started to work on the deep cut on Embele's forehead. There was a considerable lump beginning to rise from its centre.

'I've switched everything off,' Piet said. 'But it'll take another fifteen minutes for the water pressure to drop.'

He put some butterfly stitches on the cut and warned Embele about concussion.

'I'm okay, Boss,' he replied.

Typical of the man, I thought and gave him a thumbs up.

Steyn checked me out and reckoned I'd been lucky, nothing more than bruised ribs. It was strange to feel fortunate with this much pain.

'I thought I told you and Piet to stay above ground,' I said.

Steyn sat next to Stremsen and Socket who still looked shaken.

'We did, but Van Heerden rang us up and told us to get down here before you started up the MK6.'

Stremsen looked up. 'Why?'

Steyn shrugged his shoulders. 'He said it might be dangerous.' He gave Socket a look to kill. 'It looks like he was right.'

Then he turned to look at me. 'What happened?'

'I didn't see much,' I said. 'How about you, Embele?'

He shook his head. 'Not much, Boss. I began the start-up process, watching the pressure rise, then something seemed to break.'

'I heard that,' I said. 'Like something ruptured inside the Stabiliser?'

'Yes, Boss, followed by an explosion. Something hit me on the back of the head, and I hit the control panel.' He pointed to the stitches on his forehead.

'That was the water that hit you,' I said. 'It's a wonder you weren't killed. How's your head now?'

He gave me a rare smile and looked at Piet. 'Thanks, Boss.'

Piet patted his shoulder. 'Don't mention it, seems we're always getting you into trouble.'

I looked at my watch. 'It all seems to have calmed down out there. We need to find out what happened.'

Embele started to get up.

'You stay here,' I said. 'Take things easy for a while.'

I looked at Socket and Stremsen, they'd finally begun to calm down.

'Terry, this is your opportunity to explain what went wrong.'

The five of us stepped outside the pump-room and walked towards the MK6, Stremsen and Socket less

BREAKING POINT

enthusiastically than the rest of us. The floor was waterlogged, but the Stabiliser was at rest.

Apart from our footsteps splashing in the water, the only sound was running water coming from the front end, where the control panel was situated.

As we approached, we could see it was running out between the primary flanges holding the front and centre sections together... only they weren't.

Three of the bolts had sheared off completely, and the front was splayed out at an angle. Low-pressure water was still pouring past the seal and flooding the floor.

Piet pointed to one of the severed bolts embedded in the sidewall. It was next to the control panel, close to where Embele had been standing. I looked at Socket, but he turned away.

'Whatever was going on inside the Stabiliser has put this front section under enough pressure to crack it open,' I said. 'You still believe this kind of failure was due to the collapse?'

I was asking Socket outright.

'We've been through all this, Core,' Stremsen was about to give his usual response, but I wanted to hear Socket's opinion; in front of witnesses.

'Come on, Terry...' Putting him on the spot always niggled him, especially coming from me and I could see his neck glow.

'You and I have tested enough Stabilisers over the years,' I shouted. 'Tell everyone here, after what you've just seen, are you still saying that the MK6 wasn't involved in the deaths of nine men.'

None of us heard Embele emerge from the pump-room.

I pointed to the fractured bolt embedded in the sidewall.

'Tell us that the new bolting pattern is fit for purpose, even though it nearly killed another man today.'

None of us heard Embele walking up from behind.

'Tell us that your reduced safety factor is robust enough to prevent another catastrophe...'

Then he blew.

'Still trying to deflect the blame, Core! Who the fuck are you anyway? Yeah, I'll tell them it's *your* fucking database that we used to determine the safety factor.'

He was close now, pointing at my face.

'And I'll tell them it's *your* fucking calculations that got used in *your* 3S Initiative. Just a coincidence, is it?'

My teeth were clenched, but I knew if I goaded him enough, he might reveal something... I was still hopeful.

'Terry, leave it there.' Stremsen tried to shut him up.

Piet and Steyn watched on fascinated, unaware that Embele was standing right behind them.

'No, Fred, it's about time his friends learnt about the real Danny Core. How he killed his son and abandoned his family.'

I wanted to react, *but not yet.* I felt Steyn grab my arm and out of the corner of my eye, I saw Piet looking at me strangely.

'None of that's relevant,' I said. 'I'm asking you to tell everyone here that the MK6 wasn't involved in the deaths of those nine men.'

'Fuck you, Core. There's plenty more blacks where they came from, and you know...'

Before he finished the sentence, Embele was on him. He grabbed him by his overalls and raised him off the floor. All I could see were Socket's eyes bulging and heard him gasp as the punch hit him full in the face.

There was a huge splash as he hit the floor and lay semi-submerged in the water. We all managed to jump on Embele, who was already moving in for another go. Steyn, Piet and I were hanging on to him, shouting and swearing until the weight of numbers told in the end and we got him to the ground.

All three of us were gasping for air, but we daren't let him go, his teeth were clenched, and he was straining to get free. I didn't want to imagine what he was capable of doing in this state.

BREAKING POINT

Stremsen was lifting Socket's head from the wet floor; he was out cold.

'Go and check on him, Piet,' Steyn shouted, as we dragged Embele to the pump-room and sat him down.

'What the fuck are you doing!' I'd never seen Steyn so angry.

Embele looked up at him. 'I'm not sorry, Boss.'

'You can't do things like that. We might not like them, but they're our guests for Christ's sake!'

'What will happen, Boss?' He looked at me.

'I'll do all I can. But after today, I might not be here to help.'

Steyn grabbed me. 'We deny it happened, it's our word against theirs. Piet will agree.'

'What about Socket's injuries?' I asked, scarcely believing we would get away with it.

'We'll say he fell off the mezzanine.'

'And Stremsen,' I asked. 'We'd have to leave him down here?'

'Mmm, it's tempting,' Steyn replied and then smiled at Embele.

'You got in just before me. But don't worry, we'll find a way to sort this out.'

As we exited the pump-room, a voice shouted over.

'I'll report you for assault, you black bastard.' Socket had come around, but his nose was streaming with blood.

Steyn winked at Embele. 'You didn't kill him then?'

'Enough of that!' Piet pushed Socket back into the water.

'You were out of order, man. Now unless you want to be left here, show some respect.'

The journey back to the top was a solemn affair. Socket's eye was closing nicely, and Stremsen was surprisingly quiet. I spent the time trying to determine what caused this second failure.

I still believed everything pointed toward the MK6. Again, I knew they would continue to argue that this second failure was as a result of the effects of the collapse on 120. And I'd lost any opportunity to dispute the fact by agreeing to strip down the original MK6.

After returning to the changing rooms, we had a quick shower. I left Piet, Steyn and Embele to get some food while I took Socket and Stremsen back to my office.

We hadn't said anything to each other on the return journey. There was nothing else to say.

I was still up to my neck in it.

BREAKING POINT

Chapter 62

'**You look awful.**' It wasn't the most flattering welcome I'd had.

'Thanks very much, Laura, you should see the other guy,' I nodded behind me as Socket walked in.

'I think you should get some ice on that,' I said. But he ignored me.

I turned to Laura. 'What's going on? Steyn said something about the MK6 being dangerous.'

'Something's happened,' she said. 'They're in the middle of a conference call right now.'

Stremsen looked up, his eyes wide. 'What about?'

His mouth seemed to quiver with the question.

'I don't know,' she replied. 'They received some faxes from the UK, and they've been locked away ever since. It looks serious.'

Then it was Socket's turn. 'What faxes?'

He was very subdued, and I don't think it was to do with his injury.

She shrugged.

I looked at my watch, Van Heerden could be talking with the police authorities for all I knew.

Laura looked at Socket's eye and winced. 'I'll get an ice pack for that.'

We stood around while she got some ice and wrapped it in a towel.

'Shit...' He flinched as she applied it to his face.

'Hy is net 'n groot baba, Laura.' *He's just a big baby, Laura.* I rarely used Afrikaans in front of English speakers, but I'd had enough of the two of them.

Laura smiled and nodded back at me.' Ek hoop jy was nie betrokke nie.' *I hope you weren't involved.* I shook my head.

'What are you saying?' Stremsen sounded twitchy.

'She's asking if you want a cup of coffee,' I lied.

'We haven't got time for that,' said Stremsen. 'Terry and I need to go in and explain what's been happening.'

I tagged on behind as they pushed their way into the room.

Three sets of eyes turned on us, none of them friendly. A voice, I thought I recognised, was explaining something through the speaker-phone.

'Hold on Mr Jones, the three gentlemen have just arrived.' Van Heerden waved us in.

Socket went straight across to him, pointing to his eye. 'See this?' he said. 'One of your blacks assaulted me.'

Rik Last took off his glasses, squeezed both eyes with his thumb and forefinger and looked up. He looked dishevelled. 'Sit down, both of you.'

Stremsen pushed forward.

'He was punched, Rik...'

'For *fuck's* sake, sit down!' Shouted Last.

Likky Rast had left the meeting.

The outburst shocked everyone, and Stremsen and Socket fell into their chairs.

'Sorry about that, Danny.'

What was Last apologising to me for?

I was confused and looked at Van Heerden, but he gave nothing away.

The speaker in the middle of the table, hissed in the background.

'We've received some distressing news,' Last continued. 'Under normal circumstances, I would prefer to carry out this next part of the investigation in private.' He looked across at Van Heerden. 'But due to its serious nature, Thys has asked that he and Danny Core be allowed to take part.'

'What, *next part of the investigation* are you talking about, Rik?' Stremsen looked as bewildered as I felt.

Last picked up his notes and leaned back with a sigh.

'Carry on, Luca.'

BREAKING POINT

The tension in the room was unbearable as Majori cleared his throat.

'Billy Jones has found a discrepancy with the material certificate for the MK6 bearings. Do you know anything about that, Fred?'

That sent a shockwave through Stremsen that made him catch his breath.

'No, that's Billy's domain.'

'So you're not aware of a forged document?'

I swallowed hard... *forged document?* This next part was going to be an interrogation.

'Why would I be?' answered Stremsen.

Luca passed two sheets over to him and two to Socket, who was doing his best to hide behind his ice pack.

The speaker continued hissing in the background.

'The two sheets you have in front of you should be identical,' continued Luca. 'The first has been supplied by the foundry, Almeja Fundicion, which shows the material as Super Duplex 193. The other is a forgery of the first, where the material has been changed to Super Duplex 198.'

I watched their eyes flash between the sheets of paper... *Surely not,* I thought.

This was becoming uncomfortable for everyone concerned, and I still couldn't decide if Majori was defending or prosecuting?

I looked at Van Heerden, again he gave nothing away.

'Are any of you involved in this?'

I was relieved Luca was only looking at Stremsen and Socket.

Both shook their heads, Terry more rigorously. Stremsen spoke first.

'It must be an administrative error; they've got the numbers mixed up.'

'Can I borrow your magnet, Danny?' Luca held out his hand.

How does he know I have a magnet? I thought, as I searched my pocket and passed it over.

He held it over the nearest bearing, and it drew away from his fingers with a metallic, *click*. Then he looked across at me.

'Did you do a similar check on all the bearings underground, Danny?'

'Yes,' I replied, still confused as to how he knew I had a magnet.

'They were all magnetic,' I replied, still not knowing if that was a good thing or a bad thing.

The speaker suddenly burst into life. 'We've checked the Mathers stock, and they're all magnetic as well.'

It was unmistakably Billy Jones' voice.

'I have a right to know what's going on,' said Stremsen.

Billy answered. 'Super Duplex 198 is non-magnetic. The evidence leads us to believe that the MK6 bearings are made from an inferior grade, 193, which happens to be magnetic.'

'So what?' said Socket. 'It passed all the database calculations.'

That was rich coming from Socket, an hour ago he was dismissing it as… *your fucking database*.

Billy continued, obviously in his element.

'It's got nothing to do with material strength,' he said. 'It's about galvanic corrosion. The flange and bearing materials are incompatible. From the day they were installed, the MK6 Stabilisers at Rinto Gold were a ticking bomb.'

I couldn't believe what I was hearing. My whole body went weak, and I felt my eyes filling up. I couldn't help myself and started sobbing. Searching my pockets for a handkerchief, I ended up wiping my eyes with the arm of my overalls.

'Are you okay to continue, Danny?' Van Heerden passed over his handkerchief. He was smiling, which made me blub even more.

I couldn't speak and waved for them to continue.

The delay didn't help Stremsen.

BREAKING POINT

'It's Jack Smelt's fault,' he pleaded. 'He was the one who designed the bearings.'

'Yes he did,' Billy replied. 'And he specified Super Duplex 198. It's all detailed in the PMT documentation.'

Hoist with his own petard, I thought, as I regained some composure.

'Thanks, Billy,' Last replied, pulling out his comb and running it through his hair with the familiar sequence. He glanced at the faces around the table, adjusted his glasses and lifted his notes.

'Now that we've established the certificate *is* a forgery and the bearings *are* made from inferior material. We need to examine culpability.'

His voice broke a fraction, and he took a sip of water before continuing.

'Billy has spoken with Dwight Kerbow, the Quality Manager of Machine Inc., and he's admitted forging the document from Almeja, before sending it on to Mathers.'

'Why would he do that?' I asked.

'Fred, would you like to enlighten us?' Last looked across at him, but Stremsen just shook his head.

'Okay,' continued Last. 'Billy, can you take up the story please.'

Billy carried on.

'Dwight Kerbow has admitted accepting money from Fred Stremsen. He was asked to forge the documents passed through from the Almeja foundry before sending them on to Mathers.'

'That's a lie,' shouted Stremsen. 'Why would I do that, what did I have to gain?'

Rik Last looked at his notes. 'You had a considerable bonus for achieving the cost-saving target on the MK6 project, ten times what you paid Kerbow.'

Billy's voice came through again. 'Kerbow also told us that you were arranging to send more business his way on future projects.'

'I've told you, he's lying,' said Stremsen.

'I wish he was, Fred,' Last sounded weary. 'We've got everything recorded, including this written statement from Kerbow admitting it all.'

He passed over the sheet to Stremsen who didn't bother to look at it. 'The CEO of Machine Inc. has been updated and is now threatening to take legal action against yourself and Heron Inc.' Last's whole body seemed to deflate.

'All these lies and deceptions to steal money and protect your precious PMT, Fred. I backed you... trusted you.' Last slammed his fist on the table... *Bang!*

'What the *fuck* were you thinking!'

Stremsen couldn't speak, his head hidden in his hands. Then his shoulders began convulsing.

I looked at Socket. The ice pack was giving him good cover so no one could see his expression as the deception played out.

'Did you know about any of this, Terry?' I asked.

Everyone seemed to come out of a trance and turned to look at him.

He pulled the ice pack away; his eye was now closed and he looked wretched. His hands were shaking.

'Fred only told me a few days ago, but I wasn't involved in any dealings with Machine Inc.'

'And yet you still tried to blame me,' I said.

Billy's voice came through again.

'That's why he offered you the Worldwide Quality Director role isn't it, Terry? In the end, you're just as culpable.'

'I thought the material was strong enough,' Socket's voice was pleading. 'I genuinely thought it had nothing to do with the collapse. I would never have agreed if I'd known it was dangerous.'

I looked across at Rik Last.

'I believe him,' I said. 'He's a spineless bully, but even he wouldn't go that far.'

BREAKING POINT

Last turned to me. 'I'm not sure I could be that pragmatic in the circumstances, Danny, I admire your spunk.'

Then he turned his venom on Socket.

'Whoever did that to your face gets my full support,' he said. 'Just be sure not to press any charges, or you'll find yourself in the same industrial court as him.' He pointed across at Stremsen.

Socket mumbled something and hid behind the ice pack again.

Van Heerden stood and looked out from the window toward the grey, concrete tower of the winding house. The signs were glinting in the early afternoon sun. *Rinto Gold* in black letters and *Concorde IV* in red.

I watched his familiar routine, lining himself up, dead centre.

'There's still a negligent manslaughter charge to be resolved.'

He was addressing the vista beyond the window, but we all knew who it was directed at.

'Danny Core is exonerated...' My whole body shivered with the words. 'But I still have to submit my report to the police authorities in the next...' he looked at his watch. 'Ten hours.'

'You're not suggesting that Fred's going to be charged, Thys.' Last looked shocked, but not as much as Stremsen.

'It's still an open case in South African law.' Van Heerden replied, staring out of the window.

Stremsen was physically shaking and turned to Last.

'I... I'll admit to all the charges, Rik, but don't make them keep me here. I'm an American citizen, for God's sake. My family...'

Tears were rolling down his face. There were times when I'd hated the man, but to see him pleading like this was pitiful.

Van Heerden turned in that theatrical way of his, but there was no elation in his features. His eyes were cold and pitiless, and I realised, for the first time, the depth of his anger.

'You were willing to see an innocent man go to jail.' His words were laced with contempt.

'Thys!' Last stood up and faced him. 'He's an American citizen and will be dealt with in an American court. Perhaps Luca and I can discuss a more reasonable way of resolving this terrible business.'

Van Heerden looked across at me and gave another wicked smile.

The bastard was going to make them pay.

BREAKING POINT

Chapter 63

I stepped from my car and looked up at the sky. It was bright blue apart from two vapour trails running parallel to one another. I left the engine idling and walked around the front to lean against the warm bonnet and look out over the magnificent panorama.

This was high ground, and the wind had picked up. A cold shiver ran through me, goosebumps raising the hairs on my arm. My reflex action six months ago would have been to light a cigarette, but not now. I'd given them up six months, two weeks and five days ago… and counting.

I crossed my arms, half-listening to the car radio playing through the open window, the DJ prattling on with the usual nonsense. The soothing vibrations from the bodywork of the car, coupled with the warmth from the bonnet, were the perfect combination to relax and take stock.

Then the record changed, and my stomach turned over.
London Burning by The Clash.

It was the first time I'd heard it played since the accident on Concorde IV. After the initial surprise, I hummed quietly along. But it would never be the same… too many memories.

Or maybe I'd just outgrown it.

I raised myself up and made my way back to the driver's door. Slipping back into the seat, I turned the engine off, *no point in wasting petrol.* The radio went silent, and I was left with my thoughts.

I looked at my watch. It was 9am, Saturday morning. I instinctively knew Steyn would be into his weekend shift, six thousand miles away… *God, I missed the old bugger.*

I looked beyond the road, out over the Brig Uchel mountain range. It seemed softer in the low sunlight; the gorse adding colour and definition to the rolling contours. I knew above the tree-line, there would be a spiteful wind which would drop the temperature by more than ten degrees. I was rubbing my distorted fingernails as though my hands were cold.

I'd left South Africa and Rinto Gold a week ago to take up a new post with Mathers. It had been an easy decision to make and allowed me to be near both my sons.

The Technical Director's job had become vacant, and I'd accepted the offer from Rik Last. Luca Majori had sounded me out three months before when I agreed to support Mathers in the correction processes required to make the MK6 fit for purpose. Rik was retiring at the end of the year, and Luca was taking over as CEO.

Billy Jones had decided to take up a new role within Mathers as Chief Metallurgist and seemed happy with the news of my appointment. I was looking forward to working together.

Terry Socket was given two options after he arrived back from South Africa; resign immediately and keep your CV clean, or face the sack and deal with the fallout. The last I heard he was going through a messy divorce and working somewhere in Scotland

I'd miss my friends in South Africa, particularly Steyn, who I loved like a brother. Before I'd left, he made me promise to come back to visit him. His first experience outside South Africa hadn't been good, but I'd do all I could to persuade him to return and show him more of the country.

I remember Embele's face when I told him that Piet Reiss had asked me to promote him onto his maintenance team, such was the impression he'd made. It was another of those rare moments when he smiled.

Van Heerden knew Rik Last would pay to protect Heron Inc's reputation, and he was right. He set up a fund for all the families affected by the collapse, regardless of colour, and got Heron to commit $2 million.

He also got Heron to replace the two MK6 Stabilisers and squeezed them for a percentage of Rinto Gold's lost production costs. I'm pretty sure Machine Inc. got something to keep them quiet as well.

It all added up to a great deal of money, but less than the cost of a tarnished reputation.

It had proved more challenging to close the case with the South African police authorities, and Van Heerden had to call in a lot of favours before they finally relented.

We never spoke after he left the meeting at Concorde IV, which I thought was unusual given what we'd both been through.

I'd be a liar if I said I wasn't bothered.

The 3S Initiative was cleared of any involvement in the collapse and was being extended to other Rinto Gold mines. The accident at Concorde IV was blamed on a pressure burst caused by abnormal seismic activity in the area. Tragic but unpredictable.

Fred Stremsen returned to America in disgrace. He was dismissed immediately and is currently facing charges of bribery and corruption in a US Industrial Court.

John Dread did keep in touch after I was cleared, though he and Julie had parted ways not long after. It had been amicable, in his words, and he still kept in touch with Paul.

He never admitted what he'd done, and I saw no reason to bring the subject up. It was in the past.

Knowing John as I did, it would have been difficult living with the guilt, but I would always be grateful for his help. He'd asked me for a reference when he was head-hunted by a company in the north of England. I was genuinely glad for him.

Out of the corner of my eye, I caught sight of a front door opening and pulled myself out of the car.

'You can come in,' Julie shouted from the door. 'We won't bite.'

Ian Holland

'I didn't want to be late,' I said, walking up the path, and stepped through the front door as Paul came down the stairs in his football kit.

'Local derby today, Dad. You've picked a good one to come and watch.'

I grabbed him as he tried to make his way to the kitchen and squeezed him close. His hair smelt of shampoo and burnt toast.

'Tell him to let go, Mum.' He giggled as I nuzzled his neck. 'We'll be late.'

He disappeared into the kitchen and reappeared with a lump of toast sticking out of his mouth.

'Come on then, Dad.'

I followed him to the door and watched as he ran to the car. *Shirt-tails and loose-laces,* it seemed a long time ago.

'You'd better get going.' Julie came up beside me.

'He's been talking about this ever since he found out you were coming back.'

'Nice to know someone's glad I'm back,' I said.

She laughed and pushed me out the door.

'*Billy no mates*, feeling sorry for himself? I'd better cook some lunch for the two of you.'

As I opened the front gate, I thought I heard her say, '*I'm glad you're back.*'

But before I could reply, the door had closed.

About the Author

Born in Glasgow, Ian Holland has spent most of his life in South Wales. After working in engineering for several years, he moved to South Africa to work for a major gold mining company. Returning to Wales for twelve years, he was on the move once more, this time to work in America. Following his retirement, a story he had begun to sketch out ten years before, felt ready to be completed.
He lives with his wife in South Wales.
If you enjoyed Breaking Point, please consider leaving a review.

Acknowledgement

The making of Breaking Point has been an ambition of mine for a very long time. To finally realise this makes me thankful for the support of family and friends. Writing is a solitary, selfish process, and makes demands on those closest to us. I am grateful to my wife Pat, for her patience, understanding and unbending support during my hours of self-imposed isolation.

Afterword

The book is very much a work of fiction. Gold Mining is a very complicated business, and I've taken liberties with some of the technical data. The metallurgical characteristics have some basis in fact but have been stretched out for creative and storyline purposes. Crossways and Harmonie are fictitious towns, as are the characters appearing in the book. The Recycling Stabiliser is a figment of my imagination.

Printed in Great Britain
by Amazon